LORD OF THE ATLAS

CHAPTER 1

London, 1893

What a place, George thought. Greasy, grim and ripe for murder.

It was summer, the night was hot, and the air thick as treacle. Not like England at all, more like being back in India. He turned down a side street, past a couple of dimly lit bars. Shadows huddled in the corners and the doorways, women and sailors and young thugs looking for easy marks. Well, they won't find one here.

He followed the sound of coarse laughter. Two men in capes and bowler hats smoked cigars outside a nondescript building with no windows. They looked out of place among this crowd. George knew he had found what he was looking for.

He climbed some narrow wooden stairs and went along a short passageway, grimaced as he pushed through the curtain into the gambling room. The taint of fear and sweat mingled with the putrid fug of stale cigar smoke and made the bile rise to the back of his throat.

George took his watch from his waistcoat pocket. Just after two o'clock in the morning.

I should be in my bed.

He looked around the room, the moth-eaten red velvet, the fake Vicenzan mirrors, the cigar burns on the scaly Turkish carpets. It looked like the salon in a brothel he had once visited in Alexandria. Now that was an experience he didn't want to be reminded of.

There were four or five tables with various card games in progress. A few of the players glanced up at him briefly and returned their attentions to the cards.

Then he saw him, at the far table, facing away from the door. They had said he would find him here when he asked at the public house down at the docks.

He's always there, that one. Every night.

Harry had his waistcoat unbuttoned, his tie loose. He hadn't aged a day since George last saw him and yet he looked a hundred years old. He'd seen that look once before, after giving evidence at a court martial, on the face of a young man who had been sentenced to a firing squad the next day.

There were two men watching him from the other side of the rope that separated the tables from the rest of the room. One of them had the build of a wrestler and the look of a schoolyard bully, as if he couldn't wait to find someone to pummel. His companion was small and devilishly thin, he reminded George of one of the first cadavers he had seen in medical school, a criminal executed for killing his mother and younger brother with an axe. Could have been the corpse's twin, right down to the slightly bluish death pallor of his skin.

The bully's gaze settled on him for a moment, then moved away again, discounting him as a threat. Another degenerate come to lose all his money on the cards or the whores, the look seemed to say.

George moved to the side, kept to the back, didn't want Harry to see him just yet. Not much chance of that, he thought. The state he's in, I don't think he'd know his own mother right now.

It was late, and most of the players had left the table. Only three of them now, just the drunk and the desperate at this time of night. The croupier – he looked half asleep - used a flat wooden spatula to lift the cards across the baize and drop them in front of the other players.

George didn't understand much about the game but by the look on Harry's face, he was losing, and badly. The players faced their cards.

The croupier used the rake to push his chips to the right, then to the left. He looked as if he had swallowed cold fat. He reached into his jacket pocket and took out a silver cigarette case. His hand shook as he lit a cigarette.

Harry stood up and walked out of the room. He moved so quickly that the two men, who had been watching him through the whole game were caught off guard. They almost fell over each other going after him, got themselves in a tangle in the red velvet curtain. In other circumstances it might almost have been funny.

George followed the two men through the curtain and down the passageway. A man got in his way and he shoved him aside, heard him cursing after him as he ran down the stairs.

The street was empty. Yellow light from a single gaslight glimmered on the cobblestones. He heard a commotion down one of the alleys and he ran towards it, his Malacca cane with its rubber tip bouncing on the cobbles.

He saw shadowy figures in the alley. It looked like Harry had walked, or run, into a trap. Two men were at the far end of the alley, blocking his escape. Bully boy and his cadaverous friend from the gambling club had followed him from the club and now had him backed against the wall.

Bully boy produced a wooden club which he slapped against the palm of his left hand. 'What's the hurry, me old china?' he said to Harry.

'Forgot to feed my cat,' Harry said.

George smiled. Penury hasn't taken away his sense of humour. A good sign.

It looked as if Harry thought he could fight his way out of this. He ran straight at the big fellow, took a swing and missed, which allowed the smaller man to grab him from behind. He put one arm around Harry's neck and jerked him backwards, off balance. The two men who had been guarding the end of the alley ran up to help them. They each grabbed an arm and forced Harry against the wall.

They held him there while the thin one started beating him, slowly and methodically, with his fists. He took his time between punches, picking his spot. The first punch went into Harry's ribs, bending him double, making it easier for the second blow to land on his nose. Harry didn't make a sound. There was no pleading, no yelling.

George could imagine him thinking that he wouldn't give them the satisfaction.

Already there was blood streaming from his right eye and his nose. Harry would only really be upset if they broke any teeth, he had always been quite vain about his looks.

'Gentlemen, I think you should stop right there,' George said.

The thin man turned around. He looked over George's shoulder to see if he had any friends with him, and when he realized he was alone, he said something to the others, and they all laughed. They took in his clothes - the evening dress, the polished shoes, the silk bowler, the Malacca cane - and concluded that he was a fop and therefore harmless.

The big fellow said: 'You should do well to stay out of this, matey.'

George took a step forward. A casual flick of the wrist expelled the rubber tip of the cane, and even in the dull glimmer of the gaslight, the glint of steel at its tip seemed to make an impression.

The thin one changed his tune. 'Who the fuck are you?' he said.

George didn't have a Victoria Cross, like Harry, he was more accustomed to cleaning wounds than causing them, but he had been around long enough to know what a man had to do in a street fight. It was all about speed and aggression, not standing around gawping like these fine fellows.

One quick sweep of the cane and the thin one squealed and reeled back, clutching at his face. Blood spurted through his fingers. While the others stared at this in shock, George flicked his wrist a second time and Bully Boy gasped and looked down in horror at the slash on his arm. The blade had gone right through the sleeve of his coat. He found he no longer had the strength to hold the billy club. It clattered onto the ground.

'The tendon I have just bisected is crucial for movement. Its Latin name is *flexor carpi ulnaris*. You need use of it in order to flex your hand, and hold things, such as the weapon you just dropped on the cobblestones there. I'm afraid it will take rather a long time to heal. Would you like another anatomy lesson? An incision to your patellar ligament should be most instructive.'

The big man turned and ran away down the alley, clutching his arm. He would be no more trouble. The two toughs holding Harry for the beating decided that whoever was paying them for their trouble was not paying them nearly enough.

They ran off.

Without them holding him upright, Harry sagged against the wall and sat down onto his haunches.

The thin man was still clutching at his face with his left hand. He fell to his knees and scrambled for the billy club with his other hand. George stood on his fingers and he squealed in pain and panic. George put the blade of the cane tip at his throat.

'I am being impolite. A few moments ago, you asked me who I am. I'll tell you who I am. I'm the man who will take out both your eyes with one flick of his wrist and present them to your wife as earrings if you don't let go of that club.'

He did as he was told. Blood dripped down his arm and onto his coat. With his one good eye he looked around for his associates. They were long gone.

George kept the point of the blade pressed into the thin man's cheek just below the eye.

'I'm going to bleed to death here.'

'It's all the same to me,' George said. 'Do as you like.' He nodded towards Harry. 'Do you know who this man is?'

'He's a drunk who doesn't pay his gambling debts.'

'This is Captain Harry Delhaze of the Royal Horse Artillery. He was awarded the Victoria Cross for bravery at the battle of Tell el Kebir.'

'I don't care who he is. He should pay his debts.'

'How much does he owe?'

'Fifteen pounds, ten shillings.'

'Fifteen pounds? You would do a man serious injury for two month's rent? What kind of a cockroach would earn his living that way?' He looked at Harry, who had struggled back to his feet. 'Harry, these gentlemen appear to have dropped something.'

Harry grunted and picked up the billy club. George put the cane under his arm, took out his wallet, and dropped some notes onto the ground by the thin man's feet. 'Take your money and go.'

The man crumpled the notes in his fist and put them in his pocket. He stumbled away, still clutching his face.

'We should get out of here, are you ready?'

'I'll just be a moment. I have to rearrange my nose.'

'Your nose is fine. Let's get going.'

Harry seemed to be having some trouble walking and breathing. George couldn't really see the extent of the damage in the dark, and there wasn't much he could do about it here, even if he could.

'George, what are you doing here?'

'This is a conversation for later. First, we have to get you home. Do you live far?'

'Just a short and pleasant stroll.'

He took a step and stumbled. George put an arm around him. 'Come on,' he said.

They reached Waterloo Bridge, and George searched for a hansom cab. He propped Harry against the wall, took out his cigarette case, lit two cigarettes and put one between his friend's teeth.

'Been a long time,' Harry said.

'Four years.'

'Your appearance was opportune.' He coughed and spat blood onto the pavement. 'I think the bastards broke my ribs.'

'You were lucky that's all they broke.'

'Are you going to tell me what you're doing here?'

'First, let's get you home. I don't think we're going to find a cab.'

'We'll walk.'

'You can manage?'

'I'm a war hero.'

'No, you're lucky. They're two different things.' He put a cigarette in his mouth and leaned Harry's weight on his shoulder. 'Okay, show me the way.'

It wasn't not the kind of place to wander about at night, with its darkened doorways and piss-smelling alleys. The miasma that rose from the sewer grates caught the breath. George held his cane ready as

Harry directed him to an anonymous doorway. There was not a light burning anywhere, and they had to stumble up a narrow staircase in the dark. Harry fell over twice, smashing his shins on the edge of the stair.

He fumbled with his keys and finally got them inside. The first thing George noticed was the smell of stale tobacco and rising damp. There was no electric light, Harry had to grope around in the dark to find the gas lamp.

Harry pointed to the bedroom and George half carried him in and threw him on the bed. He was snoring even before George got his boots off. He threw a blanket over him and debated whether to go back to his hotel or sleep on the chaise-longue.

He decided to stay. Harry would need fixing up, and besides, if he left him alone for even an hour, there was no telling the trouble the bastard could get into.

George shut the bedroom door and looked around. What a mess. There were dirty plates piled on the floor, a mountain of cigarette stubs in a cheap tin ashtray, a painting of a naked harem girl above the mantle. A piece of the plaster ceiling had come down and was propped against the wall.

He went into the kitchen to look for coffee. The bread and milk were on the bench by the window, the bread was covered in mould, the milk was soured. It was all there was.

George went back into the living room, found a blanket in a cupboard. He would have to use his coat for a pillow. He was about to turn out the gaslight when he saw some framed photographs on the mantle and went over to take a closer look. There was a solemn family group in the garden of their house in Devon, another of Harry as a teenager with his brother and parents climbing in Wales. George was surprised to find a miniature of Harry's father, looking suitably stern in his goatee beard and *pince-nez*.

He turned out the light and curled up on the chaise longue, wondered about the man snoring to wake the dead in the bedroom. How had he fallen this far? He had so envied him when they had been at school and had tried to emulate him at military college. How could Harry have allowed this to happen to himself? If his creditors didn't kill him, then he'd die of the cold before the winter was over.

It was not the most uncomfortable night's sleep he had ever had; that would be the night he had spent sleeping in a trench being eaten alive by sand flies in Egypt. He finally dropped off to sleep, only to be woken a little while later by the horn blasts of an early morning tramway car.

CHAPTER 2

Harry woke with a start. He sat up, gasped with pain. It all came back to him, in a rush; another bad night at the tables, the men trapping him in the alley, giving him a good beating. A miracle if they hadn't broken half his ribs. He felt around his mouth for his teeth with his tongue. It seemed like they were all still there.

Well, that was unexpected. The old Delhaze luck still holds, he thought.

He went to the window, saw a man down in the street turning off the gaslights. At seven, the organ grinder started his rounds, a little capuchin monkey tied to a string, gibbering and shrieking. Trying to get away from the noise, he supposed. For God's sake, Harry thought. What I wouldn't give to be back in the Army. I'd shoot the bastard.

George put his head around the door. 'So, you're awake.'

'George. It is you. I didn't dream it.'

'You look like hell.'

'Thanks.'

'Let me have a look at you. Get your clothes off.'

He did as he was told. The shirt was ruined, the laundry would never get the bloodstains out. His suit was covered in filth from the alley.

George came back in with a flannel and an enamel bowl of cold water. He bent down, looked in his mouth. 'Well, your teeth are all still there, though a couple of the molars are loose. Your lip's split but at least your jaw's not displaced.' He wiped the blood off his face, held up three fingers.

'How many fingers?'

'Twenty-nine.'

'Close enough.'

There were bruises on his ribs, both sides, already turning blue.

'How do you feel?'

'It hurts to cough.'

'Don't cough.'

'It even hurts to breathe.'

'Don't breathe, then. It's your choice. Perhaps next time pay your debts.'

'That's your professional opinion?'

'That will cost you more.'

'What about my nose? Is it broken?'

'Yes, but not badly. It's bent at a rather dashing angle, once the swelling has gone down, it will give your boyish good looks a rougher edge. Like someone who actually looks like they deserve a medal.'

'Could you straighten it?'

'I could if I had my equipment with me. Or you could go to the hospital.'

'Is it going to hurt?'

'Oh, yes. Quite a lot.'

'Well, let's not bother. What do you think, doctor, will I live or die?'

'It depends.'

'Depends?'

'It depends on whether you give up playing cards. How many other gentlemen do you owe money to?'

'A few. I wouldn't call any of them gentlemen.'

'Then I'd say the prognosis isn't good. You were lucky this time. Your ribs will hurt like hell for a while but then you should be fine. If I hadn't come along when I did, the beating would have been much worse. They were the sort of men anyone with good sense would try to avoid.'

'It was only a few pounds. I was going to pay them back.'

'How? Do you have a job, Harry?'

'You sound like my father.'

'I feel like your father, God help him. Come on, get dressed. I'll buy you some breakfast and we can drop by my hotel afterwards and get that cut over your eye fixed up.'

'You still haven't told me what you're doing here. Last I heard of you, you were headed home to deliver babies and treat little children with measles. You didn't just stumble into the gambling hall last night, did you? Not your kind of place at all. And you're a long way from home.'

'You're right. I came looking for you.'

'Even I can work that out.'

'I came to offer you a job opportunity.'

'A job? I'm not a doctor.'

'This has nothing to do with medicine. It's a chance to do what you do best.'

'Get into trouble and disappoint my father?'

'Something like that.'

'First, I need a hair of the dog. There's a place on the corner. The owner's a friend of mine, should be, I keep him in business.' He staggered to his feet, got a jacket and hat, and headed for the door.

There were market carts jogging towards the bridge, headed for Covent Garden, tangled with the sprawl of hansom cabs and double decker buses along the Waterloo Road. The air was pungent with smoke from the train station.

Outside *The Crown*, potmen were polishing the huge swinging lamps and plate-glass windows and barrels of beer were being lowered into dark yawning cellars from the brewers' dray. A jellied eel cart had set up outside. Breakfast for some. Harry went ahead, pushed through the queue and headed into the saloon bar.

They took a seat in the snug by the window. George got a half pint of ale. Harry said, 'the usual, Bert'. The 'usual' turned out to be a double gin.

Harry's hands shook as he picked up the glass. He lit a cigarette.

'Steady,' George said.

'Can't start the day without a hearty breakfast,' Harry said. He picked up yesterday's copy of the *Times*, scanned the obituary column.

'What are you doing?' George said.

'First thing, every morning, make sure I'm not listed. Way I feel, can't always be sure.'

'What have you been doing with yourself since you left the army?' George said.

'You know what I've been doing. You don't have to be delicate.'

'I was told you'd been chasing the bottle. It looks like you caught up with it a few times.'

'I needed a rest from soldiering.'

'Is this what you call a rest? You look like you've just crawled out of the sewer.'

'Thanks.'

'Well, you told me not to be delicate.'

'Did father send you?'

'You know better than that.'

Harry took a swallow of gin. He coughed and clutched at his ribs. 'How did you find me?'

'I'm still in touch with a lot of the fellows from the old days in Cairo. They love to talk.'

'I bet they do.'

'You make a wonderful rumour.'

'Well, I'm glad you did find me. I owe you a great debt. I think those fellows might have put me in the hospital if you had not appeared.'

'Let's call it returning a favour. You got me out of countless scrapes at school.'

'Well you were younger, then. Smaller. And you didn't have a cane with a razor blade in the tip.'

'They should give them to every schoolboy when he starts a new school.'

'It would solve the bullying problem. Are you back living in Bristol?'

George shook his head. He took a sip of his beer and grimaced. Bit early for him. 'No, here in London. Looked everywhere for you, then found out we'd only been living a few miles apart.'

'How's your papa?'

'He died. Last year.'

'Oh. I'm sorry to hear that. He was a good man. There are not many of us left now.'

George smiled, despite himself. 'You may joke about it, but you had more in common with him than you think.'

'Your father was a sainted man. He and I had nothing in common with each other, and I say that with some regret.'

'He wasn't as perfect as everyone thinks,' George said.

'Who is?' Harry caught a glimpse of his own reflection in the mirror above the bar and the shelf of dusty bottles. Wherever you went, there were mirrors. 'Do you ever hear anything of Lucy?'

'Must we talk about her?' George said.

'It is an innocent enquiry is all.'

'You know there is no such thing. You mustn't keep tearing the stitches from the wound.'

'I'm merely curious. It really doesn't bother me anymore.'

'She caught syphilis from one of the junior officers in the regiment, the general threw her on the street with her baby and now she sells herself in Piccadilly for three shillings a time against the wall. You see, I saw you smile. You are not over it at all.'

'Do you see my father very much?' Harry asked him.

'I called on him when I got out of the army. I thought it was the proper thing.'

'How is my dearest papa? In good health?'

'For his years.'

'Did he ask after me?'

'Of course he did.'

'Well, I had to ask. He has two sons, it's a lot for him to remember. What did you tell him about me?'

'There wasn't much I could tell. I knew of your situation, of course. But I thought it best to be discreet.'

'My sainted brother, was he there?'

'He was at the factory when I called. He works long hours, so your father told me.'

Harry laughed.

'What?'

'Sometimes I don't know if I am jealous of him, or if I pity him. I hoped your news of dear Tom would have been different.'

'Different? What would you have liked me to have said?'

'That he had fucked the mayor's wife and lost all my father's money on bad investments and been imprisoned by the government for tax irregularities. Then I should have been pleased.'

'That's not likely, is it?'

'That doesn't mean I don't wish for it from time to time. Still, perhaps working twelve hours a day in my father's office is destiny enough. I should be glad that I avoided it.'

'He simply remains true to his character.'

'Well, that is enough of small talk. Now tell me why the hell you've gone to all this trouble to find me?'

'How would you like to turn things around, Harry? You can if you play your cards right.'

'If I could play my cards right, I wouldn't be in any sort of mess. Come on, no more games. What are you talking about?'

'I've got an offer for you, a chance to make a lot of money very quickly, putting your skills to good use.'

'Someone is going to pay me to drink and lose at cards?'

'Your skills as a gunnery officer are still valuable to certain people.'

'Sorry, I've left the army.'

'But you still know how to command a battery of artillery, don't you?'

'I do, but I don't want to.'

'What would you say if I told you that the Sultan of Morocco needs two good men to command his artillery?'

'I would say, how did the Sultan of Morocco come by artillery?'

'They were a gift.'

'Right. So he needs two men to command his new guns. And who is this other officer?'

'Me.'

'You? You don't know one end of a cannon from the other. You were in the medical corps.'

'The Sultan doesn't know this. The deal is this: I go along as your *aide de camp*, wear my old uniform, strut around a bit, and collect my share at the end.'

'For doing what?'

'For getting you the job.'

'So what do we... I... have to do for this?'

'They want one year of your life, Harry. That's all. For one year, they'll pay you ten years' wages. The way you live, you'll probably gamble it all away in six months, but that's up to you.'

'Ten years' wages?'

'Two thousand pounds.'

'Each?'

'*Each.*'

'That's madness. Who would pay four thousand pounds for two artillery officers?'

'The Sultan of Morocco.'

Harry let out a sigh and sagged back in his chair. 'How many guns are we talking about?'

'The Sultan has three muzzle-loading cannons. He put two Spanish army officers in charge of them, but these gentlemen have apparently disappeared. So he needs two experienced officers to take their place.'

'To what purpose?'

'Apparently, he needs to put down a few native rebellions in the provinces and he is willing to pay handsomely for such assistance. You have no idea how rich this man is, Harry. This is a once in a lifetime opportunity.'

'Wait, wait. Muzzle-loading cannons?'

'They were gifts from the United States government. The sort of equipment that would be unlikely to trouble a modern army. But the Sultan was delighted, they tell me.'

'Muzzle-loaders? They're museum pieces.'

'Probably. Do you know how to fire one?'

'Well of course I know *how*. Is that what he wants me to teach his army to do? Fire museum pieces at natives?'

'Do you still have your uniform?'

'In a trunk somewhere.'

'We should go back and get it.'

'You want me to put it on?'

'Not now. When we reach Marrakesh. It will impress the Sultan.'

Harry looked into George' simple, honest face. Had he caught a fever in the Far East and gone completely mad? Did he really believe all this nonsense? 'Where's Marrakesh?'

'It's in the south of the country.'

'How far south?'

'Just north of the Sahara. Two weeks' ride from Tangier. Perhaps three.'

'An entire year, then, chasing around the desert?'

'What else will you do with your time, Harry? You have no money, no life. You're living in a flat that stinks of piss and boiled cabbage. You've got rising damp and the walls shake every time the train comes through. You have no prospects. I'm offering you a lifeline here.'

'I'll have to think about this.'

'Take your time. Think about it all you want.' George took out his fob watch and flipped open the case with his thumb. 'There's a boat for Gibraltar leaving Tilbury docks at four o'clock. We have to be on it.'

'You give me no time to organise my life!'

'I've seen your life. What is there to organise? You have no job, no wife. You do not even have anything in your larder. Everything you own you can pack in a suitcase. Do you owe rent?'

'A bit.'

'I'll leave the money with your key on the table as we leave. I've already booked two berths on the ship. We'll go back now and pack your things. Then we'll go to my hotel, I'll stitch up your eye and we'll catch a cab to the docks.'

'And then what?'

'We catch a ferry to Tangier. The Sultan is sending an escort up from Marrakesh to meet us. We will ride down the coast to Rabat and then head inland to Marrakesh. The Sultan is marching there with his army for the start of his summer campaign.'

Harry felt the stirrings of panic. Yet this was a way out, as George said. Two thousand pounds! He might actually be able to pull his life back together.

Only, what was the point?

Harry drained his glass and stood up. 'It was good to see you again, George.'

'That's it? You're saying no?'

'I appreciate the offer.'

'You're mad,' George said. 'What's next? Back to the tables and the bottle?'

Harry went to the door, put on his hat. It had a dent in it from the night before. He tried to punch it out. He looked up. It was starting to rain. The sky looked grey and filthy, as if it had been dragged through the mud.

The dustmen hadn't been around yet and there was an old man sorting through the tubs of bar refuse. A gang of urchins, none of them older than ten, was throwing rubbish at him, some bits of broken glass, a cabbage head they'd found in the street. The drunk was cursing at them, but they kept right on at it.

Harry went over and chased them off. 'What was that about?' he said to the old tramp. He muttered something unintelligible.

He looked like he was part blind and all the way crazy. There was vomit or old food in his beard and he stank like the river at low tide. Harry dug in his pockets and found some coins, pressed them into the man's hand.

That was it. All he had.

He looked back at the bar.

Hell with it. A year chasing around the desert? Not even for two thousand pounds.

He stepped onto the road. A trolley bus went past, bells clanging, he felt the rush of air on his face. It missed him, but only by inches.

He took a step back, stood there on the pavement, shocked at how close he had come to a sudden, meaningless obliteration. He looked around. No one had seen what had just happened, except the old tramp, and he was laughing and slapping his knee, as if it was the funniest thing he'd ever seen.

When Harry went back into the Crown, George was about to leave. They bumped into each other in the doorway.

'Changed your mind?'

'I don't want to kill anyone,' Harry said.

'Of course not.'

'I'll teach them how to fire their damned cannons if that's what they want. But I've had enough of butchering.'

'No killing.' George said. 'My word on it. This will be the easiest money you've ever made, like taking sweets from a baby.'

CHAPTER 3

Marrakesh, Morocco

Snow-covered peaks pushed their way through a mist of clouds in the far distance. Snow! For Harry, covered in sweat and dust, his mouth gummy with thirst, the moment seemed unreal.

'The Atlas Mountains,' George said, as he rode up beside him.

He'd heard of them, of course, the forbidding mountains that stood like a rampart across the Maghreb, separating Morocco from the great deserts of the Sahara and the salt road that led to Timbuctoo and the heart of Africa. He'd never thought to ever come back to Africa, see these mountains for himself.

'Where's Marrakesh?' he said.

'There,' George said, and pointed to a thin ochre tower just visible among the groves of feathery palms below them. 'That's the Koutoubya mosque.'

They had not seen a town of any size since they had left a little fishing village called Casablanca. They had occasionally glimpsed a group of peasants gathered about a well, or a white *koubba* - what the locals called the tomb of one of their countless saints - in the middle of nowhere. There had been a few *fondaks*, or fortified farms, but most nights they had slept under the stars, two of their escort keeping guard around the campfire.

The riders the Sultan had sent to fetch them from Tangier called this vast expanse of saltbush plains the *bled*. They saw no towns, no mountains, no great rivers. From time to time they had glimpsed a caravan of mules or camels going the other way. They appeared to float on the shimmering heat haze, as if walking on the surface of some great lake.

The landscape was familiar to Harry from his time in Egypt, the humbling distances and never-ending sky. He was even accustomed to the hardships of the journey, from his soldiering days; what tormented him day and night was the need for a drink. It was like a toothache, an actual physical hurt. Some days, it was all he could think about.

He'd brought some supplies with him before he left England. He'd had some bottles of Gordon's gin in his luggage, and they might have seen him this far at least, but some porter-wallah had dropped them on the rock while they were getting ashore in Tangier. Lost the lot. He could have killed the man on the spot.

He thought about the old soak sorting through the tubs outside the Crown. That fellow hadn't simply woken up one morning in the gutter. It would have happened to him by degrees, one denial at a time, until one day he was a drunk in rags, urchins throwing garbage at him.

George was right, he thought. I got out of London just in time.

Below them, the valley stretched away through the heat haze to the foot of the mountains, the vast oasis green with crops and date palms.

'Tell me it's not another mirage, George.'

He laughed. 'No, this is it, Harry. We've arrived.'

'Do you think that mosque down there has a saloon bar?'

'Of course. And a casino with dancing girls.'

They followed their escort down the scarp. Three weeks since they had rounded Cape Malabat and the bad-tempered brute that Harry had been given to ride had made the harrowing journey almost unbearable. Some horses, like some men, were better companions than others.

And these Moorish saddles were magnificent to look at, with their embroidered tassels and coloured stitching, but in his estimation, they were second only to the rack as a form of torture. The peak, before and behind, kept the rider in the saddle, but was as solid as iron. There were perhaps a dozen layers of felt between the saddle and the poll of the horse. The short stirrup leathers that the Moroccans used made any ride longer than an hour or two a complete agony. He had once ridden a camel through the Algerian desert in far greater comfort.

Unfortunately for them, their escort had the idea, as did so many Moors, that a rider should rest as few times in a day as possible. They said that mounting and dismounting tired a horse more than a league of road, so they had not stopped to rest all that morning.

It was another hour of riding through the oasis before they reached the walls of the city. They entered through the *Bab el Debagh*, the Gate of the Tanneries, and suddenly they were in a different world. The buildings crowded in on every side, and many of the streets were arched with overhanging vines, the trellises so low that they had to bend over in the saddle to get through. The stink was overpowering. Harry pulled his *cheiche,* the Berber headscarf he had taken to wearing, tighter around his face and nose. One moment there was the smell of baking bread or meat roasting over hot coals, the next he was assailed by the stench of piss and ordure so overpowering he thought even his horse might object.

It was nothing as he had imagined. The alleys were narrower and more tortuous than anything he had seen in Tangier. The people were mostly dressed in rags. There were milk-eyed beggars with running sores and men without arms or legs huddled in the doorways of dilapidated mosques, moaning for alms. Inside the doors he caught a brief glimpse of the worshippers, seated on the floor in rows for their midday prayers. Dirt-crusted urchins went ducking and weaving through the crowds.

It was worse than anything he'd seen in Cairo. There were camels, carpets, skinned sheep hanging from hooks. Madmen with their eyes rolling in their heads wandered among the crowds beside women covered head to foot in black chador, so that all that was visible was their eyes. There were fat merchants in tarbooshes and *djellabas*, slave traders leading lines of black slaves, stinking of sweat and misery, chained at their hands and feet, their heads down, faces blank with despair.

A group of hawk-nosed tribesmen in filthy sheepskins stared at Harry as he rode past, fingering the ancient swords they wore tucked into their belts. Every one of them looked as if he would like to cut out his liver.

'It seems they don't like unbelievers in this place,' Harry said.

'Is that why they looked at you like that?' George shouted back. 'I thought it was because you owed them money.'

A string of camels bullied their way through, jamming them against the walls. Not a thing even the Sultan's escort could do about it.

They were shepherded through a warren of dusty yellow alleys and crumbling hovels and gloomy bazaars with tiny boxlike shops. Their horses were jostled on every side by the crush of mules and carts. The Sultan's riders tried to clear a path, shouting at anyone too slow to move, sometimes using long canes to whip people out of their way. It was a rude shock after their three long weeks of solitude, an assault on all the senses.

And the noise; after so many days and weeks of the rush of the wind and clip of horses' hooves, the noise made Harry recoil. Everyone in the city seemed to be roaring and haggling and screeching at one another.

At last they came out on a wide square under the tower of the Koutoubya. One of their escort told them it was called the *Jemma el-Fnaa*, the Place of the Dead.

It was clear that this wasn't another Arab city like Tangier. He saw a few bearded *sharifs* riding mules, but most of the faces in the crowds belonged to wild Berber mountain men, or Sudanese with their smooth sweat-shining faces, some pure blood Africans from the Draa and the Sus.

'Looks like an excellent place to get your pocket picked,' George said.

'Or to catch every kind of pox,' Harry said.

'You'd know more about that than me.'

Village women squatted on mats in the dirt, next to pyramids of purple eggplants, branches of golden dates, bright green watermelons, orange pumpkins, stacks of flat bread, or rough bags of thistles, fodder for the mules and donkeys. Half-naked water carriers, dressed in goat skins, with strings of brass bottles around their necks, wandered through the crowds, crying *'Alma, alma!'* Camels lurched about, having wandered off from their owners, foraging for themselves in the dust. Around the edges of the square, there were a few wooden sheds where merchants hawked waistcoats and kaftans in gaudy colours.

Some people were crouched in a circle around a storyteller. A little further on they passed another crowd staring at a performing ape on a long chain. It was dressed in a red tunic and wearing a tarboosh. Harry thought about the organ-grinder in Lambeth with his little capuchin performing on the end of its string. Whatever way you looked at it, the entertainment business wasn't kind to monkeys.

From somewhere, he heard the sound of tom-toms, and a Moorish flute, played very badly. But it seemed to delight his horse, it raised its head and stepped sideways, as if it were dancing in time with the music. It was the first time it had shown any sign of a more pleasing disposition.

The musicians seemed to be in the employ of a snake charmer. They stood behind him, making up for in noise what they lacked in technique.

As they rode past, Harry saw the man produce a snake from his basket, making a horrified face as if he really believed the poor creature might actually bite him. He reined in his horse to watch. The serpent, he knew from his time in Egypt, was a common African house snake, and no more dangerous than a three-day-old kitten. But the man was putting on a real show, shaking violently as he danced around the crowd, groaning and crying as if he was in actual fear of his life.

Suddenly he put out his tongue and let the snake fix its fangs into it, and he ran towards Harry, the snake dangling from his mouth, while his spectators gasped and backed away.

Harry felt in his pockets, all he had was a penny. He tossed it to him. 'Next time you're in the Crown in Lambeth, get yourself a quart of gin!'

One of the musicians broke away from the rest of his little orchestra and started to go round the crowd, collecting coppers in his tambourine, as the charmer brought a cobra from its basket, holding it carefully by the neck while he showed it to the bystanders, letting them admire its fangs. No doubt he had milked off its venom first. Harry had taken Lucy to witness such a performance in Alexandria, and she had squealed and called the snake charmer unladylike names when he thrust a serpent in her face.

'Harry!'

He turned around. George and their escort were waiting for him. 'What's the rush? We're here now.'

'I can't lose you. You're the only one who knows how to fire a cannon.'

As they left the square, an air of desolation descended over the city, many of the mud-brick buildings were in ruin. It was like a city that had been sacked by invaders and had never quite recovered. There were large tracts of dirt and rubble filled with offal and refuse, the precinct of snarling cadaverous yellow dogs, wild as jackals.

There was sand everywhere, in the lanes, blowing in drifts over the ruins of mosques and long deserted hovels. It grew unbearably hot as the sun rose to its zenith, and within an hour of entering the city they were covered in the grime and dust thrown up by their horses' hooves.

Everything seemed to be the same gloomy dun-grey colour; a city, as George muttered to him, that looked as if it had been built from dried camel dung. And then, turning a corner, they came upon a stunningly beautiful fountain, decorated in vivid green tiles, fit for a Sultan's palace.

The fountain had inscribed on it, *Shrab-u-Shuf.* The Arabic he had learned while on service in Algiers had come back to him during their journey from the coast and he read: '*Drink and Admire*'.

Finally, they emerged into the richer quarter, with dusty open spaces and walled gardens. He made out the tops of palm, olive, and orange trees, and the slender green stems of cypress.

The walls of the Kasbah rose ahead of them, they rode through a stone gateway into a massive square and were greeted with a blast of trumpets. The great wooden doors slammed shut on the hellish vision outside and they found themselves in a paradise of flowers and fountains and sudden, shocking silence.

Their escort led them through a gateway into another court, with a mosque on one side. They followed a long, straight road, past the soldiers' quarters and finally reached what they were told was the Sultan's palace.

Palace was perhaps the wrong word, Harry thought. He had expected something more imposing, on a grand scale, like Versailles perhaps. Instead there was a number of pavilions and kiosks, faced with Moorish arches, scattered among a vast and rambling garden of orange and lemon groves. There were pointed roofs of glazed green tiles, the golden globes on the top of each one gleaming in the sun.

George pointed out the Sultan's green flag flying from the tower. 'It seems we have arrived,' he said. 'Hopefully, they will bring us water.'

'A glass of gin would be even more welcome,' Harry said. Sand crunched between his teeth. It was everywhere, in his hair, in his clothes, under his fingernails.

They drew up their horses under an orange tree, George closed his eyes for a moment in the cool shade and breathed in the scent of the blossoms. 'I feel the worst of it is over.'

'Thank God,' Harry said.

Their four-man escort wheeled away and left them. Three weeks they had spent in their company and still they didn't even know their names.

'Not even a fond goodbye,' Harry said. 'And they've been such charming companions.'

He rocked in the saddle. He would have happily tumbled onto the ground and curled up there. He just wanted to sleep.

'I swear two of my cheeks are raw from the sun, and the other two feel like they are welded to the saddle.'

George swung gingerly down from his horse, and Harry did the same. He uttered a grunt of sheer relief. His breeches felt like sandpaper. It hurt even to walk.

There were guard tents dotted about the courtyard among the orange and olive trees. Negroes in red tarbooshes and white kaftans sat about drinking tea, playing cards, and paying them not the slightest attention.'

'The *Bokhara,* I believe,' George said. 'The Black Guard, the Sultan's hand-picked men. Perhaps you can teach them to play baccarat. You might win some money.'

'More likely, I'll lose it. If I had any to spend.'

An iron-barred gate swung open, and a man appeared, crossed the court towards them with the curiously waddling gait of the obscenely fat. He looked more like a corpulent Irishman than an Arab, Harry thought with his red beard and pale skin. He wore a snow-white *haik* over an emerald green kaftan, and there was a ruby the size of a billiard ball in the middle of his turban.

He had with him an escort of soldiery in white gowns and turbans and curved swords.

'The welcoming party,' George said.

'Looks more like the food taster. For the entire army.'

'Not so loud. He speaks English.'

They made the customary welcome, placing their right hand on their hearts followed by a swishing, open gesture. *'Assalamu alaikum.'* Peace be upon you.

The Vizier returned the gesture, carefully avoiding the word *'alaikum'*. After all, a good Muslim would never wish peace on a dog of a Christian.

His name, he said, was Haj Hammad al-Mansur, Chief Vizier to the Sultan. He made a short welcoming speech – Harry didn't catch it all, his Arabic was still a little rusty. It seemed they were to be directed to rooms in the palace and had been offered a change of clothes and a bath.

The formalities complete, the vizier went back inside with his retinue. They were left in the care of two black slaves, who ushered them into an inner courtyard, then led them up some narrow stairs to their rooms.

Their quarters were palatial, at least. They each had their own bedroom, with an enormous salon in between that looked out over the flower gardens. It was blessedly cool after the furnace heat of the city. The air was ripe with orange blossom and jasmine and remarkably tranquil. The only sounds were the bubbling of a fountain and the screech of a peacock as it rustled its feathers in the marble flagged courtyard below.

'Look at this,' George said, turning in a circle, looking at the fretted panels of cedar, the shining marble floors, the bronze doors with their ornate bosses, the arabesque ceramics of interwoven geometric design on the walls. The salon even had the intricately decorated ceilings that the Moors called *muqarnas,* a honeycombing effect quite unlike anything Harry had ever seen before.

'It will do, I suppose,' Harry said. 'Not quite the style I am accustomed to.' He walked into his bedroom. They had laid out some clothes for him on the bed, a linen shirt, a smock, loose white cotton trousers. 'Are we going native?' he called out to George. 'You told me to bring my dress blues.'

George leaned in the doorway. 'I suppose these are for comfort around the palace.'

The doors flew open, and two slaves entered carrying silver trays with honey cakes and melon. Another one came in with a silver pot and two glasses filled with tea and mint leaves.

They went out onto the balcony. Some pigeons cooed around the deep baths and pools, other arcaded apartments like theirs looked over the shadowed cypress trees and tunnels of jasmine flowers. It was a languid world of greenery, water pools and swooping swallows. Hard to believe that on the other side of the walls there were beggars with no feet pleading for alms in the filthy alleys, Negro slaves in steel chains being herded behind strings of camels.

'Well, this will do for a few weeks,' Harry said. 'In fact, I might get to like it. No offence, but a few times on the ride down from Tangier I was ready to murder you.'

'I told you. Money for old rope.'

'I think my arse is about to drop off. How long do you think we'll be here?'

'Few weeks at least. They have to give us time to train up the artillery.'

An hour ago, Harry had thought he would sleep for a week. Now, a bath and a good stiff drink and he might begin to feel like himself again.

They explored the corridors, found a stairway that led up to the roof. The city lay stretched in front of them, like a vast nomad camp, a shabby oasis surrounded by a green belt of palm trees and featureless scrubland. The noise of the great market square rose, sometimes loud, sometimes faint, changing with the strength of the breeze.

It was not a city you could wander, he thought, there were drifts of sand on every corner, you would need a mule just to reach the medina. In fact, there was nothing remarkable at all about it except for the startling dark red minaret at its centre. No matter where he looked, his eye was always drawn back to the Koutoubya, the only stone building in this ruinous desert heap of dried mud and sand.

Just below the parapet was a band of black and green iridescent tiles. It appeared as if there had once been tilework in all the many niches on the face of the tower, but most of these had crumbled away with time. On the summit, were three metal globes, arranged one above the other and decreasing in size, glowing golden in the setting sun.

'This is nothing like I imagined,' Harry said.

'You expected Cairo?'

He lit a cheroot. 'Well, not pyramids. But something grander than this. Look at it. Sand everywhere, even in the streets.'

The sun started to sink down the sky, the palms and minarets throwing long and deep shadows. The glittering snow peaks of the High Atlas turned pink, then mauve.

And as it dipped below the horizon, the first of the *muezzin* began his plaintive call to prayer, followed by the wailing of another, then another, until the city echoed with a dozen, two dozen voices, chanting their ancient song from the parapets of a dozen mosques.

When the last strains died away, there was a shockingly brief twilight and then the city and the valley fell to a profound silence. In London, he thought, I would just be getting started. There were days when I was only now risen from my bed.

George pointed towards the mountains, now fading into the dark. 'That is where we're headed. The Atlas Mountains. They are ruled by warlords, they call them *Kaïds*. They pay nominal fealty to the Sultan, depending on their mood. On the other side of the mountains is the Sahara, and that's part of Morocco too, but it's quite lawless.'

'What about the rebellion?'

'All I know is that the rebel chief is a man called Bou Hamra. He's hiding in a fortress up there somewhere. Our job is to blast him out.'

Harry shook his head. 'Never thought I'd find myself in uniform again.'

'Life is full of surprises.'

'I hope there aren't any surprises on this commission. All I want is to get my money and go home.'

George slapped Harry on the shoulder. 'You look all in. Too much debauched living. You're out of shape.'

'You can't have too much debauchery, George. Only not enough.' He stubbed out his cheroot, put the stub back in the tin for later. 'I'm going to kick off my boots and sleep for a week. You don't think our vizier friend could get me a bottle of brandy? Medicinal purposes.'

'It's a Muslim country. You'll have to make do with mint tea.'

Harry went back down to his room, to silk coverlets, soft pillows and gentle breezes cooled by the murmuring fountains below. He was asleep before he had even got his boots off.

He woke about an hour later to the sound of a pitched battle.

It was dark and he couldn't remember where he was. He staggered out of bed, realised he only had one boot on. A massive explosion briefly illuminated the room, and he saw his other boot lying on the carpets. He sat down and worked it back on.

He still felt foggy from sleep. 'Morocco. I'm in Morocco.'

He went looking for George.

There was another crash, followed by a shower of sparks. Perhaps it's the rebels, he thought, a pre-emptive attack on the city. 'George?' He wasn't in his bed. 'George, where the hell are you?'

The corridor outside was lit by gas lamps, he followed it until he found the stairs to the roof. He saw a familiar silhouette leaning on the parapet, and the glow of a cigarette.

'George. What's happening?'

'So you're awake. When I got up, you were snoring fit to wake the dead. I thought you were going to miss the show.'

The sky was ablaze with the colourful explosion of rockets, reds, silvers, golds, greens. The smell of gunpowder carried on the hot summer breeze, it reminded him of other nights, in Egypt, whole towns and villages aflame.

'What's going on?'

'You still think we're overpaid? Imagine what this little display costs. And they say he does this three or four times every week.'

'Fireworks?' Harry said.

'His latest craze. He has them shipped to Tangier, then hauled down here on a camel all the way from the coast. Must have cost a king's ransom. Plus there's insurance to cover the freight and every step of the way someone adds their commission. Believe me, our wages are nothing compared to what he spends on all his little fancies.'

Another crack, like a rifle volley, as a wall of Catherine wheels exploded into flame, a waterfall of fire in various shades of pink and green.

'Haj Hammad, was up here earlier. He told me that they brought an expert from England to stage these little shows. The Sultan has made him a permanent member of his court.'

After the Catherine wheels, there was another crack of rockets, dozens of them, one after another, trailing coloured sparks over the clustered flat roofs and the brooding tower of the old mosque. The night's grand finale.

There was an eerie silence when it was over, Harry could hear the shouts and screams from the crowd in the great square, the glow of torches, the drift of the smoke across the crescent moon.

'I wonder what the people here think of it,' George said. 'One rocket would feed a family for a month. It's an outrage. Don't you think so?'

'It's just fireworks, George.' Harry lit the stub of the cheroot he had saved from that afternoon.

'All these beggars in the street. And he wastes his money on firecrackers.'

'You're a better man than me. Here I am living in a palace, there are slaves bringing me dates and watermelon and if I had a bottle of Gordon's I wouldn't give the poor a second thought.'

'That's not true.'

'I think you overestimate me.' Harry watched the smoke from the fireworks drift across the shallow moon. 'How long did you say we'll be able to rest up here. A few weeks, was that what you said?'

'Something like that. Well, maybe not a few weeks exactly.' George seemed vague about it.

'Didn't you ask this Haj Hammad?'

'You know what these fellows are like,' George said. 'They only tell you what they want you to know.'

'A bit like you, George.'

'What do you mean by that?'

'I mean, you would probably be a better gambler than me, you know how to keep your card close to your chest. For example, you never told me how you found out about this commission. You left the Army a long time ago.'

'Do you remember Peterson?'

'Should I?'

'We all graduated from Sandhurst at the same time.'

'Wait a minute. The weedy-looking fellow with the moustache that looked like an albino caterpillar?'

'He's a major now.'

'Well, that's the Army for you.'

'I bumped into him one day, in the Strand. We went for a drink and he told me he'd been on secondment with our consulate in Tangier. He was the one who told me the Sultan was looking for retired artillery men, asked me if I knew anyone that was interested. I said I would act as a sort of intermediary and give him a percentage.'

'Wait a minute. You never told me anything about percentages. Do I have to give him part of my two thousand pounds?'

'No, of course not. You're doing all the work. I'll take care of Peterson's share.'

'Right.' Harry ground his cheroot out under his heel. 'But why did you pick me, George?'

'The truth?'

'Well, alright then. But sugar coat it first.'

'There wasn't much choice. Most of the fellows from our regiment are either still in the Army or have got themselves jobs, families. They have too much to lose.'

'So I'm the only one who's basically wasted his life and has nothing more to lose.'

'Is that sugar coated enough?' The hubbub from the Jemma el-Fnaa had died down, and the ancient city settled again to silence. 'I'm going back to bed,' George said. He turned for the stairs, hesitated. 'You know, this might be what you need. To turn things around, I mean.'

'Are you trying to save me, George? Is that it? Am I a charity project, saving up your good works for heaven?'

'Well, why not?'

'Forget it. In the end, we are what we are. Still, I'm grateful for you showing up that night, and I'll be glad of the two thousand pounds if we get it.'

'Goodnight, Harry.'

As Harry watched George disappear down the stairs, he felt a wave of gratitude. It was good of him, even if he did sound like his old Sunday school teacher sometimes. He didn't want to let the man down. It wouldn't be easy as George thought, for him to hold his end up. He looked down; his hands were shaking. He could feel the sweats coming on. That was the trouble with Africa, not a drop of good liquor to be had anywhere, even in a palace.

He heard someone coming up the stairs. He thought it was George coming back.

'Don't tell me you found me a bottle of brandy?'

'I am afraid not,' a high-pitched voice, said in perfect English. 'These Moors, they don't know how to enjoy themselves.'

He got to his feet. He couldn't see the man's face, but he knew by the size of him that it must be the vizier, Haj Hammad.

'Sorry. Meant no offence,' Harry said.

'There is none taken. Although the Koran prohibits the drinking of strong liquor, I have been known to partake of a little myself when I travel to a Christian country. To grease the diplomatic wheels. You enjoyed His Majesty's display of fireworks?'

'You speak good English.'

'Thank you. I can speak French quite well, also. And your friend says you have some Arabic?'

'I'm a little rusty. I was posted to Cairo for several years. I picked it up then.'

'Cairo, yes. Your colleague informs me that you were in the British Army there.'

'Yes.'

'He also tells me that you are a highly decorated soldier.'

'They gave me a medal once. It was nothing, a rush of blood. I'm not a particularly brave man.'

'Well, bravery can be overrated. Most brave men of my acquaintance died young. I, however, am still here.'

Alive, and eating well, Harry thought.

'You were a captain in the artillery.'

'Is there anything he didn't tell you?'

'Yes. He didn't tell me why they stripped you of your medals and sent you home in disgrace.' Harry didn't answer and Haj Hammad gave a small but apologetic laugh. 'You must excuse me. You must understand, an employer doesn't hire a man he knows nothing about. I made some enquiries of my own.'

'I wasn't sent home in disgrace. I resigned my commission.'

'And why did you do that?'

'I was ordered to.'

'Ah.'

'There was a problem between me and a certain general of our army.'

'What sort of problem?'

'The sort of problem that required me to leave.'

Haj Hammad waited for Harry to elaborate. When he didn't, he said: 'Your colleague has told you why *Sidna*, our Sultan, has hired your services?'

'He said that you wished us to help you put down a rebellion.'

'Yes. Unfortunately, there are always rebellions. It is a large country and almost impossible to administer. The people object to paying taxes, and we object to not receiving them. It causes tension. So, the Sultan is required to take his army into the more distant parts of his dominions every two or three years to impose order. But this year the need for our intervention is far more urgent. There is a usurper.'

'Bou Hamra,' Harry said.

'Yes? How much did your friend tell you about him?'

'Very little.'

'Bou Hamra has attracted quite a large following. He has great charisma and dazzles his followers with a few cheap magic tricks. He is like a magician.'

'He pulls rabbits out of hats?'

'Instead of pulling rabbits from hats, as you say, he raises the dead from the grave. Or so they say. He also claims to be a direct descendant of the Prophet.'

'Doesn't everyone?'

Haj Hammad laughed. 'A good point, but we should take care not to blaspheme. The point is, this man has gathered many followers, and the problem must be excised at its root.'

'Or blown apart with the three new cannons you have acquired.'

'Precisely. They are truly beautiful weapons. You will gasp when you see them.'

'Gasping costs extra. Where did you get them?'

'They were a gift from the Ambassador of the United States in Tangier.'

'And these Spanish artillery men who preceded us. They have already trained some men for the gun crews?'

'Of course, and they eagerly await your arrival. They are already quite proficient. I think you will be surprised.'

'If they know one end from the other, I will be amazed. What happened to the two Spanish gentlemen who preceded us?'

'They are no longer in our employ,' Haj Hammad said waving a hand airily in the air. 'Well, I will wish you goodnight now. I hope you find your quarters to your satisfaction.'

If only you knew, Harry thought. 'They are adequate.'

'I'm pleased to hear it. Enjoy your rest.'

Harry stayed on the roof for a while longer, lit another cheroot. This was the time of day he hated most, when he was alone with his thoughts, had nothing to keep him company but his dreams and the whisperings of his soul. He often wondered how contented men spent their nights. It must be pleasant to be untroubled by your own mind.

He closed his eyes and thought about the dusty rows of gin bottles on their glass shelf in the saloon bar of the Crown. For a long time now it had been the only way he could get to sleep. Without a good stiff drink the nights were endless, spent rummaging around in his interminable thoughts, trying to find something of comfort, or value.

There must be something in the world worth caring about.

He only wished he knew what it was.

CHAPTER 4

He supposed he must have fallen asleep sometime during the night, though it was still only half-light when he woke. He looked through the window, saw a pair of swallows swooping through the painted cedar beams in the corridor, preening themselves on the balustrade. He watched them for a time, heard the soft pad of bare feet outside the door, the palace slowly coming awake.

One of the palace slaves came into his room and seemed perturbed to find him still in bed. He said something to him in Arabic. He talked so fast Harry had to make him repeat it three times.

You must come. Get dressed. Follow me.

Harry looked for George. His bed was empty. Perhaps he had already got dressed and gone. What on earth was going on now?

He reached for his cotton trousers and kaftan, but the man shook his head and pointed to his dress blues. Someone had retrieved them from his luggage while he slept and had them laundered and pressed. They hung in the cedar *armoire* in the corner of the room.

He put them on, quickly examined his reflection in a mirror. Quite impressive, with the gold buttons and braiding and the polished black knee length boots, even though he'd probably die of sunstroke before the day was out like half the men at Kassassin. He slipped on his field cap and straightened his shoulders. An officer and a gentleman again.

A long time since he had been that.

'Alright,' he said. 'I am ready. Lead the way.'

He followed the man down the stairs and through a door with peeling vermillion paint. It led to the outer court. George was waiting for him, in his blues, astride a white Arab stallion. Two turbaned cavalry waited with him.

'What's going on?'

'Sorry about this. The vizier sent for me an hour ago. I was still half asleep myself. Apparently, we have to inspect the artillery.'

'At this hour? It's barely light.'

'You know what it's like down here. In a couple of hours it will be too hot to do anything.'

They rode through the dark, as the *muezzins* sent up their dreadful wailing over the city. Harry saw silhouettes moving in the shadows, the smoke from cook fires, men in *djellabas* pissing in alleys, cats stretching and yawning on walls in the first splashes of sunlight.

They rode out through the city gates.

Thousands of the Sultan's troops were drawn up on the plain.

Harry was surprised; not that some of the regiments looked like ruffians press-ganged from the East End docks, but that some were decently turned out, in smart uniforms and in good order, drilling with Martini-Henry breech loading rifles.

They all wore red tunics with yellow braid, blue baggy trousers reaching to their knees and rakish red fez caps. They had jaunty yellow shoes on their feet. They each wore a small crimson cloak, a *tarboosh*, despite the heat.

A regimental sergeant shouted a command in what to Harry's untrained ear sounded like a dialect of English heavily accented with Arabic. He knew a little bit of the language from his time in the Army, but at first, he couldn't make out what they were saying. '*Prezim Achram*!'

George leaned over. 'I think that's "Present arms",' he said.

'They're well drilled.'

'The Vizier calls them his *askaris*,' George said. 'They're his standing troops, the infantry. Their general is a British major,

MacLean. He was with the Ups and Downs.' It was a reference to the 69th Lincolnshires, whose regimental number read the same way, whichever way you looked at it. 'Kaïd McLean, they call him.'

'Where is he?'

'He's in the Rif, somewhere to the east of Fez, putting down another rebellion.'

'What's an Englishman doing here?'

'The same as us, Harry. The Sultan hired him to train his army.'

'Did he now?' Harry said. He nodded away to his right. 'Not all of them, by the looks.'

Along with the *askaris*, there were a number of regiments of irregulars. They looked to Harry as if they had been dragged by their feet out of the nearest medina: there were grey-beards side by side with boys no older than twelve, the lame leading the way for the wall-eyed, and all of them marching out of step, chatting away to their neighbours as if they were in the camel market. They were dressed mostly in rags. Harry's soldier's instincts took over and he took inventory of their weapons, a mishmash of rusted swords and ancient muzzle loading flintlocks he hadn't seen since the wars against 'Urabi.

'Look at this lot,' Harry muttered. 'Robbers and cutthroats. Where have you brought us, George? The uniform isn't very…'

'Uniform?' George said.

'That fellow has bare feet. Where are his shoes? And there's a whole row there, barely a tunic between them.'

'I am told they sell their uniforms to buy food.'

The sun had risen over the city walls, and Harry had to shield his eyes. Up ahead, there was a slight rise, where a group of riders were waiting under a single judas tree. The man at the centre sat hunched in the saddle of a black stallion. He had a sparse beard and despite the silver and jewels on his horse's caparison, he wore only a turban and a simple kaftan, with no chains or medals or any other kind of decoration. A near-naked Sudanese stood beside the stallion holding a giant sunshade of red velvet, while other slaves used long ostrich fans to wave away the flies. There were two mounted Black Guards on either side.

The man was surrounded by officers with plumed horses, court officials that Harry recognised by their white robes and crimson tarbooshes.

'The Sultan,' George said.

One of the officials broke away and rode towards them. Harry recognised him. It was Haj Hammad.

He immediately felt sorry for the vizier's horse. It was a fine-looking stallion, but he'd seen mules in the market with panniers piled as high as two men who had looked happier with their burdens.

After the ritual greetings, Haj Hammad said something in rapid Arabic that Harry couldn't follow. George turned to him. 'The Sultan wishes to see what progress we are making with the cannons.'

'Progress? What's he talking about? I haven't even seen the cannons yet.'

Haj Hammad launched into a long speech. Harry got the impression George was being harangued, though his Arabic was still so rusty he could only make out a few words. Why couldn't he use English? He saw the Sultan watching them and supposed the old boy didn't trust his Grand Vizier as far as he could kick him.

It sounded to him as if the Sultan were planning to leave on his campaign the very next morning. That couldn't be right, surely.

'What was that all about?'

'Among other things, he said their gunners are very well trained. They just need someone to help them refine their skills.'

'So he says. I talked to him last night, asked him about the two Spanish officers who were here last year.'

'Did he tell you what happened to them?'

Harry shook his head. 'Wouldn't say.'

There was a din of pipes and drums followed by the thunder of hooves. He turned in the saddle, saw the banners and glinting spears of a squadron of cavalry at the van of a column emerging from the city gates.

'Good God,' Harry said.

Three horse drawn caissons and limbers galloped across the plain towards them. A troop of gunners ran behind, in smart red uniforms and tarbooshes. The cannons were unhitched from the caissons and swung into position. There was an old tomb crumbling to ruin about a quarter of a mile distant. It seemed they were about to use it for target practice.

Harry got down from his horse and walked over. George followed. Haj Hammad was helped down from his own horse by two black slaves, who supported him, one on either side, as he followed them over.

'You see, I told you. Magnificent, are they not?'

Well, he understood that much Arabic. Harry chose his reply carefully. 'I have never seen anything quite like them.'

'When Bou Hamra sees them, he will tremble and fall to his knees. Their names are *al-wahsh*, *al-raed*, and *al-iirhab*.'

'The Monster, the Thunder and the Terror,' George translated.

'When were they last taken apart and oiled and examined?'

Haj Hammad ignored the question. 'The Sultan is most eager to see what you can do,' he said and nodded to the two slaves who helped him back to his horse. He rode back to the huddle of officials alongside the Sultan.

'Do you know these guns?' George said.

Harry walked along the line. He pointed to the largest of them, the one the vizier had called *al-wahsh*, the Monster.

'This beast here is known as a Napoleon 1857. They used a lot of them in the American Civil War. It's light enough for cavalry, I suppose, but if we get into the high Atlas, I don't know what we're going to do with the damned thing. It's really designed to use cannister shot against infantry. Still, they say you can fire anything out of it. Coconuts if you have any. It's cast bronze so it probably won't kill anyone standing behind it. This one was made in the Union.'

'How can you tell?'

'The muzzle swell. See how it's flared at the end? The Confederates used straight muzzles.'

He walked down the line. There were two smaller cannons. He stopped at the first, *al-raed*, the Thunder. He squinted at the plate on top of the barrel. 'This one's over fifty years old. The Bulldog, the Americans called it. They probably used it against their Red Indians.' He looked along the muzzle. 'Another bronze smooth bore.'

He turned to the gunner standing behind the trails. 'Where's the ammunition for this?'

The man pointed to the caisson. Harry went over, opened one of the ammunition boxes. 'Twelve pounders, explosive shells, they can do a bit of damage. At five degrees of elevation you can fire it, say, a thousand yards. At least it's a proper mountain gun. You can break the whole lot down into three loads, put them on the back of a mule or a horse.'

He went to the last cannon, *al-iirhab*, the Terror. He shook his head.

'What is it?' George said.

'A Parrott.'

'Can you teach it to talk?'

'Very funny. I'll tell you what it would say, if you did: *Whose turn is it to die today?* Because it could well be you or me.'

'What do you mean?'

'See this wrought iron reinforcing band? All the Parrott rifles have it. It's there for a reason.'

'I don't understand.'

Harry slapped the barrel with the flat of his hand. 'It's made from cast iron.'

'What difference does that make?'

'A cannon needs to be strong enough to withstand the explosion that reduces gunpowder to a propellant gas. Those bronze cannon need a bigger charge because they have what's called windage between the shot and the barrel. What that means, is that there's space for the gases to leak out, which is bad, but it also means there's less stress on the barrel. Because bronze is more flexible, the barrels hardly ever burst. Cast iron is stronger but more rigid. They can burst at the muzzle or near the trunions. Even if they've been properly maintained, they're dangerous as hell.'

'Well, the Sultan is expecting more fireworks.'

'He may get more than he bargained for. Us, too.'

'It would be unlucky, wouldn't it? After all, what are the chances? We only have to fire three rounds.'

'George, you are talking to a man who has made a very close study of the laws of probability, and to be frank, if you stand next to one of these guns, you'd better make sure your affairs are in order.'

He looked along the ranks of the Sultan's gunners; their looks of cheerful optimism struck him as somehow tragic. There were five men to each cannon and at first inspection, Harry had to admit, they looked as if they might know what they were doing.

He walked back to *al-wahsh*, the Monster, and nodded. The gun team sprang into action. He and George walked a little way up the rise to watch.

One of the gunners cleaned the vent with a long spike, while another man wormed the barrel. It was just for show, he knew, the cannon was cool, there were no hot embers to fire the gunpowder. But they seemed eager to impress.

The ramming gunner put the charge down the barrel while another man - in his battalion they referred to them as powder monkeys - fetched a round from the limber and brought it forward in a leather pouch for the gunnery officer to check.

He carried it over to the ramming gunner who put the round in the muzzle and used a long rod to push it down the barrel.

The gunnery chief stepped forward and checked the sight. He signalled to the man at the thumbstall who moved the trails to the left using a hand spike. The officer fiddled with the elevation and stood back, apparently satisfied.

The man at the thumbstall cleared the firing hole and the gunner stepped forward with the friction primer. It was attached to a lanyard. The commander shouted an order and the other gunners stood back. The gunner inserted the primer, leaned away from the gun, and pulled the lanyard.

The gun roared, jumping back several yards with the recoil.

Harry looked up at the tomb. The ground erupted in dirt and sand almost fifty yards to the left.

'I think I shall go down and render assistance,' Harry said.

George put a hand on his arm. 'It's too dangerous.'

Harry removed his hand as if he were removing lint from his sleeve. 'If it all goes wrong, I want you to read the eulogy. I don't want a dry eye in the house afterwards.'

Harry walked slowly down the hill. The men at *al-raed* had loaded a twelve-pound spherical shell into the muzzle and the commander had stepped forward to sight it. Harry tapped the commander on the shoulder and he hastily moved aside and saluted.

Once Harry had the cannon properly sighted, he stepped back and nodded to the gunner to prime the firing pin. There was an argument between the gunner and the man at the thumbstall, who was trying to take the lanyard away from him.

George had followed them down. 'What the hell are they jabbering about?' Harry said to him.

'This one thinks it's his turn to fire it. Says he's tired of just standing there with his thumb on the hole.'

'Tell him he'll do what he's told.'

George barked out an order. The man didn't look very happy about it. He glared at Harry. He's trouble, this one, he thought. He had dark eyes and a full red beard and there was something about him Harry didn't like.

He wouldn't turn his back on him on a dark night.

'Remove yourself, George.'

'We're in this together.'

'Well at least, take ten steps backwards. He counted him back, ten paces, then nodded to the gunner who spiked the firing pin in the hole.

'Fire!' Harry shouted.

No one moved.

He tried again, in Arabic. Still nothing.

'Try it in Spanish,' George shouted.

'What the hell is Spanish for fire?'

'Fuego?'

'No, that's 'flame'. I remember. *Dispara el arma!*'

The cannon roared and when it landed there was another roar as the timed fuse exploded and the tomb blew apart. A piece of the white curved roof cartwheeled through the air and landed in the branches of an argan tree a hundred yards away, sending a herd of goats scattering in all directions.

Harry heard a smattering of applause. It came from the top of the hill, where the Sultan was watching with his officers. The gunners all grinned at each other, except for Redbeard.

Harry and George walked back up the slope to the horses. 'See, I told you,' George said. 'Nothing to worry about.'

They watched the third team go through their drill. The commander spent more time sighting the piece, shouted a command, the gunner leaned to the side, putting tension on the lanyard.

And the cannon blew itself to pieces.

They ran down the slope, through the billowing cloud of white smoke. As it cleared the first thing Harry saw was the gunnery commander, lying on his back, twenty yards from the cannon. There was not a mark on him, just his head was gone. Blood had soaked into the dirt from his severed neck veins.

The barrel of the cannon had torn itself off the rails and lay beside the wheels, the breech and a part of the barrel gone, right above the reinforcing band. Pieces of rusted iron lay in an arc for about fifty yards. 'Where's the gunner?' George said.

'I think I may have trodden on a piece of him,' Harry said.

The other men seemed to be unharmed, but they were all holding their heads, shaking them from side to side, deafened by the explosion. They were the lucky ones.

The vizier appeared through the smoke. Two of the cavalry officers rode down with him. He looked at the decapitated man, then at the cannon.

'What have you done to our beautiful gun?' he said.

'Your gun? What about me? I could have been killed,' Harry said.

'You are replaceable, the gun is not.' He shook his head. 'I must inform His Majesty,' he said, and rode back up the hill.

Harry turned to George. 'You know something, I've changed my mind. I'm going home.' He started to walk back to his horse.

'You can't,' George said.

'What do you mean, I can't?'

'They won't let you.'

'What?'

Haj Hammad rode back down the slope. His shadow fell over Harry. 'This is very bad,' he said. 'Fortunately, the Sultan does not wholly blame you for the destruction of his cannon.'

Harry knew enough Arabic to understand that much. 'Doesn't blame us?' he said.

'That is correct. He is willing to pay you the same fee for commanding two cannons as three, provided you can make the men fire them faster. And please be more careful in the future.'

'These cannons are death traps.'

'There is nothing wrong with them.'

'They need to be taken apart and properly inspected.'

'How long will that take?'

'A week.'

'Impossible. We leave first light tomorrow to hunt Bou Hamra. Sala 'am gentlemen.'

And he rode away.

CHAPTER 5

Harry and George waited side by side, on their horses, in the pre-dawn chill. The sun inched above the horizon, turning the minaret on the Koutoubya rose pink. Their horses fidgeted, twitching at the flies.

The court was a vast expanse of bare ground, with a covered colonnade of Moorish arches on one side. The army had been drawn up facing an arched gate in the wall on the opposite side, the infantry in the right and centre, the cavalry on the left, each man standing dismounted beside his horse's head. The gates swung open, and a regiment of the Sultan's Black Guard rushed out and formed themselves into a long line either side of the archway.

The soldiers all dropped to their knees, to a man, shouting: *'Long live the Sultan. Victory to the Sultan.'*

'Here they come,' George murmured.

The first rays of sun hit the walls, flashed on the brocade and silk banners of the cavalry as they led the way through the southern gate, the Bab-er-Robb. A wild lot, Harry thought, never mind their plumed horses and pretty saddles. Their faces were half-hidden in the hoods of their robes. They formed themselves up into a square.

'I shouldn't like to face them at the charge,' Harry said.

'If all goes to plan, they'll be charging the other way.'

'This is Africa, George. Anything could happen.'

Another bugle, another elegant fuss. A squadron of soldiers ran out of the gate leading a line of saddled horses. His Highness's officials scurried after them in their white robes and turbans, surrounding a crimson palanquin. As the cavalry square opened, Harry could make out the Sultan lying inside it, reclining on a royal blue divan.

Groomsmen trotted out a line of black stallions and paraded them before His Majesty. The Sultan pointed to one of them and the horse he had chosen was led over. It was sleek and glossy black, with a bonnet of primrose yellow tassels.

'Imagine if we did this for the general every time we went to war,' George said.

'At least we won't be following that bloody sedan chair the whole way.'

There was a melee as the Sultan attempted to mount the horse. Slaves rushed to help him, one of the mounts reared up in panic, a vizier or two almost tumbled from their saddles. Pandemonium, a cloud of dust, finally the resumption of something like calm.

'Is it going to be like this every time we set off?'

'Think of the money,' George said.

The vanguard formed up, an official holding a sceptre rode out in front. The standard bearers followed, with banners of brocaded silk and gold thread. The poles were topped with golden orbs, and they flashed in the morning sun. Two young goatherds watched from under a grove of palm trees as they trotted past, their mouths open, their goats scattering in all directions.

The sultan followed behind, a solitary white figure on his splendid horse. Black slaves ran alongside, fanning him with long white scarves to keep the dust and flies off his sacred personage. Another soldier rode behind him, holding aloft the Imperial parasol of crimson and gold, to shade him from the sun.

They finally set out along the dusty road towards the Bab-el-Hamar.

The horses' hooves kicked up clouds of dust, which created a romantic gauze over their procession, the glimmer of the Sultan's banners, the cavalry in their long white robes, the sumptuous velvet saddles. The vanguard was followed by a long line of veiled and white-robed women, mounted on mules. Every man in the army turned their head away as they passed.

It was breath-taking, a sight he knew he should never forget, but he was impatient with it. Surely, this was not the speed they would approach the mountains. One of these blind and lame beggars at the gates could drag themselves there quicker.

And here at last were the soldiers, the ones who would actually do all the fighting, Harry supposed, while the sultan ate figs under his parasol. The irregulars were as irregular as he could have imagined, tribesmen carrying muskets that would have been ancient at the time of Napoleon. He saw spears and axes and God in heaven, maces. The Chief Vizier said the army numbered over ten thousand, but Harry reckoned it must be at least double that number, if you counted the Sultan's harem, as well his privy councillors, and the rabble of hangers-on that trailed after them. 'You said six months, at most,' he said to George.

'In rough terms.'

'Six months and the end of the line still won't be out of the gate.'

A shrug. 'It is the way they do things here.'

Haj Hammad made his way back along the line towards them, on a mule.

'Who are all these people?' Harry said to him. 'I understand the camp followers, every army has need of a few of those. But what about these fat men in tarbooshes? Some of them have families larger than my old battalion.'

'They are merchants, from the capital. They go with the sultan everywhere.'

'And the beggars?'

'They follow the merchants. On holy days, the merchants give them alms. You do not do this in your country?'

The procession from the gates seemed to never end. The city will be empty by the time we leave it, Harry thought. Finally came the artillery, or what was left of it. Harry stared gloomily at the two remaining cannons. They had been mounted on the backs of mules, a troop of mounted infantry following as escort.

And then, the most astonishing sight of all, *al-iirhab*, a jagged hole in the brass barrel, strapped into a harness on the back of a camel. Mobs of young women followed it out of the gates, ululating as they ran.

'What the hell,' Harry said.

'Our lord Sidna, the Sultan, refused to leave it behind,' Haj Hammad said.

'But it's useless. He does understand that it cannot be repaired?'

'It's a symbol of the sultan's divine power. It cannot be abandoned.'

Harry turned to George. 'Well this should strike fear into this Bou Hamra fellow,' he said. 'It's not a military campaign. It's a travelling circus.'

'But the Ringmaster holds the purse strings,' George said. 'Shall we ride?'

The further they travelled from Marrakesh, the drier the ground, nothing but grey sand and stones. They passed a few thatched hovels and ragged tents, where knots of women with matted hair stared at them with blank faces. There were a few dogs and some naked and dirty children. They had nothing to fear from the Sultan because they had nothing worth stealing.

They passed a number of waterwheels, which at least allowed them to water the animals, then pressed on.

There were no roads to follow. The army spread out across the plain, raising a vast cloud of dust as it went. Haj Hammad told them the Sultan's expeditions into the bled-es-siba, the lands outside his direct control, were called, in Arabic, a *'harka'*. It meant, literally, 'the burning'. That was the way it looked to Harry, a vast conflagration turned south from Marrakesh, destroying everything in its path. They stretched from horizon to horizon, an array of men and horses and lumbering mules and swaying camels fading into the haze.

How the people who live here must loathe him, Harry thought. No surprise that there is never any peace in this country. He may be God's representative here on earth, but he must seem to them more like a heavenly curse than a blessing. You'd be better pleased to see a plague of locusts heading your way.

The land was as uncompromising and dull as he remembered from his time in Algeria. They crossed a vast plain, with a few olive groves, the domain of goats, sheep and a few miserable looking cattle. The looming ramparts of the mountains rose in front of them, forbidding yet also promising a welcome relief from the deadening heat.

It was as much as he could do to keep in the saddle. He thought he was used to privations, he had soldiered in the desert and in the jungles in India, but by the afternoon even two thousand pounds seemed a pittance for such torture. The *sirocco*, the desert wind that blew from the Sahara, whipped up stinging clouds of red dust. He was glad of his *cheiche*. It kept off the worst of the sun and protected his face from the grit and sand.

He had promised himself once he would never drag himself behind another general ever again. He thought he was through with all this.

He stared at George, in his colourful scarf, with what looked to be a much better horse. You bastard, you did this to me.

Why did I ever let you talk me into it?

Early the next morning they started up the valley. The mountains rose up the sky, and as soon as they reached the foothills, the country around them began to change. There were houses of stone and plaster, nestled among groves of palms and olive trees, even villages with walls and flanking towers. The air was clamorous with insects.

The road ahead coiled ever upwards into the mountains and started to narrow, becoming increasingly dangerous. It was nothing more than a goat track now, in some places no more than two or three feet wide, the loose stones slipping beneath the feet of their horses and mules, a cliff on one side, a sheer drop to a boiling ribbon of river and boulders on the other. The *harka* snaked through the mountains for miles.

Progress was slow, but finally they emerged onto a wide plateau, where they followed the broad green banks on the upper reaches of the river. It was wilder here, littered with boulders, and the mountains towering above them, the peaks glistening with snow even this far into the summer. They had left behind the palmetto scrub, were surrounded by conifers, pines and evergreen oaks.

As the country changed, so did the people. The Arabs of Tangier and Marrakech wore beards and long robes with mud-stained hems. But these mountain men had short black cloaks revealing sinewy calf muscles and tough rawhide sandals. Many of them shaved their heads, leaving just a ringlet over each ear, with white cloths or strings of camel hair wound round their temples. They were mostly gaunt and smooth-cheeked, with just small, pointed beards on their chins.

The biggest difference was in the women. The Berber girls reminded Harry of the gypsies he had seen selling heather around

Covent Garden, in their faded hand-me-down smocks of red, blue and green. They didn't cover themselves up like the Arab women of the Maghreb, they even decorated their hands and faces with henna, in intricate swirls and patterns, and even the poorest girls had pendants and bangles and anklets, silver or coral and amber.

They all wore woollen leggings, but he guessed this was less to do with modesty and more to protect themselves while walking from the thornbush, which was everywhere. When he looked at them, they looked right back, and he swore a few of them even smiled and tried to flirt with him.

Haj Hammad referred to them and their language collectively as *'shillah'* – the outcasts. 'They are a proud people,' he said, when Harry asked him about them. The vizier's lip curled into a snarl. 'They have no cause to be.'

Towards evening they arrived at a fortified town, perched on a crag high above the river. A pretty little village crowded down the mountainside below it, row upon row of yellow mud houses nestled among the olive groves. The minarets of several small mosques were silhouetted against a backdrop of snow-capped mountains, dazzling against the cobalt sky.

Harry looked back over his shoulder, realised how far they had climbed. In the distance, framed by the green valley walls, lay a stunning panorama of rolling desert of sand and stones. Several oases of palms and white houses were dotted across the plain and in the far distance he could make out the pink tower of the Koutoubya mosque rising above the city of Marrakech.

The *harka* stopped to pitch camp, so that the local chieftain, the Kaïd, could ride out and make his obeisance to the sultan.

The Sultan's enclosure was erected first, nothing could be done until the golden globe was raised above the great lord's tent. His quarters were hidden behind a nine-foot-high wall of white canvas at the middle of the encampment. They were told that no one save the Sultan's women and their female slaves could enter.

When it was done, the rest of the army moved into action, and the entire *harka* came to rest remarkably quickly and quietly. The tents of the soldiers were spaced around the Sultan's, then came the *hoi-polloi*, the camp followers and merchants and beggars and the rest. It was like a city of itself, that packed up and moved with the coming of every dawn.

Soldiers hurried here and there, bright specks of colour in their often-ragged uniforms, horses and mules and camels kicking up clouds of dust, the piercing blast of bugles and drums.

The vizier had arranged for slaves to erect Harry and George' tent each evening, all they had to when they finally eased themselves down from their horses was take their place in the folding chairs that had been placed in front of them.

The tent was seven paces wide, luxurious really, with a number of thick carpets thrown across the floor, and a camp bed for each of them. There was also a square table, covered with a striped Moorish cloth, for their looking glass and shaving mugs, even a folding wash handstand.

'You never had this kind of luxury in Egypt, did you Harry?' George said.

'No, but at least we could console ourselves with loose women and cheap gin.'

'A touch of sobriety will do you a bit of good.'

'And abstinence?'

'I do believe your heart needs as much rest as your liver.'

'I wasn't talking about my heart,' Harry muttered.

As the sun sank down the sky, he saw a figure appear at the balcony of the minaret, heard the *muezzin* begin the call to prayer, his voice echoing through the valley.

The whole army came out of their tents to pray, ten thousand, twenty thousand men on their knees, all facing towards the east. It was a remarkable sight.

'I think we could get to like it here,' George said.

'You're out of your mind,' Harry said and went back into the tent to dream about how much Gordon's he could buy with two thousand pounds of Her Majesty's sterling.

Night fell, and Harry was summoned to supervise the firing of *al-wahsh* outside the sultan's enclosure, the signal that the Sultan was retiring to bed. It passed off without incident, to Harry's relief, and the camp fell to complete silence, except for the Sultan's musicians playing outside his enclosure. Pretty it was too; Harry recognized the *oud*, a sort of lute, and a *kamenjah*, 'that stand-up violin thing', as George called it, and pottery goblet drums. But after a while one of His Majesty's personal musicians produced a banjo, and Harry wanted to tear his ears off.

It was unlike any army camp he had ever seen. Not a single soldier was fighting or swearing. Even the camp followers respected the silence. The discipline was extraordinary. Harry wondered if it would be the same on the battlefield.

He and George sat around their campfire, the flames throwing shadows on the claw-like branches of an ancient olive tree. The tent city was dotted across the plateau, lit with thousands upon thousands of lanterns.

The sultan's orchestra finished serenading their *grand seigneur*. The only sound was the river rushing over the rocks hundreds of feet below them in the gorge.

'Listen to that,' Harry said.

'I can't hear anything,' George said.

'Yes, that's what I mean, the silence. Even the beggars have stopped their moaning.' He lit a cheroot, the last of the supply he had brought with him from London.

'Your hands are shaking,' George said.

'Nonsense,' Harry said and clenched his right hand into a fist.

'It will be like that for a while. The tremors, I mean. It will pass.'

'I haven't got the shakes. You're imagining things.'

'My father said that if a man could stop drinking for a month, he could stop drinking for a lifetime.'

'I never said I wanted to stop drinking, George. I said I wanted some quick money so that I can drink even more. I still haven't given up hope of finding a bottle of absinthe hidden in one these mosques.'

'You're a better man without it.'

'You've never seen me sober before, so how can you be so bloody sure?' Harry flicked ash from his cheroot into the campfire. 'Let's talk about something else, for God's sake. Tell me about home. How are your sisters? What were their names again? There was Jean, Agatha, Margaret and...'

'Camilla.'

'That's it, Camilla. She was the dark one.'

'No, she was the blonde one. The youngest. You always ignored her whenever you came by the house.'

63

'I never did.'

'I'm afraid it's true. She was in love with you, of course.'

'In love? With me?'

'You were oblivious. She would cry every time you went home.'

'She was only a little girl.'

'She was fourteen. Old enough.'

'What happened to her?'

'She married a painter.'

'That was bad luck.'

'In fact, he ended up doing rather well. Became a friend of Collier and the Huxleys and that crowd. I thought his stuff was pretty dull, but he exhibited at the Royal Academy and won all sorts of medals and prizes. They have three children now and live in Paris.'

'Turned out for the best, then.'

'The others are all married. I'm the only one that can carry the family name.'

'Not much hope there, then.'

'I may not have your natural charm with women, Harry, but I like to think all is not lost yet.'

'Well, good luck with all of that. My brother carries all my father's hopes, and he's welcome to them.'

'I don't think you quite mean that.'

'Well there's not going to be any little blond Harrys running around anytime soon. I'll leave the burden of carrying the family name to brother Tom.'

'You know it's a shame, don't you?'

'What is?'

'You Harry, your life. Every man should have a purpose.'

'I did have a purpose, once. I was going to inherit the family business and be a rich man. But it was decided that my brother should have a purpose instead.'

'You would have hated it, sitting in an office, adding up rows of figures in a ledger book.'

'I would have liked the chance to find out.'

'If you'd stayed in the army, you would have been a major by now.'

'I am a major. A major disappointment. I don't know why everyone minds so much. I don't.'

'I used to talk about you, in the officer's mess, in Alexandria, after you went home. When I said we were friends at school together, everyone wanted to buy me drinks.'

'They were consoling you.'

'Harry, you were a *hero*.'

'No, I wasn't.'

'There's not many men would have done what you did. I certainly couldn't have done it. I'd have ridden off with the rest of the gun crew.'

'It was nothing. A bit of a scrap with a couple of Egyptian fellows, all over in a few minutes, and the officer I was trying to save died anyway, so it was all pointless, wasn't it?'

'They don't hand out the Victoria Cross for nothing, Harry.'

'They take it back for nothing though, don't they? You've never asked me, by the way.'

'Asked you what?'

He finished the cheroot and tossed it into the fire. 'If I did it. If I stole that money.'

'You are a lot of things, Harry. You're reckless with money, you drink too much, and there's been far too many women. But one thing you're not, and that's a thief.'

Harry cleared his throat and sat a little straighter. 'Right. Well, that's the elephant out of the room.'

'The problem with you, Harry, is that you've lived your entire life for an audience of two people. Three if you count Lucy. You know what I think? That day at Tell El Kebir, I think you wanted to die. I think you wanted to sit at the back at the funeral and gloat while your father and your brother threw themselves over the coffin and wept buckets.'

'Don't forget Lucy. She has to be there as well. And I want the union jack draped over the bier.'

'You're impossible.'

They heard a sentry snap an order outside the Sultan's canvas-walled enclosure, saw a figure in white make his way through the ring of Black Guard, and head through the camp towards them. They couldn't see his face in the dark, but Harry knew by the waddling gait that it had to be the Chief Vizier.

They stood up. Haj Hammad performed a perfunctory *temennah,* which they returned.

'I have news.'

'Bou Hamra?' George said.

'Our spies tell us he is not far from here. He is trying to recruit some of the local tribes to his cause. We believe he is hiding in a town called Azdouz. The local Kaïd is sympathetic to him.'

'We will hardly take him by surprise.'

'That is why I have decided that we will split our force. You will go ahead with the artillery along with the *maghasen* and two thousand of our best *askaris*, reach him before he expects, and cut off his line of retreat.'

'We need to overhaul the cannons before we use them in a battle,' Harry said.

'Overhaul?' He worked his prayer beads between his fingers.

'Take them to pieces, check the barrels for cracks. It's the reason the first cannon blew up. Metal fatigue exacerbated by corrosion in the cannon's bore may have reduced its material strength to the point that it was no longer able to contain the pressure of firing.'

'The first cannon blew up because God wished it. *El hamdu billah.* Also, because you were out of practice. Fortunately, the Sultan saw fit to forgive you.'

'It was nothing to do with me. Those cannons are ancient.'

'How long will this 'overhaul' take?'

'A day,' Harry said, 'perhaps two. Also I need more time to train those men. And two replacements for the men who were killed.'

'We will give you more men. We have plenty of men. But we do not have time. The Sultan will never agree to this. Anyway, you fire the cannon every night, as the Sultan retires.'

'A blank round.'

'What is the difference? The cannon fires.'

'Perhaps you should tell the Sultan what I have said and ask him for his thoughts.'

'I am his adviser. I know what the Sultan will think because I will tell him to think it. No, tomorrow we go after Bou Hamra with the cannons. I wish you a good night.'

He turned and headed back to the enclosure. After he'd gone, George gave Harry a look. 'Must you incite the man?'

'Just make sure you are out of the way when they fire the cannon, George. No point in both of us going home in a cigar box.' He sighed. 'Well, if we're going to war tomorrow, perhaps we should go to bed and get some sleep. If I'm going to die tomorrow, I want to leave behind a good-looking corpse.'

CHAPTER 6

Early the next morning they started up the valley towards Azdouz. Harry reckoned they had about a third of their force, which Haj Hammad assured them would be enough. By the next night, he said, they would have Bou Hamra in chains and he and George could go home. The caissons were dispensed with and the mountain gun, *al-raed,* was dismantled. The pieces were mounted onto the pack saddles of some long-suffering donkeys.

The path soon narrowed to a dirt track, the rocks crumbled away, treacherous underfoot. Harry and George dismounted and walked their horse along the track. It wound its way up and around a spur. When Harry peered over the side, he could see a river rushing over the rocks hundreds of feet below. He nudged George on the arm. 'Who has the hardest job, the vizier's slaves or our donkeys?'

George looked where Harry was pointing. Slaves helped Haj Hammad clamber down from his mule. He was wheezing as if he was the one who had carried his considerable girth all the way up the mountains. Four of them picked him up and started to carry him up the narrow path.

'I think I'd rather carry *al-wahsh*,' George said.

They reached the highest point of the defile. It opened onto a valley, a river boiling between fields of ripening corn and groves of walnut trees. There were two stakes planted in the ground, each had something impaled on it. It was impossible to make out what they were, the birds and insects had been at them, and they had turned black in the sun. The smell was appalling.

'What the hell is this?' George said.

'They look to me,' Harry said, 'like heads.'

They heard someone laughing behind them. Haj Hammad told his slaves to let him down. They were blank with exhaustion and soaked in sweat all of them.

'Ah, your predecessors!' Haj Hammad said. He put his hands on his hips and shook his head.

'What?' Harry said.

'I believe these are the Spanish artillery officers. They came with us last year on our *harka*. They were careless. I did warn them, but they allowed themselves to be captured.' The vizier took a closer look. 'They have not aged well,' he said and gave another chortling laugh, astonished by his own wit.

'How do you know it's them?' George said.

Haj Hammad pointed to something lying on the ground at the base of one of the stakes. Harry saw what he was pointing at and stooped to pick it up. He clawed some of the dirt off it with his fingernails. 'It's an epaulet,' he said.

'I thought Bou Hamra might keep him alive. The captain was very knowledgeable about artillery but insufferably arrogant I'm afraid. Perhaps he got on his nerves.'

He rapped out a sharp command and the slaves picked him up and carried him down the other side of the defile.

Harry looked at George. 'Like taking sweets from a baby, you said.'

'Don't believe him. He's making it up.'

'This looks genuine enough to me.' He tossed the epaulette away. 'You alright?'

'I don't want to die, Harry. Not here. For nothing.'

'Everyone dies for nothing, in the end. Have to take the long view. Come on.'

They remounted their horses and made their way with the rest of the column towards the mouth of the valley. A range of steep, low hills rose in front of them, funnelling them towards a steep ravine. The army drew to a halt and a rider was sent back along the line to order George and Harry forward.

The vizier needed to speak with them urgently, he said.

Haj Hammad was lounging on a divan that had been set up in the shade of a walnut tree. A black slave had produced rosewater, another had a fan to cool him. Two of the army officers were with him.

'We are going to be ambushed,' he said.

'What?'

He pointed to an open ledge of green grass halfway up the ravine they were about to enter. 'Up there.'

'How do you know this?'

'Because it always happens. Every time we pass this way.'

'Why don't you go another way?' Harry said.

'That would show weakness. No, we will let them ambush us. And we will teach them a lesson. We will fire the cannon at them.'

'You can't,' Harry said.

Haj Hammad sat up, tossed the watermelon rind to one side. 'Why not?'

'By the time you've got the mules in there, got the cannon assembled and into position, we'll lose at least half of the gun crew to sniper fire.'

'You will fire the cannon at the rebels. It is what we are paying you for. If I wish you to fire the cannon, you will fire it.'

Harry looked at George.

'Hide behind a rock. Let the men fire the cannon.'

'They'll all die.'

'As God wills,' the vizier said, cheerfully. '*El hamdu billah!* We have plenty more men. As the lieutenant says, just tell them what to do and stay out of the way.'

They went back to the horses. Harry saw his gun crew unslinging *al-raed* from one of the mules, reassembling the carriage, bringing up a pair of horses.

'You heard what he said,' George murmured, 'Stay the hell out of harm's way.'

'Of course,' Harry said.

They rode into the ravine single file, following a regiment of the Sultan's *askaris*, who led the way on foot. The cannon followed, bumping and clattering over the rocky ground, half a dozen mules behind them with the boxes of shells. They were escorted by a detachment of cavalry.

The walls of the defile rose around them. The air crackled with heat. It was early in the afternoon and the light was blinding. They were marching directly into the sun. Harry couldn't see anything.

He felt the hairs standing on the back of his neck. He looked up, thought he saw something glinting on the grassy ridge above them, the spot that Haj Hammad had pointed out to them as the likeliest spot for the ambush.

The cavalry officer in front of him fell off his horse.

The sound of the rifle shot was delayed, it was still echoing around the defile seconds after the cavalry officer had dropped from the saddle. The horse bolted in panic, dragging its rider over the rocks, the man's foot caught in the stirrups. Either it was a lucky shot or there was a marksman up there and in a couple of minutes they'd all be dead.

Harry leaped from his horse. George was slower to move. Harry grabbed him by the arm and dragged him towards an outcrop of rocks. He heard something zip through the air close to his face and kick up the dust in front of him.

He threw himself behind a boulder, pushed George's head down when he tried to peer over the top to see who was firing at them. Snipers loved the curious.

'This is unacceptable,' Harry said.

'What?'

'I did not agree to getting shot at. It is not part of our contract.'

'We should have stayed back there with the vizier.'

'And leave these clowns with the cannon?'

He could see the gun crew setting up *al-raed* away to his right. There was something about their childlike enthusiasm that made his heart bleed. There were at least a dozen men with rifles up on that ridge, and judging by all that black smoke, the guns they were using were antiques, but they'd had plenty of practice with them. He saw one of the men get a shell from one of the mules and put it in the satchel around his neck. He'd taken just a few paces when a bullet hit him in the back, and he fell face first in the dirt.

The gunner with the red beard abandoned his post at the thumbstall and ran over to him. Harry thought he meant to drag him clear. Instead, he pulled the satchel off his shoulder and went back to the cannon, pushed the shell down the barrel. Another of the gunners stepped up with a ramrod, immediately screamed and fell back, clutching his face. Redbeard picked up the rod, settled the shot in place and then he turned around, clearly looking for someone.

He's looking for me, Harry thought. He can see me hiding here behind the rock.

But this isn't my battle. Or my country. I'm not even supposed to be here. I'm only being paid as an adviser, not to risk my neck in a skirmish of no account to anyone.

He heard George shout: 'Harry, no!'

He was already up and running towards Redbeard and the cannon. Ten strides and he was there. He crouched down under the sight, turned the screw to raise the elevation, shouted instructions to Redbeard who had gone back to his position at the trails. 'Left, to the left!'

Something zinged off the barrel and he felt a sharp pain in his cheek, ignored it. He turned to the man at the lanyard, was surprised to see him still standing there, bolt upright, as if they were on the training ground.

Harry scrambled clear. 'Fire!'

The concussion sent the cannon jumping back on its wheels. Harry looked up at the ridge. There was a flowering of dirt and smoke and half the mountain tumbled down into the valley in a landslide of stones and earth. At least half a dozen bodies went with it. The firing stopped.

Redbeard stood up, brushing dirt and sand off his robes. Harry grinned at him and clapped him on the shoulder. 'Well done.'

Redbeard scowled and spat in the dirt. He muttered something as he walked away. He had heard it spoken behind his back a thousand times, in Morocco and Algeria. 'May God destroy your grandfather and your great grandfather in the flames of the eternal regions.'

George came up behind him and clapped him on the shoulder. 'Good to see you still know how to win the loyalty of your men.'

'It's a gift.'

'What the hell were you doing? You could have got yourself killed. This isn't your fight, Harry. We're just here to collect our two thousand pounds. Try and remember that.'

'Do my best,' he said, but George somehow knew that he wouldn't.

Azdouz slept in the sun. Harry took out a field glass and surveyed the town. It guarded the entrance of the valley, situated on a small hill in the crook of the river. The kasbah appeared rose-pink in the late afternoon sun. There were guard towers along the crenelated walls.

The plain in front of it was dotted with olive groves. Some cattle had come down to drink by a shallow river. It looked peaceful enough for now, but appearances could be deceptive. Harry could see a goatherd running his goats towards the gates before they closed, the flock raising a cloud of dust. The local Kaïd was ready for a fight.

There was a man standing on the walls, a pair of glasses held to his eyes also. His guards stood either side of him. For a moment he and Harry regarded each other across the plain.

'Bou Hamra,' Harry murmured.

George held out a water canteen. Harry took a swallow at it, wishing it were red wine.

At least it was cooler up here after the baking trek across the plains. If this was as bad as it was going to get, then it still seemed like a decent enough bargain. They'd blast this Bou Hamra out of his nest, take the money and head back to Tangier. If one of those blasted cannons didn't take off his head.

'You're bleeding,' George said. 'Sit down under that tree over there, let me have a look.'

Harry did as he was told, George fetched his black medical bag, squatted beside him. He used tweezers to pick some pieces of iron out of his cheek. 'The bullet must have hit the barrel, and ricocheted away,' he said. 'Another foot to the right, and we'd be burying you over there in the olive grove with the captain of the cavalry.'

'What would you put on the headstone?'

'Good for nothing, died for nothing. Thought he was immortal.'

'Perfect. Write that down.'

'Haj Hammad told you to keep your head down. Why would you do something like that?'

'I didn't want to look like a coward in front of that man with the red beard.'

'I'd rather be alive and stupid than dead and brave,' George said. Harry winced as he bathed the cut in some tincture, he said it would keep the wound clean. 'The Sultan is making his way up the valley with the rest of the army. We will have to wait until he arrives before we attack. Then we'll take our money and go home.'

'One skirmish, a few days in the saddle, if the cannon doesn't blow us up tomorrow it will have been worth it.'

'I don't know why you're in such a hurry to go back. All that's waiting for you are the bully boys and the bottle. Next time there may not be anyone to save you.'

'That would trouble you?'

'It would seem a terrible waste.'

'Thank you for saying so.' George packed away his bag and Harry got back to his feet. They heard the plaintive wail of the *muezzin* calling the faithful to prayer from the minaret inside the walls. A star appeared in a sky blue as gunmetal.

'One more day.'

'You'll lose your two thousand pounds at the tables within six months.'

'No,' Harry said and laughed. 'It won't take me that long.'

CHAPTER 7

Harry was awake before dawn, decided to smoke his last cheroot. It was an extravagance but another week at the outside and they would be back in Tangier, and he could buy as many as he wanted. George had found coffee; it was black as tar and strong enough to wake a dead man.

The town looked beautiful in the dawn light, the kasbah silhouetted against the snow-dusted peaks of the High Atlas. The smoke of the morning cookfires drifted up in the still morning air.

Out on the plain, the Sultan's infantry was falling in, bugles sounding in every direction, as the Sultan's army prepared for battle, all the sounds and smells he had tried so hard to forget over the years: horses, gunmetal, drums, camp smoke, fear.

'You have to stay well back,' Harry said.

'What?'

'I don't trust those guns. No point in both of us getting blown up.'

'You said it was only the bronze castings that were unreliable.'

'I wouldn't be surprised if *al-wahsh* was last used at the Battle of Gettysburg and no one's thought to oil it or clean it since. Would you trust it?'

'We're in this together. I will be standing right there beside you.'

There was shout from one of the officers, taken up by ten thousand throats: '*Ah! salih en-Nebi, Rasoul Allah!*'

The prophet is great, he is the messenger of God.

The same shout came from the walls, fainter on the wind.

'So we both have God on our side,' George said.

'Of course. Have you ever been in a battle where nobody had God on their side?'

Harry raised his field glasses, could make out the glint of rifle barrels along the parapets. The Sultan's *askaris* were within a thousand yards now, out in the open, there was no cover. They were advancing slowly, as if they were getting ready to run at the first crack of rifle fire, which they probably were.

The morning air was still; he could hear, even from this distance, the commanders shouting instructions, ordering their men to keep formation.

There was a sudden volley of rifle fire from the walls, a rapid, nervous spitting of Mausers, and the lines of *askaris* seemed to shiver and break as some of them lost their nerve. A few of them fell.

The *askaris* raised their own rifles and fired back, their bullets pinging harmlessly into the mudbrick walls. Harry realised that the rebels were actually better armed, for the *askari* lines were soon shrouded in black smoke from the gunpowder they were using. He supposed that most of the infantry were like his own gunners and had never fired a shot in anger before today.

There was a blast from a bugle, somewhere on the plain, and the *maghasen,* irregular cavalry made up of wild tribesmen from the boondocks, galloped in. They waved their flags and fired their ancient Mausers at the red *pisé* walls, then rode away again.

'They might as well throw sand for all the good they are doing,' he said to George.

'I think we are needed at the guns, Harry.'

They rode to the rear, where the two cannons had been drawn up, a thousand yards from the walls and directly in front of the gates. Off to the side, there was a forest of flags and banners, the sultan's commanders, their horses caparisoned in bright silks and brocades.

They looked magnificent and were safely out of the way of any stray bullets.

The *askaris* had attacked in two columns, leaving them a clear field of fire. Harry got down from his horse and walked over. The gunners were all waiting for him, standing eagerly at attention beside the two cannons.

Harry glanced at Redbeard. He had a dagger at his belt and looked like he would like to slit Harry's throat with it. By the look of things, he had promoted himself to ramrodder on *al-raed*.

A phalanx of riders separated from the sultan's coterie and trotted over. It was the Chief Vizier. He had marked today's occasion by exchanging the mules and slaves for a white stallion, with a burgundy saddle and bright yellow tassels around its ears.

'Are you ready, captain?'

'To do what?'

'Once you bring down the walls, our troops will advance and take the town. We will capture Bou Hamra, and your commission will be finished. Your friend assures me you are eager to be home.'

'You and your fellow commanders should take up a position a little further away. I cannot vouch for their safety even at this distance.'

'Bou Hamra's men cannot hit us from there.'

'I don't mean the enemy, I mean the cannons. A piece of iron from an exploding breech can take a man's head off at a hundred paces.'

Haj Hammad nodded and rode away. Harry saw him consult with the sultan and his fellow ministers. They withdrew even further, almost back to their encampment.

'Are you sure you don't want to go with them?' Harry said to George.

'I got you into this. I'll stick it out to the end.'

Harry went to *al-raed*, the smaller of the two guns. He nodded to the man at the thumbstall – no more than a boy, really - who opened the firing hole and cleaned it. The rest of the crew completed the priming and loading of the shell and stood back.

Harry stepped forward and sighted the barrel, adjusting the elevation wheel, while the number three gunner used a lever to adjust the rails. As Harry stepped back, he felt someone brush his shoulder. Redbeard was standing almost directly behind him.

'Back to your post, gunner,' Harry said.

'You have aimed too far to the right,' he said.

'Back to your post or I'll have you flogged.'

Redbeard gave him the devil's look and stepped back.

Some of the *askaris* were already retreating, a wild look in their eyes, dropping their ancient muskets and rusted swords as they ran. An officer pursued them. He raised his revolver and fired at a man not ten paces away from him, missed. The man kept running.

It doesn't fill you with confidence, Harry thought.

He knew Redbeard was watching him. I should step to the side, he thought, if the barrel cracks, and I'm standing behind it, they will be sweeping me up all morning. He saw the look of contempt in Redbeard's eyes. Their eyes locked.

Al-raed's gunners covered their ears. Harry smiled at Redbeard and gave the order to fire. The man at the lanyard took a step to the left and the cannon roared and jumped back on its rails.

Harry waited for the smoke to clear and brought his field glass to his eyes. He was gratified to see that one of the gate towers was rubble, the massive, barred gates now no more than splinters. He strode to the other cannon, supervised the loading.

'Let me do it,' Redbeard said.

Harry stared at him in astonishment. If we were in the Corps, he thought, this man would already be stretched over a cannon, having his back striped for his indiscipline. But I only have eight trained gunners left, I need him. And despite himself, there was something about this black-eyed cutthroat that he admired.

Harry sighted the big gun, straightened, strode back several paces, again standing directly behind the barrel. He heard George shouting at him to get clear.

He looked at Redbeard, standing to the side with his ramrod and murderous eyes and smiled.

Then he turned to the gunner at the breech. 'Fire,' he said.

Harry strode towards the Sultan and his coterie of advisers, watching from their horses on the slight rise above his position. Haj Hammad walked his horse forward.

'I think you'll find the gates are down,' he said.

'I am impressed,' the vizier said.

'You didn't expect to be?'

'I had no opinion on the matter.'

Haj Hammad turned his horse away and nodded to one of the cavalry officers. Trumpets blasted across the plain.

The vanguard, most of them expendable, just tribesmen from the provinces, had renewed their charge in a brilliant flash of colour. He heard their ululations on the still morning air, even from this distance.

The *askaris* had also taken encouragement from the bombardment and were running across the plain towards what remained of the gates. White smoke blossomed along the walls as the defenders opened fire. Futile, Harry thought. It's all over for them now.

George was waiting for him, back at the guns.

'Nicely done,' he said.

'Like hitting a camel with a watermelon in a grocer's shop. When do you think they'll give us our money?'

The *maghasen* poured through the hole they had blasted in the northern gates, the *askari* following close behind. It was like watching the tide run towards a race, an irresistible surge of men and horses. The view of the walls was obliterated by the smoke from the cheap cartridges the *askaris* were using, but the battle for the town didn't last long.

In minutes, the roar from inside the walls turned from the sounds of battle to unholy shrieks and screaming as the Sultan's men went about the serious business of killing and looting. A glow rose up the morning sky from innumerable fires, deliberately lit, quickly followed by black billowing smoke.

The Chief Vizier and a few of the officers walked their horses across the plain. The Sultan remained behind. Harry and George decided to follow,

Their horses picked their way through the smoking rubble and the ghastly hedgerows of bodies at the gates. How many of these corpses am I responsible for, Harry wondered. Add their ghosts to all the others who haunt my dreams.

He drew his *cheiche* across his face. The thick smoke drifting through the streets was choking. The cobblestoned yard behind the gates was littered with more bodies. It seemed the *askaris* were more proficient with bayonets than they were at marksmanship.

The killing wasn't done. He could hear the familiar sounds of screaming and killing from further inside the town. Some *askaris* went past them, already headed back to camp, stumbling under the weight of loot. One had a thick carpet over his shoulder and was trying to balance a tea tray with teacups, while his companions staggered along with sacks of flour and painted wooden chests on their shoulders. Another had a canary in a cage.

'Aren't you going to stop this?' George said to Haj Hammad.

He looked at him blankly.

'The looting.'

'It's their wages,' he said.

Harry heard a noise, it came from close by, sounded like a child's cry. He saw a boy, perhaps ten years old, standing at the doorway of a house. It was well ablaze. He was trying to get inside, but the heat was driving him back. What was in there, that made him want to go into that inferno? A toy, a pet, a mother, a sister?

Black smoke was billowing from the windows. No one could survive that.

He jumped down from his horse and ran over, just as the roof fell in with a crash in a shower of sparks. The child screamed and took a step back, tried again to run inside. George shouted a warning.

One of the walls toppled in a white cloud of dust, and the boy disappeared under it.

Harry started to tear at the fallen stone with his bare hands. 'Help me!' he shouted.

George leaped out of his saddle. The bricks were too hot to touch with his bare hands, so he kicked them aside with his boots. Harry had hold of the boy's shoulders, and he helped him carry the boy clear.

In seconds, the building blossomed in flame and crumbled to nothing even while they watched. When they were safely clear, they laid the boy gently down on his back. He was covered in white dust, and there was blood on his face.

'Are you both mad?'

They turned around. Haj Hammad was watching them from his horse.

'Why would you do such a thing?'

'We couldn't watch and let him die,' Harry said.

'Why not? It was your cannon that set fire to his house. Now you want to save him?'

They didn't have an answer for him.

'Well, he's your problem now. But I will tell you now, it would be better for him if you threw him back in the flames.'

He and the rest of the officers spurred away and rode towards the square to find Bou Hamra.

CHAPTER 8

Harry heard the din of drums and trumpets and stepped out of the lean-to, wondered what fresh atrocities he might have to witness next. They had been kept awake all night by the hair-raising screams coming from the *askari* camp.

A smoke haze hung heavy in the air. The *askaris* were burning everything, crops, houses, bodies. The *harka* was earning its name. The town had been reduced to a rubble of timber and mud brick, like a child's trampled sandcastle on the beach.

Only with the putrid smell of burned flesh.

'I swore I'd never put myself through this again,' Harry said.

George came to stand beside him. 'At least it's stopped now.'

A scarlet and green pavilion had been erected outside the royal encampment, A solitary figure, dressed all in white, walked slowly through a line of officials, all of them with their foreheads pressed to the dirt as he passed. He took a seat on a royal blue divan inside.

The *askaris* and the irregulars were drawn up on the plain in front of his pavilion along with what remained of the former population of the town. They all fell to their knees.

'May God prolong the life of our Lord,' they chanted in unison.

Prisoner's heads had been piled so high on and around the two cannons, that the muzzles of the two guns could no longer be seen. Harry had tried to stop them, but several Black Guards had shoved him away and would not let him close.

Soldiers, weighed down with loot, would stop to toss another head on the pile beside the cannons, shouting 'May Allah bless our Lord Sultan!'

One of the officers threw them five silver *douros*, the going rate.

Meanwhile, local Berber chiefs had been riding in all morning with their escorts to pay fealty to the sultan. Harry watched through his field glasses as one of them climbed down from his horse and was escorted to the sultan's tent, barefoot, by an escort of Black Guards. He prostrated himself in the dirt and crawled the last twenty yards.

The Kaïd of the town watched on from a tiny cage that had been built from the barrels of Mausers taken from his own dead soldiers. He had been stripped down to his trousers, as miserable a human being as he had ever seen,

He turned away and went back into the lean-to, where George was bent over the little boy they had rescued from the burning shanty the day before.

'How is he?'

'I've cleaned his wounds with silver salts, sutured the cut on his head with catgut thread, debrided the burns as best I can. He's sleeping. I've given him some laudanum for the pain.'

'Will he live?' A shrug. 'If he does, what are we going to do with him?'

'I've no idea.'

'He has no family, no money, his home's been destroyed. I wonder if we did him a favour by saving him.'

'Would it have been better to let him burn to death under the rubble?'

'Can you imagine how life treats kindly with an orphan in this country?'

'If it comes to it, I'll take him back to England with me.'

George stared at him, speechless.

'Well, why not?'

'We do not have time to go through all the reasons why that is a very bad idea.'

'Are you saying I couldn't do it?'

'Harry, you can't even look after yourself.'

'How dare you?'

'Are you saying it's not true?'

'No, it's true, of course it is. But how dare you say it.'

The boy's eyes suddenly blinked open. He frowned in confusion, then bewilderment. When he saw them, he gasped and sat up, crawled to the other side of the tent, eyes wide, his knees drawn up to his chest.

'We won't hurt you,' Harry said to him in Arabic. He had saved some bread and honey from their breakfast and he held it towards him. 'Are you hungry? Do you want something to eat?'

He shrank further away into the corner.

'Perhaps he doesn't understand,' Harry said. 'Do you know any Berber?'

'No, do you?'

They heard a commotion outside. They turned around, it was the Vizier, he had of course half the Sultan's bureaucracy with him, and a platoon of the Sultan's Black Guards. He rode the hundred yards or so from the royal enclosure on one of his long-suffering mules.

A slave helped him down and another fanned him with a palm leaf, to keep off the flies.

'*Salaam*,' he said and executed a swift *temennah*. 'The Sultan sends his felicitations.'

Harry pointed to the two cannons, and the pile of human heads that surrounded them. 'What is this?'

'It is tradition. The soldiers are accustomed to making such offerings in gratitude for the victory.'

'They stink,' Harry said. 'They stink worse than the gentleman's lavatory in the Crown hotel in Lambeth. I never thought anything could.'

The heads had turned a greyish purple in the heat and had attracted thick flocks of ravens and buzzards that were squabbling and shrieking over this unexpected windfall. Or headfall, as George had called it.

'It's medieval,' Harry said.

The vizier's smile dropped away. 'The customs of other people always appear strange if you are not accustomed to them. The *askaris* are paying tribute to you and your guns for bringing us victory yesterday. You do not do this in your country?' He looked over George' shoulder into their tent. 'How is your new slave?'

'He is not a slave.'

'No? Then what are you going to do with him? Let him go? The *askaris* will be pleased. They have run out of fresh meat.'

'I know. We heard them celebrating last night.'

'You are a seasoned warrior, captain. Surely you understand the nature of war.'

'I understand it, but I don't have to like it. What's going to happen to that fellow?' Harry nodded towards the Kaïd in his cage under the trees.

'He will return with us to Marrakesh on the back of a camel for public exhibition.'

'Why don't you just kill him now?'

'That is not our way. The people must learn to fear the Sultan if they are to obey him. He must suffer his fate in public.'

'Do what you want, as you say, it's your country. We've done our job. Now it's time to go home.'

'The job, as you call it, is not completed.'

'We had an agreement,' George said. 'Once you had found and killed Bou Hamra, we would be rewarded and escorted back to Tangier.'

'Bou Hamra is still very much alive.'

'You said your spies told you he was inside the town,' Harry said.

'Our spies were wrong. We think he escaped hours before we arrived and has fled further into the mountains, looking no doubt, for other sponsors for his madness.'

'What does that mean?'

'It means we must go after him. And you will come with us. Your artillery has proved a great success. The Sultan may even pay you a bonus once this commission is completed.' As he turned to go, he stopped and pointed to the lean-to, and the little boy huddled inside. 'I believe you have created for yourself an unnecessary burden.'

He waddled back to the mule and four of his slaves helped him clamber back on the poor animal's back. He trotted back to the royal enclosure, surrounded by his clerks and sycophants. George went after him.

A few minutes later, he came back, looking flushed.

'Everything alright, George?'

'I told him we'd had enough.'

'What did he say?'

'He said he would sell us two horses to ride back to Mogador, if that was what we wished.'

'Wait, *sell us* two horses?'

'He quoted a fair price and I agreed.'

'Well, I didn't.'

'What? We could be wandering around this damned desert for the rest of the summer.'

'I don't care, George. Look, it can't be for more than a few weeks. We've come this far. I'm not going home without my two thousand pounds and that's the end of it.'

CHAPTER 9

The rider picked his way carefully up through the snowbanks and icefall in the forest. The fortress loomed from a ridge high above, in the shadow of the great *Jbel Toubkal*. Finally, he dismounted and led his horse up the narrow rocky path for the last steep ascent. A kestrel hawk circled above, its sharp staccato cries following his progress.

The entrance to the kasbah was guarded by massive oak-barred doors the height of four men. The Keeper of the Gate hurried across the inner court with a key the length of his forearm and inserted it in the lock. Slaves set their shoulders to the wood to jar one of them open just wide enough for the rider to enter. The iron hinges groaned with the strain.

The rider kept his head down, to shield himself from another flurry of snow and sleet.

Rows of dark stables lined the curtain wall on the south side. Above it, castellated lookouts ranged the walls, under the brooding shadow of the mountain. There were three colours; the whitewash of the stables, the ruddy stain of the bricks, the grey of the mud; in the pall of this winter afternoon all the colours seemed to have been leeched away.

The Keeper of the Gate had scores of keys on his belt, they were so heavy he wore a heavy silk rope over his shoulders to help support their weight. He shivered inside his heavy woollen *djellaba*, pulled the hood over his face as protection from the worst of the wind.

The rider followed him through the labyrinth of the castle, there were twenty-three doors to unlock. The slave knew the kasbah better than anyone, but even he had to stop every now and then to go to a window and peer out, in order to orient himself.

The salon into which the rider was ushered, was a contrast to the austerity of the fortress itself. The room was hung with panels of silks and brocades, intricately worked, while other decorations were so crude, they could have been the work of a small child. The walls were paved with painted tiles, the yew ceilings were bright with carved flowers painted in yellows and aquamarines.

Amastan sat by the fire, on a low divan, almost completely covered by his blue-black robes. His *cheiche* hid his entire face except for his eyes. And such eyes, the rider thought. Even here, at his repose, he wore a scimitar at his belt, a handle of mother of pearl and a blade of damascened steel.

'Zdan,' Amastan said and continued to stare into the fire. 'What news do you have?' His voice was soft and sibilant.

'The Sultan is only ten miles away.'

'He did not find Bou Hamra?'

'He has chased him all through the mountains as far as Zagora. Bou Hamra would not dare risk a confrontation with him. He plays the flea, biting hard when he can, then jumping away.'

'Very wise.' Amastan stood up, kicked one of the juniper logs in the hearth, making the flames jump. There was precious little warmth in it. He opened one of the shutters. Snow and sleet blew in, where it melted slowly on the rugs. 'I hope the sultan does not feel the cold.'

'The snows are early,' Zdan said. 'He would have hoped for better luck on his way through the pass.'

'Still, good fortune for the buzzards, I suppose.'

'He is losing hundreds of his men every day and even more to Bou Hamra's raiders.'

'You think our Sultan is in danger?'

'His advisers were telling him to return to Marrakesh weeks ago, but he wouldn't listen. He wanted to finish with Bou Hamra. Now Bou Hamra may well finish with him.'

'You really think so?'

'There are two thousand rebel tribesmen gathering at Taroudant. If they overtake the Sultan now, he is finished.'

'There is opportunity here, Zdan. There is also great danger. Do they still have the cannons with them?'

'Two. The third was destroyed before they left Marrakesh.'

'And the two Englishmen?'

'They are alive. Barely. As is the rest of the Sultan's army.'

'You have seen these cannons? You are sure they still have them?'

'It slows their progress, but the Sultan will not leave them behind for Bou Hamra.'

Amastan slammed the shutters closed again. His breath clouded on the air. Move more than a dozen paces from the fire, Zdan thought, and you might as well be standing on the top of the mountain.

'What should we do about this, do you think?'

'They will not reach Marrakesh in their present state. The Sultan's men are dying by inches. Unless we help him, he will lose his army, he may even lose his life. We can finish him off, take the cannons for ourselves, and then deal with Bou Hamra. When he is proclaimed the new sultan, he will be most grateful to us.'

'Bou Hamra would not know gratitude if it roared up in front of him in the shape of a giant lion and bit him on his sacred member. We will have to find another solution. Warm yourself by the fire. There is only one course for us. I will start to make the preparations.'

Four months they had chased Bou Hamra around the Atlas and into the fringes of the Sahara itself. Always he was able to stay one step ahead of them. The Sultan's army was too cumbersome, too slow. Harry and George had followed the *harka* as it burned a swathe across the lands of anarchy, the *bled es-siba*, the Sultan accepting the fealty of the tribal chieftains as they went, knowing they would rebel again the moment his army was again beyond the horizon.

They ventured as far as the Sahara itself, a torture of heat, thirst, and frustration. And still they had not found him.

Finally, his viziers persuaded him that he must go back. The great army turned around and headed back towards the Atlas Mountains.

But they had left it too late. The first snows came early, while they were still climbing up through the foothills. The snows were accompanied by a driving wind, that flung down the valley from the summits, howling and shrieking, laden with sleet. In the space of weeks, the pink dirt that had crumbled under their feet in powdery clouds when they had descended during the late summer, now became a freezing glutinous swamp under a rutted crust of ice. The *askaris* stumbled on, bundled in blankets and sheepskins.

Every day saw thigh-burning hikes deeper into the mountains, up vertiginous tracks made even more perilous by the snow. Every climb was followed by a sharp descent into another valley, slipping on ice and loose shale, the breaks for rest and boiling tea growing briefer as the Sultan and his viziers became more panicked.

The burning had become a freezing. The retreat was transformed into rout.

Soon they had climbed so high there were no longer any trees and so no wood for the fires. The camels and horses and mules grew weak with starvation, some of them stumbled into snowdrifts and died.

Soldiers hacked feverishly at the carcasses, loaded what little meat remained on the starved animals onto the backs of the beasts that yet survived. Soon all that stood between all of them and starvation was a little horsemeat and some camel steaks tough as goat hide.

Black clouds of ravens and vultures rode the icy currents above them, silhouetted against a sky the colour of pewter. Soon men started dying as well, from frostbite or exhaustion or exposure, were left unburied in the snow, stripped of their boots and their clothes.

Finally even *al-iirhab*, the useless bronze cannon that the Sultan's harnessed slaves and camels had hauled halfway across the Atlas and the Sahara was finally dragged to the edge of a precipice and allowed to tumble into the gorge below, so that Bou Hamra could not retrieve it and harness its magic.

Bou Hamra.

He had remained elusive. But now they were exhausted, and the Sultan's army was on its knees, he had instead found them.

Shots echoed down the passes every day as his snipers harassed their retreat and there was never a night that a few *askaris* weren't found the next morning with their throats cut.

For the first time Harry wondered if he would ever see England again.

The wind shrieked and howled as it drove through the high passes. Harry stopped to check that George was still behind him. He saw him, head down, stumbling as he led his horse up a face of frozen scree, the boy behind him, wrapped in a *djellaba* he had found or stolen, many sizes too big for him.

Harry heard someone shouting his name. It was the boy from *al-raed*, the one he had privately nicknamed 'Thumbstall'. He was lying in the snow, Redbeard and the rest of the gun crew were standing over him.

'What's going on here?' Harry shouted over the roar of the wind.

Redbeard had wrenched Thumbstall's jacket half off him. Thumbstall was clutching his stomach and the rag of a bandage that had been wrapped around his middle. It was seeping blood.

'What happened to him?'

'Musket ball,' Redbeard said. 'One of Bou Hamra's snipers.'

'Can't you help him?'

'What's the point? He's a dead man. We need his clothes.'

'I'm not dead,' Thumbstall groaned.

'Of course you are,' Redbeard said. The others started digging a shallow grave, clawing at the snow with their hands.

'Don't... don't.'

'You can't bury him. He's still alive.'

'You're not a doctor,' Redbeard said. 'What do you know of medical matters?'

One of the other gunners came over, the ramrodder on *al-wahsh*, put a hand on Harry's shoulder, lowered his voice to a whisper. 'The thing is, captain, we can't leave him here. Bou Hamra's men, they will cut off his head and take it as a trophy. Do unspeakable things to him, even if he's still alive. It's better this way.'

'Can't you bring him with you?' he said.

'He has a belly wound. Anyway, look at us. We can barely drag ourselves up this mountain.'

There was a yell. Redbeard and the others had kicked Thumbstall into the grave. They started shovelling the dirt and snow on top of him. Redbeard picked up Thumbstall's jacket and cloak and walked away.

He stared at the grave. The earth moved, a feeble shifting of stones.

What should a man do in such a position? What should a good man do?

He stood there in an agony of doubt. If I uncover him, then what do I do for him. They're right, I can't take him with me, it is as much as I can do to look after George and myself. He'll die of the cold anyway within a few minutes now they've taken his jacket and his cloak.

What should a good man do?

He went back to his horse, took the Martini-Henri from the holster on the saddle, and went back to the grave.

CHAPTER 10

The cold was so intense, he and George dismounted and walked beside their horses to try and keep warm. He made his way by instinct, his mind numb, concentrating on putting one foot in front of the other, trying not to think about the cold ache in his belly or the screaming of his leg muscles. He was so tired now that he kept slipping, grabbing rocks and thorn bush to keep from sliding back down the mountain.

His fingers were numb with cold. He wished he had gloves. He was shivering, a bad sign. He had to remind himself he had been through worse. In Egypt, at the Kassassin Lock, instead of ice and hunger and snipers there had been heat and thirst and dust storms. The principles were the same. If you have to walk through hell, one of his commanders had told him once, it makes no sense to stop.

He looked around for George, saw him slump to his knees. Where was the boy? He couldn't see him. He grabbed George by the arm and hauled him back to his feet.

No trumpets now, no drums, no banners, no camp followers. Harry looked back down the mountain. Their *harka* was reduced to a pitiful line of a few thousand, most of them lost among the low cloud and flurries of sleet, each engaged in his own individual battle as they struggled through the high passes. Bodies littered the trail. Ravens stood on the flanks of fallen horses, their beaks red with gore, the beast's entrails staining the snow.

An *askari* dropped his musket and stumbled on, too weak to carry it any further.

Two men went over to one of the dead soldiers, rolled the corpse over with their boots. Harry realised he knew them. It was Redbeard and Ramrod from *al-wahsh*.

'Look at him, we take off his hams, there's enough there for all of us for our dinner.'

'Walid was sick before he died.'

'Well, go hungry, I don't care.'

He took a curved dagger from his belt and cut two hunks of meat from the dead man's haunches. He wrapped the bloodied pieces of meat in cloth and put them in his pack.

He saw Harry and grinned. 'Dinner,' he said.

Dear God.

He was too exhausted to try and stop them.

As the sun slipped behind the mountains, they burrowed a deep hole in the snow, foraged for a few sticks to light a fire, tried to roast a little of the salted meat they had brought with them over the cold blue flame, tore at the half-frozen hunks of dry bread with their teeth.

This high in the mountains there were no trees, they had no wood for fires, just a few meagre embers here and there where soldiers had fired some bracken in an effort to heat some water for tea.

One of the *askaris* saw Harry watching them. 'In summer,' he said, 'it is so hot up here, there is only sand and lizards. Up here, there are only two choices, die of thirst or die of cold!'

The boy had managed to find a few dry sticks. They started a small fire but there was scarcely any heat in it. 'It's because of the altitude,' George said. They huddled around the poor blue flame, imagined a roaring log fire.

He had proved loyal and surprisingly resilient, the boy. They had learned his name was Mohammed, but George called him Mou. He had recovered well from his burns and the knock on his head and now he followed George everywhere and scavenged food and blankets for them from around the camp. George had given him a lecture about stealing, which had been received with wide-eyed bewilderment.

But sir, he had said, if we don't steal, how do we ever live?

'Why do you do this?' Harry said to him.

'Why do I do what, *sayeed*?'

'You get wood for the fire, you steal food for us, blankets.'

'You said that you will take me with you to England.'

'But why don't you hate us? I was the one who ordered the guns to fire on the town where you lived, it was me that killed your mother and father.'

'It wasn't you, *sayeed*. It was the will of God.'

'God had nothing to do with it.'

Mou put a finger to his lips. 'You should not say such things! Everything is the will of God. *Inshallah!* My father told me this, and so did the *imam*. We can say, *I will do this*, or *I will do that*. But it is God who decides if we will succeed, or if we won't, and it is God who decides when we have had time enough in our lives. So if the shell lands on our house, it is not you, or Mister George, it is God who says it should be so. It is written.'

It is written.

I wonder what is written for me here in the Atlas, Harry thought. Not another losing hand, I hope.

'What are we going to do about the boy?' George said, as they watched him cook some salted meat over the meagre blue flame in the fire.

'We have to get through this alive first.'

'Let's be optimists and say we do. What then?'

Harry shook his head. 'I don't know yet.'

'I suppose we could give him to an orphanage in Marrakesh.'

'No, George. I won't countenance that. Even back home, those places are no better than being in prison. If they don't bugger him to death, he'll be picking pockets in the Jemma-el-Fnaa this time next year. He deserves better.'

'Be careful, Harry. He thinks you're his new father. What's going to happen when he finds out you're going back to England and leaving him behind?'

'I'm not going to leave him behind.'

'Harry, a child needs a home, stability. Not gin, late nights and a procession of women.'

'Well, he'll want all that later. I just have to get him through the slow times, until he's old enough.'

'This isn't funny.'

'I'm not leaving him behind, George. And he's not our main problem right now. If we don't get over these bloody mountains, it's all a moot point, isn't it? How did we end up here? *The easiest money you'll ever make!* That was what you said.'

'I may have overstated my case.'

'I'm freezing to death, George. How did this happen? I always remember North Africa as being too damned hot. Now here I am, I have never been so cold in my whole life.' His feet were numb, and his boots were practically in the fire. He couldn't stop shaking. 'How many men have you saved, George?'

George shrugged, confused by the question. 'I have never counted.'

'You should. You're a doctor. Should keep a tally. I keep count of how many I have killed.'

'Why would you do that?'

'I never planned to. But, you know, these things come to you at night, and they won't go away. Of course, the exact count is always difficult when you are in charge of artillery. Did you kill ten or a hundred with that last salvo? You're too far away to be sure. But those men I killed in Tell el Kebir. I was close enough to see their faces.'

'It was you or them, Harry.'

'True. But when you wake up in a screaming sweat in the middle of the night seeing those men's faces, it doesn't seem to count for anything. What other dreams do I have to look forward to? Mou's parents, his mother, his father, I know about them. That's two more at Azdouz. Those men who ambushed us in the valley. The *askaris* found six bodies. That's nine. How many shall we say in Egypt? A hundred? Round figures.'

'It's war, Harry. You're a soldier. It's your job.'

'You were a soldier, too. But you saved lives, you didn't take them. For every life I take, you save one. I'd like to balance up the scales one day. Not unreasonable to want to do that, is it?'

'I doubt I have saved a hundred.'

'Well, give or take a few. The point is, no matter who you're fighting, you're always on the side of the angels, George.'

'I doubt that.'

'Of course you are. Tell me this. You hear a man groaning, he has been buried alive, he is trying to shift the earth off his body, to get to the light, to breathe. Yet he is badly wounded. If you help him, he will die anyway, from his wounds, from the cold. But if you leave him there, suffering, then bandits will come and torture him till death overtakes. What would you do?'

'I would put him on my back and carry him until I myself drop of exhaustion.'

'Yes, I believe you would.'

'I'm joking, Harry. I would do what you and I have both seen some fellows do, what no one talks about. I would find a way to put him quickly out of his misery. Why are you asking me?'

'No reason. It's just a question.'

Harry heard someone coming towards them in the dark, it was Ramrod, he had a hunk of meat wrapped in a piece of bloody cloth. He handed it to Harry. 'For you,' he said.

'What is it?'

'You eat,' Ramrod said.

Harry unwrapped it and sniffed at it. 'It's fresh. Where the hell did you get this?'

'You don't want?'

George snatched it back. 'It's horsemeat probably. For God's sake, Harry, we need to eat. Throw it on the coals, or else I'll eat it raw.'

Ramrod disappeared back into the dark.

George unwrapped the meat and held it over the fire with his knife. The flames were barely hot enough to sear it, and George was impatient, after a few minutes he cut it into three bloody pieces with his knife.

'Here,' George said.

Harry hesitated.

'For God's sake man, you'll starve.'

Harry took it.

It was the rarest steak he had ever eaten. It hardly filled their stomachs, it was just enough to remind them how hungry they all were. Mou finished his first, licking the grease from his fingers, then stared at the meat on the end of Harry's knife, he had a look like a rabid dog. Poor kid.

Harry took one last bite and handed it to him.

'Do you think that was mule or horse?' George said, licking the cold grease from his fingers.

'God knows,' Harry said, and hoped it wasn't Thumbstall.

He was shaking all over, there was ice in the wind, it bit through his greatcoat and the thick woollen *djellaba* he wore on top of it, even the sheepskins the vizier had brought for them weren't enough to keep them warm.

They piled anything they could find on top of themselves, a prayer mat they had found abandoned, some sacking they had offloaded from the mules. Every time Harry drifted to sleep from exhaustion, he was woken again a few minutes later by the shivering of his own body.

Snow had melted and seeped into his clothes. He saw Redbeard huddled by one of the cannons, the ragged bundles of the other gunners around him, they were snoring. How did they manage to sleep in cold like this? Hard men, these, who never expected anything better. He didn't expect to outlive any of them.

The night seemed endless, and they got no sleep. It was almost a relief when one of the guards shook him by the shoulder, told him it was time to go. Soon after, they heard the trumpets and drums, the order to march.

Men mounted horses and slung their rifles. Silent as wraiths, the army rose from the snow, as the first grease-grey streaks of light leaked across the eastern sky.

Harry could not feel his face. There was ice in his beard, he tried to pull it out and his whiskers snapped off in his fingers, frozen solid. Well, he thought, at least I won't have to shave now.

They stumbled on, hardly a man speaking, all of them alone with their own struggle and their own misery, saving their strength for the march. Harry kept sliding and falling on the snow, now stamped into a highway of muddied slush and ice by thousands of feet. They staggered on blankly, except for a few rest periods around the middle of the day, some men fumbled with frozen fingers to light small fires, and boil water for tea. They soon learned it took all their time just to coax a small flame from some meagre, sodden brushwood, and by then it was time to march again.

CHAPTER 11

Harry listened to the jackals calling in the mountains. He was too cold to sleep, occasionally he would slip into a few minutes of fitful dream then wake with a jolt, shivering. George woke him at some time in the night for his turn at the watch. He stamped his feet, trying to get warm. They had mounted a guard on their horses, suspecting that if they didn't, someone might kill them during the night and butcher them for the meat.

He spent the rest of the night shivering with cold, alone with the ghosts of all the men he had killed. Now that one of them had a face and a name, the rest would not leave him alone.

He winced at the pain in his feet. The blisters had broken days ago and now the worn leather of his army boots was rubbing the raw flesh of his heels. He couldn't afford to do anything but keep walking in them, they were all that stood between him and frostbite.

The river was swollen, launching itself down the mountain in torrents, bringing with it fallen trees, dead animals, and huge sheets of ice. Harry and George stood on the bank with their horses, staring at black rush of water.

'I don't fancy it much,' Harry said. 'That water looks damned cold.'

'Not much choice though, is there? Unless we want to stay here and freeze to death. Bou Hamra would love to hang your head on his wall. Something for his guests to talk about over dinner.'

Harry drew the hood of his *djellaba* closer around his face. He was cold, he was tired, he was dirty, he was exhausted. He looked at Mou, George had put him on his horse, he seemed completely unafraid, so eager to survive. His determination was touching but Harry no longer shared his enthusiasm for the struggle.

'I don't know how we're going to get the cannons over that,' George said.

'I don't care what happens to them. They're not my problem anymore.'

Redbeard and the half dozen men that survived from their original gun crews were busy building a raft of logs to float the cannons. They had found some stunted cypress pine in a gully, barely enough for the job. Several of the Sultan's commanders were supervising the work, even Haj Hammad was down there, his slaves helping him through the snowbanks.

It took them the best part of the morning to lash the bronze barrels to the log rafts with ropes. 'They'll do anything to keep those cannons,' George said.

'Madness.'

No one could make the crossing until the Sultan himself was safely across. He went in astride his horse, the stallion surrounded on all side by his Black Guard. A line of Negro slaves stood, hands linked, downstream, in case the royal personage should meet with misfortune and be swept away. Some of them were neck deep in the water and all of them were shaking with cold.

They won't last five minutes in there, Harry thought.

The cannons were next, more Negro slaves were conscripted for the job, some of them in bare feet and wearing nothing but white tunics and trousers. They dragged *al-raed's* barrel down the bank and supported the raft through the fast-flowing water and over to the far bank where it stuck fast in the mud. It took scores more of them with ropes to haul it out.

The remainder of the gun crew set off with another contingent of slaves to try and save *al-wahsh*. Halfway across he heard Redbeard shout a warning, as a massive tree trunk scythed through the swollen floodwaters towards them. It smashed into several of the slaves lined up on one side of the raft, within seconds there was blood in the water, men screaming in panic. The raft almost tipped, then swept loose and headed downstream to the human chain across the river.

'Oh, good God,' George said.

It was like trying to stop a runaway horse. Three of the slaves, unaccountably brave, tried to get in front of the runaway raft. Harry winced and turned away.

The men died for nothing. Fifty yards further on, there was a bend in the river and the raft careened into the bank and lodged there, tangled in the branches of a fallen tree. More slaves were sent into the water, they waded across and were soon swarming around it like ants, the Chief Vizier and the commander of the horse screaming instructions at them from the bank. They used ropes to drag it up the bank to safety.

'I wonder if they'll send slaves in after us,' George said, 'if we get swept away.'

'The vizier will hoist up his skirts and jump in himself,' Harry said.

It was time for the rest of the army to go across. The *askaris* waded in, then the cavalry, there seemed to be no order to it, just a confusion of men and mules, the horses shrieking, yells, more panicked shouts as men disappeared under the freezing water. But most of the army made it across, crawling and sprawling up the muddy quagmire banks on the other side.

Harry thought about the majestic carnival atmosphere the day they left Marrakesh. It seemed like so long ago.

They walked their horses in side by side, Mou clinging to the croupe of George' saddle. They were halfway across when Harry saw a large sheet of ice heading towards George' horse. He shouted a warning, George pulled hard on his horse's reins, but the stallion lost his footing, and they went in. Harry reached over and grabbed the boy, Mou clung on to his saddle. George was swimming, he still had a grip on the reins, made it into the shallows.

'My medical kit,' George said.

Harry looked back, saw the leather satchel floating away on the fast-running water. Without a word, Mou went in after it. There was nothing he could do. Harry pulled his horse up the bank, sat down on his haunches, shaking with cold.

George held tight to his stallion's reins, to keep him from bolting. 'The boy!' he said. 'We've lost the boy!'

'No, we haven't,' Harry said.

He emerged from the river, a hundred yards downstream, his hair plastered to his face, and covered in mud. He held the satchel over his head and let out a huge whoop.

'He's saved the medicine,' George said.

'Looks like the little rascal could be useful after all,' Harry said.

CHAPTER 12

What a pathetic ragged band. They were strung out over the valley, the Sultan's commanders had ordered no outriders, no scouts.

There had been a snowstorm overnight. If they didn't make it through the mountains soon, they would all die here, Harry thought. If Bou Hamra's riders didn't finish them, then the frostbite would.

He knew the raiders who had been dogging them since they left the desert were only waiting for the right moment. He wondered when, not if, an attack would come.

Later that afternoon, they were in a valley, steep ridges on either side. He heard the crack of a rifle, and an *askari* twenty yards in front of him stumbled forward onto his knees then slowly pitched forward onto his face. They had been harassed by snipers for weeks, but so far they had concentrated their attentions on stragglers at the rear of the column. This was something new.

'There,' George said, pointing to a ridge halfway up the pass, and the puff of black smoke from the ancient powder Bou Hamra's men were using.

Something made Harry turn, look in the opposite direction. Perhaps it was a sixth sense, an artefact from his years campaigning in Tonkin, or perhaps he felt the vibration of the hooves even through the saddle of his horse. The raiders seemed to come from nowhere, he guessed they had been hiding in a *wadi*, lying in wait for them.

They were rebel horsemen, a hundred, perhaps two hundred, hard to tell for they were already tangled with the Sultan's cavalry at the rear. The snipers were a ruse, an effective one. He felt the sting of bullets in the air, heard them cracking into the rocks, or the clang as they struck one of the cannon barrels, tied on the backs of the pack mules.

They were helpless. The *askaris* assigned to protect the cannons were exhausted, the cavalry too far away. Harry drew his sabre from its sheath. George wheeled his horse around and did the same. He pushed Mou from the saddle. 'Go and hide!' he shouted at him.

An *askari* in front of him looked up at Harry in dull surprise. There was a bullet hole in the middle of his forehead. He swayed back and fell.

'What should we do?' George shouted at him.

Harry wasn't of a mind to guard the Sultan's cannons. This was simply a matter of fighting for their lives.

The riders were on them before he could shout back. One of them came at him with a spear, he swayed out of reach in the saddle, spurred his horse around and swept at another with his sword, heard the man scream and clutch at his arm.

George had two of them on him, there was plenty of fight in him, but he was no warrior. He lunged with his sword at one of the riders, missed. The second rider saw his opportunity and stabbed at him, got through his guard. George swayed in the saddle, Harry thought he was going to fall. He spurred his horse after the rebel horseman, came up from behind, stabbed down between his shoulder blades with his sabre. The man dropped from the saddle and disappeared under his horse's hooves. Harry grabbed at the reins of George' horse and dragged him clear.

George was white with shock, and he was clutching at his shoulder.

The raiders wanted the mules with the cannons and the rails but the *askaris*, backed by Redbeard and the other gunners, were holding them off. For men who had a few moments ago been staggering from hunger and exhaustion, they were making quite a fight of it. He saw Redbeard leap onto the saddle of one of the raiders and wrestle its rider to the ground. The *askari* escort was getting slaughtered where they stood but they weren't giving ground, they were fighting and dying right under their hooves.

As one of the rebels reached the mules, there was a trumpet blast, and a squadron of mounted Black Guards appeared over the rise and swept in. Their charge took them through the ranks of Bou Hamra's riders, who lost their appetite for the fight and fled.

Harry led George' horse away from the fray, jumped down, caught George before he fell from the saddle. There was blood all over his leather cloak. He dragged him away from his horse and laid him down in the snow.

When he looked up, the horsemen were gone, vanished as quickly as they had come. They left behind a litter of bodies in the snowy fastness, the only sound the cawing of ravens.

They had put up a tent against the wind, Haj Hammad had sent a slave with a pile of sheepskins and he laid George on those. There was a gaping wound at the junction of his chest and his shoulder. Harry knew little about battlefield medicine, but he knew enough to know that the wound needed stitching.

George had lost a lot of blood. Harry poured silver salts from George' medical kit to clean it. He wrapped it as best he could with a bandage he found in the satchel.

Mou watched over his shoulder, his face creased with worry. 'You will help him?' he said.

'I don't know how. Go and find Haj Hammad. Tell him the English lieutenant is badly wounded.'

The boy was gone in an instant.

Mou returned just before evening, the Chief Vizier said that their sage – their *hakkim* - had died two nights before and there was no one else who could help.

Harry hardly slept that night, forced to listen to George groan and cry out in his sleep. Within hours he was burning with fever, even though it was icy inside the tent. Mou burrowed under the sheepskin next to him. For comfort or to warm himself on George' fever? Who could tell? Perhaps both.

Long before daylight he heard the camp stir, though it was still pitch-black outside. He still hadn't slept. Perhaps I'll dream in the saddle, he thought.

The tents were struck, men moved about in the dark like wraiths, mules and horses screamed in protest as they were saddled for another day's ride. The moon was still high, glittering on the snow, shimmering on the white canvas of the Sultan's enclosure. His tents were the only ones that remained, the last to be struck. The army was ready to march, the plain bobbing with cavalry, pack mules and grunting camels.

It was all deceptively beautiful against the ruddy glow of campfires, a smudge of smoke hanging like mist in the still air.

Harry looked up into the high passes. They still had to cross the highest part of the massif. Such a long way still to go. He doubted now that any of them would make it. Was this his day to die?

He felt a shiver along his spine, he knew that somewhere up there, eyes were watching them, and waiting their moment.

CHAPTER 13

'Wake up, sir. Wake up!'

Someone was shaking him by the arm. He couldn't open his eyes. His head felt too heavy to lift. He wanted to be left alone.

'Please sir, everyone is leaving. Get up, get up!'

It was Mou. He tried to shake the little pest off, but he kept at it. His mouth felt gummy and dry, the bones of his skull were splitting apart. Leave me alone, for the love of God.

'Sir, sir!'

He forced his eyes open. He could hear people moving about outside, it was cold, he could hear bugles and drums. He couldn't remember falling asleep. Where was he? What was going on? He put his head down.

'No sir, no, you must get up, get up!'

The boy was pulling at his shoulder.

He heard George' voice, calling him. They had hold of him, Ramrod and Redbeard, they were manhandling him out of the tent. George' head fell back over his shoulder. Where were they taking him?

The boy was still tugging at his arm. It was cold, so cold. The boy held a mug of water to his lips. He tried to turn his head away, but he made him drink it.

'You do not drink enough water.'

'Don't want any.'

Redbeard and Ramrod came back and grabbed him by the arms. He said to them, leave me, they wouldn't listen. They dragged him outside, into the pitch dark and the cold. He smelled horses and snow. They lifted him up into the saddle.

It was barely light, the sun still behind the mountains, the cold white peaks of the massif turning to a soft and roseate pink with the dawn. Harry heard the drumming of horses' hooves on the frozen ground, looked up and saw them, many more than last time, a dark line stretching from east to west on the ridge above them. They swept down, as one. How many? Well, it didn't matter. He doubted that the *askaris* and the Black Guards would have strength or will enough to fight them off a second time. Bou Hamra had won.

He heard the ululation of their war cries. By instinct he reached for the sabre at his side, but he didn't have the strength to draw it from its scabbard.

Bugles sounded up and down the line. There was frenzied activity around the Sultan's enclosure, he imagined the fat viziers raising their robes like old women and being hefted onto their horses, in a last panicked bid to get away with the Lord of the Faith. The royal bodyguards gathered into a defensive line in front of the royal tent, while some officers rallied a pitiful ragtag of *askaris* into a skirmish line.

The charge stopped, suddenly, a hundred yards from the *askaris*. They were quite still, hardly a murmur, the horses snorting and fidgeting, their breath freezing on the air in clouds. Finally, one rider walked his horse forward, and dismounted.

Two of the Black Guards rode out with torches. The rider had dropped to his knees beside his horse, pressed his forehead to the snow. The guards jumped down. He allowed them to haul him to his feet and drag him across the open ground towards the sultan's tents.

The Sultan appeared, supported by slaves, all in white. The guards forced the rider's head into the snow at his feet.

Harry heard him, as he was supposed to, as he supposed he meant the whole camp to hear him: 'Lord of all, be pleased to rest with us a while; Lord of all, accept our humble homage; Lord of all, be pleased to accept what little your slave can offer; Lord of all, be gracious, and with your illustrious presence lighten the darkness of my kasbah; Lord of all, bestow the favour that I may feed your *harka*; Lord of all, bestow your blessing upon my will to be your slave; Lord of all, tell me how I may serve you.'

Feed your *harka*? The man has food!

It must be a trick, Harry thought. I am hallucinating.

He started to slide off his horse. And that was the last thing he remembered.

Bou Hamra sat on the back of his white stallion and surveyed the litter in the snow, the dead camels, the headless bodies of men, discarded rifles. If it wasn't for Amastan, the Sultan might have lost his throne without another shot being fired.

He looked down at the prisoner one of his men had brought him. His hands and feet were black from the cold. His face was grey, he had bled profusely from a belly wound, he would have thought him a dead man except that his lips were moving, mumbling something, and his arms and legs were still twitching.

They had found him in a shallow grave, somehow still alive. The riders threw him almost naked in the frozen mud at Bou Hamra's feet. Their fellows had a handful of other prisoners and were busy hacking off their heads. When they were done, they would take them back to the fortress, the Jews would salt them, ready for hanging on the walls with the rest.

This one had slumped to his knees, was still trying to say something.

'What was that?' he said to the soldier holding him up.

'Lord, I think he asked you to be merciful.'

'What is wrong with him? Why is he covered in slime like that?'

'They buried him, Lord.'

'While he was still alive? That's barbaric. Do you think that's the actions of a civilised men, soldier?'

'No. Lord.'

'What's he saying now?'

'He says he can be useful to you.'

'Really? How does he think that?'

The soldier leaned closer to try and make out what the man was saying. 'He said, Lord, that he is no ordinary solider. He was with the Sultan's artillery. He knows how to fire a cannon.'

Bou Hamra laughed. The other soldiers laughed too, even though they didn't understand the joke. 'Ask him if he was the commanding officer.'

'He says no, Lord.'

'Of course he says no. Do you think a wretch like this could command artillery? Idiot. Ask him about the men in charge. Are they Spanish?'

The man gabbled something, the soldier got frustrated and kicked him. 'I'm sorry, Lord, I can't make out everything he is saying. I think he said the two men commanding the artillery are English.'

The man crawled towards him, touched his boots with the blackened claws of his fingers. 'Please. Be. Merciful.'

Bou Hamra understood that well enough.

'For your good service, I won't take your head, you shall go to Paradise complete,' Bou Hamra said. He looked at his captain. 'This man is freezing cold. Warm him up. Take him back where you found him and cover him up.'

He watched two of his men throw him back in the grave and kick the snow and dirt over him. When it was done one foot stuck out of the ground. Was it still moving? Hard to tell.

He turned to his captain of the horse. 'We need artillery and instructors. Can you think of a way?'

'Perhaps,' he said. 'We have a friend, inside Amastan's kasbah. He may be able to help us.'

'Good. Let's call in the friendship. Pay him whatever he asks. Just find a way of getting those cannons. And get the two Englishmen, too.'

When Harry came round, he was lying under a mountain of sheepskins next to a raging log fire. He stared at the flames, watched the sparks fly, enchanted. He felt as if his soul had returned to his body. A good thing, a bad thing, he wasn't sure. He had some strength in him again.

A man in a *djellaba* was crouched over George. Mou was kneeling next to him, watching intently.

He saw the man squeeze the flaps of the open wound on George' shoulder between his index finger and his thumb, and then turned to the boy, who was holding open the lid of a small wooden box. The man reached in and when he withdrew his hand, he had a small red insect pinched between his fingers. He held it over the wound.

'No,' Harry said and would have stopped him, but he was still too weak to move.

The ant closed its jaws around the ridges of skin. The man in the *djellaba* promptly picked up the small knife that lay beside him and decapitated it. The insect's mandibles remain closed, holding the two edges of skin together.

'Don't worry,' the man in the *djellaba* said to him in Arabic. 'We are closing the wound. These will hold it together so that it can heal.'

Harry watched, fascinated, as the man repeated this process four or five times more.

The man said his name was Zdan and that he was the Kaïd's deputy, his *Khalifa*. He had performed such operations countless times, he said. After he had closed the wound, he applied a resin he called *el Elk*, a paste he said came from an acacia tree, that had been mixed with red hematite. It will help with the healing, he said.

'Will he live?' Harry asked him.

'Perhaps,' he said. '*Insha'Allah*. If God wills it.'

He had a weathered face, craggy as a mountain cliff, cracked with cold. He was brown as a walnut. Who the hell are you, Harry thought, and where are we?

When he had finished tending to George, Zdan put his hand on Harry's forehead. 'Look at you. I have seen corpses with better colour. The boy says you have not been drinking enough water.'

'What do I want with water? It's so cold up here.'

'That's how a man dies, my friend. I have told the boy to make you drink. Do as he tells you. Who is he anyway?'

'Mou?'

'Yes. Is he your slave?'

'No, when we get out of these mountains, we intend to set him free.'

He seemed to find that amusing. 'No man is free. Him, even less. No one is free until they are dead.'

'Where are we?'

'You, my friend, are in the kasbah of Aït Karim, the eyrie of Amastan el-Karim, Lord of the Atlas. Without him, you would both be dead and Bou Hamra would be the new sultan of Morocco.'

Harry remembered now. The horsemen riding down from the ridge, their leader making obeisance in the snow.

'Bou Hamra?'

'He cannot harm you here.'

'I just want to get out of these mountains.'

'My friend, you are further into the mountains now than you can ever be. This is the very heart of the Atlas and with all this snow, who knows when you will leave? But first you must get back your strength. Sleep well. And pray for your friend.'

CHAPTER 14

Harry woke to silence. He stood up for the first time in days, staggered to the window, jarred open the wooden shutter. The sky was a startling blue over the white stillness of the mountains. The only sound was the raucous cry of a kestrel somewhere overhead.

The air was so bright, so clean, he imagined one sweep of a sword could shatter it, like crystal.

George was asleep. He knelt down beside him, sniffed at the bandages. He could make out no putrefaction. He was cooler. His colour was better, there was colour in his cheeks again. Whatever Zdan had done, had worked.

George opened his eyes. 'Harry?'

'So you're alive. I wouldn't have put money on that for either of us a few days ago.'

George tried to sit up, groaned, and put a hand to his shoulder. He glanced down at the linen bandage. 'That doesn't look like your handiwork.'

'It's not. One of the locals patched you up.'

'Where the hell are we now?'

'We're the guests of someone your saviour refers to as the Lord of the Atlas.'

'Where's Mou?'

On cue, the door burst open and the boy ran in. He was wearing a new tunic and *djellaba,* looked pleased with himself. Someone had shaved his head, no doubt worried about lice. Otherwise he seemed to show no ill effects from their recent experience.

'Ah my sirs, you are awake. At last. You have missed so much!'

'What have we missed?' George said.

'The *diffa*!' he said, using the Moroccan word for a banquet. 'There were spiced chickens, and pigeons, hundreds! And whole roast sheep, so many you could not count so high!' He touched his pursed lips with his fingers. 'And almond pastries, I ate so many I thought I would burst, and sweet mint tea. Never have I seen so much food. I ate and ate, long after I couldn't eat any more.' He dramatically threw out his stomach so they could see for themselves how fat he had become in three days. 'And the dancing! Boys, some of them younger than me, they had painted their faces and they had gold-embroidered belts, and tambourines and they made *click-click* with their fingers with little brass cymbals in the courtyard around this big bonfire, never have I seen such a fire. And the best of all was the dancing girls, they swung their hips like this.' He put one hand behind his head, another on his hip, and danced in a circle, swinging his hips. 'They were so beautiful. My eyes are sore from all the looking. One day I will have my own harem and I will have a hundred girls like this!'

'You are not old enough to think about harems,' George said to him.

'You sound like my father,' Harry said and smiled. He patted Mou on the head. 'We're glad you had such a good time, Mou. Now go and find Haj Hammad, tell him the two English officers wish to speak with him. Urgently.'

'I cannot.'

'No one's going to hurt you. You are running a message, that's all.'

'But sirs, I cannot because the vizier is not here. The Sultan and his counsellors and his whole army have all gone home.'

George groaned, clutching at his shoulder. 'They've gone back to Marrakesh without us?'

'Why didn't anyone tell us?' Harry said. 'Why didn't *you* tell us, Mou?'

'Because I don't want to go to Marrakesh.'

'*We* want to go to Marrakesh.'

'You were asleep, you were sick. Both of you. And Zdan said it was no point to wake you, because you cannot go to Marrakesh anyway.'

'What does he mean, we *cannot*?'

'Zdan said the Sultan has given the two cannons to the Lord of the Atlas in gratitude for how he saved us all from the snow.'

'And are we a part of the gift?' Harry said.

'He said a cannon is no good without...' He couldn't remember the word in Arabic, so he made one up. '... cannoners.'

George swore under his breath.

'We're still stranded here,' Harry said. 'God knows when we'll ever see England again.' He turned to Mou. 'Get Zdan. Tell him we have to talk to him.'

CHAPTER 15

Unlike the houses in the town below, the fortress was built of large blocks of squared stone, unlike anything they had seen so far in the mountains. The town was surrounded by a curtain wall, with towers at every corner. He imagined he had seen nothing quite so majestic or imposing in all of his time in Morocco.

Their rooms, while not as luxurious as those given them at the Sultan's palace in Marrakesh, were comfortable enough. There were thick embroidered rugs on the floor and the walls had been whitewashed, so they somehow seemed much more spacious than they actually were. The ceiling was supported on stout and rough-hewn walnut timbers. There were even some narrow shelves with a teapot, some brass cups and saucers and a copper tray and kettle. The only other decoration was two antique German cuckoo clocks. They were broken.

A window looked out over a small, paved courtyard, with orange and lemon trees clustered around a tiled fountain. Food was brought, *couscouso*, with boiled turnips and some boiled chicken, a huge honour, Harry realised. Afterwards, there was tea and dates.

Harry and George picked at the food without appetite. What they wanted was to talk to this Amastan. Mou watched them, wide-eyed, and pounced on any leftovers.

Zdan did not return until the next morning. It was snowing outside, and the air was frigid, even inside the Kasbah, but his legs were bare, and he just wore sandals and the same short cloak and trousers he had seen other Berbers wearing when they had passed through the mountains in the summer. These people didn't seem to feel the cold at all.

'You are both looking much better,' he said and clapped his hands, called for slaves to bring coffee and bread. 'I think you will live. Why the long face, captain?'

'We need to see your Lord of the Atlas,' Harry said.

'There is something wrong?'

'We want to go home,' George said. 'We are British nationals. The Sultan has traded us as if we were common slaves.'

Zdan affected a look of great concern. 'I am sure no one has done anything of the sort.'

'Then why has the *harka* left for Marrakesh without us?'

'You wanted the whole army to wait for you? Besides, that is something you should perhaps discuss with Amastan el-Karim himself.'

'Precisely. And when will that be?'

'I'll see what I can do.' Zdan turned for the door then hesitated. 'You know, and I say this as your friend, even *British nationals* should mind their manners when they address the Lord of the Atlas. It might go better with you. Try to remember that.'

They were escorted through a series of courtyards, there were wild-looking tribesmen and black slaves in snow-white cloaks milling about. They all bowed to Zdan as he passed.

They reached the ground floor of the kasbah and ducked their heads to enter. The ground floor seemed to serve as stables, while the next floor seemed to serve as a kitchen, its walls blackened with smoke. There were a number of women crouched over open cook fires tending huge copper cooking pots, while others were weaving on hand looms. A fug of figwood charcoal hung in the air in choking clouds. There were cobwebs in the rafters, and even they were blackened with smoke, making them appear monstrous.

As they climbed the stairs to the upper floors, they had to feel their way, there wasn't much light, as there were few windows, just a few slits and loopholes for use of the Kaïd's archers in the event of a siege.

They went down a small dark tunnel and up a vertiginous set of stairs to a stone landing. Now they were at the very top of the kasbah. Through a narrow window Harry had a dizzying view of the roofs of the fortress and the medina far below. The wind howled through the embrasure in the stone.

A guard pushed them through a heavy green door into a large, furnished room, unlike any they had seen elsewhere in the kasbah. It was dominated by a chimney set against the far wall and there was a roaring log fire at the heart of it, and the sudden warmth was shocking. The floors were covered with carpets, earthy colours and covered with the complex almost Runic Berber designs. There were leather-covered cushions, instead of chairs, in the manner of the Maghreb, a number of large chests and an intricately carved low mahogany table inset with mother-of-pearl.

There was even glass on the windows, a sign of unthinkable opulence up here. They were thick and tinged with green, so that it was almost impossible to see out of them, but they kept out the draughts and let in the light. There was even a clerestory in the vaulted cedar ceiling, with red, yellow and blue glass, diffused coloured beams of light angled across the carpets, lighting up the particles of woodsmoke that hung in the air and lent the great lord's eyrie the feel of a magician's lair.

Instead of arabesques and ceramics inlaid with verses from the Koran there was instead a pair of German field glasses and a series of

English sporting prints, with such titles as "Gone away," and "Tally ho!" A Belgian breech-loading pistol hung on a nail on the wall. It was double-barrelled, nickel-plated and clearly considered something of a prize.

The Lord of the Atlas himself reclined on cushions in front of the roaring fire. He was dressed entirely in black, and even within the confines of his private rooms in the Kasbah he wore a black *cheiche* which covered almost all his face except his eyes. He did not look up when they entered, neither did he give any indication that he knew they were there.

'This is our Kaïd, Lord of the Atlas,' Zdan said. 'He is sheikh of the mountains and valleys as far as you can see and beyond. Even to the sands of the Sahara. He is supreme in all the qualities the Prophet demands, except that he lacks patience. It would be best not to try it.'

There was a low table with *msemen*—traditional pancakes dripping in honey—and a silver pot of sweet mint tea. Zdan poured tea into two glasses and left the room.

'*Maha babicum,*' the Kaïd said. Welcome to our door.

He waved a hand towards the cushions in front of them. George squatted down beside the table and tried one of the *msemen*. 'You should try the pancakes,' he said. 'They're really rather good.'

Harry hesitated, then joined him at the table. He drank some of the tea. It was scalding hot and flavoured with peppermint leaves.

Amastan el-Karim turned around. 'So,' he said, in Arabic, 'you are the English advisers.' His voice was soft, sibilant, like a snake slithering across a tiled floor. It took Harry by surprise, he had expected something deeper, more commanding. Yet he supposed, it was hypnotic, menacing even, in its own way.

'Captain Harry Delhaze,' Harry said, 'and this is Lieutenant Doctor George Marriot.'

Amastan turned to George. 'You are recovered from your wound?'

George touched the bandage on his shoulder. 'It aches, but the wound is healing well.'

'You are fortunate. You both are.'

'We thank you for your medical aid and for giving us shelter,' Harry said. 'We do not wish to seem ungrateful, but what are we still doing here?'

'Allow me to explain. Before he left, our Sultan, may God bless him and grant him increase, he saw fit to make me his personal *Khalifa,* his governor, in all of the Atlas. This is a great honour. It means that no other chieftain in these mountains can challenge me now without offending the Sultan himself. The other tribes must bow to me for I have his authority on this. He made me one further promise. When I bring him the head of Bou Hamra, he will make me the new pasha of Marrakesh.'

'That was very generous of him.'

'Well, he was very grateful for my help. He and his army may all have perished in the snows had I not chosen to intervene.'

'That does not explain our continued presence here.'

'The Sultan's vizier did not explain your situation?'

'He left before we could wish him a fond farewell.'

'That is unfortunate and shows bad manners. What can you expect of a former slave?'

'Never owned a slaved, so I wouldn't know,' Harry said. 'It did strike me, though, that Haj Hammad, God keep him and grant him increase, couldn't lie straight in a cannon barrel.'

The corner of Amastan's eyes crinkled, perhaps he was smiling under the *cheiche*. 'It is as you say. That is why I got from him something more valuable than promises.'

'And what was that?'

'I told him that if I were to defeat Bou Hamra, I would need his cannons, *al-wahsh* and *al-raed*. As you know, they are the only heavy weapons in all Morocco outside the Imperial Chereefian Army. I said I would also require the caissons and the ammunition as well as two properly trained officers to maintain them, repair them and supervise their operation. He also left me what remained of his gun crew, to continue in my service.'

'With respect,' George said, 'he has gifted you something it was not in power to give. Us.'

'You contracted with the Sultan to assist in the successful capture of the rebel Bou Hamra. Bou Hamra is not yet in chains, so the contract is still unfulfilled. Therefore, he has passed your contract on to me. It is commerce. I am sure you understand the concept in your country?'

'We wish to cancel the contract and return to Marrakesh,' George said.

'That will not be possible.'

'What about our money?'

'You had a verbal agreement with the Sultan, I think?'

'Haj Hammad guaranteed us the equivalent of two thousand British pounds. Each.'

'Is that what he promised you? Well, as you say, the vizier is a notorious liar. This is not to revile the man, mendacity is a virtue in any good counsellor. I will tell you your new salary. You will help me bring Bou Hamra back here in chains and in return I will feed you and give you shelter and let you live. At the end of your service you will be given two hundred English pounds in silver between you and two horses so that you might ride to Mogador and find a boat to take you back to England.'

'Two hundred? We agreed two thousand.'

'I remind you, your agreement was with the Sultan's vizier, not with me. I have no money to give you, though you will be entitled to a share of any treasure we find when we take Bou Hamra's fortress. But feeding the Sultan and his army and giving him and his household and his army provisions to complete their journey to Marrakesh has emptied my treasury. You are free to leave, of course. How you will fare in the winter in these mountains, without food and without horses, I do not know. Or you can remain here as my guest and provide me with the assistance I require.' Amastan stood up and went to the window, threw open the shutters. He was not as tall as he had expected, Harry noticed, but there was a swagger to the way he walked, a man accustomed to command.

He pointed down at the battlements. They heard the cawing of ravens as they fussed over something that had been impaled on a stake on the wall. 'I must warn you. If you prove troublesome, your heads may soon decorate our walls.'

'You can't do that,' George said.

'I am Lord of the Atlas. I do as I please.'

'We are subjects of the British Empire!'

'Zdan said you would bring that up. Look around you, gentlemen. We are not in the British Empire. We are not in Cairo or Calcutta. Your army has no sovereignty in these mountains. You are under my roof, and you will be well treated. In return, you will make sure the Sultan's cannons are ready for battle. It is my final offer, and I do not think you are in a position to bargain.' He looked at Harry. 'And what about you? Are you unhappy with my arrangements also?'

'When I was at school,' Harry said, 'we had a headmaster who enjoyed caning us if we were unruly.'

'And you were unruly?'

'Oh yes, on many occasions. Some of the other boys would go in his study and when he brought out the cane, they would plead and make excuses for their behaviour.'

'But not you?'

'Well I always thought, if you're in for a flogging, just grin and bear it. The old bastard's never going to change his mind anyway.'

Hard to tell, but he thought Amastan smiled under the *cheiche*.

'How long will we be here?' George said.

'It is winter. Nothing can happen until spring. Until then, stay close to the fire, and enjoy our hospitality. You cannot escape, so do not consider it. Thank you, gentlemen.'

He clapped his hands. Two guards came in and he said something to them in the Berber dialect that Harry did not understand.

'Leave me now.'

George was about to protest, but Harry put a hand on his arm and shook his head. It was pointless to argue further.

'One word of advice,' Amastan said, as they were leaving. 'You would be wise not to trust anyone in this place. Remember. No one.'

They followed the guards through the labyrinthine corridors to their accommodations. Neither of them spoke until they were back in their rooms and were once more finally alone.

'That man is a scoundrel,' George said.

'Don't worry,' Harry said. 'We'll get our money.' And he went up to the battlement on their roof, to stare at the mountains and brood.

Harry couldn't sleep. It was dark in the room, but slivers of bright moon found the gaps in the wooden shutters and threw chevrons of light across the floor. He put on his heavy wool *djellaba* and boots and treading softly, he went up to the terrace on the roof. The moon was huge, it seemed close enough that he could reach out and take it out of the sky.

The snows on the mountain peaks shimmered in the dark and the wind carried with it the scent of ice and cedar wood. A bird glided right over his head, startling him.

Just an owl.

The cold scared him now. It reminded him of death. He couldn't endure it for long. He went back inside. There were oil lamps flickering along the corridors, he thought he could easily find his way back to their room, but soon he was lost.

He turned down a darkened corridor and found himself suddenly stepping into space. There was a hole cut into the brick, the incomplete fenestration cut right to the floor and no balcony, a sheer drop over the side of the cliff to the valley below. He gasped and clung to the brick with his fingertips, swayed into the chasm for a moment before he found his balance. He stared down into the darkness, heard the rush of a river torrent far below.

For a moment he was a soul, rising from the earth. He could smell the ice in the air, drew it deep into his lungs, held it, savoured it as his last. How sweet it was.

He had never experienced so much space, so much breath, so much air. This is what eternity is if I wish to be a part of it. The darkness extended beyond the mountains, even shivering with cold he sensed the lapping sands of the deserts to the south, the great yawning mass of

Africa beyond, the rolling, foaming black sea somewhere out there, just beyond his reach.

He was no longer a prisoner, not in this Kasbah or in this life.

All you have to do is step out and it will be all over, he thought. You won't be a failure anymore, you won't have to think about Lucy or where she is and what she's doing, you won't have to worry about your creditors back in London. No more cold, no more privation.

You can be done with it all if that's what you want.

He swung an arm and a leg free into the dark, imagined death in his shadowy robes, down there in the abyss.

'No,' he whispered to the night and as he said it, felt a sense of timelessness and elation. 'Not yet.'

Something was waiting for him in this land of sand and ice, he felt it in his bones. He had come here for easy money, but there was something else here, something far more valuable, even though he didn't yet know what it was.

'You will have to wait,' he said to the waiting dark.

His fingers slipped on the crumbling brick, and he felt himself falling.

You see, something whispered to him. Do not toy with me, make your decision and be sure, or I will make it for you. A reflex drew him back, his heart hammering wildly in his chest and he clawed for another handhold and pulled himself back from the edge.

He swung back inside and followed the flickering corridors of light inside the kasbah back to his rooms and another day of life.

CHAPTER 16

Harry soon realised that when Amastan told them they could not escape, it was not a mere boast. Aït el-Karim was one of the bleakest, loneliest places he had ever seen.

The fortress itself possessed a sort of faded beauty, forever silent. Decades, perhaps centuries, of stark cold and withering heat had racked the walls, the bolts and hinges on the many cracked and twisted doors were rusted and gave a banshee shriek whenever they were opened or closed. It was a labyrinth of empty courtyards, and dark and narrow rooms, most of them empty. Narrow stairs led up to carved cedar cloisters that led nowhere. The tiles that lined the floors and walls must once have shimmered with glaze but were now stained and cracked. The Lord of the Atlas had not lied. For all his power, it was clear that he was flat broke.

One step outside the walls, and it was as hostile an environment as he could imagine and for weeks after the Sultan's departure it appeared as a vision from Hell, as vultures and jackals feasted on the bones of the countless sheep that had been slaughtered to feed the sultan and his army. There was not a blade of grass, not a tree, not a bush, not even a mule track through the barren whiteness of the mountainside. A few outcrops of rocks pushed through the snow, some crumbled walls and scattered shepherds' shelters that appeared deserted.

It was as desolate an eyrie as Harry could imagine. There would be no caravans passing through here until spring, Zdan told them. Until then, they were cut off from the world beyond. Even Marrakesh, no more than three days ride away in summer, might as well be as distant as the moon.

When they asked Zdan if they could explore the town, he shrugged and nodded, and sent a bodyguard to escort them out of the Kasbah and into the warren of narrow lanes that led into the medina below.

As soon as they were outside, people came running from everywhere. Some gave them shy smiles or made a sign to ward off the evil eye. Others stared at them with undisguised hostility, as if they were wild animals running loose.

Already, Harry had learned a few words in their language, which they called Tamazirght. It was not as guttural as the Arabic that Harry had learned in Egypt. '*Aman*' was the same as '*el ma*' in Arabic, water. '*Asardoun*' was a mule, and '*asif*' was a river. Many of the Berbers could converse freely in both languages.

He overheard two small boys talking about them as they went past.

'What are they?' one of them said.

'Apes,' the other one said.

He smiled to himself and didn't mind. He didn't even want to correct them for he knew that apes were held in higher esteem in the Maghreb than *arroumi* - Christians.

Children followed them wherever they went, never daring to come too close, but never far away. Whenever they stopped to get their bearings, they would hear giggling and saw little heads peering at them from around a corner or popping up from behind a wall.

Harry amused himself for a while by making a face and roaring at them like a bear and watching them run off, shrieking with terrified laughter.

Their bodyguard's chief purpose seemed to be to chase and thrash whatever of the small boys he could catch, cursing their grandmothers and grandmother's grandmother in the traditional manner. Harry thought he would be better served just making sure they didn't get lost.

'I wonder sometimes if we would attract less interest if we wore a burnoose and *djellaba*,' George said.

'We might, George, but we would also lose some of our aura. The hard helmet, these elastic-sided boots, the braces, the two-carat watch chains, they're like *al-iirahb*. I've no doubt they're actually quite useless, but to the Moors they mark as out as somehow special, even dangerous. We are a walking Maxim gun.'

'That is an interesting theory.'

It was different here from Tangier or Marrakesh, in the cities the only women they had seen had been slaves, servants, a few peasants from the country, all veiled and wrapped in black and brown.

Here, the women did not veil their faces like the Arab women of the Maghreb. They mixed freely with the men and laughed and talked quite amiably. They were mostly very pretty, even coquettish, and made themselves appear even more exotic with the henna tattoos on their face and hands and the dark kohl they wore to accentuate their eyes.

Most commonly they had five streaks from the top of their foreheads to their eyebrows, with a triangle on each cheek. A black smudge of kohl was worn on the tip of the nose, each corner of the mouth and the point of their chins. Some of them even tattooed their necks as well.

They wore dresses of indigo cotton, with a cord of red wool looped several times around their waists, the ends hanging down in long tassels. Often, they were barefoot, even on the coldest of days.

'Please don't,' George said, when he saw him staring.

'What?'

'We are in enough trouble as it is. Don't start making eyes at the local women or we'll end up like those two Spanish artillery officers, with both our heads on a stake.'

'It does no harm to look.'

'Every harm starts with a look, Harry.'

They passed under a crumbling archway where men were shoeing horses and mules and were soon swallowed up by the warren of streets and tunnels that burrowed under the upper stories of the houses above, all the way down the severe mountain's edge. The houses hung over the street, ancient beams and buttresses supporting each other from tipping and blocking out what dim light there was from the leaden skies. Few of the houses had windows, just iron-barred slits stuffed with rags. There were cats everywhere, bare-ribbed and scrawny, darting in and out of the black doorways.

The streets were full of little box-like shops. The shop owners sat cross-legged, running their prayer beads through their fingers. It all reminded him of the flea markets down by the quayside in the summer, they all seemed to be full of junk, old brass and copper kettles, chains and screws. It was so gloomy that most of them were lit even in the middle of the day by oil-lamps. He never saw anyone stop and buy anything and the shopkeepers appeared as if they didn't care less.

Forbidding and black and reeking staircases and alleys led God knew where, winding under the overhanging eaves of houses, past the richly painted and carved doors of a mosque and then into a tunnel and under more houses. Yet even without their bodyguard, Harry did not believe they could ever truly get lost. The brooding dark tower of the Kasbah always loomed above them, no matter where they were inside the walls.

'It feels as if we've stepped off the edge of the earth,' Harry said.

'There are times,' George said, 'when that is exactly what we all need to do.'

It was dusk, and Harry was standing on the roof terrace, watching the colours fade over the valley, rose to grey to dark. The wind moaned through the stone battlements, there was the piercing cry of a kestrel soaring over the valley. He saw a herd of wild goats skipping nimbly between the ice and rocks far up the mountainside.

He was suddenly aware of a figure standing on the parapet of the kasbah. Amastan. He was staring at the mountains in the gathering violet dusk.

He turned and looked around, and for a moment Harry had the sense that he was looking straight at him. It was surely just his imagination; he could not see him from up there.

But then he suddenly raised a hand in salute. Harry returned the gesture.

It was only for a moment, and then the Lord of the Atlas turned and disappeared inside.

CHAPTER 17

There were some days that Mou went missing from breakfast until the evening prayers, *al-maghrib*. At first, they were too preoccupied with their own concerns to pay him any attention, but his reaction alarmed them when George casually asked him one day: *So, what do you do with your time?*

He had lowered his eyes, mumbled something into his hand and fled.

The next day, when he was gone, they searched his bed and found a jewel diadem and an embroidered pink slipper hidden under his sleeping mat.

'Where did he get these?' George said.

'I'm no expert,' Harry said, 'but that, unless I'm very much mistaken, looks like a harem slipper.'

'What the hell has that boy been doing?'

'I don't know. I think we should find out.'

The *muezzin* had already begun the evening call to prayer when Mou sauntered back into their rooms. He saw George standing by his bed holding the slipper and the diadem and immediately turned to run, but Harry stepped out from behind the door and blocked his retreat.

Harry grabbed him by the ear. 'What have you been doing, Mohammed?'

'I haven't done anything.'

'You may be a terrific thief but you're a terrible liar.'

'Let me go!'

'Not until you tell us where you stole these from?'

'I didn't steal them, I found them!'

'Just tell us where you found these, Mou.'

'By the fountain in the courtyard. Someone must have left them there. I just picked them up.'

George looked at Harry. 'I think we should tell Zdan,' beginning the speech they had rehearsed earlier. 'We don't want anyone to think *we* stole them.

'What do you think they'll do to him?'

'They'll flog him, to start with.'

'How many lashes?'

'For stealing? At least thirty.'

'Do you think they'll cut off his hand as well?'

'That's the usual punishment, I think.'

'No! You mustn't tell anyone! I'll put them back! I promise!'

'Put them back where?'

Mou took a deep breath. Harry pinched his ear even harder to persuade him. 'The harem!'

George shook him by the shoulders. 'You've been into Amastan's harem?'

'Only once.'

'The truth.'

'Twice.'

Harry pinched his ear again.

'Every day!'

'Are you crazy? Why would you do this?'

'I like looking at the pretty ladies. I didn't go in there to steal, I swear. It was an accident.'

'How do you get in?'

'You want me to show you?'

'No!'

'You can't tell anyone! Look, I can help you. I know everything about the kasbah, every door, every way in, every way out. Please.'

Harry let him go. 'He's right,' he said. 'He's the size of a cat and about as nimble. He probably can slip in and out of places we couldn't go.'

'You have to stop stealing,' George said to him. 'Do you hear what I say?'

'You can't tell me what to do, you're not my father!'

'No, I am!' Harry said. And that was it, it was said, and he saw the hope dawn in the boy's eyes.

'You will let me stay with you?' Mou said. 'I promise I won't steal anymore! I will be your slave. Do anything you want.'

'What can you do,' George said, 'apart from take what doesn't belong to you?'

'I can carry,' Mou said. 'I'm strong. Look.' He flexed his arm and squeezed the muscles. 'I can carry firewood. Make fires. I know how to load a donkey so the straps don't chafe and you make your donkey sick. My father taught me.'

Harry looked at George, saw the disapproval in his eyes. 'You can stay with us for now.'

'Harry,' George said. He switched from Arabic to English. 'You have to tell him how it is. You can't feed him false hope. He can't come back to England with you.'

Harry nodded, then said to the boy in Arabic: 'Do you have an uncle, a grandfather perhaps, who can look after you?'

Mou shook his head. 'I only had a sister.'

'A sister? What happened to her?' When he didn't answer, Harry said: 'Was she in the house when the cannon shell hit the gate?'

He nodded.

Harry winced. 'Another ghost for my dreams,' he murmured.

'It was God's will,' the boy said. '*El hamdu billah.*'

'It was our cannon that orphaned him,' Harry said to George. 'I have a duty to him. I have to help him.'

'We can't even help ourselves right now.' Harry shrugged his shoulders and looked away. 'You have an idea?'

'I only know we have to try and get out of here. We could be trapped up here for God knows how long and get nothing for our troubles. They treat us like slaves. Suppose we defeat Bou Hamra, who will say that this Amastan will honour the agreement, give us even the meagre few hundred pounds he's offering us? He's not the Sultan. He doesn't have a bottomless treasury. It would be cheaper for him to put our heads on a stake once we're no longer of use to him.'

'There is no way out of this place.'

'How do we know for sure? If we can find a way down to the valley, we could steal two horses and make our way to the coast.'

'But what would we do for money?'

They both looked at the boy. He saw them staring at him, he almost smiled, wondering if the deal had been made in his favour.

'You're right,' Harry said, in Arabic now. 'He can do something for us. He can be our thief.'

'And our spy. Perhaps our guide as well.'

Mou nodded. 'You will let me stay with you?'

George looked at Harry. Harry nodded. 'You can stay with us,' he said.

CHAPTER 18

Harry patrolled the terrace, mapping the terrain around Aït Karim in his head. It seemed clear that the only way up or down was from the valley to the south. There was flat ground to the west that led to the foot of the mountain, it was littered with boulders and scree. There was a river between the fortress and the mountain spur, it was still running, but it was partly concealed beneath treacherous caves of ice. Beyond it, the cliff face was sheer and scarred with deep ravines.

Using his eyeglass, he could make out a number of shepherds' huts dotted among the trees below the walls. He wondered if they were abandoned, or if Amastan had men posted down there at night. He had never seen campfires. That didn't mean there weren't guards patrolling the ridge.

Well, tonight he would find out.

He ate without appetite. The food was barely better than field rations anyway; olives, potatoes, some chicken flavoured with fragrant yellow spices but so tough it must have been alive when Napoleon was a boy. There were dates, which he slipped into his pocket for later.

'If I find a way down,' Harry said, 'tomorrow night we will make our move. We take whatever food Mou can steal for us, and try to get down the valley, out of these mountains. We know what it's like. This time we won't have to worry about Bou Hamra.'

'You think we can do this without horses or mules?'

'We only have to reach the nearest village. There will be horses or donkeys.'

'You think we can use the jewels Mou stole to buy some?'

'No, the people won't help us, we're the only white faces in the whole of the Atlas Mountains. They'll know where we came from. If they help us, Amastan will put their heads on the walls for the crows. We will have to get our transport by other means.'

'That's dangerous.'

'George, the whole enterprise is dangerous. If we want to be safe, we can stay here until there's white in our beards.'

'We'll have to steal food as well.'

'We can survive as long as we have water. We only have to get to Marrakesh.'

'Do you think the vizier will still be there?'

'Perhaps, but I'm not sure the Sultan will help us. There's a chance he could send us back to Amastan. He needs Amastan's help now more than he needs ours.'

'What do we do, then?'

'One of us goes to the Vizier. The other tries to trade the diadem Mou stole for horses and food.'

'What about him?' George said and nodded at Mou, who was staring at them, looking frightened and hopeful.

'We promised to take him with us. At least as far as Tangier. Then we'll have to think again.'

'It's three weeks' ride to the coast.'

'Once we are clear of the High Atlas, Amastan cannot harm us. Our problem will be avoiding bandits and finding shelter. The cold won't be nearly as bad when we get out of the mountains.'

'All we have been through. Nothing to show for it!'

'Do you want to change your mind about this?'

'No. We have to get out of here.'

Harry turned to Mou and said, in Arabic. 'You're sure you know a way out of the Kasbah?'

'There's a door, you have to go down a long tunnel under the fortress. I know the way.'

'Once you take me there you come back here and wait, with George. If there's a way out of this valley, I'll find it.'

'What about the snow?' George said. 'If you leave tracks, Amastan's men will see them.'

'I've thought about that. I'll follow the rocks below the kasbah walls until I reach the north-east corner. There's a goat track, it's well-trodden and there's not much snow cover, it leads up to a ridge. I'll go up there and down the other side, no one will be able to see my tracks from there.'

'How long will you be gone?'

'I don't know. Maybe an hour or two, perhaps all night. If I hear the muezzin, I'll know I've left it too late.'

'There's jackals, wolves out there.'

'I'll take my chances. As you said, we don't have much choice.'

They went to bed, but none of them slept. The mountains fell silent, an all-enveloping hush, Harry imagined he could hear the stars breathe. A cat screeched in the rafters, chasing a mouse.

He heard the guard snoring in the corridor. He touched Mou on the arm and he was up and on his feet in an instant.

George reached out and gripped his arm in the dark. '*Bon chance,*' he whispered. 'Good luck. God be with you.'

Luck. He hated relying on luck. When had that ever worked for him?

And God? He'd always been on the other side.

Once they were outside, Mou led the way, keeping to the shadows under the wall. Harry could see the silhouettes of the guards on the parapet walls above them, but the courtyard was empty. As they slipped past the stables, the horses smelled them and snickered and stamped their hooves.

Mou led him down a dark passage, under the west tower, it was narrow and cold as death, barely high enough even for Mou and Harry had to bend double as he ran to get through it.

Within a few steps it was pitch black. He followed the boy's footsteps, feeling the cold stone brushing his shoulder, couldn't even see his hand in front of his face.

'How did you find this?' Harry said.

'In the day, you can see the light at the very end. Not far. It's down here.'

Mou kept going, Harry sensed they had turned down another passageway. He could hear water dripping. Every small noise they made echoed along the walls.

'Here,' Mou said.

It was not as much a door as a wooden hutch. Mou pushed it open. The ground, bone hard and frost bright, sloped away towards the rocks. Harry squeezed through the opening and he was outside the walls.

'Go back to George and wait,' Harry said. 'You'll freeze if you wait here.'

'You can find your way back, *sayeed*?'

'If I don't, you'll know where to find me in the morning,' he said, pulled the door shut and started off into the night.

Harry gulped air into his lungs, it was so cold it felt as if it was burning his throat with every breath. The mountain coat Mou had 'found' for him stank of sheep. He waited there for a few minutes, steeling himself, getting his bearings in the dark. A quarter moon in the sky, a perfect night for plotters and fugitives. He bent into a crouch and set off.

He kept to the shadows until he reached the corner of the north-east wall and waited. He could hear the guards talking to each other on the parapet above him. He couldn't make out what they were saying but their conversation went on for a long time, any longer and he would have frozen. Finally, they broke off and headed towards the main gate, away from him.

Harry headed up the goat track, he had only gone a few paces when the muscles in his thighs started to burn and he couldn't get air into his lungs. But he couldn't stop. He only had a few minutes to get out of sight. It seemed to take forever. He pushed himself on, reached the top of the ridge and almost threw himself over the other side. He lay on the frozen ground, the stars spinning above his head.

He waited until he had his breath back then sat up and planned his next move. Once he had made up his mind, he set off towards some trees to his left, tracking around the snowdrifts, jumping from rock to rock where he could, trying not to leave too many tracks behind him.

Harry made his way up towards another ridge. Suddenly he found himself waist deep in a snowbank, could barely move his legs. His heartbeat pounded in his ears. Stay calm, he thought. He crawled out the way he had come, looked for another way. It was so cold he knew he had to start moving again soon.

He scrambled over the icy rocks, back the way he had come. Already, he was shaking so hard with cold that it was affecting his balance. His sweat was freezing to the linen shirt inside his clothes. The physical effort was harder, much harder, than he had even imagined. The air was so thin he had to drag it into his lungs.

He kept his eyes on the ground, jumping over snow patches where he could. But the shadows were deceptive in the moonlight and he yelled as he tumbled into another drift. He had to fight his way out, panicked. For a moment he thought he would suffocate. He even thought of calling out for help.

He finally got himself back onto the rocks, lay there for a long time, chest heaving, staring up at the sky.

He heard voices, saw silhouettes on the battlements of the fortress. Had the two guards seen him? So why hadn't they fired?

There was one other way. A steep gorge fell away on one side of him, there was a horseshoe ridge behind it, and if he could climb it, he thought he might make his way down to the valley from the other side.

It would mean doubling back, climbing perhaps another few hundred feet, another hour at least. He didn't know if he had the strength for it.

He had to try.

The climb down into the gorge was difficult, scrambling and sliding on ice, small rocks and scree. Twice, he lost his footing and for a moment he thought he was going to tumble over the edge. By the time he reached the bottom he was almost spent. He lay on his back in the snow for a long time, the stars spinning crazily around the sky, his breath sawing in his lungs. He thought how easy it would be to lie there and fall asleep and let it all go.

Something made him stir. He looked back up the slope. A few hundred yards. That was all.

It might as well have been Mont Blanc.

He set off, scrambled two steps, slid one, had to stop every few yards to get his breath, clawing at the ice and the rock. His fingers were numb with cold but when he looked at them, he was shocked at the state of them, they were raw and bleeding and he had torn off two of the fingernails. Now when did he do that?

Stones and scree skittered down into the gorge below him. He was past caring. He didn't think the sentries could hear him from where they were, but if they did, well that was it then, wasn't it? He couldn't stop now.

He rested a few yards from the crest, gathering his strength for one final push. He hadn't felt as exhausted as this since he climbed his first mountain with his father when he was fifteen.

He crawled the last few yards.

He peered over the lip of the crest, into a sheer snowbank, the ice glittering in the moonlight. It tumbled hundreds of feet down into the darkness.

Going down there would be suicide.

Harry lay on his back, felt the ice melting and seeping into his clothes, past caring, the strength gone out of him. Well, what was the point anyway?

As he lay there, he wondered, and not for the first time, about God. Was there such a thing, and if there was, what did he look like and where was he, and had he even heard about Harry Delhaze? He doubted it, very much.

His father had always told him to be afraid of God, that much at least made sense, because if God was a man then he probably frowned a lot and would have disapproved of most of the things he had done, much as Father had.

He could imagine both of them, God and his father, sipping their cognac and smoking their cigars and shaking their heads and muttering: *Well, see, this is what he deserves for the kind of life he's lived. I warned him!*

When he had set off a few hours earlier, he had made a landmark so that he could find his way back. There was a stretch of wall behind the west tower that rose ten or twenty feet straight up, and the ancient door was directly below it. Harry stumbled towards it. All he wanted was to get warm again, to sleep.

Now there was no hope left, he felt curiously free.

When he got back to the kasbah, the guard was still snoring by the fire in the corridor. He stepped over him, slipped into their bedroom, and collapsed onto his sleeping mat, too tired to take off his clothes, too tired to move.

George sat up, lit a candle. 'Harry. Oh my God, what happened to you?'

He heard Mou's voice. '*Sayeed*?'

He was aware of them undressing him, piling dry sheepskins on top of him, trying to get him warm. George tried to dress his torn fingers as best he could by the light of the candle, dabbing at them with tincture, tying linen bandages around them.

'It's hopeless,' Harry murmured. 'We are stranded here. We are lost to the world.'

CHAPTER 19

The door opened and two of Amastan's guards appeared with rifles. Zdan walked into the room. 'On your feet,' he said.

Harry tried to remember what had happened. That's right, he thought, they have found out I tried to escape. He felt groggy, his head was splitting, as if he'd drunk too much brandy and played cards all night.

He tried to sit up, grimaced at the pain in his fingers, looked down at the thick linen bandages, brown with blood.

Mou yawned and stretched as if men putting rifles in his face first thing in the morning was the most natural thing in the world.

'What's this about?' George said.

'I don't know. But Amastan sent me to get you.

The three of them got to their feet.

'Not you,' Zdan said to Mou.

The boy shrugged, pulled a sheepskin over his head, and went back to sleep.

George dressed, threw on a *djellaba* over his tunic, helped Harry struggle into his clothes. Harry couldn't do it himself because of the bandages on his hands. His legs and knees were crisscrossed with deep scratches. Zdan stared but didn't say anything.

'The guards have reported me,' Harry said to George in English as they made their way through the kasbah.

'What do you think they're going to do?'

'Dock our salaries perhaps?'

Amastan was waiting for them in his eyrie in the kasbah's south tower, prowling the carpets, wildly changed from the cold, enigmatic man they had met on their arrival. He was still wearing the *cheiche* that covered his face. Did he never take it off? Harry thought. He would like to see what this demon looked like.

'Which one of you is the wise man?' Amastan said. 'Is it you?' He pointed to George when they didn't answer him quickly enough.

'Hardly wise.'

'Zdan said you were a *hakkim*, a sage.'

'I'm a doctor in England, yes, if you think that's the same thing.'

He nodded at Zdan and he and the two guards left the room.

'I need your help,' he said.

'My help?'

'For my sister. She has a *djinn* inside her. A bad spirit.'

'A bad spirit. I don't know if they taught us what to do about that in medical school.'

'Why do you smile? Have I made a joke?'

'Not at all. What does this bad spirit do to her?'

'Sometimes she falls. She shakes. It is like a demon has taken hold of her entire body. There is nothing any of my mullahs or sorcerers can do for her. Sometimes she stops breathing, many times I have feared she would die.'

'How long does this shaking go on?' George asked him.

'Sometimes just a touch of the hourglass, sometimes on and on as if it will never stop. It is happening more often now. I am very afraid for her life. You are a magician. You can help her.'

'I will do my best. First I must examine her?'

'You mean touch her? Of course not. She is a woman.'

'How can I discover what is wrong with her if I cannot...'

'It is forbidden! She has a *djinn,* that is tormenting her. That is all you need to know. Do you have some magic to remove a *djinn*?'

George looked at Harry.

'Do you know what's wrong?' Harry said.

'It's impossible to *know* if I cannot see her. It sounds like epilepsy, but I can't be sure.'

'Can you help him?'

'I think I have some bromide in the medicine box that may help. It may stop the seizures, if that is what is troubling her.'

'Well, you have to do something.'

'You have an amazing talent for stating the obvious.' He turned back to Amastan. 'I have medicine that I can give her. It cannot take away the *djinn* completely, but it may make the spirit less troublesome. Though it would be better if I could...'

'You cannot. Did you not hear what I said? She is my sister.'

'Well, I will see what medicines I have. I can bring it to you myself, later perhaps and explain how best to administer it.'

'Very well. If you can do this, then perhaps I will reconsider the matter of your payment.' They turned to go. 'What have you done to your hands, captain?'

'I fell.'

'You should be more careful. Perhaps do not go out at night. It is easier to see your way in the daylight.'

Harry could not tell if he smiled, because of the *cheiche* that covered his face. But he suspected that Amastan had just made a joke, at his expense.

'Well,' George said, as they followed the guards back to their quarters, 'that was unexpected.'

CHAPTER 20

It was a different room from the one where they had first met the Lord of the Atlas, not as stark, the walls and ceiling were fretted with cedar and the rose-pink embroideries and intricate needlework of the furnishings were almost female. The windows had panes of brightly coloured glass and there were gaudy divans ranged around the walls. The room was dominated by a huge carpet, burgundy red, unlike the native Berber carpets in his eyrie, something George imagined he might find hanging in the bazaars in Tunis or Algiers or Fez.

Several of the shutters had been thrown open, affording a view over the flat roofs of the medina, that tumbled down the edge of the mountain like a staircase of mud brick. The massif, white and crisp, ranged along the entire northern horizon.

George thought at first that the room was empty, and then the Kaïd stepped out of a dark corner, like a wind shadow, a ghost. George had hoped that he might dispense with the *cheiche* for their meeting, but he was dressed as he was on their first encounter, in black *djellaba* and scarf.

Amastan went to sit at a divan by the window. Wordlessly, he invited George to join him.

Two slaves brought the tea while Amastan reclined on the cushions, watching them, ensuring the ceremony was properly adhered to. On the tray was a brass kettle, a sugar box, some tiny cups and glasses and several silver spoons.

One of the slaves took a handful of green tea and put it in the pot, along with several teaspoons of sugar and then the boiling water. They allowed the brew to stand for a few minutes and poured out half a glass of the tea and tossed it out of the window. This, George knew was supposed to remove any poisons, such as copper, that might have been used to colour the tea. The slave then poured out another half glass, which he then drank rather noisily and enthusiastically, George thought, to show that it had not been poisoned by either the tea-maker or the host.

Finally, George was handed a glass of the tea, in one of the tiny brass tumblers. It was like green syrup, and far too sweet for his tastes, but he knew etiquette required him to drink at least three cups of it if he did not want to offend his host.

He waited for Amastan to sip from his own cup, so he could see his face, but the tea was merely a formality, it seemed. Amastan made no attempt to remove the *cheiche*.

Figs and walnuts were produced. Finally, they could get down to business.

'You have the magic elixir?' he said.

George took the bottle from his pocket and placed it on the the low brass table between them, along with a small metal spoon.

'It is not magic,' George said. 'This is called potassium bromide. It is not a bad spirit that ails her, but something we call epilepsy. At least, I think so, without seeing her, I cannot be sure. You must give her one spoonful of this medicine every day, no more than that.'

Amastan stared at the bottle on the table between them and nodded.

'It will banish the *djinn*?'

'In some cases, it lessens the severity and frequency of the seizures.'

'Good. Thank you. If this helps her, I shall reward you.'

'Reward us?'

'I can perhaps double your fee when the contract is finished. Five hundred pounds in silver.'

Well, that was something. George stared at him. Such intense eyes and made the more striking when the rest of his face was hidden. They sent a chill through him.

Amastan continued to stare out of the window, as if he had something of great weight on his mind.

'Is there anything else I can do for you?' George said.

'You can tell me about your friend.'

'Harry? What is it you wish to know?'

'You know him well?'

'I have known him since we were schoolboys together in England.'

'Is he a good man?'

'A good man. How does a man count as good?'

'Does he have courage? Honour? Loyalty?'

'Well, he certainly has courage. He was awarded the highest honour for bravery that our country can give a soldier for his actions in a place called Tell El Kebir. His artillery unit were exposed by a cavalry attack and were ordered to withdraw. As they were hitching the guns to the horses the commanding officer was badly wounded. He was wounded here.' George pointed to inside of his thigh. 'The other gunners panicked and were going to leave him behind, but Harry stayed with him, tried to stop the bleeding. Three enemy horsemen broke through and he fought them off.'

'That is remarkable. What happened to his commander?'

'A bullet had shattered his femoral artery. There was nothing anyone could have done. He died.'

'Still. Your friend, they gave him a medal?'

'Yes.'

'What else should I know about him?'

'He is an accomplished climber. He climbed some of the highest mountains in Wales and Scotland when he was younger.'

'As high as here, the Atlas Mountains? As high as Mount Toubkal?'

'Perhaps not quite as high.'

'And loyalty?'

'Yes.'

'Why do you smile?'

'He is loyal to a fault.'

'Loyalty can be a fault?'

'When we were at school, there was a boy, Stiles. He was the size of a house. He made my life hell. Harry saw him beating me up in the yard one day and he intervened.'

'And?'

'Harry got himself thrashed. Still, the bully left me alone after that.'

'That leaves honour. You are frowning.'

'Because the British Army says he has none.'

'You said they gave him a medal for his courage.'

'And a year later they took the medal and made him resign his commission.'

'Why?'

'I don't know all of it and even if I did, I don't think he would want me to talk of it with others.'

'I don't understand.'

'He can be reckless when it comes to women.'

'Ah, a woman. Is this why he has such pain in his eyes?'

George shook his head. He didn't know how to answer him. Was it so plain that everyone could see it, even a Berber chieftain who had only met him once?

'The real pain, I suppose, comes when a man has been gifted with a privileged life, and he doesn't know quite what to do with it. When he feels he's not good enough to fit into it.'

'Did his father not teach him?'

'His father, I think, is a part of the problem.'

'You knew his father?'

'I did.'

'Was *he* a good man?'

'In my estimation, no.'

Amastan nodded. What was he thinking? When all you can see are a man's eyes, George thought, you are always at a disadvantage. It is as if he can see into me, while I can divine nothing of him. He sipped at the tea the slave had brought him, not because he needed refreshment, but to avoid the Kaïd's gaze.

'Why are you here, Englishman? Here, in Morocco.'

'Because we were offered a good deal of money.'

'Money itself is nothing. If you have enough, you can store it in a cave, piled to the roof, and you will not be any richer. The purpose of money is for making dreams and desires come true. It is a sword to strike down your enemies or a stonemason to build your palace. What are you going to do with yours?'

'I am going to keep a promise to my father.'

'A good answer.' Amastan picked up the bottle on the table between them and examined it. His hands were rough from riding horses, but the fingers were surprisingly long and delicate. 'We have much in common, you and me. Once you have helped me with the cannons, perhaps we will see if I might help you also.'

'In truth, I know nothing about artillery. I was a doctor, in the Army. Of the two of us, Harry is the warrior. I am surplus.'

'No, a *hakkim*, a healer, like yourself. You are useful, in a limited way.'

'I shrink before such extravagant praise.'

'If your elixir can chase away the *djinn* that torments my sister, you will have earned my thanks. I will make sure that you are rewarded.' He stopped, clutched at his stomach.

'My lord?'

'It's nothing.'

'Are you ill?'

He winced again and shook his head.

'If I might be permitted to examine you?'

'No, you may not. It is nothing. Thank you for the elixir. You may go now.'

'But if there is…'

'You may go!'

George got up to leave. As he reached the door, Amastan called him back. 'Your friend. The captain.'

'Yes?'

'Tell him, the next time he wishes to go out at night, he should use the main gate. It will be easier. I will have the guards serve him hot tea when he returns.'

And he laughed.

Harry looked up when George came back from his meeting with Amastan. He was surrounded by screwed up balls of paper. Zdan had found him some scraps of porous, parchment-like paper and writing materials and he had been trying to write a letter to his father, but no words would come. He had tried to write instead to Lucy. After a few attempts, he had given up in disgust.

'I had not expected you back so soon,' he said. Harry tried to make out the expression on his face. 'Were you able to learn anything about him?'

'He is canny. He found out more about us than I discovered of him. Well, in truth, you were the one he was interested in.'

'Me? What did he wish to know?'

'Everything.'

'I hope you were discreet.'

'I told him you were a wastrel and a womaniser with no redeeming qualities.'

'Thank you.'

'It's easier to dissemble when you don't have to lie.'

Harry laughed at that.

'What did he want?'

'He was grateful for the bromide. He still thinks it is some kind of spirit that troubles her, like she is possessed or something. He believes all kinds of superstitious nonsense.'

'Nothing else?'

George shook his head.

'Did he offer you anything in return?'

'He said he would double our fee if we could help his sister.'

'Well, that's something, at least.'

'Not really. The bromide may not work. It may not even be epilepsy. This is all guesswork. The only thing I'm sure of is that it's not an evil spirit, as he believes.'

Harry saw Mou put a hand to the cheap *khamsa* he wore around his neck on a leather thong. It was the shape of the palm of a hand, but with three fingers and two thumbs. They had seen them everywhere, there was scarcely a house in all the Maghreb that did not have one painted on its wall or a doorpost, to avert the evil eye and keep away the *djinn*.

'Why are you shaking your head, Mou?'

'But *sayeed*,' the boy said. 'If the Kaïd says she has been possessed by a *djinn*, then that is what it must be.'

'There are no such thing as evil spirits,' George said. 'It's just superstition.'

'Have you ever even seen an evil spirit?' Harry said to Mou.

'Yes, sirs, of course. He was the height of six men, with black horns and red eyes.'

'It was a bad dream.'

'No, it was a real. I saw him with my own eyes.'

Harry was about to answer him, but George put a hand on his arm and shook his head. 'Don't even try,' he said. 'This is another world. We would do well not to forget that.'

CHAPTER 21

As the weather grew warmer, they started eating their meagre breakfasts in the courtyard, and were always joined by a number of sparrows. They were quite fearless and picked crumbs off their plates and their sleeves, even perched themselves on the edge of their tea glasses. In Morocco, the little birds were believed to be sacred and were never harmed. There was one with a malformed leg and Harry picked him out for special attention, so that after a while he could feed him breadcrumbs by hand.

It seemed to George that his friend had a special affinity for birds.

There was a whitewashed wall, where the slaves hung the carpets to air in the sun. A large silver cage with a massive grey parrot hung from the branches of a nearby orange tree. Harry would always stop by after breakfast and feed it pumpkin seeds or bits of orange or banana that he had rescued from the sparrows.

At first the parrot was shy of him, but Harry's bribes had their effect and soon it started to sidle up to the edge of the cage whenever it saw him. It was soon so tame that he tried to teach it to talk.

'God save the Queen,' he said to the bird.

George shook his head. 'Harry, you can't teach him that.'

'Why not?'

'Too many words.'

Harry turned back to the bird. '*God Save the Queen*. Come on, say it.'

The parrot chewed on a pumpkin seed, one claw holding the treat to its beak, its eye watching Harry with something like suspicion.

'*Fuck off Bou Hamra!*' Harry said to it.

George laughed, despite himself.

'What's the bird's name?' he said to the slave.

The man looked at George as if he were crazy. 'It's a bird. It doesn't have a name.'

'If it doesn't have a name,' Harry said, 'I'll have to give it one. I'll call it Algernon.' Algernon was the name of their old battalion commander. He turned back to the bird and said: 'Come on, Algernon. Say it for me. *Fuck off, Bou Hamra!*'

'I'll bet you five guineas you can't do it,' George said.

'I accept. Algernon and I will practice. Won't we, Algernon?' He gave the bird a piece of banana. *Fuck off, Bou Hamra!*'

The bird ate the fruit, and when it had finished, it came to the edge of the cage, looking for more. For weeks it went on.

But it didn't say a word.

The two cannon had been left inside a storeroom in one of the *fondaks*, which served as an inn for the innumerable caravans that stopped here between Marrakesh and Timbuctu in spring and summer. It was a beautiful and ancient building, with four storeys, and open in the centre, surrounded by galleries of carved wood. It smelled strongly of spices: cinnamon, vanilla, and cloves. There was another taint, unmistakeable, fear and sweat, they had kept slaves chained in this room on their way to the market in Fez.

Garlands of herbs hung over the muzzles of both guns, there were offerings of fruit and flowers around the wheels. Two young Berber women sat astride them, kissing the barrels and shouting incantations, their hands held to the heavens.

As they entered, the women screamed and ran out. Harry and George watched them scatter across the courtyard and disappear.

'What the hell were they doing?' George said.

'They were praying for children,' Zdan said.

'To the cannons?'

'Of course. The cannons have the power of *baraka*, of blessing, they can cure disease, they help a woman have babies, everyone knows this.'

The two cannons were a grim proposition in the dull yellow lamplight. The wooden trails on *al-raed* were all but rotted through, it was a wonder they had managed to drag it this far through the mountains. The breech was corroded, and the axle was bent.

Harry ran his hand over *al-wahsh's* barrel, it was pale green with age, to be expected. It was only slightly better, larger, sturdier, how they had dragged this monster over the massif, how many slaves had died carrying it over the high passes, he did not like to imagine.

'What do you think?' George asked him.

'You see this? Put your hand here. See this powdery spot, how it flakes away if you scrape it with your fingernail. That's bronze disease.'

'Is that from the cold?'

'No, humidity causes this. This was there before we set off from Marrakech. God knows how long they've been left untended.'

'Can you fix them?'

'I hope so. I don't want to be standing next to one if we fire it in anger in this condition.'

'The Sultan has cheated us?'

'What did you expect?'

'What can we do?' Zdan said.

'We need some good smithies. And we need time, because we'll have to pull these things apart, screw by screw.'

'We will get you the men you need.'.

'Time,' George said. 'That's something we have in abundance.'

Amastan sat by the window, cross legged on the carpets. Oil-lanterns twinkled down in the medina, the light retreating across the slopes of the mountain as the sun slid down the sky. He shut the heavy glass window, against the cold. He pulled a leather pouch from his robe, took out the letter, unfolded the parchment. It had been folded three or four times.

He read the familiar words: *My beloved, my forbidden, my lost.*

He winced and looked away.

How many times had he read those words? They still hurt him.

It is so long since you have written to me. But I will not allow you to forget. I cannot let you forget. It doesn't matter that you have forsaken me, I will not, I cannot leave you behind. You will always be a part of me, and I will, always, be a part of you.

I will not let you forget.

I have patience, I will wait forever.

He threw back his head, tore the *cheiche* from his face, as if he was fighting to breathe. He stared at the ceiling for a long time, as the shadows crept over the carpets, and the light withdrew from the room.

He winced at the cramping pain in his belly. He could tell this time it was going to be bad. He wondered if it had anything to do with the Englishman. The pain subsided, and he looked down at his hand. It had curled into a fist crumpling the letter into a ball.

He unfolded it, read it one final time. Then he held the letter to the candle, twisted it in his fingers as he watched it burn. When it was fully alight, he let it drop to the stone on the windowsill. The ashes he crushed with his fingers.

The crew that Zdan had assembled were a ragtag bunch. They were unlikely engineers standing there in their tatty turbans and dirty *djellabas*. Zdan told Harry they were the best smithies and carpenters that they had.

'Well?' he said.

'First, we have to take them apart, completely,' Harry said. 'We have some basic tools in the caisson, or we did, unless someone dropped them in the river on the way from the mountains. We need to build new trails, for both of these cannons. That one,' he said, pointing to *al-raed*, 'it's smaller, it should be no trouble. This one will take some work. We'll need to make new wheels. But first we go to work on the barrels. We need salt, flour, vinegar, and lemon juice. Lots of it. You can do this?'

'In the winter when there is barely enough to eat?'

'It's up to you. What is more important to you, the cannons or salt?'

Zdan nodded. 'Whatever you need.'

'Good. Let's get to work.'

'Need an assistant?' George said.

'What do you know about cannons?'

'Nothing, but I'm willing to learn. After all, it's going to be a long winter and I've nothing else to do.'

Harry clapped him on the shoulder. 'Good. Keep those healing hands away from the hammers and you'll be fine.'

CHAPTER 22

'Have you seen Mou?'

They had been in the stables all day working on the cannons. It was late in the afternoon, they were tired, their fingers numb from the cold. The carpenters had built new rails for *al-wahsh*, to replace the originals that had rotted through and they had spent the whole day re-fixing them.

'I told him to follow Zdan, keep his ears open. I said he could be our little spy.'

'As long as he doesn't try and get back into the harem.'

Harry sat down, took a needle from the medical kit, and started to work at the splinters in his fingers and hands. His hands were so cold, he couldn't hold the needle. He went to the fire to warm them.

'There's flames and there's no heat.'

'It's the altitude,' George said.

'What good is a fire if you can't get warm?'

There was still so much work to do on the cannons, they still had to lamp the rusted patches on the barrels, check the metal for cracks. It was a miracle they had come this far, without being lost in a ford or disappearing down one of the innumerable gullies they had crossed between here and the Sahara.

Amastan's smithies had done their best, but what they needed was a proper foundry and smithies with the right tools. After so many years of neglect, they needed more than a few running repairs up here in the middle of God knows where.

They heard yelling outside, they looked at each other, that sounded like Mou.

'What's he done now?'

They went outside, the Chief Black Eunuch, a huge man with fleshy jowls, had him by the ear and was marching him down the corridor towards them.

'What's going on?' George said to him.

'Tell him to stay away from the harem. Next time he'll get a good flogging.'

'The harem?'

'If he were a few years older, he would have been put to death on the spot.' The eunuch threw him into the room and rounded on them with a snarl. 'It's his last warning.'

'Last? He's done this before?'

'He's trying the great lord's patience. You've been warned.'

After the eunuch marched away, they went back into the room. Mou sat cross-legged on the carpets, looking surly rather than sheepish.

'Is this true?' Harry said to him. 'We told you to stay away from that place. You promised us!'

'I was just looking. I wasn't doing any harm.'

'Looking at what?'

'The girls. The *girls*. They are beautiful!'

'You are too young to look at girls,' George said.

'Who said so?'

Harry shrugged. 'Come on, George. He's right. A man's never too young or too old to look at girls.'

Mou made a face at George. 'You are jealous. It was worth a sore ear!'

'You heard what that man said. It's the lord's harem! Next time they'll cut your head off.'

'It's your fault,' Mou said.

'How is it our fault?' Harry said.

'You told me I had to spy for you. I was doing spying, like you said.'

'Spy on Zdan, find out what's going on with Bou Hamra and in Marrakesh. Not spy on Amastan's wives!'

'I do spy on him. All the time!'

'How did you get into the harem anyway?' George said to him.

'There's a wall. It's an old wall, where the bricks and plaster have fallen out, you can climb. You can see everything from up there, into the ladies' *hammam*, everything.'

'Well, that's enough climbing for you. This is the last time. You are never to do that again.'

Mou's ear was glowing red where the Chief Eunuch had pinched it. When the boy didn't answer, Harry grabbed him by the other ear. 'Swear to us!'

'I promise, *sayeed*,' he said.

He ran off.

The repair work on the cannons was progressing far better than Harry had expected.

He had made a paste from lemon juice, flour, salt, and vinegar and showed the two smithies how to rub it into the corroded spots on the copper barrels and flake off the corroded metal. They didn't have brushes soft enough for the freckling, so the men improvised and used raw potatoes. Zdan looked pained when he saw what they were doing – more food going to waste on the damned cannons – but he didn't try to intervene.

They soaked some rags in the solution and left them on the barrels to soak, cleaned away the residue with fresh clean water – they put clean snow in some buckets and let it melt – then let the barrel dry. They did it again and again until all the affected areas were clean of corrosion.

It was long and painstaking work. Harry had been concerned at first that the work might expose cracks in the barrels or breech blocks that would be impossible to repair outside of a metal foundry. He was heartened to find that the damage was not too extensive.

It was impossible to examine the insides of the barrels, they put a sponge on the end of one of the ramrods to clean the inside of the barrels as best they could, and one of the smithies fashioned a bore brush to loosen and remove the corrosion and residue from inside the tubes. *Al-Raed,* smaller, shorter, was more easily restored to something like its former glory.

Al-wahsh had iron trails, which were heavily corroded, Harry had the smithies scrub the rusted patches with sand and wire brushes, soaking them with the same paste they had used on the brass. When he was satisfied, they hoisted ropes over the rafters and lowered the trails into a huge vat of boiling water. It was hot work, and they were sweating, and stripped down to their trousers, even as snow and sleet flurried through gaps in the doors from the gale outside.

When they were cool, any loose oxide was carded off and the rags soaked in sheep tallow laid over them to soak. It wasn't perfect, but it might keep the rust at bay for a while longer.

The carpenters fashioned two new wheels for *al-raed*, along with brand new trails, and then went to work on the caisson. Their work belied Harry original impression. They might look like goatherds, but they knew their craft.

CHAPTER 23

There hadn't been a snowfall for weeks. Occasionally they saw glimpses of sun through the clouds, and the thick crust of snow in the *maydan* started to melt. On some afternoons, instead of snow there was a freezing mist of rain, and from the terrace Harry saw the streets in the medina turn to a quagmire of mud.

Zdan came to their rooms every day. Some days he brought some of the local black tobacco or *kif* and enquired after their welfare. At first, they had asked him for news, but there was none to bring, and they had long ago stopped asking for any. He had given Harry one of the local pipes, made from goat horn. As they sat and smoked, he asked them questions about England, and they asked him about Aït Karim and the Lord of the Atlas.

He told them that the slaves they saw around the Kasbah – and that the Sultan owned in their thousands – came from the Sudan or from Timbuctu. Even the sheikhs of the humblest villages owned a handful.

As for the harem, yes, the Kaïd was a Berber. He was also a great lord and it was a matter of great pride that he had a grand household to rival those of the pashas of the *mahkzen*. The Kaïd's own father had had just one wife, it was only towards the end of his life that he had established the el-Karim family as pre-eminent in the Atlas. The women, of course, were of all colours and races – the only Berber woman in the lord's harem was his sister, Wafa.

It was all ephemeral, he said. Should the Kaïd fall out of favour with the Sultan or should Bou Hamra - may his testicles turn into argan fruit and be eaten by goats – become *chereef* of all Morocco, then Amastan would lose it all. His women, his sister as well, would be taken into some other lord's harem, his wealth would be forfeit, Aït

Karim would be razed to the ground and the Kaïd himself would be left to rot in a dungeon. That is how it is here. You win all, or you lose all.

'Who is this Bou Hamra?' Harry asked him. 'Why does the Sultan hate him so much?'

'You don't know? What did the vizier tell you?'

'That he was a rebel who wanted the throne for himself.'

'He didn't tell you why?'

'No.'

Zdan lit his pipe and settled back in the cushions. 'The reason the Sultan hates him so much is because he is afraid of him. Bou Hamra is his brother.'

'His *brother*.'

'Some say he is the older brother, the rightful Sultan. But in Morocco, the throne does not always go to the eldest boy, the sultan himself can decide which of his sons will succeed him. His father chose against him, in favour of his younger son, Moulay. When the last Sultan died, Moulay threw Bou Hamra in prison, but he escaped to the south, to Mauretania. Nothing was heard from him for years. Then a couple of years ago he reappeared in the deserts south of here, impressed some of the local people with cheap conjuring tricks. Now they believe he is not only the rightful sultan, but that he is the *Mahdi* himself, something like your Jesus Christ, come back to earth to restore justice and defend the true faith. That is how he got his name. 'Bou Hamra' means 'the man on the she-ass'. There is a legend here in the *Maghrib* that says when the *Mahdi* returns he will appear from the west, mounted on an ass.'

'That is why Amastan sided with the sultan?'

'He felt he had no choice.'

'He could have slaughtered us all on the mountain and given the Sultan's head to Bou Hamra. He would have been richly rewarded for it.'

'Is that what you would have done?'

'It's what some men would have done.'

'First, Amastan trusts Bou Hamra as he would trust a cobra in his bed. But also these other tribes who have already allied with him, they are our rivals here in the Atlas. Bou Hamra has promised them he will bring down Amastan and make them Lords of the Atlas in his place, if he becomes Sultan.'

'I thought the Sultan had no real power here.'

'He has power enough. He decides who is pasha of Marrakesh and every lord of the atlas covets being lord of the plains as well. That is the path to true power.'

'This Bou Hamra, does he have cannons, does he live in a fortress like this one?'

'Not yet. But you must understand, Amastan's money and power comes from the taxes he levies on the caravans that pass this way from Timbuctu. Bou Hamra is disrupting that trade route, raiding the caravans, stealing the gold and the ivory and the slaves. If he is not stopped, Amastan's treasury will be empty and then he becomes vulnerable to attack.'

'That's why he needs us,' George said.

'Yes.'

'Where is Bou Hamra now?' Harry asked him.

'He has taken refuge with one of the other families here in the Atlas. They have a fortress, almost as tall as this one. But they don't have cannons. We do.'

'So what will happen now?'

'In Spring, when the snow clears, we will go and find Bou Hamra. Once we have settled with him, we will bring his head to the Sultan. Once that is done, our Kaïd will become second only to the sultan himself in all Morocco.'

'And what month is it now?' Harry asked him.

A shrug. 'It is winter. When the snow clears, it will be Spring. What more do you need to know?' He finished his pipe. 'That is enough talk for now. It has been a long day. I wish you goodnight.'

CHAPTER 24

Harry woke to the sound of a dog barking somewhere in the valley, the braying of a pack mule. He heard the chirping of women's voices as they made their way out of the gates to the fields, the chink of kettles and pans from the kitchens off the courtyard below, the acrid smell of wood smoke.

There was tapping at the wooden shutter. When he unlatched it, a small bird flew off in a flash of yellow and white. A finch. A sign of spring though the air outside was still bitter and the sky was clear and pale blue.

Winter began to loosen its cold gunmetal grip on the mountains. There were days he could stand on the terrace and feel almost warm for an hour or two until the shadows chased the sunshine across the hills. The thick crust of snow on the mountain spurs began to melt and began their slow retreat back up the mountains and then they had a week of rain. The winding alleys in the medina below turned to mud, only to freeze over again at night, leaving deep corrugations from the donkey carts and sheets of black ice.

They hadn't been given any meat for weeks, not even any of the tough and stringy chicken, their meals consisted of flat bread with a few beans and rotten vegetables. One morning, when Zdan walked in while they were eating their meagre breakfasts, Harry asked him if they were on prison rations.

'I'm sorry for the food. You are not prisoners, you are our honoured guests. You eat better than most.'

'I'm sorry,' Harry said. 'I didn't know that.'

'At least we have bread,' George said, holding up a leathery piece of flatbread.

'Actually it's mule dung mixed with some barley and wheat,' Zdan said. 'You'll get used to it.'

'As long as it's prime dung,' Harry said.

'The Sultan's army ate almost everything we had,' Zdan said. 'We have hardly any fresh meat, and the granaries are almost empty. The Kaïd has been forced to place armed guards in front of the doors to keep mobs from the medina from trying to break them down. The rations we can distribute among the townspeople are getting smaller every day.'

Only Mou didn't seem to mind. He said it was the first time in his life that anyone had ever fed him three meals in a day. Even bread made out of mule dung tasted good to him.

'It was a risk then, to take the side of the Sultan.'

'It was, but the people here are accustomed to hardship. It is part of life here. I am sorry there is not more food for you. The Kaïd has instructed me to ensure your comforts. He is very grateful for the help you have given him.'

'We have done nothing yet,' Harry said.

'No, his sister Wafa is much better. He says the *hakkim's* magic has banished the *djinn.*'

'The *djinn*, as he calls it, will return, I'm afraid,' George said. 'She is not cured.'

'It has not possessed her since you gave him the elixir. He is fulsome in his praise.'

'How old is his sister?' George asked.

'She has twenty-five, twenty-six summers. An old woman, well past marriageable age.'

'Then why is she still in the Kaïd's household?'

'Who would have such a woman? She is cursed with a devil.'

'Not even for a tactical alliance?' Harry said. 'He is, after all, Lord of the Atlas.'

'He has five other sisters. All the alliances he needs have been made.'

'And no brothers?'

'He is the last of his line. I am his eldest cousin. If not for fate, I would have been Lord of the Atlas in his place.'

'Does that bother you?' Harry said.

'As God wills,' Zdan said. '*El hamdu billah.*'

'What about the Kaïd? How many children does he have?'

'He has a son.'

Harry was astonished. 'Just one son? There must be more than a hundred women in the harem.'

'How would you know that?'

Harry glanced at Mou, who stared back at him wide-eyed. I shall have to be more careful with what I say, Harry thought. 'A guess. I thought that was your custom.'

Zdan glanced at Mou, then at George. Did he know? 'The Kaïd is an unusual man.'

'In what way?'

'In ways you do not need to know. Finish your breakfasts. I have work to do. Take your ease.'

After he had gone, Harry and George exchanged a look.

'What did you make of that?' George said.

'I'd say that if I had a harem of a hundred women, I'd have more than one son.'

They settled down to rest. The work on the cannons was done, and without anything to occupy his time, the days seemed endless. There was nothing to drink, no women, no opportunity to lose money he

178

didn't have. It was a torment. He had spent the better part of life searching for and finding distraction, and now he was left alone with only his thoughts for company. He thought he would go mad.

He looked up. Mou was standing at the window, watching Zdan make his way across the courtyard below. 'I do not like that one,' he said.

'Zdan? He's alright. He helps us.'

Mou ran a finger across his throat. 'Don't trust him,' he said. He finished his breakfast, curled up in a ball and went back to sleep.

CHAPTER 25

The river below the Kasbah became a roaring torrent, blocks of ice and broken trees tumbling end over end over the rocks and down the gorge. The mountainside started to return to its natural colours, here and there were patches of green showing through the crusts of snow.

As the snow melted, the carcasses of the thousands of sheep and goats that had been slaughtered to feed the Sultan's army were exposed and every scavenging bird in Morocco came to feast on the thawing remains. Vultures, kites, and crows wheeled on the currents, for days the sky was dark with them, and the parapets and terraces, courtyards and laneways were fouled with splashes of bird excrement.

Harry watched them from their window, jostling with each other, shrieking and spreading their black wings at the jackals that came down from the eyries for their share of the feast.

Every day the snow retreated a little further. Children ventured down to the river, now a torrent rushing headlong over the boulders and rocks, swollen by the melt waters. For months it had been silent, hidden under a vast bank of snow but now the roar of it muted every other sound in the valley. A cavern had formed at the widest part, stalagmites creating a forest of columns and arches, and children threw shards of rock and ice at it, trying to knock pieces into the sun-bright water. One day the whole architecture came crashing down, and they shrieked, and ran laughing back up the hillside and didn't stop until they reached the gates.

'Zdan came to see me this morning,' George said.

'What did he want?'

'He wants to know if I have any more of the potassium bromide for Amastan's sister.'

'Do you?'

'No.'

'What will happen?'

'She'll start having convulsions again and he will see what I have been trying to tell him all along, that I am no sorcerer, just a simple provincial doctor.'

Harry came to stand at his shoulder and lowered his voice, even though he was using English. You could never be sure in this place what languages people knew, and how much they understood. 'Mou brought me some disturbing news this morning. He doesn't seem to have taken mind of our admonishments not to go back to the harem.'

'You're not serious. After what we told him last time?'

'He's incorrigible. He gets it from his father.'

'You are not his father. This is not funny, Harry. Doesn't he understand what they will do to him if he is caught in there again?'

'Don't worry, I gave him a good talking to. Even so, what he claims to have seen is disturbing.'

'Amastan?'

'No, Zdan.'

'What about him?'

'He says he saw him go in the harem by a little-used door. He swears to me it's true.'

'If the slaves see him, Zdan will lose his head.'

'He says it was the Chief of the Eunuchs himself who let him in.'

'That is a dangerous thing to know. Almost as dangerous as not knowing it.'

Harry nodded. True enough. 'Sooner or later Amastan will find out.'

'And then it's Zdan's head. Unless he wants a fight, and he is getting ready to be the next Kaïd.'

'What should we do, do you think?'

'Nothing, except make sure we don't make an enemy of either of them. Not if we want to see England again.'

'I'll take your advice but George, I must tell you, I have already given up hope of seeing old Blighty again. Ever.'

In London, the changing of the season meant only that you could take your drink outside on the benches instead of huddled inside the snug well away from the door and the draughts.

But here, with the coming of spring, the entire landscape was transformed.

The snow disappeared and the white wasteland around the Kasbah turned to green pasture and fields, and the irrigation channels ran with bright cold snow melt.

After a few weeks, as soon as the scavenger birds had picked the bones of the slaughter clean, the women and young girls began venturing down to the forest with mules and pack horses and returning with fresh water from the wells or bundles of dry sticks. Shepherd boys in striped *djellabas* drove their herds of goats and sheep into the foothills, looking for fresh feed. Boulders and rocks appeared through the melt, alongside the curled horn of a goat, picked clean now by the jackals and crows.

There were smudges of colour on the trees and in the rock crevices as the first buds appeared.

It became Harry's favourite time of the day, listening to the *muezzin* calling the townspeople to prayer from the minaret in the town, watching the swallows wheel and arc between the walls of the Kasbah.

He even started to feel at ease with himself. There hadn't been a drop of hard liquor to be had since they left Tangier, and his eyes had never looked clearer. His hands didn't shake in the morning. He was almost as fit as he'd been when he'd been in the army.

The rains set in. Harry stood on the terrace watching the people in the descending laneways beneath the Kasbah, the children with mangy shaved skulls, the women with their hennaed faces, the men in their sheepskins, long daggers at their belts. He felt as if he had descended into some netherworld where other mortals couldn't go, but his golden fleece, his two thousand pounds, was as far away as ever.

He imagined going home with two thousand pounds, starting his own business becoming richer than his father, his brother, proving to everyone they were wrong about him. Lucy would beg him to take her back, her father would shake his hand and tell him he had underestimated him. Even papa would come, cap in hand. 'I misjudged you so, boy. I shall make it up to you.'

Just a fantasy, of course. He supposed he would never see any of them ever again.

He certainly wouldn't see the money they promised him.

He took out the hollow bone pipe that Zdan had given him and plugged it with the thick black tobacco these Berbers smoked. His mind wandered from an imagined future to an imagined past, thinking about how his life might have been, if he had married Lucy, if her father hadn't got in the way, if she hadn't let him. He supposed that was what hurt, not that the general didn't think he was good enough for her, but that she had agreed with him.

You'll never be good enough, he thought. No matter what you do.

He let his mind run away with itself, imagining them together in Greece or Switzerland. Once he thought she was his destiny, that fate had brought them together. The thoughts tumbled over in his head, fantasies of how his life could have been in the past, what it might be in the future. But here was his cold reality.

He was a drunk and a gambler, and he had nothing.

A dog barked somewhere down the valley and lights flickered on in the medina, as the first cook fires were lit. A stork settled on its nest on the roof of the Kaïd's mirador.

In the very top of the eyrie, he saw a man silhouetted against the glow of a candle.

Amastan.

The Lord of the Atlas settled himself on some cushions. It was late in the evening and he would not be disturbed. He sat by the open window, midges dancing around the light, listened to the cough of a jackal in the dark somewhere high up the mountain.

He opened the drawstrings on the pouch and took out the parchment. The author of the letter had a beautiful hand. It seemed a pity that its ultimate destiny was the fire.

He read:

'Solitude was my choice. It was your choice also.

I live in this body that God gave me, knowing there will never be hope of true happiness of any kind. My desire will reside with me in aloneness, and one day will die with me stillborn.

You could have saved me. It was within your power to do it. You chose the will of another over your own will. You chose the destiny designed by another over your own heart.

I am the one who must live with that choice, day after day.

Tell me it has been worth it. Just a word from you will end my pain.'

He held the letter to the candle with trembling fingers and let it fall to ash. He blew the ashes to the wind and they disappeared into the darkness.

He took his time composing his reply. The moon had almost fallen behind the mountain by the time he had finished, yet he had written only a few lines.

'Your last letter disturbed me greatly.

You have no right to judge me.

Yes, solitude was my choice also, and I know I must live with it, without hope of anything, except obligation. There is only one traitor to duty, and it is called desire. It is a flimsy, ephemeral thing. But reputation, dynasty, these live on for ever in the memories of countries and of empires.

You must stop now. I have made my decision. It is done.'

He let the ink dry and rolled the parchment back inside the pouch. Tomorrow he would conceal it in its hiding place, and he promised himself that after that, he would never go there again.

CHAPTER 26

Although the snows had started to melt, the ground still refroze every night, so for a few hours it was still hard enough to hitch the caissons to the horses and drag them out of the kasbah with the two cannons.

Not much after dawn and already Zdan had *al-wahsh* and *al-raed* drawn up on the *maydan*, the meadow below the fortress. They were in their firing positions, their muzzles aimed at the ridge below the mountain.

Harry and George rode out, accompanied by Zdan and a squadron of Amastan's Berber horsemen, all of them armed with muskets and rifles. 'Don't try to escape,' Zdan said to them. 'They won't shoot you, you're too valuable. But they have orders to shoot your horses from under you. They're good horses. You don't want that, do you?'

It was the first time Harry had seen what was left of his gun crews since their rescue in the mountains. There were just three of the old guard, all that was left of the two five-man crews that had left Marrakesh. Three had deserted, the other four had died on the trek, food for the buzzards, their bodies under the snow up there in the high passes.

Redbeard was there, of course, he imagined it would take more than frostbite and wholesale slaughter to kill him. Ramrod was next to him, in rags and grinning like a snake oil salesman, and the one with the milk eye. They were all drawn up in a line, more or less, with seven men of various ages that Zdan told him had been hand-picked as replacements for the lost crew. All Berbers by the look of them, they had bad teeth and murder in their eyes.

'I need men who can follow simple instructions,' Harry had told him.

'It is hard to find a Berber man who will follow orders,' he had said. 'I'll try and find a few who won't take out their knives if you yell at them.'

Harry swung down from his horse and looked them over. His Arabic had improved since the last time he had addressed them, and he surprised them with a few well-chosen insults.

Stand straighter you sons of dogs. I scrape you from the bottom of my shoe!

That got a reaction. Only Redbeard didn't flinch, just scowled back at him.

Harry split them into two crews; he put Ramrod and Redbeard in one crew on *al-raed*, Milk-Eye with the others on *al-wahsh*. When he directed Redbeard to his place at the thumbstall, he got a murderous look.

He muttered something under his breath.

'What did you say?' Harry said to him.

'I said, I am the most experienced here. I should be the gunner.'

'You'll go where you're told.'

The two crews formed up in positions at the cannon.

'Why did you do that?' George whispered to him. 'That one with the red beard. He's right. That isn't fair.'

'I don't like him,' Harry said. 'He's a troublemaker. It's written all over his face.'

'If he's a troublemaker, you're only encouraging him to make more.'

Harry took the first crew through their drill.

Redbeard cleaned the vent with a long iron spike and covered the flash hole with the thumbstall on his leather glove. 'It's too easy for me,' he said.

Harry ignored him.

'Tell the new men. What's the purpose of what you just did?'

'It stops the air getting in and lighting embers from the last shell. You could train a monkey to do this.'

He nodded to Ramrod who took a pole with a sheep's hide wrapped around one end and plunged it into a bucket of water. He wormed the barrel with it, spinning the pole around in his fingers before withdrawing it.

'Tell the men what you're doing,' Harry said.

'I am removing any debris and hot sparks from the barrel before we load the next round, *sayeed.*'

'Correct. What happens if there are still embers alight in the barrel?'

'It could set off the gunpowder when we reload the gun.'

'Show them how to grip the rod.'

Ramrod showed them, his fingers looped lightly around the pole.

'And why do you hold it that way?'

'Because if there is any charge left in the barrel, the pole could blow backwards.'

'And what will that do to your hand if it gets in the way?'

'It will blow if off, *sayeed.*'

'Again?'

'It will blow my fucking hand off, in the name of the Prophet.'

'Exactly. It will blow your fucking hand off. Have we all got that?' He looked around at the faces gathered around the cannon. 'How many times should you do it?'

'Many times, *sayeed.*'

'That's right. Many times. Until I tell you to stop. Carry on.'

One of the new men, a Berber, realised everyone was staring at him. He was holding a long pole, similar to Redbeard's. He was about to plunge it into the bucket of water, but Harry stopped him and took the pole from him. 'No, son. You now need a dry sponge to go down the barrel to remove all the water residue that could cause your cannon to misfire.' He slammed the pole back into the Berber's arms.

Once that was done, he nodded to Ramrod, who put the sack of gunpowder charge down the barrel and used the ramrod to tamp it down.

'Why did you use one hand to tamp the powder. Tell them.'

'I have told them.'

'Tell them again.'

'If the embers are not all doused, it could blow up, and then, God help me in my sorrow.'

'Exactly. So you use one hand, and a nice, loose grip. Do you all understand?' He had Zdan repeat it to them, in Tamazight, for the new Berbers in the crew who couldn't understand his execrable Arabic.

The number-three plunged the sponge into the bucket of water and used both hands to ram it down the barrel.

'No!' Harry shouted, and grabbed it out of his hands. He turned to Zdan. 'Tell this man he is not fucking his donkey, he has to spin it, and hold it loosely, one hand, like this. There may still be hot embers in the barrel.'

Finally, the number-three did it as he was shown, his eyes dark with resentment. Zdan was right. These Berbers didn't like taking orders.

He nodded to the powder monkey, a man named Faizal, who went to retrieve one of the cannonballs from the caisson. He put it in the satchel around his neck, but he was so frightened that as he was running back with it, he tripped over and fell. The ball landed in the snow. Everyone except Ramrod and Redbeard threw themselves to the ground in terror.

Harry went over, picked up the heavy ball and rolled it down the barrel.

'Get up, you sons of dogs!'

They all shuffled back to their feet.

Ramrod stepped up with the pole end of the wet sponge and pushed the round all the way down the barrel and gave it a sharp tap to seat it properly against the breach.

Harry grabbed the Wormer and pushed him towards the trails. 'On my command you will move the cannon to the left or right with that hand spike.'

Harry went to the gunsight and sighted the barrel on a boulder just below the ridgeline. He first made sure there were no goats or sheep or small children in the way and adjusted the elevation with the screw. 'A little to the right,' he said. 'I said a little, that's almost ninety degrees. Move it back. Not that far. Oh for God's sakes.'

'That man couldn't find his nether regions with both hands and a map,' Redbeard said. 'Why don't you let me do it?'

Finally the gun was aimed. The Berber at the lanyard had bumfluff on his cheeks and a look of utter bewilderment on his face. Harry showed him how to fire the gun. 'You don't pull. There's thirty pounds of pressure here. You lean. Like a penguin.'

'I doubt if anyone here has ever seen a penguin,' George laughed.

'Like this.' He went back to the gun, waited for Redbeard to stand aside, and withdraw the thumbstall. He did it, albeit reluctantly. Harry pushed the pointed end of a bronzed looped rod into the hole to pierce the cartridge.

He handed the lanyard to the gunner and stood to the side. 'Prepare,' he said, and Ramrod stepped to the side of the gun, leaned back and covered the ear nearest the gun. A few seconds later, at the urging of his comrades, the number four did the same.

Harry yelled fire, and the gunner pulled on the friction primer. Nothing.

'One leg out and lean, *lean*,' Harry shouted at him. 'Try again!'

Finally.

The cannon roared and jumped back a yard on its trails. The shell blew the boulder to fragments and the men gaped in astonishment and cheered themselves hoarse.

He ran through the procedure with the second gun crew, they were all new except for One-Eye, and he took more time over it. After several minutes, they had the cannon loaded and another boulder was blown into pieces.

This time he heard ululations and wild cheering from behind them. He looked around. The whole of Aït Karim had come out to watch.

'More,' Zdan said.

'They need more practice before we fire any more live rounds,' Harry said.

'No, do it again. The people want to see it.'

'The more live rounds we fire, the more dangerous it is.'

'The danger doesn't matter.'

'Not to you, perhaps.'

'Do it again,' Zdan said.

They did it again. *Al-wahsh's* crew had a little experience with the gun by now and they fired another round without mishap. Harry turned to George who was timing them with his fob watch. 'How long?'

'Six minutes and twenty-seven seconds. How long is it supposed to take?'

'G Battery in the Royals could manage one round every forty-five seconds.'

'Close.'

The second crew went through their second drill. He saw the man on the thumbstall peer over the barrel to watch what the number three man was doing, just as he was ramming the shot down the barrel. He was using both hands. Harry yelled at him to stop, but it was too late.

Either there were still embers in the barrel, and they were ignited by air getting in the vent, or the number three slammed the shell too hard against the breech. The gun roared, everyone cheered, the women set up another long ululation; and when the smoke cleared the number three gunner was running in circles, clutching at his left arm, which had been blown away below the elbow.

Harry turned to Zdan. 'I told you they weren't ready.'

'Don't worry,' Zdan said. 'We'll find you a replacement. We have plenty of men.'

George was already running down the slope, by the time he reached *al-raed* the number-three had collapsed. His comrades stood around, looking interested but not unduly alarmed. All except Redbeard.

George took off his belt and tied it around the man's arm as a tourniquet.

Harry ran over. 'How is he?'

'I think I've stopped the bleeding.' He looked up at Zdan. 'Have your men carry him back to the fortress.'

'Why?'

'If we don't, he could bleed to death.'

'*Insha'Allah.*'

'I can save this man.'

Zdan frowned. 'Well, if that's what you want. But this man, he will probably prefer you let him die. What use is a one-armed man?'

He rapped out an order to the Berber crew and four of his comrades picked him up and carried him back up the hill towards the fortress.

They carried the injured man back to their rooms in the Kasbah and laid him on the floor on top of the carpets. Soon there was a crowd of people watching from the doorway, servants, *askaris*, the rest of the gun crews.

'Can you get them all out of here?' George said to Zdan.

'What are you going to do?' Redbeard said.

Harry turned around, saw him standing in the doorway, refusing to move, like some malevolent *djinn*.

'Leave us,' Harry said.

'That's my cousin,' Redbeard said.

Harry looked at Zdan, who nodded. 'He was one of the Sultan's *askaris*. He persuaded us to recruit him for the guns, to replace one of the men you lost.'

'What's his name?'

'Idrissa,' Redbeard said.

George brought his satchel from the window shelf and laid out what he needed on a clean cloth. 'I need bowls, towels, rags,' he said to Zdan. 'And a table. A proper one. I can't do this squatting on the floor.'

Zdan rapped out an order and one of the servants ran off to get what he wanted. 'Why are you doing this?' he said to George. 'You don't know this man.'

'I'm a doctor, I can't let him die. He's going to bleed to death if we don't do something.'

'You think you can save him?'

'It's not the first time I've done this.' He looked up at Harry. 'I'll need you to help me. You've seen battle wounds before?'

'No, I always looked the other way. It made me feel sick.'

'Well, not this time. Mou, you're going to help us as well.'

The boy nodded eagerly. Some excitement at last.

'Zdan, can't you get all these people out of here?'

'I want to help,' Redbeard said.

'Good,' George said. 'You can hold one of his legs.'

The servants came back with what George needed, manoeuvred a table into the room and then lifted Idrissa onto it. He had been only half conscious when they carried him in, but now he was coming round, he'd started to jabber and scream. His face was white as chalk, and he was shaking.

'He's going into shock,' George said.

Harry dared a look at the man's arm. He had lost his hand and most of the lower arm, it was still pumping blood from a charred mess of meat and skin. He felt the bile rising to the back of his throat. He'd seen enough of this in Tonkin.

'What are you going to do?' he said to George.

'I don't have a bone saw with me, I'll need to make an incision at the elbow joint and ligate the arteries. We'll need to work fast.'

'What are his chances?'

'Better than if we do nothing.'

He handed a gauze pad and a bottle of chloroform to Harry. 'Soak some of that onto the pad and hold it over his mouth and nose until he passes out. Alright?'

Harry nodded. He didn't trust his voice. George poured some antiseptic solution into a blue porcelain bowl, gaily coloured with blue flowers, and soaked his scalpels and arterial forceps in it to sterilise them. Harry looked away. All the things he'd seen in his life, he'd never got used to this.

'Mou, you hold his right arm, you,' he said to Zdan, 'you hold his arm still while I cut and you,' he said, pointing to Redbeard, 'you hold his legs. He may kick a bit, even when he's unconscious. That's it, grab his ankles. Lean on them if he tries to kick. Try not to break any bones.'

The wounded man twisted his head right and left, but Harry kept the gauze clamped over his mouth. He twitched a few times and lay still.

'You can take the pad away now,' George said. 'We don't want to suffocate him, that would defeat the purpose. If he looks like he's waking up, give him some more.'

George splashed carbolic acid solution over his hands, took a scalpel from the bowl and made a small incision, to test the man's reactions, and then cut cleanly through the skin past the elbow. 'With luck there's enough viable skin tissue for a flap. It's a while since I've had to do this.'

He pulled the skin from the flesh in strips. There was a low groan. Harry thought it came from the wounded man and was about to give him more chloroform. But it was Redbeard.

'If you think you're going to vomit, go to the window,' George said to him. 'Do not throw up on my patient or I shall amputate something of yours.'

Harry took another deep breath and looked away, saw Mou leaning in so far for a better look that George had to shoulder him out of the way.

George grunted as he worked.

'Hard work?' Harry said.

'Ever tried to cut through a chicken leg at the joint? It's like that.'

He talked to himself as he clamped off the arteries. 'Brachial, okay, that's the main one, radial, medial collateral, superior ulnar, inferior ulnar collateral. Done.'

He released the belt around the upper arm, blood spurted into the air and over his face, he seemed oblivious to it. He found the bleed, clamped it. Harry felt light-headed. Perhaps it was the chloroform.

'Drip a little more anaesthetic on the cloth, please,' he said to Harry.

Idrissa gave a sharp, strangled cry through the gauze and started to kick his legs. 'He's waking up!' Redbeard shouted. 'You must stop this now, he's awake.'

'He can't feel a thing,' George said. 'It's just a reaction from the nervous system.'

'I'll give him some more chloroform,' Harry said.

'No, we don't want to kill him.'

'For the love of God, you're torturing him!' Redbeard shouted.

The door opened and Zdan walked back in. 'What's going on?'

George nodded towards Redbeard. 'Tell that man to get control of himself or shoot him.'

'What?'

Redbeard stared wide-eyed at George.

'Hold his legs!' George shouted at him and Redbeard did as he was told.

George worked quickly, using silk ligatures to tie off the blood vessels. He tossed what was left of the arm onto the floor, bent to examine the wound as best he could, the light from the window was barely enough. 'I think we have secured all the bleeds,' he said. He sewed the flaps of skin over the stump and reached for the layers of wet gauze he had soaking in a bowl of carbolic acid. He laid them over the wound, then some waxed gauze from his medical bag.

When it was done, he straightened, wiped the sweat and blood out of his eyes and took a deep breath.

'How long do you think?' he said to Harry.

'I don't know, I don't have a watch.'

'My fastest amputation was eight minutes and forty seconds. I must have come close.'

'Are we done?'

'Now we wait. I have left a drainage hole. There's bound to be pus forming in a day or two.'

'George, only tell me what I need to know.'

Zdan looked down at the arm. 'What shall we do with it? The arm?'

George shrugged his shoulders. Zdan picked it up.

'What would you like to do with it?'

'We can feed it to the goats,' he said.

Redbeard put a hand on the knife at his belt and gave George a murderous look. 'My cousin is going to be alright?'

'Insha'Allah,' George said.

Harry grabbed Redbeard's wrist, and pulled it away from his knife. 'And don't threaten us or I'll tie you to the end of *al-wahsh* and blow your black heart all the way to the Sahara.'

After Zdan had escorted Redbeard from the room, George looked down at his sleeping patient. He had stopped moaning and thrashing about, but he was grey as a fresh corpse and snoring like a hog in mud.

'When he wakes, he'll be in a lot of pain,' George said. 'I have some laudanum, though I doubt it will be enough. The dangers now are some sort of surgical fever. There's a sort of blood poisoning called pyemia, if he gets that, there's nothing I can do for him. There's also tetany, hospital gangrene, you name it. I sterilised the sutures but if they get infected, they could rot through the artery and he'll bleed to death anyway.'

'What are his chances?'

'In the army, the mortality rate was about one in three. And even in the field, the conditions weren't as bad as this.'

Harry clapped him on the shoulder. 'Well, you did your best.'

'Are you alright?' George said.

'That was fun,' Mou said, his eyes bright with excitement.

'What about him?' Harry said, nodding towards the unconscious man lying on the bench in the middle of the room, among the detritus of blood-soaked swabs and tattered tiny bits of flesh.

'Let's have our lunch first,' George said.

The slaves brought them in some stringy pieces of chicken and chickpeas, hard as grapeshot. Mou tucked straight into his.

'You do not want your lunch?' he said to Harry.

Harry shook his head, his senses reeling from the coppery reek of blood and the stink of chemicals. He didn't know how anyone could eat with a badly wounded and mutilated man lying in the middle of the room. Perhaps he was getting soft.

He went up to the terrace and gulped in the cold air, listened to the sound of a flute coming from somewhere in the Kasbah, and wished he was somewhere, anywhere, else.

CHAPTER 27

Harry woke to the sound of a woman screaming.

'What the hell is that?' George said. He got up and lit a candle, took it to the window and threw open one of the shutters. 'There's lights in that tower over there. What is that?'

'The harem,' Mou said from the dark behind them.

'What's going on, do you think?'

'The *djinn* has come back,' the boy said.

'More like someone being murdered. When you're living with bandits, bad spirits are the last thing I worry about.'

The screaming stopped, started again a few minutes later. She sounded as if she was being tortured. Sleep was impossible. Harry tried to plug his ears with his fingers. It made no difference.

Dawn crept up the sky, Harry peered out, saw shadows moving about the court below them. The *muezzin* began the call to prayer. *'Prayer is better than sleep, come and pray.'* The melodious chanting was interrupted by the piercing shrieks coming from the harem.

He heard voices outside in the corridor and then slippers padding on the stone stairs that led to their rooms.

He turned towards the door and waited.

A moment later it opened, and the Chief Eunuch walked into the room. He was a brute of a man, any muscle he had once had now turned to fat, his skin was smooth as basalt, coal black and the size of one of the granary doors.

'Are you the magician?' he said, looking at Harry.

'Well, I can make money disappear in no time, but I think that is the man you're looking for.'

The eunuch fixed his solemn eyes on George. 'You are to come with me. Bring your magic with you.'

George dressed quickly and picked up the satchel with his medical kit.

'This doesn't sound good,' Harry said. 'I should come with you.'

The Chief Eunuch put a hand on Harry's chest and pushed him back into the room. 'Just him,' he said.

The woman screamed again.

'I'll be alright,' George said. He sounded a lot more confident than he looked. Harry felt someone squeezing his hand, hard. He looked down. It was Mou.

'Everything will be alright,' he said to him, as the door slammed shut again.

The sky was gunmetal grey as the first light crept across the sky, brushed with mare's tails. George followed the eunuch across the court and into a labyrinth of passages and patios, past slaves in shabby *djellabas* who flattened themselves against the walls and lowered their faces the moment they saw them.

It was a maze of dank laundries and smoky kitchens. He felt eyes watching them from the dark, but when he turned his head, the figures scuttled away, back into the gloom.

They climbed a narrow staircase. George was hoping for a glimpse of one of the exotic beauties that Mou claimed to have seen, but there were only a few ragged slaves. He supposed that Amastan's women had been ordered to shut themselves in their rooms and stay out of sight.

They went up a dark winding staircase, then another, and another. Despite his size the eunuch took the steps easily, two at a time. George felt dizzy trying to keep up with him.

Finally they came to a heavy wooden door with cracked blue paint. The eunuch pushed him inside. It was dark, the shutters were closed, the only light came from two small oil lamps. There was a strong smell of sandalwood, incense used to cover the taint of corruption and sweat, smells all too familiar to him by now.

'Englishman,' a voice said. 'I find myself in need of your help once more.' It was Amastan.

As his eyes adjusted to the gloom, George made out a large lattice screen, shadows moving behind it. There was another shriek, it was so close and so loud that it startled him, and he realised the poor soul they had heard screaming all night long was on the other side of the screen.

'Who is she?' George said.

'This woman is one of my household,' Amastan said from behind the screen. 'She is in terrible pain. I hoped that you might know how her suffering might be relieved.'

'I might be able to, if you would let me examine her.'

'I am afraid that will not be possible. You know this.'

'Surely, there are- exceptions?'

'She is one of the harem, one of my wives. It is forbidden for you to see her. It is written.'

'Then how can I possibly help her?'

The woman screamed again, so loud and so close that George flinched.

'Where is her pain?' George said.

'In her belly.'

'Where in her belly?'

'On the left side.'

'Where on the left side? High, low?'

'Low.'

'Is she pregnant?'

He heard Amastan say something to the woman on the other side of the screen, heard her sobbing an answer, most of it mumbled, *yes, yes, perhaps*.

'She says there has been no blood for two moons.'

The woman screamed as another spasm of pain hit her.

'Is she bleeding now? From her…' He searched his memory for the Arabic word for vagina. '*Almuhabil*?'

'Yes, there is a lot of blood. I can see it.'

'Is it dark red or bright red?'

'Dark. Dark red.'

'What else?'

He heard the woman moaning. *I cannot keep my food down. I feel sick all the time.*

'She also complains of pain, much pain, in her shoulder,' Amastan said. 'What is wrong with her? Is it a *djinn*? Can you give her an elixir, like you gave my sister?'

'It is not a *djinn*,' George said.

Three things, he thought. She has a disease, or there is a rupture in her bowel, or it is a malformed pregnancy. 'I *must* be allowed to examine her.'

'No!'

'At least a hand, then. So that I can feel her pulse, her skin.'

His patient screamed again, you would think I would be used to this by now, George thought, all the operations I have performed, all the battlefield wounds I have treated. But never have I been in a situation like this.

There was a hushed conversation on the other side of the screen.

Finally Amastan said: 'Very well. Nour will allow you to examine her hand. You may approach the screen.'

George put down his satchel and took a few hesitant steps forward, into the dark. He could smell the woman, sweat and fear and blood and urine. A hand appeared through the screen, and the brocaded sleeve of her gown fell away.

Her hand was tiny, like a child's. She was wearing a silk glove, and her fingers were adorned with heavy silver rings. She was shaking. 'May I remove the glove?' George said.

'Be brief.'

George peeled off the glove and the rings. The girl's hand was tattooed with henna, the nails had been painted also, though he could not make out the colour in the dark. 'Bring me the lamp!' he snapped at the Chief Eunuch.

The big Somali, unaccustomed to getting orders from anyone except Amastan, hesitated. Amastan snapped at him to hurry and he did as he was ordered.

George felt for the girl's pulse, it was weak and thready. Several of her nails were broken, he imagined her clawing at the walls in pain and breaking them. Holding her hand was like holding a small, wounded bird. Her gold wrist bangles jingled as another spasm of pain hit her, and her hand clenched in spasm, she had surprising strength, or perhaps it was the intensity of the pain, he heard one of his own knuckles crack.

'Bring the lamp closer,' he said to the eunuch.

He chipped away the paint on her thumb with his finger, pressed on the nail bed. The blood was slow to return.

He replaced the glove and rings. The hand slipped back through the screen, a beetle scurrying from the light. 'May I reach through the screen and touch her forehead?'

'It is necessary?'

'It is necessary.'

'Quickly, then.'

He put his hand through the screen, Amastan took it and guided it to Nour's forehead. It felt as if it she was lathered in cold grease. Not a good sign.

'Nour,' George whispered. 'The pain. When did it start?'

'Last... night.'

'Before sunset?'

'After.'

'Your stools. They are loose?'

'You cannot ask her that!' Amastan growled.

But he heard her groan: *Yes.*

'Withdraw your hand,' the Chief Eunuch said over his shoulder.

George did as he was told. He stood up. Daylight had started to creep into the room. He searched for inspiration in the shadowed rafters. Not bowel, he thought, not with the blood flow from her vagina.

He suspected the worst.

'If you can help her,' Amastan said, 'I will give you your two thousand pounds in silver and I will have some men escort you back to Tangier. You can go home.'

'What about my friend?'

'I need the captain to look after the cannons. He will follow you later.'

'I won't leave without him.'

'That is your choice. What about Nour? Can you help her?'

'I can. But only if you allow me to operate.'

'What are you saying?'

'Sometimes when an infant grows, from seed, it does not grow in the proper place, inside the woman. If it grows outside the womb, it will burst an organ called...' He did not know the word for 'Fallopian tube' in Arabic and supposed it would make no difference to Amastan, or to the outcome, even if he did. 'The baby must be removed, the tear must be repaired, or she will bleed until she dies.'

'It is not a *djinn*?'

'No. It is simply nature making a mistake.'

'What is this, 'operate'?'

'I can sedate her and make an incision in her abdomen and...'

'No. That will not be possible.'

'You don't understand.'

'I understand very well. It is not permissible. You cannot touch a man's wife or see her nakedness. You must find another way. As you did with my sister.'

'There is no other way.'

Amastan growled an order, there was scuffling on the other side of the screen, he imagined black slaves picking Nour up from the divan, carrying her away. She cried out as they moved her.

Amastan waited until they were gone.

'The Chief Eunuch will see you back to your quarters.'

'Wait!' George said. He went back to his satchel and took out a bottle; the laudanum tincture - the precious little he had left. Still, it would be enough for what he proposed.

'Take this.' He passed the bottle through the screen. 'It is very bitter, but a spoonful should ease her suffering.'

'Thank you.'

'Why won't you let me help her? I might save her life.'

'Men die taking life, women die giving it, it is the way of things. You cannot sully her honour, or mine. I'm sorry. It is our way.'

He heard the rustle of Amastan's robes as he moved away from the screen.

'If you wish,' George said. 'There is another way.'

'To save her?'

'No, not to save her. If you give her three spoonfuls it will help her to Paradise quickly without needless suffering.'

Amastan said nothing. George felt the Chief Eunuch's hand on his shoulder. He turned and followed him out of the room.

CHAPTER 28

A slave brought them their meagre breakfast, Harry had no appetite, he gave the bread and goat's yogurt to Mou. He saved George his share, listened to the intermittent screams coming from the harem and wondered what in God's name was going on. Zdan wasn't around to answer any of his questions and he was more than a little relieved when he heard footsteps on the stairs and heard George' voice.

He was pale when he walked in, threw his medical satchel in the corner, and slumped onto the carpets.

'Are you alright?'

'Harry, when I took my oath as a doctor, I swore to protect life. I have just given that man the authority and the means to end one.'

'That screaming, it's one of Amastan's harem girls?'

'Yes. I might save her if he would allow me. But it seems that the touching of any woman is forbidden, even at the cost of her life.'

'What did you do?'

'I gave him the rest of our laudanum and advised him of the nature of a fatal dose.'

'It seems to me you had no choice.'

'If I had let her suffer, it would have been on my conscience. Being the means of her death is hardly less so.'

He laid a hand on his shoulder. 'You couldn't let her suffer like that.'

'I'm supposed to be a doctor, not an executioner.'

I suppose you are no mood for breakfast?'

A shake of the head.

Mou jumped up and grabbed the plate from Harry's hands and ran off with it.

Harry took out his bone pipe and filled it with the strong black tobacco the Berbers smoked, plus a little of the hashish Zdan had given him. He went and sat by George, lit the pipe, and passed it to him.

'You can't save the whole world, George.'

'You won't want to hear this, but he said that if I could save Nour – that was her name – he would give me my money and let me go.'

'Not me?'

'He needs you to command his artillery.'

He handed back the pipe. Harry sucked on it, gave this some thought. 'A good offer. You should have taken it.'

'No.'

'Why not?'

'We're in this together. I got you in, I have to get you out.'

'Me, I would have taken it. Give me a horse and the silver, I'd ride off without even a look over my shoulder.'

'No, you wouldn't.'

Harry laughed. 'No, you're right. Before we started this, perhaps. Now, as you say, we're in this together. Let's hope we get it out of together, too.'

Idrissa's face was drawn with pain, his cheeks hollowed, the whites of his eyes had turned yellow. He stared at them, without blinking, his gaze followed them, almost imploring them for something. What does he wish for? Harry thought. Death or hope? He must be in unbearable pain, but he is stoic in the face of it, I'll give him that. And against all expectation, he is still alive.

For days he had slipped in and out of a drugged sleep, Zdan had given him a pipe, laced with hashish. Between the *kif* and the laudanum, it had got him through the worst of it.

They had found another room for him to sleep in. George had insisted that he not sleep on the floor, he was afraid that rats and roaches might gnaw at his bandages. That's the least of his troubles Harry thought. At least they were spared him moaning all night.

He winced as George peeled back the bandages. He had seen enough of these kind of wounds in the tropics and knew what to expect. But the stump didn't stink as much as he thought it would, there wasn't the disgusting oozing he had seen in the hospital tents in India.

George threw the old dressings in a ceramic bowl.

'There's a little laudable pus. See here? It's thick and creamy.'

'I'd rather not look, all the same to you.'

'No, it's a good thing. When it's thin and bloody it's more likely to be malignant. He might still develop pyemia or tetanus. He's not out of the woods yet.'

'Out of the woods? I'd say he's in the swamp, up to his neck.'

'No, there are positive signs. This fellow seems to have luck on his side.'

'If you call having one arm, lucky.'

'It's better than the alternative, surely?'

He took a bottle from his medical kit and some lint. 'Labarraque's chloride of soda,' he said. 'We apply it to the mortified surface, to limit the extent of slough.'

Harry turned away. 'I know you enjoy yourself at my expense but unless you wish me to revisit my breakfast, you'll stop now.'

'Hand me that ointment, will you?'

He reached for the bowl that George had brought with him. 'Good God. What is it?'

'Zdan gave it to me. I'm running low on silver salts and I decided to try it, after all, I supposed this fellow had nothing to lose by it. Apparently, it's made from the cream of goat's milk and the roots of some sort of desert grass that they pound up in a pestle. They swear by it.'

He dipped some lint in carbolic acid solution and placed it over the stump, then a new pad. He gave their patient some quinine for fever and turned away, apparently satisfied.

'His cousin may yet be persuaded not to come after you with a knife one night.'

Harry smiled. 'Oh, I don't think anything will stop Redbeard from trying to kill me one day. I can see it in his eyes.'

CHAPTER 29

Al-wahsh and *al-raed* gleamed dully in the light of the oil lamps. They smelled of sheep fat and freshly cut timber, and he supposed they looked better now, here in this lonely *fondak* than they ever had in all their years in the Sultan's service. Harry patted the barrel, flicked away an errant piece of straw.

'Your men did a good job,' Harry said.

'They will talk of it for years to come. Their wives think they will be blessed with dozens of children now and pester them for sacred joinings from dawn till midnight.'

'I am glad we could be of some service to them. You have found a replacement for Idrissa?'

'Replacement?'

'The guns must have at least five men each, trained in their duties.'

'He does not wish to be replaced.'

'But he lost his arm.'

'That was a long time ago.'

'A month.'

'Well, his wound is healed now. And he says that you told him it is better to clean the barrel with just one hand. He says that now he is the right man for the job as he is perfectly equipped.'

'What if he loses his other arm?'

Zdan seemed intrigued by this possibility. 'Then he will die. A man cannot live without arms.'

'This does not worry him?'

'The Timbuctians say that death is how God keeps us honest. Also, how he reminds us that we are free.' He turned to George. 'Idrissa owes you Englishmen his life. He will be the best gunner you ever had. You have his loyalty forever.'

'Is there news of Bou Hamra?'

'He is still here, in the mountains. He has wintered with a Kaïd called Abdel ibn Hidi. His kasbah is called Aït Isfoul, it is twenty miles from here, though it will take many days to get there, as you will see.'

'What does this Kaïd hope to gain from siding with him?'

'Ibn Hidi owes his allegiance to Amastan, but now he has rebelled, hoping that if Bou Hamra succeeds, he will reward him by making him overlord of the southern Atlas. Every village chief with ambition of his own has gathered there with him, willing to throw his fate in with Bou Hamra's.'

'That is quite a gamble,' Harry said.

'Ibn Hidi and Bou Hamra have attacked the spring caravans from Timbuctu, and their taxes are a vital part of our revenue. This cannot be allowed. The other chieftains will be watching what happens very closely. We have to stop him now.'

'When do we leave?'

'We leave in the morning. The snows have melted. We must catch Bou Hamra before he tries to run away again into the desert. With luck, you will be back in London before the summer is out.'

CHAPTER 30

There were still patches of snow on the ground when they set out.

Harry travelled as light as he could, just a small leather bag, which he had bought in the medina, that fitted easily over his shoulder. He had a toothbrush, a few sheets of writing-paper, a pencil, and the pipe that Zdan had given him with some wads of tobacco.

Around the kasbah he had taken to wearing a white cotton shirt and loose trousers, like the Berbers, under his striped *djellaba*, but now he reverted once more to his officer's uniform, under the grey army greatcoat he had brought with him from England. The grey is better than blue, Zdan had told him. It will make you less attractive to snipers.

It was hard going, as Zdan had warned them. They made their way up the massif, past massive foldings of purple and grey and white shale. Once they left the Kaïd's valley, they came out on a plateau, bare of vegetation except for a few wind-stunted conifers. They were surrounded by craggy mountain peaks, crusted with snow and ice, the slopes below them covered with stunted thornbush.

Around sunset, Amastan ordered a rest under the shade of some trees. Harry slumped against the trunk of an ancient cypress, sweat beading on his face, soaking into his shirt. Spring had brought a riot of colour to the Atlas Mountains, the slope below almost entirely purple from the buds of wild thyme. He closed his eyes, the air rich with their scent, started to doze.

'A month from now,' George said, 'we'll be sitting in a bar drinking cold beer and *pastis*.'

Harry nodded and smiled. 'I can taste it now.'

There was no road, each day began with a long climb followed by an equally taxing descent down a steep gorge, then another climb.

Many of the tracks were too difficult for their horses, they had to lead their stallions by the halters up the worst of it, the shale crumbling away beneath their feet, two steps up and one back. Spending all winter inside the kasbah had weakened them both, after a day their thigh and calf muscles were cramping, and Harry couldn't get enough air into his lungs. He kept stopping every few minutes, lathered in sweat, had to force himself to keep going.

Amastan's men were like mountain goats, leaping from rock to rock, their rifles slung easily over their shoulders, laughing and talking among themselves even up the steepest terrain.

It wasn't just him and George slowing them down. The mules carrying *al-raed* and its trails and ammunition were finding it tough going. Even a mountain gun like that weighed about six hundred pounds, and they had to keep shifting the bronze barrel between the pack mules during the day, giving some of them a chance to rest.

It was worse going down than it was climbing up and after a couple of days George' left knee started to swell from the constant jarring and Harry found a blister on his right heel the size of his thumb. George heated a knife in their cook fire and lanced it.

They had only the provisions they had brought with them, some salted semolina and unsweetened pancakes. At the end of each day Harry didn't feel much like eating anyway. All he wanted to do was roll up inside his blanket and sleep.

Amastan travelled with them, but they hardly saw him. He led from the front, with Zdan, and never came to the rear to talk to them, even at night. He kept much to himself, aloof even from his own men, an enigmatic figure in black, whom the men seemed to regard with a mixture of awe and cool respect.

They crossed several shaky wooden bridges, the rivers swollen by the thaw, rushing over rocks and boulders far below. One of the mules took fright halfway across and refused to take a step further or back. *Al-raed* swayed perilously on its back. Harry and George could only watch on helplessly from the far side of the bridge.

'The whole lot's going to go in,' George said.

'I hope not,' Harry said. 'If it does, we're out of a job. There goes our payday.'

'There's still *al-wahsh*.'

'You won't get that beast up any of these tracks. No, they'd better get *al-raed* over, or we're surplus.'

The entire gun team, Redbeard, Ramrod and the rest set to work, pushing, pulling, swearing, trying to persuade the beast to move. One of them made the mistake of getting too close to its hindquarter, went down howling, his shin smashed by one of the hooves. It took the other four men, two pulling and two pushing, almost an hour to finally get the mule across.

They passed what Harry at first thought were glaciers, glittering in the cold sun around deep tarns of black water. He realised they weren't ice sheets, these were Amastan's salt mines. Half-naked men swung away with pickaxes, stripped and sweating in the frigid mountain wind. Others piled the slabs of raw salt into panniers on the backs of sturdy little mules. The miners seemed to defy gravity, scrambling down almost sheer cliffs of crumbling shale, keeping their balance with long sticks, their donkeys behind them.

They struggled over a rock-strewn track for hours, it was as much as they could do to keep the horses and mules on their feet. The mountains towered either side of them, cloaked in pine, and oaks, cliff soaring upon cliff, precipice upon precipice. The snow lay in deep drifts on the upper reaches, and though the sun was hot, the wind still bit deep as winter, freezing the sweat-stained shirts to their backs.

The roaring of the river in the gorge below them drowned out every other sound.

Now and then they found themselves looking down on the flat roofs of poor Berber villages, with poor gardens of walnut trees and terraces of vegetables.

The track twisted in and out of the escarpments, among huge boulders and the twisted trunks of wind-bent evergreen oaks until they finally reached the top of the pass, and Harry stopped and looked around, awestruck. The entire panorama of the Atlas Mountains lay below and around them, in every direction.

'My God,' he murmured.

George pulled up his horse beside him, but the Berbers kept trudging on, without a single glance.

'Look at that,' George said.

From where they were, they could see the woods and forests of the northern Atlas spread out behind them, wooded valleys with olive and fruit trees. In front of them, the southern Atlas lay bare and bleak, a dreary wasteland of black and grey shale, baked by the Sirocco in the summer, where no rain ever fell. There was no sign of life anywhere.

'We're at the top of the world,' George said.

'And headed into the fiery pit,' Harry said, and spurred his horse on, following the rest of the Berber army down the track towards the Sahara, somewhere down there beyond the mountains.

On the third afternoon, the weather was appreciably hotter. Harry dispensed with the greatcoat, draped it over his stallion's saddle, and to hell with snipers.

They had left the trees and greenery behind them, save for the occasional wind-bent stump of an evergreen oak. Wild snow-capped limestone peaks soared around them.

Their rest stops became fewer and shorter, as Amastan urged them on, eager to arrive at Ibn Hidi's eyrie at Aït Isfoul before Bou Hamra could escape. Every hour, another gorge, another climb, another knee-jarring descent. Harry and George climbed down from their horses, guiding them over the treacherous shale.

They followed the rocky banks of a river for over a mile until it opened out unexpectedly into a wide, salt pan. They were finally able to remount their horses, Amastan gave orders to reassemble the cannon, and attach it to the trails, to speed up their progress. When it was done, they set off again, keeping to the river, which led them to a range of burned orange foothills. They rounded a spur and were afforded their first glimpse of Aït Isfoul.

Even this early in the afternoon, it lay in the shadow of the mountain above, as foreboding as the steep ochre cliffs that surrounded it on three sides. The town sprawled up the spur of the mountain, surrounded by sheer mud brick walls, and crowned by the grim square tower of the kasbah.

George reined in his horse and shook his head. He turned to Harry. 'How does the Lord of the Atlas propose to take that, do you think?'

Before he could answer, they heard a commotion from the rear.

The cannons.

They rode back along the line, saw the gun crew gathered around *al-raed*, the new carriage had cracked on an outcrop of loose rock. One of the gunners kicked it with his boot, in a time-honoured tradition. Harry smiled. He hadn't even had to teach him that.

The mules stood patiently in the traces, flicking off the flies with their tails, ears twitching.

'Bring up the carpenters,' Zdan said. 'Let's hope we can get this fixed before dusk.'

They stood on the hill beyond the river, staring at the yellowish mud-built walls and towers, the height of three men. The Kasbah itself looked unassailable there on the ridge above the town. Harry was glad he was not one Amastan's fighters. Taking the town was going to be costly.

The towers were decorated with patterns of diamonds and squares, turned golden with the setting sun, stark against the black cliffs and cedar forests behind it. A pinpoint of light flashed from the green metallic tiles of the town's minaret.

Corn fields stretched from the walls to the yellow cliffs behind it, on the other the river wound bright and sparkling across the valley floor. There were orchards of cherry, walnut and almond trees. A camel slept under a palm tree outside the gates.

It looked deceptively peaceful, hardly the home of a warrior chieftain and a bloodthirsty rebel.

Zdan had said Amastan would come and join them there, to discuss tactics. But when the Lord of the Atlas arrived, it seemed any mention of an open and democratic discussion was a little optimistic.

'Are you ready?' he said.

'For what?' Harry said.

'To blow away the main gate.'

'Is that what you're planning?'

'You don't need to know my plans.'

'What about my tactical advice? Would you like that?'

'I need you to do what you are being paid to do. Fire the cannons.'

Harry saw George shrug behind Amastan's back. Just do what he says, his look said.

'You can position the cannons there,' Amastan said, pointing to the near bank of the river. 'You will be out of range of their flintlocks. Can you hit the gates from here?'

Harry raised his eyeglasses. The great gates of timber and iron were four hundred yards distant, in his estimation.

'There are two flies on the gates, a green one and a black one. Which one do you want me to hit?'

He glanced over to see if he had at last made Amastan smile, but the Kaïd's face was hidden behind the black *cheiche* and it was impossible to tell.

'The black one,' Amastan said.

'You have a preference of which wing?'

'I leave that to your discretion,' Amastan said, and walked away.

'What do you think?' George said to him, after he had gone.

'I think he is making a serious mistake. As he will not be persuaded, I think to let him find out for himself.'

CHAPTER 31

Harry stood behind *al-raed*. He had told Amastan that an initial bombardment of thirty rounds should be enough to reduce the gates and the walls to rubble. It would give his boys practice. If he would make any difference to the outcome, he was unconvinced.

The first shell was loaded, and he sighted the gun. He stood back and gave the order to fire. The first round landed short, the second was more accurate, the small gun had a rifled barrel, more accurate over longer distances than *al-wahsh*. The gate exploded and Harry watched a plank of timber arc end over end through the billowing smoke.

The boys knew their jobs. Even Idrissa, with his one arm, bent his back to it as if he had been doing it all his life. The fourth round destroyed the other half of the gate. Harry directed the rest of the rounds against the walls, it was a little like firing musket rounds into a sandbag, but when the guns finally fell silent, he studied the damage through his eyeglass and saw that the defences had been breached in three places.

He shouted: 'God is great!' to his gunners in Arabic and they responded in kind. Then he turned around and went up the hill to where Amastan was waiting, astride his horse, with Zdan and George.

'I hit the black fly,' he said. 'But I think the green one got away.'

Not even a flicker.

Amastan raised his sword and his men rose from their hiding places in the bushes and started across the river towards the fortress. With shouts of *Allahu Akbar*, his horsemen galloped towards the walls. They splashed whooping through the shallows, but there was a deep channel halfway across that forced the horses to swim twenty or so yards. By the time they struggled to their feet again in the shallows, slipping on the river stones, they and their riders were in range of the musket fire from the fortress walls and the honeycomb of caves that pockmarked the cliffs on either side of the town.

'Oh my God,' George said. 'It's a shooting gallery.'

None of them got to within fifty yards of the gates. The river slowed the charge enough so that the defenders had time to load and reload their flintlocks and lay down a withering field of fire. Within minutes it was clear that the attack would not succeed. Harry looked at Amastan, sitting motionless astride his black stallion.

Horses and men were milling in confusion in the river, bodies floated away with the current, some of the fighters who had not yet reached the river were already turning back.

Amastan gave a signal to the trumpeter who was standing ready by his horse, waiting for the signal. He blasted a single plaintive note on the trumpet, and below them the horsemen spurred their horses back across the river, overtaking the soldiers still splashing through the shallows, gripping the hems of their *djellabas* in one hand, their rifles in the other.

George had commandeered one of Amastan's pavilions for the wounded. Harry stood in the doorway, watching him work, astonished and a little humbled by the man's dedication. George knelt beside a man who lay unconscious and bloody on a scrap of filthy blanket. He was feeling around inside a bullet hole with his finger for the musket ball that had lodged in the man's chest.

There were perhaps a dozen wounded, most had been left behind, in the quiet he could hear a few of them groaning and calling out for help, though there were less doing it now than there were an hour ago.

Some had drowned in the river; others had been used for target practise by the defenders on the walls or had simply given up and died.

George had asked Zdan if he could send a party to fetch them. Zdan shrugged and said there is no point, they would be in range of the flintlocks, you will only be making more work for yourself.

George had said he would try anyway but Zdan shook his head. 'I have been told not to let you or your friend out of the camp. You are too valuable to get yourself shot.'

That, at least, was reassuring.

Mou had volunteered to help George. The boy seemed to take cheerfully to any task they set him, and the blood and flies and filth didn't seem to trouble him at all. As he walked in, he looked up at Harry and grinned. There was a spray of blood across his face, like freckles.

'Do you need assistance?' Harry said to George.

'I need many things,' George said. 'I need more chloroform, I need carbolic acid, I need dressings, I need catgut for sutures. I'll settle for just a pair of hands to hold this man still while I try to get this musket ball out.'

Harry looked around, there was a man lying on his back with blood bubbling through a bullet hole in his chest, another screaming, as two of his comrades struggled to hold him still, his knee was minced red meat and glistening bone.

He thought of the hospital tents he had seen in his time in the Army. The smell, the screaming, you never got used to it.

He had always avoided the sick and wounded over there; if it was one of his men, he tried not to think too much about them until they got back to the battalion. Sometimes they did, sometimes they didn't.

He was afraid if he got too close to it, the suffering, the crippling, he might lose his nerve.

He couldn't turn his back this time. George made him feel diminished somehow. Harry was the one with the medal, but of the two of us, he thought, George is the better man.

'I'll help best I can,' Harry said, took off his jacket and rolled up his sleeves.

CHAPTER 32

Harry made his way to Amastan's tent, past a corral of horses, hobbled by their legs in the local custom. Riders jostled their way through the camp, some mustering flocks of sheep, others holding chickens and even small goats by their feet, all the result of the raids they had made into the surrounding country, looting from farmers and villagers too slow to have found sanctuary inside Aït Isfoul.

Amastan's tent was not a great deal humbler than the Sultan of Morocco's, more a pavilion, lined on the inside with rich green velvet. Harry thought he could have held a regimental lunch inside it. Amastan was attended by Zdan and a number of his captains and other brigands, masquerading as high officials.

It was lit by huge tallow candles, as large as one of the shells he had fired that afternoon at the fortress. They had been arranged around the tent in tall brass candlesticks, the yellow glow reflected on the shining black faces of the slaves who sat in groups by the door, waiting for Amastan to only raise a finger for them to scurry over to him.

His captains and counsellors were seated on thick carpets and cushions, while the slaves served them green tea flavoured with mint and strong black coffee some of the tribesmen seemed to like. One cup was like a kick from a horse.

Amastan was laying out the plans for the next day.

'Tomorrow, we will try again. Instead of an attack across the river, we will cross further down and come upon the town by the western approaches.'

There were murmurs of approval around the circle of men, though several of them looked fiercely at the carpets and he could see by their faces that they didn't agree with their Kaïd's tactics.

Harry took that as encouragement enough. 'That won't work,' he said loudly, from the back of the tent.

They all stared at him as if he had interrupted God in the middle of dictating the Commandments. Damn them, he'd had enough of watching men get killed for no good reason.

Amastan peered into the darkness, looking for him, must have known by his accent and his execrable Arabic that it was him.

'You have something to say?' Amastan said.

'It doesn't matter if you cross further down the river. I can blow up all the walls, if you want me to, but when you approach the perimeter you will still have to cross two hundred yards of open ground. You are also in range of the caves on the hillside, and the snipers hidden up there. You have an insufficient force to attack an entrenched position up a steep slope. I tried to tell you that this morning.'

There was a long silence.

'You have a better plan?'

'Yes, I do.'

'I should like to hear it.'

'The weakness is the north wall.'

A few of the Berbers started to laugh. The Englishman wasn't serious, surely?

'It's a sheer cliff face,' Zdan said.

'Not that sheer. I have completed more difficult ascents when I was a teenager in England.'

Amastan sat forward. 'What are you talking about?'

'I'm talking about scaling the wall, at night. Good men with daring and skill are always more effective than cannons.'

'You are serious?'

'Give me ten of your best Berbers, mountaineers, men with experience.'

'Even if you could scale the wall,' Zdan said, 'what good would it do? Our army cannot follow you up there.'

'Once we are inside, we light fires, create panic. At that moment you launch an attack on the main gate. Meanwhile we go looking for Bou Hamra. You don't have to kill everyone in there. Just one man. Am I right?'

'How will you know where to find him?' Amastan said.

'He will be in the Kasbah, When the fires take hold, he and his bodyguard will come out to take command of the defenders. And we will kill him.'

Amastan thought about this.

'That is suicide,' Zdan said.

Another man said: 'It can't be done.'

'No, you're wrong,' Harry said. 'I can do it.'

'This is not an idle boast?'

'When I was fifteen, I was climbing mountains higher than Toubkal.'

'I don't believe you,' Zdan said.

'Believe what you wish. If I die, what is it to you?'

'Ten men?' Amastan said.

'All I ask is that if any of them cannot keep up with me and fall off, then they die quietly. If necessary, I shall alone scale that wall and get inside and open the gate for them. Once we are inside the town, they must light the fires, and be prepared to die.'

'My men are not afraid.'

'Neither am I.'

'And in return?' Amastan said. 'Should you succeed?'

'The price for my participation is steep. It is commensurate with what you have to gain.'

'Tell me.'

'You will pay George and myself double what the Sultan promised us, four thousand sterling each, and two horses to ride for Mogador. It's a good bargain. I save the lives of many of your men, I deliver you Bou Hamra and in return the sultan will make you pasha of Marrakesh.'

Amastan looked at Zdan, who shrugged back. 'Four thousand. Each. And if you die during the skirmish?'

'Give my share to my friend. He'll probably spend it more wisely than I will anyway.'

'Very well, Englishman. You have your bargain. Let us find you your men.'

CHAPTER 33

Harry thought about when they had presented him with the medal, he in his dress blues, head bowed as he stepped up to the Queen. Victoria herself. All he remembered was a stout grey-haired woman in black. Afterwards there was the champagne and chandeliers, the speeches and the applause, such a fuss they had made of him. When they asked him why he did it, he said it was to save his brave comrades, or for England, or it was the heat of the battle.

Were you not afraid?

Sometimes he said yes, of course, sometimes he said, no, my only thoughts were for my comrade. He had tried on so many excuses, like trying on top hats at the milliner's, seeing which suited him best.

But he had not told anyone the truth. George was right, damn him. He had not been afraid because he simply hadn't cared if he lived or died. This time was different; the sudden presence of fear caught him off guard.

That day at Tell El Kebir, it was almost as if he were watching someone else standing there as those wild-eyed Egyptians came at him. He had felt icy calm, a pistol in one hand, his sabre in the other. His hands weren't shaking like this. He couldn't afford to let Amastan see it, or George, or the men he was going to lead up that cliff.

He studied the kasbah and the cliff below it, through his field glasses. It was a full moon, and the town was bright-lit with silver, they would have to wait for it to set behind the mountain before they made their climb.

What he had said in the Kaïd's tent had not been an idle boast; he had indeed completed more challenging climbs when he was a younger man. The cliff was not sheer, as Amastan had suggested. If they could scale it, it would take them to the base of a wall close to the kasbah itself. The wall would not present a significant problem, through the glasses he could see that the surface was no longer smooth, it had weathered over decades, perhaps a century or more, and there were plenty of hand holds where bricks had fallen away or supporting timbers had rotted.

The one thing he had not told Amastan was that all his previous climbs had been made with wooden spikes and safety ropes. This time, if he made even one mistake, it would mean certain death for him and anyone mad enough to follow him.

'What the hell do you think you're doing?'

He turned around. It was George.

'Would you rather tramp around the mountains chasing these rebels until our hair turns grey?'

'This is not our battle,' George said. 'You were here to supervise the artillery.'

'The artillery. A gun the size of a wheelbarrow.'

'That is not the point, Harry. We are here as advisers, that's all.'

'Come on, George. What's the worst that could happen?'

'You could die.'

'Apart from that.'

'This is not a joke. I won't stand by while you get yourself killed in another of your stupid stunts.'

'Won't you? So what will you do?'

George glared at him, his hands opening and closing into fists at his sides. 'How could you possibly think this is a good idea?'

'I don't know. I leave the philosophy side of things to you.'

'Send the Berbers up there if you like. But it's not our fight.'

'It is our fight if we want our money. Anyway, I just want to get this over with. I will tap the shoe and turn over the card, it will be the King of Diamonds or the Ace of Spades. We will either go home with our winnings, drinks all round, or you can bury me here, under those rocks. If I fall near the top, I will make a hole deep enough myself, all you will have to do is kick the dirt back in after me.'

'What happens if you die, and we still don't take the town?'

'Then you will have to learn the finer points of firing two ancient cannons very quickly indeed.'

George seemed to deflate. 'When I came to see you in London, I never meant for this.'

'What are you looking so sorry about? You saved me from my debtors in a dark alley, and a bad situation. And I have to tell you, these last few months, for all our privations, I have felt better than I have in years.'

'Can you really do this?'

'I think so. If I had ropes and spikes, I could manage it with my eyes closed. But it's been a while since I did any real climbing.'

'How long?'

'I believe I was fifteen years old. But it's too late to change my mind now. One last throw of the dice, right?'

Harry looked around the group that Zdan had assembled, all tough Berbers who looked as if they were weaned on salt and ice. His eyes rested on the one with the red hair and beard.

'What's he doing here?'

'He volunteered.'

'He's part of my gun crew. I can't afford to lose him.'

'He says he was raised in the mountains. Some of these others know him, they vouch for him. They say he's the best climber of all of them.'

Harry stared at the scoundrel, could not rid himself of the uneasy feeling about him. Why would he want to put himself in danger like this?

He supposed he had no choice but to bring him along.

They had rifles, knives, some lengths of rope, little else. They set off through the darkness, the majority of them in bare feet, Zdan said they preferred to climb that way. They made their way up through the crumbling trail to the foot of the cliff, moving slowly, trying to avoid rockfalls that might alert any of the sentries on the wall above.

It would be cold. He had left his greatcoat behind, would have to climb wearing just his shirt and loose-fitting trousers. Some of the Berbers thought they could do it in their *djellabas*. Perhaps they were accustomed to it. He knew that if he tried it, they'd be scraping him off the rocks come morning.

He had brought his sword and the Martini-Henry rifle, had them both slung over his back for the climb.

He looked up.

The track rose steeply into the flank of the mountain to a jagged ridge, the tower of the kasbah looming above them in the dark, silhouetted against the black mountain. They followed a vertiginous goat track of loose stone to the foot of the cliff, and Harry stopped to catch his breath. The man waited silently in a circle around him. The moon scuttled behind the clouds.

'*Yallah*,' he said. Let's go.

CHAPTER 34

He clung to the side of the cliff with the tips of his fingers and the thin edges of his boots. A chill wind froze his fingers. He wanted to breathe on them, warm them, get feeling back into them, but it was impossible. He searched for a handhold in the dark. The granite was smooth, like glass. That afternoon, studying the face through his eyeglass, it had all seemed so simple.

Had he taken the wrong route up the face?

He looked for a divot, a nub, any tiny crack that he could use to claw himself up. He knew the others were following him, if he had taken them the wrong way, they were all dead men. They couldn't get back down again, not without fixed ropes, it was a vertical climb.

He tried to move his toes. They were numb with cold. His knees and ankles ached from the climb through the gorges to get here.

Halfway up, he froze. He couldn't see the next hold, the cloud went over the moon, and he hung in the darkness, fighting his own mind. This had happened to him once before, the temptation to look down was overpowering. He fought to control his breathing, slow it down, push down the panic. He could feel his muscles tensing.

Relax, relax.

His body wanted to hurry, search for a move, get off the cliff. No, you have to think your way through this, he told himself. Don't rush. Don't think about falling.

He closed his eyes, concentrated on checking his breathing. Slow, steady. That's it. Deep belly breaths.

Certain thoughts, memories, came back to him, even now. When he was fourteen, he had scaled the walls of a ruined castle not far from his grammar school. He had announced beforehand what he intended to do, and the whole form had come out to watch. He had got the strap for that, from his father. Showing off, he called it. *You could have killed yourself, you stupid boy.*

But it had been worth it. His classmates had treated him differently afterwards. The boys called him crazy, they nicknamed him 'Crazy Delhazy', and the girls from the neighbouring school giggled behind their hands and whispered to each other when he passed them in the street.

Another memory: the first time he had outpaced his brother and his father climbing a mountain in Scotland. They had been tied together, for safety, and over his father's shouted warnings he cut his rope and went ahead to the peak, to prove to him that he could.

He was too old for the strap by then, so his father simply stopped taking them climbing. Reckless, his father called him. Perhaps he was. But he had done it, hadn't he, showed him there was something he could do better than his sainted brother.

He shook his head, reminding himself to concentrate. Focus on your next move.

He looked up, a sliver of moon blinked from behind a chink of cloud, he saw a scallop of rock, just deep enough for his fingers, felt with his other foot for grip, three points of contact at all times. He levered himself up, found the handhold, as he looked up it was like a spiderweb, there to there to there to there. He had his map up the cliff.

He could see his next rest position, three moves, four, and he was there.

He heard a sound somewhere below him. A gasp, the patter of rockfall, then a hollow crack, something hitting the ground below, hard. One of the Berbers had fallen. True to the promise they had all made, he had died making no sound.

He looked down and to the left, wedged his left foot into a tiny crack in the rock, tested it with his weight. He palmed the wall, pulled himself up, snatched at a crimp in the rock face, easy, easy.

It held.

Something erupted out of the cliff face a few feet above him, there was a screech that nearly sent him reeling back, he fought his instincts and instead pressed himself flat against the rock. Only a bird.

He was almost there. He could see the lip of the cliff, the shadow of the fortress wall. He was in striking distance.

This was tougher, much tougher, than anything he had ever attempted. There had always been an audience before. When he climbed the old castle walls in Dene, all his classmates had been there to watch; in Snowdonia and the Cairngorms he had climbed for his father's approval, and later, for his disapproval.

Tonight, there was no one, not even in his mind. For the first time in his life, he actually felt alone.

He raised his right foot and set the sole of his boot against a divot in the cliff face. He put his weight on it, straightened slowly, reached for the next hold. Suddenly his hand was on fire. There was a black mass crawling over his right hand. Fire ants.

He wanted to scream, wanted to take his hand away, shake them off, anything, anything. Instead he closed his eyes, looked for the next hold, found a nub of rock and switched his balance, gripped hard with the fingers of his left hand.

He took his right hand away from the ant nest.

He slowly, carefully, wiped his right hand on his trousers, grunting against the pain, conscious that even the slightest sound would betray him and the Berbers with him. They were everywhere now, up his arms, under his shirt. He had to get to the top of the cliff quickly.

He found a ledge in the rock, hauled himself up, hung there, balance, balance, his palms flat against the smooth rock, looking for the next hold. A gust of wind now would tear him off the face.

He found one, two more moves, his fingers curled around the lip of the cliff, he dragged himself over, unslung his rifle, and tore off his shirt, rubbing at the ants all over his chest and arms. Already his right hand was numb from the ant bites.

And there was still another fifteen feet of wall to go.

They all huddled together on the ledge, their breath forming clouds on the night air. Harry looked around, gathering his wits and his strength for the next part of the climb. He was shivering badly. He'd have to try and control it before they started off again.

He looked around, trying to work out which one of the men had fallen. He saw Redbeard, their eyes met for a moment. Still here.

He made another count in the darkness. Nine of them left. It would still be enough.

He pointed up at the wall above them, and they all nodded. He didn't need to brief them again. They knew what they had to do next.

Harry looked up. Just fifteen feet but this was the most difficult part of the climb. He stood up. His hand was on fire, he could feel it swelling, it was like he had a thick glove on it. The burning and itching were almost unbearable. He could feel the sweat on his skin, chilled by the wind. The pain made him nauseous. He swallowed back the bile in his throat.

He looped a length of rope over his head, then his rifle, and pressed his forehead against the wall. Let's get this done and go home.

He couldn't trust his right hand; he would have to lead with his left. Earlier that night, when the moon was up, he had studied this part of the climb through his field glasses and hadn't been able to pick out the best way up, he had been too far away. The danger in going up blind like this was getting halfway up and being unable to either go further up or come back down. If he slipped, there would be nothing to break his fall, there would be one bounce on the ridge where he was sitting and straight over the edge to the bottom.

He saw a crumbled hole in the brick two feet above his head and hooked the fingers of his left hand into it, started to haul himself up. Three or four quick moves, it was easy, too easy, suddenly he stopped, the ochre wall was as smooth as glass, as he had feared.

His left boot found purchase on a slight nub in the wall, his left hand found a small crack. He hung, searching the shadow dark for the next hold. He saw a crumbled hole where a timber stanchion had rotted, away to his right. His hand felt almost completely numb now, could he trust it?

There was no choice.

Think about the climb. Try and tense the fingers, work at it.

The brick crumbled away beneath his left boot and he made one desperate lunge with his left hand, his fingers jammed into the crack in the wall, and held on. His boots searched for a foothold, his right toe caught in a crumbled hole, he stayed there, his face against the cold brick for what seemed like an eternity.

If I move, I'll fall.

You have to move. Slowly now, gently.

He gathered his strength for the last push, felt for purchase with his right boot. He saw another hold away to his left, brought himself up, two more moves and his fingers closed over the crenel and he hauled himself up.

He lay on his back on the parapet wall for a moment, to catch his breath, then sat up, and removed his boots. There were still ants inside his clothes. He winced at another bite on his back, on his belly. Don't make a noise!

He reached inside his clothes, killed the little bastards as quietly and quickly as he could with his left hand. He couldn't see his right hand clearly in the dark but already it felt as if it had swollen to twice its size.

He would have to finish the job one-handed.

He ran silently to the end of the battlement and up to the guard tower. He waited, peered around the corner of the parapet, and looked around. There was only a single guard, he was asleep against the wall, next to an iron brazier. A few coals giving out some meagre warmth.

Harry readied himself for what he was about to do. He took a deep breath, unslung the rifle, and swung it over his head as hard as he could.

There was a crack as it crushed the man's skull through his turban. The sentry made a gurgling noise in his throat and slumped sideways. Perhaps he'd killed him. He hadn't meant to, but this was no time for philosophy.

He went back to the parapet, took the coil of rope from around his shoulders, threw one end over the wall, looped the other end several times around the brick crenel and coiled the loose end around his back, put all his weight on it. He gave it a tug, the arranged signal, come up, come up.

He felt the weight on the rope as the first man came up the wall. Harry braced himself against the parapet with his heel. This would be the worst of it. Once there was another man up here, they could haul on the rope together.

The first of the Berbers leaped over the top of the wall, and together they pulled up the third. Inside a few minutes, the rest of the Berbers were on the wall.

They were inside the fortress. Half the job was done.

CHAPTER 35

Harry led them along the parapet to the guard tower, past the sentry, sprawled like a rag doll next to the brazier. They went down some stone stairs. There was a torch burning in an iron sconce on the wall and one of the Berbers grabbed it. Four of them had sacks with oil-soaked rags on their backs. They would use the torch to set them ablaze.

There was an arched doorway at the bottom of the stairs. Harry stopped and peered around. He heard voices, held up his hand to warn the others. There was an open paved court, the kasbah and granary loomed above it, open space around it for twenty paces either side.

He couldn't see anyone. The voices appeared to be coming from the other side of the kasbah. They must be guarding the kasbah doors.

The town was sleeping, the night watch would be concentrated on the towers at the main gates and around the breeches in the eastern wall. They would be expecting another attack from Amastan's soldiers soon after dawn. Not this.

He nodded to the others, the signal for the attack to start. Six of the Berbers silently formed into three pairs and set off down the alley under the parapet walls. The plan was for them to split up, start setting spot fires all through the medina. Then they would head for the main gate, fire at the defenders from the town side, cause as much confusion as they could.

They disappeared into the shadows. Harry waited, gave them time to get well clear. He was gambling that Bou Hamra would be inside the kasbah with the town's Kaïd. They might be able to fight their way inside, but there was an easier way. Once the townspeople started shouting the alarm, the Kaïd would come out to help fight the fire. If

Bou Hamra was with him, they would be able to finish him off, and then the job was done.

He took the Martini-Henry off his shoulder, and a shell from the canvas bag at his waist. Redbeard and the two men with him started to do the same but he held his finger to his lips, the guards might hear them cock and load, they would have to wait.

He saw one of the guards come around the corner and pull up his robes. He pissed on the wall, still laughing and talking to his comrade, some ribald talk about a recent visit to a brothel in Marrakesh.

Harry grabbed Redbeard's arm, signalled to him what he wanted him to do. Redbeard nodded. He in turn whispered something to the two Berbers with him, and they handed him their rifles and slipped away, keeping to the shadows under the parapet. There was a flash of steel as they pulled knives from the sheaths at their belts.

There was a loud crack as a screen of matted palm caught alight somewhere in the medina, and a few seconds later, a plume of black smoke spiralled up the sky, followed by a shoot of orange flame. It sounded like one of the fireworks the Sultan was so fond of.

The guards stopped laughing.

'What's going on down there?' he heard one of them say.

'Fire! Quick, go down there, get someone to sound the alarm!'

'Why me?'

'Because you can run faster than I can!'

Grumbling, the man shuffled away across the court. When he reached the corner, one of the Berbers stepped out of the dark, threw an arm around his neck and dragged him into a doorway. Harry imagined the knife doing its grisly work. It wouldn't take long.

The other guard knew something was wrong, but he hadn't seen what had happened. He took half a dozen paces across the court, stopped, went back to his post outside the doors, hesitated. 'Mahmud? Mahmud, what is it?'

Harry could see the two Berbers, knives ready, still crouched around the corner of the kasbah. They needed the guard to come a little closer. They waited.

Another orange glow lit up the roofs of the medina away to the right, then another. There would be plenty of fuel for the flames, wooden slats, canvas, straw matting, people were shouting and screaming, and he heard the panicked blast of a trumpet.

Amastan would see the fires, too. He would be getting his cavalry ready for the attack.

There was no more need for subterfuge. Redbeard signalled to the two others to stay where they were and stepped out of the shadows. He put a round in his rifle, cocked it and aimed. The guard heard the noise, must have guessed what it meant, but he had no time to react.

One shot and down he went.

An orange glow spread across the roofs of the medina. This whole town is going to be a pile of ashes by the morning, Harry thought. Smoke mushroomed into the night sky from a dozen different spot fires, as flames roared along laneways of ancient, decayed wood.

Harry could hear another sound now, the distinctive crack of ancient flintlock rifles from the battered walls around the gates, it meant that Amastan had started his next attack. His men would be trying to ford the river in the darkness, head towards the breeches his cannons had made in the gates and the walls.

Harry led Redbeard and his other three men towards the iron-barred doors of the kasbah, they put their shoulders to the wood, but they wouldn't shift, they were barred from the inside. Well, if they couldn't get in, and there was no other way out, they would wait for Bou Hamra to come to them. He led the men back to the shadows below the parapet wall. He knelt down, put a round in the chamber of his rifle and signalled to them to stay quiet.

He looked up at the windows. He could see shadows moving, saw someone lean on the sill with his fists, look down at the medina, heard him shouting orders to someone inside.

He has to come out soon. There's no other way out of there.

Is there?

'Come on,' he murmured under his breath. 'Let's get this done and I can go home.'

There was the sound of heavy fighting from the gates, the distinctive sound of the Martini-Henry rifles, as the rest of his team opened fire on the defenders at the battlements by the main gates. There were screams, trumpets, the stench of wood smoke, the whole town looked as if it was alight.

And no way out, he thought. We might burn to death ourselves.

The doors to the kasbah groaned open and a dozen men came barrelling out, fumbling with swords and flintlocks. One of them even had a mace. They were led by a huge man in a turban, his face devilish in the orange glow. Harry raised his rifle and fired. His finger, swollen and numb from the ant bites, was slow to respond. The big man turned away just in time and his round hit the man behind him.

The rest of the Berbers opened fire. At this range, you didn't have to be a marksman. Three more of them fell, the big man roared an order, then turned to flee back inside the kasbah, as they fumbled to reload. Bou Hamra's men milled about in confusion, didn't seem to know who was firing at them, Harry and his men fired off another round before Bou Hamra's men could get back inside the doors.

Harry reloaded and ran for the door.

The Berbers got there ahead of him, one of the guards was trying to shut the heavy door so he could bar it closed. The Berber swung his rifle at him, drove him back. The guard was holding something in his other hand, Harry realised it was the mace, he tried to shout a warning, but it was too late, it came up in a tight arc from knee height and it hit the Berber in the middle of the chest. There was a loud crack as his chest stove in and he flew backwards.

Harry leaped over the top of him and hit the guard with his rifle butt as he went past. It snapped the man's head back and he went down. One of the other Berbers ran in behind him, started pummelling the unconscious man with his rifle, his face and coat was soon splattered with blood, and still he wouldn't stop. Harry grabbed him by the shoulder and dragged him away.

'Leave him!' he shouted.

'He just killed his brother,' Redbeard said.

'Our job is to find Bou Hamra.'

He looked around. The lower floor of the kasbah was the granary, there were a few sacks piled against the far wall, pitifully few of them, he realised if Amastan had been patient he could have starved them out.

He looked up the stairs. The big man and the rest of the guards had escaped that way. He put another round in his rifle, cocked it, and went after them.

CHAPTER 36

For all the grim medieval aspect of the exterior, the upper floors of the kasbah looked like a boudoir. There were painted cedar beams resting on panels of traceried stucco. On either side of the landing there were long recessed rooms closed by vermilion doors painted with gold arabesques and vases of spring flowers. Each of the shadowy rooms was spread with silk rugs and divans. Braziers glowed in the dark corners, fragrant with sandalwood.

Harry waited on the landing, staring into the shadows, straining for every little noise. Where were they?

He heard a yell behind him.

A guard rushed out of one of the rooms and came at him, brandishing a curved sword. Harry turned around, raised the gun, and fired.

The man dropped dead at his feet.

The Berber with him said, 'Get down,' and raised his rifle, pointing it straight at him.

Harry ducked his head and span around. He saw the big man in the turban run for the stairs, two of his guards with him. The sound of the rifle so close to his ear deafened him. One of the guards fell, clutching at his leg and dropping his sword. Another of the Berbers ran up the stairs from the granary. He ran over and dispatched the wounded guard with his knife, severing his windpipe and his neck veins like he was killing a goat for his family's dinner.

He wiped the blood off the blade onto his robes and kicked the dead man the rest of the way down the stairs where he lay sprawled horribly on the carpets.

Harry jumped over him and followed the Berber up the stairs to the next landing.

The torches threw long shadows on the walls. Harry waited on the landing, fumbled another shell into the rifle, his right hand was almost useless now, even for holding the rifle steady, and he dropped the cartridge on the stair.

He held the rifle under his right arm and fumbled in the pocket of his trousers for another with his left.

He heard a yell, the Berber in front of him was too slow to react, one of the guards ran out onto the landing and the point of his sword took him in the middle of the chest and slammed him against the wall.

Harry was still trying to reload, the guard might have skewered him as well, but he couldn't get his sword free, it was mired in muscle and cartilage, he had to plant his heel on the dying Berber's chest for leverage and by the time he had the sword ready again, Harry had the rifle loaded and shot him in the head, left-handed.

'God forgive me,' Harry muttered, cleared the breech, loaded again.

This damned hand.

He had to jam the muzzle against one of the stone steps, hold the stock under his arm, load again, everything with his left hand now. His right hand was starting to blister already, it was swollen and weeping, like he had plunged it into boiling water. Even holding the stock of the rifle was agony.

He knelt down beside the wounded man. There was frothy blood bubbling out of the wound in his chest. The sword must have pierced his lung. Fatal.

He heard the creak of a floorboard, turned in time to see the giant in the blue turban rushing at him, a massive sword raised over his head.

He raised the rifle, and he might have finished it then, but the mechanism jammed, he pulled the trigger once, twice, it wouldn't fire, he just had time to raise the rifle over his head and let the stock take the full force of the blade as it swung down.

The force of it knocked him back across the landing.

It was Bou Hamra.

The big man looked at the rifle. The cartridge was jammed in the breech, it wouldn't fire now until he had cleared it. He was at Bou Hamra's mercy.

And there would be no mercy, would there?

Bou Hamra looked down at the wounded Berber, choking on his own blood. He took a moment to savour it. He looked back at Harry, took another step, another, another, Harry wriggled back across the carpets until he felt the wall at his back, and he knew he was trapped.

'The Englishman,' Bou Hamra said.

So, this was the Antichrist of the Maghreb.

Harry couldn't decide if he was handsome or monstrous, everything about him was overlarge, his body, his lips, his nose, his teeth, strong white teeth. The indigo dye that had streaked from his turban and stained his forehead and cheeks was uneven and made his appearance even more unsettling.

He seemed reluctant to finish it.

'I could use you,' he said. 'If only I had more time.'

There was a loud crack.

A bullet slammed into the bricks a few inches from Bou Hamra's head, ricocheted around the landing, chipping brickwork. It hit a ceramic vase thirty feet away and shattered it to pieces.

Harry looked at the stairs. Redbeard stood there, his rifle at his shoulder, how had he missed from there? Redbeard snapped open the breech, fumbled with another cartridge.

Harry scrambled to his feet, lunged at the big man, who slashed at him, backhanded, and the hilt of the sword hit him on the cheek and smacked his head against the wall. He fell, raised his head long enough to see Bou Hamra running down the corridor towards one of the side rooms, Redbeard rushing up the stairs after him.

And he passed out.

CHAPTER 37

Harry opened his eyes. There was a sickening pain in his skull, and he turned on his side and retched. He tried to think where he was. Why wasn't he in his bed, listening to the muezzin call to prayer, where were the mountains, the smell of donkey dung.

Ah, that's right. He remembered now.

'He's awake,' someone said.

He thought for a moment that it was morning, the whole sky seemed to be lit up. He wrinkled his nose at the taint of smoke, remembered they had set light to the medina.

'Harry?'

A face swam into his vision.

'George?'

'He is alive?' someone else said. 'Remarkable.'

'There's a lot of blood.'

'He split his head on the wall as he went down.'

'What happened to his hand and his arms,' someone else said. 'It looks like he has the pestilence.'

'Ants,' Harry mumbled.

'Fire ants? I'd rather get fired out of a cannon.' He recognised that voice. It was Zdan.

'Do you have something I can give him?' George said.

'Some vinegar,' Zdan said. 'What we use to clean the cannons. And a clean white cloth.'

'To soak up the vinegar?' George said.

'No, to put in his mouth to stop him yelling,' Zdan said. 'I'd rather be tortured with hot irons than have fire ant bites.' He walked out.

George sat him up and wrapped a bandage around his head, there was blood everywhere, on his shirt, on his face, in his hair.

'How does it feel?' he said.

'Do something about these bites, can you? My hand feels like it's on fire.'

'Don't scratch at them. If they get infected, it will be a lot worse.'

'He could have killed me,' Harry said. 'Bou Hamra. He had the chance.'

One of the Berbers was standing to one side, watching him. It was Redbeard, of all people.

'You saved my life,' Harry said.

'I owed it to you,' Redbeard said, 'Because of Idrissa. Now we're even. No more favours. I'll find some vinegar.'

CHAPTER 38

Amastan stood by the window, watching the Kaïd's harem being led out of the kasbah, his treasure chests secured to the back of pack mules, the scene lit by the orange glow of the fire. His guards were agitated. They wanted him to leave, they said the fire was out of control now, and it was dangerous to linger.

It was as if he hadn't heard them.

He looked around as George helped Harry towards the stairs.

'You did well,' he said. 'Abdel ibn Hidi is dead. This kasbah, his lands, his harem, they are all mine now. It was your courage and skill and good counsel that brought down this fortress.'

'You will give us our money? We can go home?'

Amastan shook his head.

'You gave your word,' George said.

'I gave my word that you could leave as soon as I had Bou Hamra's head. But when my soldiers stormed the kasbah, there was no sign of the magician. The one with the red beard, he said he escaped.'

'That's impossible.'

'It seems not.' Amastan nodded towards the window where he had been standing. George steadied Harry on his shoulder, they went over and looked down. There was a rope ladder leading down to a small courtyard.

'There is another rope ladder, it must have been thrown over during the night, it leads down to the base of the cliff. It can't be seen from the river or from our camp. From the tracks my scouts found down there, it seemed he had horses waiting for him. He is far away from here by now.'

'What now?'

'We return to Aït Karim, until my spies send me message of where to find him. The hunt goes on. When I have Bou Hamra's head, or the man himself in chains, the Sultan will make me pasha of Marrakesh and Lord of all the Atlas. Until that happens, you are still in my service.'

George waited for the explosion, but Harry just gave him a rueful smile. 'This is not what we agreed.'

'It is precisely what we agreed.'

'My friend risked his life for you.'

'No, he did it for the money. Unfortunately, the gamble did not pay off. But you will get another chance. When we have Bou Hamra, and only when we have him, you can have your money and go back to England as rich men.' He pointed to the window on the other side of the Kasbah. 'The fire is getting closer. We should leave here. This time tomorrow, this place will be smoke and ashes.'

George had them bring Harry back to the hospital tent in Amastan's camp. The city was well ablaze now, and the glow rippled on the canvas walls of the tent. George bent over him, trying to work as best he could by the glow of the lantern that hung from the crossbeam.

'For God's sake, that hurt!' Harry said, through gritted teeth. 'What are you doing?'

'It is a nasty cut you have here. Keep still. I need to get the lips of the wound together or it will get infected.'

'I killed at least three more men last night.'

'You're a soldier. If you hadn't killed them, they would have killed you.'

'It doesn't sit any easier on my conscience. I am not like Amastan and Zdan and these others. They are so matter of fact about it.'

'They can't afford to be sentimental, like you.'

'What is this you have put on my arms. I smell like a hangover.'

'It's vinegar. The sort of astringent they used to call champagne in that greasy bordello where I found you in London. How do the bites feel?'

'Better.'

'Good. But I warn you now, you look like a leper. Hold still. I haven't finished stitching your head.'

'You are killing me. What are you using, copper wire?'

'I've run out of catgut,' George said. 'I'm forced to use the local remedy.'

It took a moment for Harry to realise what he meant. 'You mean...'

'Yes. Ants. Now hold still.'

CHAPTER 39

Darkness fell halfway through the afternoon, a storm broiling in from the mountains. Grey clouds rolled down the valley slopes above Aït Karim. Lightning cracked over the distant peaks.

Wafa sat on gold cushions by a low table, sheltered by the gallery above her. In the centre of the courtyard, open to the sky, fat raindrops plopped into the central fountain, pattering onto the leaves of a date tree,

Her head was bare except for a thin green headscarf. There were trinkets at the sash around her waist, and in the storm light she looked like a girl again. She wasn't, of course. There were small lines around her eyes and mouth, she should have been married by now, with a household of her own.

Amastan paced the carpets. He had dispensed with his *cheiche*, something he only did here in the harem.

'What is it, brother? Is there something I might do to help you?'

'It is nothing.'

'Is it Bou Hamra?'

A sigh. 'He is part of it. I thought I would have his head on the walls by now.'

'He cannot run forever.'

'He has been running a very long time. He shows no sign of fatigue, that I can tell.'

'You will find him.'

'But when? He is the son of a sultan. While he lives, he is dangerous.'

'The last two battles, you have defeated him. It has only raised your own reputation and weakened his. Thanks to your Englishman, he has lost the last of his allies in the Atlas.'

'When the present sultan dies, everything changes. If Bou Hamra should find a way to succeed in his claim, I will be finished. We will all be finished.'

'You have known this for a long time. Something else is troubling you. Is it the Englishman?'

'I gave my word to him and I broke it. I have to keep him here, keep both of them here, until Bou Hamra is dead.'

'I don't think he is the cause of your sleepless nights. I think perhaps it is the letters.'

Amastan froze, then turned slowly, wary of her now. 'How did you know about the letters?'

'I have known about the letters for a very long time.'

'Why have you not spoken before?' He came and sat down beside her. 'You must not tell anyone. *Anyone.*'

'Of course. You don't have to tell me that. But what are you going to do?'

'There is nothing to be done. It is as it is.'

'It causes you such distress.'

'And it will always be so. Let it be, Wafa. Let it be.'

'I should like to. Yet I worry for you.'

'Why should you worry now and never before? Nothing has changed.'

'I worry,' Wafa said, 'because of the Englishman. He is what has changed. Be careful of him.'

'What are you saying?'

'You are my blood. I know you better than I know myself. I think you know precisely what I mean, my Lord. You are in danger. And we both know it.'

The shutters were open, their rooms faced the mountains, and the wind was picking up, whipping the woollen hangings across the door. Harry went to the window, was about to close the shutters, stopped to watch the clouds rolling down the mountain, the distant growl of thunder. The sound of the *asr*, the call to afternoon prayer, echoed over the rooftops and down the valley. Six times a day, the time of prayer was announced, the *mueddhin* was the only clock these people needed.

'I'm going to miss this,' he said, 'if we ever get back home.'

'I thought you hated it here.'

'At first I did. But I see how a man might grow to love it. In Lambeth, all I ever heard was the man next door screaming at his wife and if I stood at the window like this all I could smell was piss, the stink from the drains and the river.' He took a lungful of air. 'This place is somewhat magical at times.'

'It's brutal.'

'Yes, that as well.'

'Do you think he'll keep his word. Amastan? When all this is done.'

'Which word? He's given us many.'

'What I mean is, will that cold-eyed bastard give us our money?'

'I take it from your tone that you are not truly enamoured of him?'

'The man is a tyrant. First, he says we must help him, or he will have us murdered. Then he offers us a tenth of what the Sultan offered, now he changes his mind and says he will pay us the same. He's worse than a carpet salesman in the bazaar.'

'He is just being practical.'

'I do not understand why you are so sanguine about this.'

'I don't know how to explain this to you, George.'

'Explain what to me?'

'That there are some things more important than money.'

'I know that, I didn't realise that you did. Can I ask when this revelation came to you?'

'I was hanging by my fingernails, a hundred feet up the cliff at Aït Isfoul. I discovered that I didn't want to die, after all. That I'd like to make something of myself one day. It was a priceless discovery, in the circumstances.'

'Dear God, Harry, it's what I've been trying to get through to you ever since we came here.'

Harry felt the first fat drops of rain on his face. There was a greenish tint to the air, the storm light perfused through the gathering clouds. He drew the shutters closed. As he did, he saw a shadow move in the tower above the harem, saw Zdan in the courtyard below, keeping to the shadows.

'You know, I was thinking about this girl, the one who died, what was her name? Nour?'

'She didn't die, Harry. In England, they would call it murder.'

'You did what any decent soldier would do, you didn't allow her to suffer needlessly. But that is not my point.'

'What is your point?'

'Zdan told us that Amastan is not inclined to spend much time in his harem. Right?'

'That's what he said.'

'Because, you know, if he doesn't like women, you have to wonder how Nour came to find herself with a child.'

'He was doing his duty for the family name.'

'Or perhaps the child belonged to the man who found his way into the harem under cover of the night. Just as Mou told us.'

'You mean, Zdan? Perhaps. But it's not our problem. We just have to help Amastan capture this madman Bou Hamra and then, I pray to God, this nightmare will all be over. I swear, I could not stand another summer in this damned place.'

'I had Bou Hamra in my sights, George. He was as far away as you from me and I was looking at him down the length of the rifle barrel. I couldn't have missed. But for one jammed cartridge, we would have our money and be on our way home.'

'Don't blame yourself. It was bad luck.'

'Or fate.'

'What do you mean, fate?'

'Perhaps we are meant to be here.'

A clap of thunder sounded like a shell had dropped on the kasbah. The shutters rattled in their frames and the whole tower seemed to shake in a violent gust of wind.

'He heard you,' George said.

'Laugh all you want, this has nothing to do with God, or religion. It is a feeling I have, that there is something better waiting for me at the end of all this. More than just money. I wonder if life doesn't have a plan for me.'

'I hope so. Though if you don't mind me saying so, I think if life is betting on you, it's taking quite a gamble.'

CHAPTER 40

It was Harry's habit of an evening to sit on the terrace above their rooms, take out his tobacco pouch and stuff a wad of tobacco, mixed with a little of the hashish that Zdan brought for him, into his pipe. It was not much more than a hollowed-out chicken bone, but it served well enough, and it seemed there was not a cigarette to be had in the whole of the Atlas Mountains.

He watched the sun set over the valley, listened to the clack-clack of the storks nesting in the tower above the harem, while the muezzin chanted the evening prayer. He knew nearly all of the words by heart by now, murmured them to himself as they echoed along the valley. There were cats everywhere at this time of the day, they played along the walls, screeching or pawing at each other if one strayed into another's territory.

And that was when he saw him.

It was only for a moment, Mou was quick and nimble, light as a shadow, it was why he got away with so much. They never knew what he did when he wasn't with them. George always supposed he must be getting into mischief, stealing bread or sweetmeats from the stalls in the medina. When they asked him how he spent his days, he always lowered his eyes and mumbled some unintelligible response.

How many times had they warned him? And he had promised them, by the Prophet, that he would never, ever, ever, go back to the harem.

When Harry saw him clambering over the high wall, dropping nimbly into the court on the other side, he threw his pipe away and jumped to his feet, outraged, shaking with it. It was not only that the boy had broken his promise, again; he knew that Amastan would have him flogged, or worse, if he was caught a second time.

He ran down the narrow stairs, saw the boy dodging along the corridor, could he look any more furtive? Harry positioned himself behind a pillar and as the boy went past, he caught him by the hood of his *djellaba* and swung him around.

Mou yelped with fright.

Harry crouched down so he was eye to eye with him and shook him by the shoulders until his teeth rattled. 'If I were the Chief Eunuch, you know what would happen right now. Don't you?'

Mou stared at him wide-eyed. This had given him a real fright, or at least he hoped so.

'Well, do you?'

'I wasn't doing anything,' he said, an entirely predictable lie.

'I saw you jump over the wall to the harem. What in hell were you thinking?'

'Don't tell the *Kaïd*!'

'Why not? You know what he'll do, don't you? He'll put your head up there on the wall for decoration. Now tell me, why I should care, or *Sayeed* George.'

A shuffling of feet. The boy was incorrigible.

'The women were fighting.'

'What?'

'The pretty women. Some of them were fighting, pulling at each other's hair.'

'You shouldn't be watching them.'

'It wasn't my fault! You told me to be your spy. When I heard them, I had to go and look!'

'Tell me you won't do this again.' He wouldn't look up, so Harry put his hand under his chin and forced him to look into his eyes. 'Promise me!'

'I promise.'

'You swear?'

'I swear.'

'Let me give you some advice. I was a little bastard, too, when I was your age. I thought I was clever. You think you're clever, don't you?'

'No, *Sayeed*!'

'Yes, you do. You think you're cleverer than anyone else, you think you can get away with anything. But you can't. One day life catches up with you, Mou. I'm telling you, it's true.'

Head down, solemn, a good impersonation of what a little boy who is contrite should look like. It didn't fool Harry for a moment. He let him go, and he ran off.

'Mou!'

He stopped and turned around.

'What were the pretty ladies fighting about?'

'I heard one of them shouting Zdan's name. Over and over. They were fighting about the one called Nour.'

'Why?'

'I don't know.'

No, that wouldn't do at all. Harry grabbed his hood and pulled him back.

'Mou, there is something I have to ask you. It's important. Do you understand the difference between the truth and, well, something you say to get people to like you and pay you attention?'

'Yes,' he said slowly, though he didn't seem certain.

'You told me that you saw Zdan go into the harem. That wasn't true, was it?'

'It was! I swear!'

'No one can go into the Kaïd's harem except for the Kaïd himself.'

'I wasn't just saying it. It's true!'

'Alright.' Harry stood up but held on to the boy's *djellaba*. 'If I see you in there again, I will disown you. Do you understand? I will not take you back with me to England, not ever. You will have to sleep on your own in the medina. Do you understand?'

He nodded.

He ran off. He hoped he had frightened him enough that he wouldn't do it again. But then, he'd thought that the last time.

He thought about the things Mou said that he'd seen. Why would Amastan's harem be fighting about Zdan? It didn't make sense.

CHAPTER 41

A caravan had arrived, it had travelled across the desert from Timbuctu. Zdan told them it was one of the largest they had seen for a long time; there was gold, ivory, ostrich feathers, pepper and, of course, slaves.

Ah, the slaves. Harry saw them, wretched creatures, being led through the streets towards the *fondaks*, lines of shuffling miserable men in heavy chains. Even when you couldn't see them, you could smell them, it was like a pall hanging over the entire town. He imagined the girls in the harem, the Chief Eunuch, even the Sultan's own Black Guard had all passed this way once.

They were guarded by Tuareg tribesmen, Blue Men, from the far south, the place Zdan said was called the 'land of the mirage'. They wore turbans and robes dyed a rich blue, made with ink made from Mediterranean sea urchins. But the dye was not fast and sweat made the dye run from the cotton onto their faces, staining their faces indigo blue. It made them look fearsome. Even Harry shuddered when he saw them stalking through the medina.

The caravan guides were mostly Berbers, men who knew the shifting sands of the Sahara as well as the drivers of the hansom cabs knew the backstreets of Soho and Stepney.

People had flooded into the town to meet the caravan. They came with panniers of olives and dates on the backs of their donkeys, slabs of salt on the backs of their camels, anything they could trade, leather or silk or rusty swords. He could see men of every colour, swarthy bearded men from the Souss and the Draa, Sudanese and Senegalese with skins as shiny and black as coal. Even way up here, he could hear the noise, a muted roar from their incessant bargaining.

He saw someone in the alley below the walls, his quick, furtive movements catching his eyes. It was Zdan. He took another look over his shoulder then disappeared down an alleyway out of sight.

Where would he be going?

The market square in the medina had been transformed, there was row upon row of white tents and stalls, and the lanes and bazaars were heaving with turbans and veils and peasant dresses, farmers from the valleys, nomads with nut brown faces and curved daggers in their belts, peasant women with baskets of dates and pannikins of pumpkins and onions. There was soap and carpets and freshly skinned sheep's heads and monkeys in little red tunics performing for coins. It was a bedlam of noise, everyone shouting, shoving and haggling, while dirty-faced children ducked and shrieked through the crowds, begging and stealing fruit.

At the far southern end of the medina, away from the crowds and the hubbub, there was a narrow dusty path, roofed with rushes and date palm fronds and lined with merchant stalls. Sunlight angled through the gaps in the makeshift roofing, the air filled with fine dust and tiny black flies. A big Tuareg strode down the lane leading from the main square, ignoring the cries of the hawkers and stallholders. Any that became too impertinent got a savage look that sent them scurrying back into their shops.

There was a teashop at the end, a few low wooden stools and rickety tables for the customers, who squatted together in the gloom and stultifying heat of midday, under the lean-to roof.

The Tuareg went in, waited a moment for his eyes to grow accustomed to the gloom. The shop was almost empty, just one man sat facing away from the entrance, in the far corner. He went over and sat down.

The shop owner started to approach with a pot of minted tea, stopped when he saw the look in the other man's eyes. He went away again.

Zdan looked up, a quick glance and a nod, that was all.

'Can you do it?' the Blue Man said.

'I will do what I can.'

'Not good enough.'

'Don't threaten me. The one who sends you knows I am the only one who can help him. I told him what I am telling you now. There are no guarantees, I will do what I can. But first, I want my down payment.'

The Tuareg reached inside his robes and took out a stiff leather pouch. He handed it to Zdan under the table.

Zdan opened the drawstrings and peered at the gold coins snug inside. He took one out and tested it with his teeth. He emptied the rest into his palm and counted them carefully. He put them back and hid the pouch inside his own robes.

'If you do not deliver what you have promised, you will see me again,' the Blue Man said.

Zdan leaned forward. 'You would do well to remember whose fortress you walk in. I have promised nothing. Now leave, while you still can.'

The big Tuareg stalked out. Zdan waited a few moments and got up and took out his knife. He held it under the tea seller's nose, then handed him a few coins for his silence. The carrot, the stick. It was what every mule understood best.

CHAPTER 42

Swallows flitted between the branches of the poplars.

The caravan had moved on, heading down the pass to Marrakesh. The lanes were deserted now, the *fondaks* empty, the *riads* of the wealthy left in shadowy silence below the parapet walls, a few Sudanese slaves in their pure white turbans sweeping at the cobblestone streets outside the houses. He could see between the flat terraced roofs as far as the medina, could make out a handful of Berber women squatting on their mats with their scrawny chickens and a few mouldy squash and pumpkin. The hubbub that had engulfed the kasbah for days had gone. The silence was profound, the buzzing of insects, the sound of a child playing a flute somewhere behind one of the courtyards.

It was the indolence that Harry hated the most. At least in London there were creditors to avoid, drinks to scrounge, loose women to chase. Here, there was nothing to do except settle in the scrap of shade on the roof, fill and refill his pipe, wait for his destiny to present itself.

Nothing to do, couldn't even sabotage his own dim prospects.

Beyond its high walls Amastan's harem ordinarily went about its business in utter silence, its fretted shutters closed to outside view. It was the noise that startled him first; women shrieking at the tops of their voices. One of the shutters high in the tower flew open and he saw a boy, he could have been no more than five or six years old, wearing a short smock, clamber out and balance precariously on the ledge.

He saw a woman slap at him, it looked like she was trying to push him off. Someone grabbed her and pulled her back inside. It was the

Chief Eunuch. He saw him lean out of the window, towards the child, trying to usher him back inside.

The little boy retreated further along the ledge. When he had strayed out there he had been in a panic, trying to get away from the woman. He suddenly realised how high he was from the ground and started to wail at the top of his lungs, opening his arms for someone to come and get him.

The Chief Eunuch tried to coax him back. It was clear to Harry that it wasn't do any good.

Unless someone intervenes, he thought, this can only end one way.

Harry launched himself down the narrow stairs. A number of slaves had gathered in the courtyard, they were peering up at the tower, pointing and murmuring among themselves. He pushed past them and launched himself at the wall.

This would be the easy part. He jumped and got both hands on the top of the wall and hauled himself up. He made his way along it, balanced easily on top of it.

From there, he could see down into the marble-paved court of the women's quarters. Pigeons fluttered about a central marble fountain, there were some cedar trees with marble benches, whitewashed walls, nothing as grand as he had imagined. A knot of slave women, dressed in rags, were pointing up at him in astonishment.

Several harem girls appeared from under a trellised arcade hung with linen curtains, they were unveiled, a mix of coffee-skinned Somalis and taller, darker Sudanese. They wore diaphanous silk robes, tea rose and gold and peach, there were embroidered gold slippers on their feet. Some of them had pearls in their braids, all of them had gold wrist bands and bangles on their ankles.

They looked up at the tower, shrieked in terror when they saw him standing on the wall and fled back inside.

One of the slaves pointed at the tower. The little boy had tried to make his way back to the window, where the Chief Eunuch was still trying to urge him back inside. He lost his balance on the wall and for a moment Harry thought he was about to fall.

He regained his balance, sat down, closed his eyes, and screamed. If no one went to get him, it was clear that he would be up there all day.

There looked to be just one way up there. The wall encircled the courtyard on three sides, on the fourth side there was a flat roof, which led to the foot of the tower. There was a short climb, twenty feet, no more, to the window where he had seen the boy climb out. The parapet led from the harem tower to a guard tower on the kasbah walls.

It should not be anywhere near as difficult as getting inside Bou Hamra's fortress, he thought. The first ten feet or so of the climb would be relatively easy, the problem would not be finding gaps in the brick for holds but knowing which ones would not crumble away as soon as he trusted them with his weight.

He hauled himself up.

He ran across the mudbrick roof, looked up, saw the boy still squatting on the parapet wall. He was shrieking in panic. The Chief Eunuch was shouting out of the window, which was only making it worse. There was a woman behind him, she was wailing louder than the boy, was trying to crawl out there as well. The boy's mother, Harry decided.

Any moment the little boy would do something crazy, and that would be the end of him.

The brick pisé of the tower had been worked with intricate geometric patterns and Harry used them for handholds. He reached the junction of the parapet wall and the tower, lifted himself up, was shocked to discover how narrow it was. He looked down. Twenty feet on one side to the flat roof, forty feet on the other to a tiled courtyard. Either way, far enough to kill the boy.

Far enough to kill me as well.

The boy had his hands pressed together like he was praying, his cheeks bright red with terror. His face was creased into a grimace, he was screaming, open-mouthed, and when he saw Harry he screamed even louder.

Harry smiled to reassure him, but the sight of a sweating, fully grown infidel with blonde whiskers only made him panic all the more.

'Everything will be all right,' Harry said to him in halting Arabic. 'I will help you.'

He couldn't make out what he said through the sobs. At least he'd stopped yelling.

'I can help you,' Harry said. 'I will take you back to your mother, your *umi*. Isn't that what you want? '

A nod of the head.

'Good. That's what we'll do.'

The child's shrieks subsided to a series of hiccoughs.

He could not have been more than three or four years old. He was a plump, solid little boy with tight black curls and brown eyes, skin the colour of café au lait. He wondered briefly what had happened with the other women that he got himself chased out here.

Harry eased himself along the crumbling ledge, balanced astride it. He held out a hand. 'What's your name?'

'Udad,' the boy sobbed.

'Take my hand, Udad. Don't pull, okay? Just hold.'

The boy's bottom lip quivered. Suddenly he threw himself sideways and launched himself at Harry.

'God. Jesus. Mother Mary of God. Fuck.'

For a moment he thought they were both going to fall.

He clutched at the back of the boy's smock with his right arm, fought to keep his balance with his left hand, his fingers clutching the edge of the parapet, his knees pressed into the brick trying to take the strain.

'Keep still, Udad. Keep still!'

The boy yelled and tried to reach for his mother over Harry's right shoulder. It was all he could do to hold him still. For a moment he lurched to one side, he thought, this is it, what a stupid way to die. He heard Udad's mother screaming at the window behind him.

'Hold still! Hold still, Udad!'

The boy was panting, wriggling. Harry held him tight to his chest, stayed quite still, until he had calmed down.

He used his knees to balance himself, as he would on his horse. He shuffled back, his left hand behind him on the parapet, keeping a firm grip on the boy's back with his right, coaxing him along after him.

Three, four times, they were almost there. He saw the boy's mother reach over the Chief Eunuch and try to grab the boy's shirt before the big man pushed her back inside.

'Give him to me.'

He looked over his shoulder. The Chief Eunuch had clambered out onto the window ledge, his huge frame jammed into the window space. He held the stone sill with his left hand and was reaching towards him with the other.

'You can let go of me now,' he said to Udad.

The boy only clung on even tighter.

'No, no!'

He lifted him up bodily with both hands and prayed that the Chief Eunuch was strong enough to hold him. He heard the man grunt under the strain, Udad shrieked in panic as he hung suspended, for a breathless moment, in thin air.

He saw the Chief Eunuch's face for a moment, his neck muscles bulging with the strain, the veins popping at his temples. Udad's mother grabbed the boy, pulled him inside.

Harry grabbed for the parapet, the brick crumbled, he grabbed again, this time it held, he clawed himself upright, gasping for breath, his heart hammering in his chest. He smiled at the Eunuch over his shoulder.

'We did it,' he said.

Slaves helped the Chief Eunuch down from his precarious position. He leaned out. Harry extended his hand, so that he could pull him inside after him.

'You may not enter here,' he said. 'It is Forbidden.'

The shutter slammed shut.

Harry sat on the parapet for long moments, stunned. Had he really said that?

Then he started to laugh.

If his father could see him now: *Didn't I tell you, son? No kindness ever goes unpunished.*

How the hell was he going to get down from the wall? It wouldn't be possible to climb down the way he had come. What, then?

A shutter on one of the guard tower windows flew open and Zdan leaned out. 'Englishman! This way.'

Harry gave him an elaborate salute and started to shuffle over.

From a terrace in the main kasbah, Amastan watched Zdan and George pull Harry inside the tower to safety. A remarkable feat. Twice in as many months.

Why would he do such a thing, for a child that wasn't his own?

He turned to one of the slaves, waiting by the door. 'Send word I wish to speak to the English captain tonight in my quarters. *Alone.*'

The man bowed and hurried off.

CHAPTER 43

The Kaïd's quarters were the only rooms in the entire fortress – indeed the only rooms he had seen since leaving Marrakesh – to have glass windows. He had only ever seen his eyrie before in winter, when the light had been its dullest, but now, with the coming of summer, the sun angled through the high clerestory windows, in a kaleidoscope of red, yellow and greens, making it appear almost magical.

It was too hot inside, Amastan took his ease outside, on a low divan, in the shadows of the late afternoon. Despite the heat he still wore his black *cheiche*, as always.

After the guard who had escorted Harry from his quarters had left, Amastan indicated that he should take his ease beside him. There was a silver tray with oranges and pancakes sweetened with honey.

'I like to sit here at night,' he said. 'I love the light. It is softer at this time of day. The dust of the day filters down the valley, hangs there like a mist and turns to violet.'

He has brought me here to admire the view, Harry thought. That is unexpected. It was beautiful, the swallows flitting in the orange groves, only the harsh cry from a jay bird breaking the silence. England was a million miles away.

As the sun dropped down the sky, figures started to appear on the flat roofs of the house below the kasbah, Sudanese slaves in striped turbans, beating at rugs and carpets with long sticks, then whole families, the children laughing and shouting, their parents and grandparents come up to escape the heat, sipping tea, seated on cushions.

'Why did you do it?' Amastan asked him. 'Why did you risk your life to save the boy?'

'All I did was shin up the wall. It wasn't anything. Besides, there was no choice. The lad would have made a nice mess on the marble if someone hadn't grabbed him.'

'No choice? But there is always a choice. You could have let him fall. Instead, you risked death or terrible injury for the son of a man who has, surely in your estimation, played you for a fool.'

'Is that what you have done?'

'No, but I can imagine how you might see it that way. I am the cause of much of your present sorrow and frustration. Am I not?'

Harry wondered where this was leading. He thought Amastan wanted to thank him, offer him some kind of reward for what he had done. After all, from what he knew, Udad was his only male heir. That must be worth something.

'Now you think there will be some kind of compensation for your efforts,' Amastan said, reading the direction of his thoughts.

'I had considered it.'

'Then I am sorry to disappoint you. All I can offer you is these poor sweetmeats and the view.'

'Well, it's a nice view,' Harry said.

'Yes. I hoped you would enjoy it.'

'You know, not my place to say, but you are somewhat of a contradiction.'

'Ah! Is that what I am?'

'George thinks you are a tyrant. I told him you were merely practical.'

'That is quite a mild view, in the circumstances. I expected you to be as sour as your friend. I have caused you a great deal of hardship.'

'I am accustomed to hardship. I was a soldier for many years.'

'So was your friend.'

'He was a doctor, not a soldier. He is hardened in other ways.'

'I am curious about you. Will you indulge me?'

'If you like.'

'I have watched you since you came here. You are clearly a man of great daring and resource. Your friend tells me your army gave you a medal for being brave. But then you left the army, and they took their medal back. How did this happen?'

'I think you know the answer to that. I didn't leave the army. The army left me. Is this really of interest to you?'

'Does it cause you pain to talk about it?'

He shrugged. 'I fell in love with a woman.'

'Is this a crime where you live?'

'It depends on who the woman is, doesn't it? I am sure it is the same in Morocco.'

'And who was this woman?'

'She was the daughter of a general. The highest-ranking British officer in Egypt.'

'And you were just a lowly captain. He did not approve.'

'No, he did not approve.'

'You must possess great charm around women.'

'Unlucky at cards, lucky in love. It's a saying we have.'

'But not lucky this time?'

'I had been seeing her for months, behind his back. It wasn't easy. Eventually I got sick of skulking around and I went to see him, told him that Lucy and I were in love and we wanted to be married.'

'What did he say?'

'He had quite a bit to say, as it turned out. He told me that he didn't think I was good enough for her. He threatened to transfer me elsewhere. Said I might prefer the climate in India, somewhere with rampant fever epidemics.'

'And the woman?'

'When I told Lucy of her father's opinion, she said that we should elope.'

'Elope?'

'Run away together. Without his blessing.'

'Is that what you did?'

'I bought two tickets on a packet steamer to Athens under false names.'

'I thought that in England they would shoot you for doing such things.'

'Yes. But all's well that ends well. She never showed up. So they never had the chance to shoot me.'

'What a shame. Her father must have been looking forward to a firing squad. They found a way to get rid of you anyway?'

'Of course. Her father, as I said, was a general. A few months later I was brought before a court martial on a charge of embezzling a fellow officer. Theft.'

'And did you? Steal from a fellow soldier.'

'What do you think?'

'No, I think you would steal a man's daughter, but not his money. What about your own father?'

'What about him?'

'Is he a good father?'

'I'm sure my brother would say he is.'

'Not you?'

'My father and I haven't spoken a word to each other for eleven years.'

'Ah, fathers. Their expectations of us can be a heavy burden. Your brother is his favourite, then?'

'Of course. He can add up a ledger row of figures to the halfpenny, and not one mistake. I am hard pressed to pace out the range for a six pounder.'

'I see. So, everything for the first son, yes? It must trouble you, how he treated you like a daughter.'

'What?'

'Someone to do as they were told and stay out of the way and marry for advantage if opportunity arose. Kneel at the feet of the chosen son. A daughter.'

'I never thought it of it that way.'

'Of course not.'

'I am no man's daughter. I have a medal to prove it.'

'A woman cannot be brave?'

'That was not my meaning.'

'Women are not equal to men?'

'No,' Harry said.

'No, you are right. Women are not equal. They have no say in their lives whatsoever. You have seen for yourself what it is like to be a woman in Morocco. What is it like being a woman in England?'

'I'm not sure what it is you're asking me.'

'I am curious about the ways of other countries. How it is for men, for women, in other places.'

'I think you know we treat our women somewhat differently.'

'Ah, but do you?' Amastan said. 'Are your wives really so different to the wives in say, Fez?'

'Our young ladies don't have to cover their faces. They are free to go out as they please.'

'Ah, an excess of liberty. You see, Captain, I sometimes wonder if a woman living in your London, despite her lovely dresses and fine house, might sometimes dream of changing places with a Berber wife. I see by your face that you don't believe me.'

'I mean no disrespect.'

'Of course not. But let me give you an example. My grandmother was the chief of our tribe, a Kaïd in her own right. Could one of your elegant wives ever be a general or a prime minister? I see by your face you are surprised at this.'

'I thought among you Muslims…'

'Not all Muslims are the same and a Berber is not an Arab. We praise the same God, we pray to Mecca five times a day, as the Prophet proscribed. But we all interpret the word in different ways, and we have our own customs.'

'But you have a harem,' Harry said.

'To display my wealth to the world and curry favour with the Sultan and the *imams*. A Kaïd cannot be respected in Fez or Tangier if they do not have a kasbah, and women. But such riches have come to me only lately, as a result of wars and alliances. My father could not have afforded more than one wife.'

'If a woman can be a Kaïd, like your grandmother, can she also become a Sultan?'

'No, that is not possible,' Amastan said, 'not in the Maghreb. The sultan and his viziers, they are all Arabs, and it would not be allowed. A woman can rule the Berber, but never rule the Arab. No woman in the Sultanate can be trusted with power. Even an incomplete man like a eunuch can rise higher than a woman. Such as the present sultan's Chief Vizier. Did you know he was a eunuch?'

Harry thought about Haj Hammad, that grating voice, the rolls of fat jiggling as he walked. Of course. He should have known that.

'Women can be part of a harem,' Amastan said, 'but they may never keep one themselves. That is the prerogative of a Lord.' He got up and went to the end of the terrace, leaned on the parapet. 'Come here. Look at this.'

Harry went to stand beside him. A full moon had risen, ghostly against the pale blue sky. An old man was riding along the dusty road down from the terraced gardens on an ancient donkey, two panniers of dates balanced on either side. It was a sight that Jesus and his disciples must have seen countless times.

'You see that old man,' Amastan said. 'That could be my grandfather's grandfather. He was a poor man, just a few fields and a mud house. But he had ambition for his son, that one day he would be a great chieftain. And that son had a dream, also, and his daughter became a Kaïd.'

'And what of your father?'

'He dreamed that one day I would be pasha of Marrakesh.'

'You are fulfilling his dream.'

'Yes. Isn't that what we all do if we can? If we cannot, then we try and destroy all semblance of it.'

'I suppose,' Harry said.

'What did the woman do?' Amastan asked him.

The sudden shift in the conversation took Harry off balance. 'The woman?'

'The woman you fell in love with, in Egypt. The general's daughter.'

'Lucy.'

Lucy. Harry found himself thinking of a warm night in Alexandria, the scent of cinnamon, vanilla, and cloves from the warehouses along the waterfront, the long lamentable wail of the blind beggars outside the gates of the medina, the young Arab men in bright kaftans, with roses and jasmine behind their ears, peddlers hawking lemonade and sweetmeats and golden fritters, the flower-sellers pursuing them with tight bunches of orange-blossom and little pink roses.

'Buy sir, buy, for the pretty lady.'

We will steal away on a ship for Athens, he had said to her.

But they will shoot you if they ever find you, she had whispered.

He told her he didn't care. Carried along on the storm wave of his recklessness, she had agreed, promised that she would defy her father, join him there on the waterfront the next night, start a new life. They would cast adrift from everything that had made them what they were, a British army officer, a respectable and sought after young woman.

He remembered the sky; the rags of cloud throwing a halo around the moon that hung over the palm trees skirting the dock. He could feel the pull of the ocean tide, drawing him towards the deeps, was thrilled by it. He felt her hand on his lapel, her fingertips on his cheek, her body pressed against him. She had offered him her throat, white and soft, he had felt the warm bounce of her pulse against his lips. Everything had seemed possible.

That night, in the officer's club, he had won forty guineas on one hand of *vingt-et-un*. The jack of hearts and the ace of spades, he remembered.

He had felt the gods at his back then.

'When our plans were discovered,' he said to Amastan, 'she did as her father told her to do. She refused to see me again.'

'Well, fathers can be very persuasive. We will do anything to please them. Or displease them.' The corners of Amastan's eyes crinkled. 'But you must be eager to get back to London, and your card games, and your gin. You will be pleased to know that we have found Bou Hamra. It seems he has taken refuge among the Aït Atta.'

'Who are they?'

'They are a tribe who live in the south, on the fringes of the great desert. They have always been troublesome. They are warlike and ambitious.'

'Unlike you.'

A hint of a smile. 'The Aït Atta claim descent from the *Koreish*, the tribe that gave us the Prophet. Or so they say.'

'It seems everyone in Africa is descended from the Prophet in some way.'

'No one has kept records, so why not?'

'I have found it is always an advantage, in any battle, to have God on your side.'

'Of course. Otherwise, who would ever go to war?'

'So this Aït Atta - they are Arabs, then?'

'They have adopted Berber ways, and they speak the noble tongue. But everyone knows they are the spawn of a family of horse thieves from the time of the Book, and any one of them would sell their own grandmothers for profit. Besides, they are short and dark, and they lack the handsomeness of a true Berber.'

Now it was Harry's turn to smile.

'Until now,' Amastan said, 'I chose to tolerate their presence at my borders. Most of the land they lay claim to is desert that no one else has much use for. Let them be Lords of the Lizards. But now they have joined with Bou Hamra they have become dangerous.'

'So that is where we are headed?'

'When the time is ripe, yes. But not yet.'

'How long?'

'When I am ready,' he said enigmatically, and signalled to a guard standing by the door. Where had he come from? 'My man will see you back to your rooms. Thank you again for saving my son. Goodnight, captain.'

CHAPTER 44

They were asleep when the guards woke them, shaking them by the shoulders, come, quickly, quickly. At first Harry thought it was Mou, that he'd got himself in trouble again, but when he looked around, he saw him there beside them, sleeping soundly through all the commotion. He and George slipped on their *djellabas* and followed the bobbing lanterns down the narrow stairwell, what is it, George shouted at them, what's wrong?

'Quickly, quickly,' was all they said.

They headed out of the kasbah gates and down towards the medina. Harry got a sick feeling in his stomach. It must be the cannons.

Down by the *fondaks* there was the familiar smell of horses and dung and something else, the coppery taint of blood. They followed the guards into the courtyard where they kept *al-wahsh* and *al-raed*, there were lanterns everywhere, sending monstrous shadows dancing on the walls. Amastan's men were flooding into the quarter, nervously fingering their rifles. He heard angry voices, one of them was Zdan's.

'How could this have happened? Why were there only two guards down here?'

Harry saw three bodies sprawled outside the doors of the *fondak*, there was fresh blood leaking across the cobblestones.

'What happened?' Harry said.

Zdan held the lamp over one of the bodies. He had on a blue turban, a Tuareg, almost certainly one of Bou Hamra's men.

'There were three of them. They killed the guards and spiked the cannons. Two of them got away.'

Harry grabbed the lantern and pushed past him, into the warehouse. George and Zdan followed him in.

'The guards on the tower thought they heard screams. They got here as fast as they could. They killed one of them.'

'How did they get in?' Harry said.

'We don't know.'

'The gates are closed at night.'

'They must have already been inside, waiting.'

Harry went to *al-wahsh*. Bou Hamra's men had driven a nail into the vent hole, broken it off flush with the barrel. He swore softly and went to *al-raed*.

'Well?' George said.

'Your men got here just in time,' he said to Zdan. 'This one is okay.'

'What about *al-wahsh*?' Zdan said. 'You can repair it?'

'You'd need to send it to a foundry, have it rebored and tested. Even then, I wouldn't trust it.'

'What about the smithies?'

Harry shook his head. 'You need specialised machinery to repair this.'

Zdan shook his head. 'Amastan will not be pleased when he hears of this.'

'Are there are any more of Bou Hamra's men in the kasbah?'

'I don't know. We will put a triple guard on the guns from tonight.'

'It might be wise,' Harry said. He and George made their way back to their rooms in the dark.

'What do you make of that?' George said.

'I cannot believe that Amastan would be so careless with something so important to him as those guns. I suspect he may have a traitor in his camp.'

'Zdan?'

'Keep your voice down.'

'What is his game, do you think?'

'I don't know.'

'If these men had succeeded in spiking the other cannon, Amastan would have had to let us go. We would have been no more use. Then what about our money?'

'Sometimes I think damn the money.' Harry looked up at the crescent moon, the shadow of the kasbah, the million stars. 'It's strange. When they eventually send us home, I really think I will miss this.'

'You're mad,' George said, and headed off to bed.

CHAPTER 45

The next morning, still shaken from what had happened the night before, Harry took a hasty breakfast of flat bread, honey and olives which he washed down with mint tea. George was already awake and gone. Perhaps their conversation last night had disturbed him, and he did not want to face him this morning.

For the first time in his life, Harry felt as if he was attuned to the world around him. In London, it had become his habit to rise around lunchtime, a couple of gins and then a reluctant stroll along the waterfront to clear his head. The days were a few languorous hours of *ennui*, waiting for night to fall, so he could start to live, or at least, to entertain himself.

He only truly came awake at night, and he lived by the watch in his pocket, rarely seeing his bed before four o'clock in the morning. The sun rising in the morning was merely an inconvenience, requiring him to draw the curtains tighter at his bedroom window.

Here, the people rose with the sun, early in summer, later in winter. They knew the time of the day by the chanting of the *muezzin*, and the five daily prayers, all of which had a different name. When the sun went down, they went to bed. It was a circadian rhythm, in tune with the earth and with God. He had come to find it strangely calming.

Just before sunrise the muezzin would go up to the roof of the minaret, stand with his hands on the parapet, and start to hum, in preparation for the *adhan*, the call to prayer. Sometimes he was already on the roof terrace before the chant began.

Allahu Akbar! Allahu Akbar! Allahu Akbar! Allahu Akbar!
Ashhadu an la ilaha illa Allah. Ashhadu an la ilaha illa Allah.

God is Great! God is Great! I bear witness that there is no god except the One God...

The call would set the dogs to barking, then the chickens and the goats, and then he would listen to the people come awake, women chattering as they made their way across the fields to fetch water, the bleating of sheep as the shepherd boys set out with their flocks. Smoke drifted from the morning cookfires in the soft blue light.

There was a calm to life here. Life went on as it had done for thousands of years, since the days that the Moslem and Christian prophets had walked the earth.

He felt humbled by it. Once, his horizons had been proscribed by the docks and the cathedral; here he felt the earth spread before him, he had the sense of the desert beyond the mountains, the oceans beyond the valley. He felt the massive and palpable presence of time itself, gathered around him, the centuries behind, the children yet to come.

Perhaps *my* children.

Perhaps.

Suddenly he heard someone running up the wooden stairs and Mou ran in, wide-eyed and shaking. He stood in the doorway, trying to get his breath.

'What is it?' Harry shouted at him.

He heard a commotion down in the courtyard, the Chief Eunuch and several of the harem guards, they all had their swords drawn. Amastan appeared, shouting at them: *Where is he? Where's the boy?*

'Mou, what have you done?' Harry said.

'It wasn't my fault.'

'How many times have I warned you not to go into the harem?'

'I saw him, the Lord of the Atlas. He was naked.'

They were headed up the stairs, Amastan was shouting at the top of his voice, shrill, the first time he had ever heard him raise his voice.

Harry pulled him in, put his arm around his shoulders, shut the door.

'He's not a man,' Mou said.

Harry stared at him. 'What do you mean?'

But Mou just stood in the corner, trembling and shaking his head.

Not a man?

Amastan kicked open the door. The Chief Eunuch and his guards crowded in behind.

Instinctively, Harry stood in their way, arms outstretched, so they couldn't get to the boy.

'Get out of my way,' Amastan said.

'Let's talk about this.'

'The time for talk is over!'

Amastan tried to grab the boy but Harry shoved Mou into the other corner and blocked the way. Mou curled up into a ball, yelping like a puppy.

Amastan produced a jewelled dagger. 'Get out of my way, captain, or I'll slaughter you where you stand.'

'Do what you have to do. But I'm not moving.'

Amastan seemed to consider. Finally, the dagger was returned to its sheath. He recovered his former icy calm. 'If you do not remove yourself, I will have my Chief Eunuch pick you up, put you under his arm and place you with some force in the fountain downstairs. Is that what you want? The boy is coming with me.'

'What are you going to do with him?'

'Has he told you what he saw?'

Harry shook his head.

Amastan nodded. 'You are a very bad liar. The boy has seen too much. You know what I have to do.'

'Come on. You need me and George for the guns. If you hurt the boy, we won't help you anymore.'

'There is only one cannon now. I shall have to do without it. There are some things that are more important to me.'

Mou was sobbing like a baby. Harry felt sorry for him, despite himself. How many times had he told him not to go anywhere near the harem?

'If he's told you,' Amastan said, 'I will have to do something about you as well.'

There was a commotion in the doorway. George was struggling with one of the guards. 'Let me in! Harry, what is happening?'

'Everyone out of here,' Amastan said. 'Now!'

They all filed out. George was shoved out as well. After they had all gone, Amastan kicked the door shut behind them.

They stared at each other. Amastan tore the *cheiche* away from his face. Harry stared at her in disbelief.

He had never considered the possibility. A Berber who walked like a man, rode like a man, and fought like a warrior. But was a woman.

'The boy can live,' Amastan said. 'But I have to cut his tongue out.'

'You can't do that. I saved your son. You owe me.' Even as he said it, he thought, if what Mou told me is true, then the child I saved cannot be Amastan's son. So whose is it?

'What is this dust of the street to you?' Amastan said, pointing at Mou. 'Why should you care what happens to him?'

'I was the one who orphaned him. I owe him. It's a debt. Every gambler has to pay his debts.'

A softness came to Amastan's eyes, something he had not seen when the Lord of the Atlas was hidden behind the *cheiche*. 'You are the strangest man I ever met.'

'I'll make a deal with you,' Harry said.

'What deal?'

'I'll take him with me back to England. Today. No one need ever know what he saw.'

'Why would you do that?'

'Me and George, we're all he has now.' He was asking for mercy. Could the Lord of the Atlas afford to show such weakness? 'He will speak of this to no one. No one. On my word.'

Amastan seemed to hesitate. A bite of the lip, a slow blink of the eye. 'It would be easier to kill both of you.'

'Yes, it would. Letting me live, letting him live, that would be a gamble, I admit.'

He watched Amastan's eyes. He, she, weighing it all up.

'I cannot afford to be sentimental.' Amastan said.

'I swear, he will speak to no one. I will keep him silent until we get to London. Even then.'

'How can I trust you?'

'After all I have done in your service, you still have to ask this?'

'What you did at Aït Isfoul was for the money.'

'And what I did when Udad climbed out on the ledge?'

Amastan turned away, went to the corner, stood over Mou, her hands clenched into fists. 'So much trouble for one small life.'

'There is no such thing as a small life.'

A shake of the head. 'You don't know what you're asking of me. I don't understand what you gain from this.'

'Honour, I suppose. Don't tell George I said that, he'll laugh.'

'Every nerve, every sinew, in my whole body, tells me that this is a mistake.'

'No, it's not. Don't ask me how, but you know you can trust me on this.'

Amastan seemed to make up her mind, pulled the scarf back over her face. 'You will leave now. Do you understand? This minute. The three of you. Let us see if you truly are a good man.' Amastan turned for the door. 'I shall have them fetch the horses.'

They trailed through a thick cedar forest, the trees growing so closely together that almost no sunlight could get through. The path led in and out between the trunks, and at times narrowed to about two feet in breadth. When they finally came out of the trees, they found themselves high up a mountain gorge, with a sheer drop on one side for seven or eight hundred feet.

There were six of them, Harry, George, Mou, Zdan and two of the *Khalifa's* Berber horsemen. They were both armed with breech loading rifles and swords, but Zdan said they weren't expecting trouble. These mountains belonged to the Lord of the Atlas.

They never raised their horses above a walk, it was too hot to ride them hard, and they had a lot of ground to travel before they reached Tangier.

Zdan had been riding beside Harry the whole way. Finally he pulled back, and George took his opportunity, and rode up alongside him. 'What happened back there, Harry? Was it Mou? What has he done?'

'He went back into the harem, George. Despite everything we said to him.'

'God damn him. We warned him this would happen!'

'Yes, we did. Time and time again. We should have known he wouldn't listen.'

'What did Amastan say to you?'

Harry looked over his shoulder at Zdan. Amastan's *Khalifa* couldn't understand English but he lowered his voice anyway. 'We made a deal. We are to return to England with the boy. Zdan and his men will escort us as far as Tangier, give us enough money for passage on a ship. We are not to allow him to speak to anyone until we get there.'

'Why? What did Mou see in there?'

'Have you asked him?'

'He won't tell me anything. He says you have promised him that if he speaks a word of it to me or anyone, you will leave him in the desert to die. Is that true?'

'That sounds about right.'

'Why did they let him go? Why did they let us go? I don't understand.'

Harry shook his head.

'What are you not telling me?'

'He saw Amastan, bathing. He discovered his secret.'

'Don't tell me he's a eunuch.'

'Something like that. A woman.'

George swore under his breath and fell silent. It seemed an eternity before he spoke again. 'Impossible.'

'Not among the Berber, it seems. Amastan's grandmother was a chieftain, also, not as powerful but sheikh of her tribe, just the same.'

'If his, her, grandmother could be a Kaïd, why does Amastan have to wear a disguise?'

'Because her ambition extends further than the Atlas. She wants to be pasha of Marrakech. The Sultan would not appoint a woman to such a position. If the great seigneur in Fez knew this secret, Amastan would lose her position as the Sultan's *Khalifa* in the Atlas.'

'Well, damn me.'

'Amastan wanted to cut out the boy's tongue. I proposed the deal as a compromise.'

'Why did she accept it?'

'Perhaps because I saved her son when he climbed out on the ledge.'

'But it's not her son, is he? So who fathered him?'

Harry turned around in the saddle and looked at Zdan, following fifty yards behind. 'I don't know, but I could guess.'

'His trusty *Khalifa*?'

'That's why the women were always fighting, perhaps. Jealousy.'

'Or perhaps Udad's mother was fighting with Nour. Zdan might have got her pregnant as well.'

'And Amastan allowed it to happen, so he could have children and keep up the pretence.'

They rode in silence a while longer, both alone with their thoughts, trying to balance what they had discovered with all that had gone before, reliving their adventures with the Lord of the Atlas now from a very different point of view.

'What are we going to do with Mou when we get back to dear old Blighty?' George said.

'I told you. I will take him in.'

'You? A drunk and a gambler?'

'I agree. Not much of a start in life is it?'

'You would do better to farm him out to one of my sisters.'

'You really don't think I could do it?'

'Frankly, no. And what about the money? He promised us twice what the sultan had offered us, in silver.'

'Only if we helped him catch Bou Hamra.'

'So we have endured so much and all for nothing!'

His raised voice caught Zdan's attention. 'Is everything alright, captain?'

'We're just discussing, when we get back to England, whether to go to a bordello first or a bar.'

Zdan grimaced. *Filthy infidel.* He pulled his *cheiche* further over his face to protect himself from the hot wind and settled back in the saddle.

'We're penniless now,' George said. 'What the hell are we going to do?'

'At least we have our lives, George.'

'That meant nothing to you once.'

'Well, now I have responsibilities,' Harry said.

'You're serious about this? About the boy?'

'I've given my word.'

'Have you thought of the practicalities of this?'

'I'll find a way. Perhaps I'll go back to Bristol and ask my brother if he has a job for me in the accounts department.'

'I can scarce imagine that.'

'Whatever happens, I have given my word I will look after the boy. He is in my charge now.'

'He's a liar and a thief.'

'And as you have pointed out, I'm a drunk and a gambler. Do not be surprised if we are occupying the same jail within the year.'

'Or the same morgue.'

'That's it, look on the bright side.'

'Oh, Harry. You never cease to astonish.'

'It's something of a shame,' Harry said, and he twisted around in the saddle and took a last, long look at the tower of Aït el-Karim, silhouetted against the mountains. 'I was just beginning to enjoy myself.'

CHAPTER 46

Mou had been badly frightened by what happened. A changed lad, almost. In a way, it was a shame. He had lost his cheeky smile and even in camp he never ventured more than a few paces away from either of them. On the trail he rode so close to Harry that at times their saddles were almost touching.

It grew hotter, the further they descended the valley, and Harry began to doze in the saddle, lulled by the chirping of the insects in the trees. He didn't see where the riders came from. He heard a shout from George, looked up, and within the space of a few seconds the men were almost on them.

Their two guards both reached for the breech-loaders in their saddle holsters but Zdan put up a hand to stop them. 'Too late,' he said.

There was a dozen of them, and they had black masks covering their faces. They galloped towards them, with their rifles raised. Bou Hamra's men, they had to be. They spread out over the trail in front and behind, their horses frothing and stamping.

Zdan walked his horse forward, raised a hand to the leader of the horsemen, who nodded in return. It seemed they knew each other.

Zdan turned his horse around. 'Captain. Lieutenant. I regret to inform you that you are my prisoners now.'

'What?' George said.

'We are not going to Tangier. Bou Hamra would like to meet you instead.'

'Amastan promised to send us home,' George said.

'Amastan is not here.'

Zdan told the two guards to drop their rifles on the ground and, realising they had little choice, they complied.

'Why are you doing this?' George said.

Harry answered George's question for him. 'Money,' he said.

'It is not just the money, captain. Once Amastan is dead, I shall be Lord of the Atlas.'

'Bou Hamra has offered you Aït Karim?'

'Yes, but not just the kasbah. I would not sell my services quite so cheaply. He has promised to make me his voice and his sword in the whole of the mountains south of Marrakesh once he is Sultan.'

'But first you must prove your loyalty.'

'You see? You do understand.'

'It was you who spiked the cannons.'

A shrug.

'We were so close to going home,' George said. 'I knew it was too good to be true.'

'Perhaps one day you will go back to England. But not today.'

'Where are we going?'

'It is a place called Zagora. It is on the other side of the mountains, on the edge of the desert. It is a rough place, but I'm sure Bou Hamra will make you most welcome there.' He raised his rifle and aimed it at one of his guards. He fired and the man fell backwards from his horse.

The other guard scrambled down from his saddle and fumbled in the dirt for his weapon, while Zdan took his time to reload. The guard had only just picked up his gun when Zdan shot him between the eyes.

'It is unfortunate but I'm not sure I could trust them. Come. Turn your horses. We have a long ride in front of us.'

CHAPTER 47

It was five days' ride, or so Zdan said, probably longer because they would have to avoid Aït Karim and Amastan's patrols. Zdan was courteous, even apologetic. He wished it were otherwise, but really, as practical men, they must understand his situation. He was sure they would do the same, in his position.

'Do the same?' George asked him. 'You mean, become a traitor?'

Zdan seemed surprised by the rebuke. 'A man's first duty is to himself and his family.'

'Have you no shame?'

'The only shame is to lie down at the feet of another man. Bou Hamra was born to be sultan, but his father overlooked him. Should he just accept it? No. I am one heartbeat from being a Kaïd and lord of lords in the Atlas. Do I just carry on doing Amastan's bidding, without complaint?' He shook his head. 'We change our fate, or we die. Is it not the same where you are from?'

They turned around and headed towards the white-capped bastions of the massif, leaving the two dead guards for the kites and the jackals. They were almost accustomed to the rigours by now. High passes led through craggy ravines and dark pine groves, down giddy tracks that clung to the edges of steep cliffs, back the way they had come. It was a depressing climb. They both thought they had left the Atlas behind for good.

There seemed no way back from this.

Zdan made them rise every morning while it was still dark, riding to avoid the heat of the day and Amastan's men. They skirted around the villages and settlements.

They talked little. What was there left to say? George fell into a deep depression; even Mou hardly spoke, a changed boy since the events at Aït Karim.

One morning they reached the crest of a ridge and looked out over a vast and desolate valley. The arid palmetto scrub seemed to stretch away forever on a featureless plain. They descended through wild olive groves and spiky argan trees. When they reached the valley, they were buffeted by a blistering desert wind, the black shale of the Atlas giving way to a wasteland of grit, stones and grey sand.

The heat was breathless, intolerable. The searing breath of the Sirocco came straight from the Sahara, baked them in the saddle, mile after lonely mile. Occasionally they saw a shepherd boy in a filthy *djellaba*, sometimes they got a half-hearted wave, most often the boys turned and ran, using a stick to hurry their charges in front of them. The monotony was relieved occasionally by the lonely white dome of a saint's tomb, shaded by the twisted branches of a wind-blasted fig or olive tree.

The Atlas lay on one side, a distant barrier of immense limestone peaks, capped with snow; the southern Atlas lay on the other, a forbidding rampart of black and blood red rock. In front of them, a featureless horizon shimmered in the heat, mile after lonely mile.

They were surrounded by ragged black mountains, a weary track ahead of them, through low black hills. From time to time they glimpsed a gazelle or some wild Barbary sheep so Harry supposed there must have been some tufts of rank grass in the hollows left over from the winter.

The only things that seemed to grow were some sunbaked thorn bushes. Hard to imagine anything surviving long here, Harry thought. Sure enough, they soon started to come across evidence of those who had not survived the journey, the bleached bones of a mule or the whitened skull of a goat, the curled reddish horns protruding from the sand.

On the fourth day, Harry saw a vast blue lake in the distance. After so long without fresh water, he could not wait to reach the shore and spurred his horse into a trot. Trees threw long shadows in the shallows, where a gaggle of women were washing their clothes. The white dome of a saint's tomb nestled among the palms.

When he got close enough, he planned to throw himself down from the saddle and run into the water, fully clothed. They were less than half a mile from it when he realised the oasis was just a sandy waste with a few prickly pear bushes.

He groaned aloud in disappointment.

'We are getting close to Bou Hamra's fortress,' Zdan said. 'It is one of his miracles.'

'It's not a miracle,' George grunted. 'It's just a mirage.'

'Bou Hamra is a great magician, a sorcerer, and sent by God. You will see.'

'How far?' Harry said.

'Not far.'

Later that morning, Harry saw another oasis, at first he supposed it was just another mirage until they were actually riding through it. There were forests of palm trees, and walled gardens of fruit trees, jasmine and roses. There was a handful of stone houses, even a few shops. The green fields were a balm to the soul after the forbidding grey of the desert.

They followed sandy tracks that twisted their way through the thickening palm groves, over countless bright and fast flowing streams.

'There it is,' Zdan said, finally. 'Zagora.'

It looked, from a distance, no more than a sleepy *ksar*, surrounded by groves of date palms, next to a wide and sluggish river. Strings of sad-eyed camels lined the banks, the animals watching them suspiciously as they passed.

'What are we going to do?' George said, as they rode side by side through the oasis.

'Bide our time, I suppose,' Harry said. 'Learn to be patient.'

'We have been in Morocco for almost a year and nothing to show for it. Is that not patience enough?'

'Then we will have to be patient some more.'

'This is all my fault,' Mou mumbled, his horse plodding through the sand behind them.

'Yes,' Harry said. 'It is.'

The fortress was nothing like the ones they had seen in the Atlas. There were just curtain walls of rammed earth and stone, with forbidding flanking towers. It looked more like an Arab city than a Berber one.

Behind it rose the great sand dunes of the Sahara, running east and west, shaped and rolled by the furnace heat of the Sahara winds.

The *ksar* seemed innocuous enough, but as they got closer to the adobe ramparts, Harry quickly revised his impression of the place. Perhaps it was the tribesmen that patrolled the walls, each of them cradling a Martini-Henry rifle; or perhaps it was the string of impaled heads, fixed over the gate by hooking a piece of wire through their ears and nailing them into the wall.

Some of them had fallen, and lay rotting on the ground, where the vultures were busy feasting.

The fortress was protected by a double gateway, separated by a killing ground, so that should an enemy force the outer gate, they would face the deadly assault from the men on the inner ramparts. Judging by the pockmarked walls, it looked to Harry as if they had seen countless battles.

As they rode through the gates, fanatics in filthy sheepskins, glowered at them from the doorways. They must stink in this heat, Harry thought. They entered the medina, with its market stalls domed like beehives. Tuareg tribesmen, with thick black beards and faces stained a deep, indigo blue fingered the pearl-handled daggers in their belts as they passed. A wild-eyed saint, carrying a battle axe and almost naked except for a camel's hair turban, shrieked religious nonsense in the medina. Snake charmers with matted ringlets and mad eyes hissed at the crowds that gathered around them, holding up their wicker baskets and flutes.

The houses were all connected by tunnels and covered alleys to keep out the heat. The maze of *souks* and bazaars opened onto a large square, that surrounded a bone-white saint's tomb. On the far side was a palace, its pink walls and tapering towers decorated with geometric designs.

'We have arrived,' Zdan said. 'Bou Hamra will be most eager to meet with you again.'

A large fountain bubbled at the centre of the court. It was blessedly cool here after the desert. Bou Hamra sat under a royal blue canopy in the shadow of a colonnade, on silk rugs, two slaves fanning him with palm fronds. He was dressed entirely in white, his kaftan embroidered with pearls and emeralds, rings sparkled on every one of his plump fingers. Despite the attentions of his slaves, sweat ran in rivulets from under his face and down both cheeks.

He was a huge man, fleshy and tall, with eyes that seemed too big and too prominent for his head. He selected a date from the silver plate in front of him and put it in his mouth, chewed it slowly.

Zdan approached him, whispered something in his ear. Bou Hamra nodded and waved him away.

A slave announced them.

'Sultan Bou Hamra, Imam of all True Believers and Ruler of Morocco, Descendant of the Holy Dynasty of the Alaouites, the last free ruler of Arab North Africa.'

'All I see is an impostor and his dog,' Harry said.

George groaned and put an arm around Mou's shoulders. It wasn't how he had hoped the conversation would go.

'You would do well to guard your tongue,' Zdan said to Harry.

'I was almost a free man again,' Harry said. He looked at Zdan. 'And now you expect me to bow and scrape? Go to hell.'

'Hell may be provided if you wish.' Bou Hamra got to his feet and approached them. He was of imposing size, a man who was no doubt accustomed to intimidating other men. He brought his face close to Harry's. 'I remember you. You held a rifle to my head.'

'God spared you. I would not have done.'

A sour smile.

Harry heard a low growling, looked around, was startled to see an iron cage under the colonnades on the other side of the courtyard, two beasts pacing around inside. They stank of carrion.

'Do you like them?' Bou Hamra said.

'Lions,' Harry said. 'Your pets?'

'A gift from a local Kaïd.' He clasped his hands across his ample belly and studied him. 'You are the Englishman that the Sultan and Amastan el-Karim prize so highly?'

'Prize? We have been treated like slaves since we arrived in this damned country, and now we have been kidnapped by this scabrous dog.' He looked at Zdan. 'We have had enough of you and your rebellions. We wish to go home.'

Bou Hamra smiled and looked at Zdan. 'He has fire in his belly this one.'

'Yes, but he has his uses.'

'But will he be of any use in the future?'

'What are we doing here?' Harry said.

Bou Hamra ignored the question. He assumed a dramatic pose, theatrically stroking his chin. 'Amastan el-Karim decided to send you back to England. Why would he do something like that? Even Zdan does not seem to know.'

'We had served out our contract.'

'Really? Even though Zdan was able to disarm one of his great guns, he still has the other. And he did not pay out his contract. Zdan says he searched both of your horses and found nothing. Mysterious.'

'We said we had had enough.'

'And he just let you go, like that? It is not like him to be so benevolent.'

'What do you want with us?'

'I need a captain of the artillery.'

'You do not have artillery.'

Bou Hamra settled himself back on his cushions and clapped his hands. A slave brought a silver pot, another placed a glass filled with mint leaves in front of him. After the slave had poured the tea, Bou Hamra sipped at it, sighed, smiled.

'I will give you a contract. I can offer better terms than either the Sultan or Amastan el-Karim.'

'A contract? A contract is worthless in this country. We have had fabulous sums flashed in front of our eyes ever since we got here but so far no one has paid us a single dirham.'

'Then do it because it is the right thing to do. My father was the Sultan of Morocco and I am his eldest son. The throne should have gone to me. Do you not wish to help set this great injustice to rights?'

'The world is full of injustice. Anyway, I was told that the Sultan does not have to hand the throne to his eldest son, only to the one best suited to the job.'

'Who has told you this?

'All I know is that it sounds very much like a story from my own life. I sympathise, but I think you'll find, if you examine your plight a little more closely, your father was probably right about you. It hurts, doesn't it?'

'You know, you surprise me. I thought all artillery officers knew how to test which way the wind was blowing before they sighted their guns. The wind, captain, has shifted in my favour.'

'And it brings a stink with it.'

'I cannot tempt you with justice, or with money?'

'No, you can't.'

'Very well, then you will do it because otherwise your life, both your lives, will be forfeit. That is surely encouragement enough.'

Bou Hamra nodded to one of the slaves who hurried across the courtyard to a pair of large, wooden doors. Two horses and riders were waiting patiently on the other side. As the doors swung open, they rode through, hauling a caisson and an eighty-millimetre cannon. It was so new the bronze barrel flashed gold in the sun and Harry imagined he could smell the black paint fresh on the wheels.

Bou Hamra continued to sip his tea. 'You recognise this?'

Harry swore under his breath.

How did you get it?

'I believe you commanded an entire battery of these when you were with the English army. Or am I misinformed?'

'This is impossible. How did you get it?'

'It cost a great deal of money. Never underestimate another man's greed, captain. Even English officers have been known to open their hearts and their hands to a gift, judiciously offered.'

'The Legion, in Algeria.'

Bou Hamra nodded.

'You know this gun?' George said to him.

'It's one of the latest eighty-millimetre mountain guns. It's a cavalry gun, the same size as our six pounders but it weighs a lot less. It even has an obturator, for sealing the breech.'

'Correct, captain,' Bou Hamra said.

'You have ammunition?

'Not yet. It will arrive shortly. With this gun and with you to train a gun crew and to take command of it, I can take the war to my friend Amastan. Soon I shall be Lord of the Atlas, and after that I will go to Fez and a reckoning with my beloved brother, the Sultan. What do you think?'

Harry turned to George. 'Well?' he said in English.

'I think we have no choice.'

'Really? I think we do. I think we could say that we are entirely sick and tired of being treated like slaves. We are Englishmen and I am damned if I will be ordered around anymore.'

'Harry, we are here for the money. Perhaps this one will actually pay us.'

'No, I won't do it.'

'Harry, this is not our war!'

No, not our war, Harry thought. What is the difference between the Sultan's coin or Amastan's or Bou Hamra's? It wasn't about money anymore. He did have a contract, with Amastan, who had trusted him, could have easily had Mou killed, or mutilated. That must be worth some measure of loyalty.

This had become about more than just money.

Harry turned back to Bou Hamra. 'We say go to hell.'

'Well, the dungeons here are very much like it, and I can give you a taste, if that is what you wish.'

'Is that all part of the contract?'

He smiled. 'You could be valuable to me very soon. Perhaps there are other means of persuasion.' He looked at George, then down at Mou. 'Zdan tells me you are very fond of the boy here.'

'Leave him alone,' George said. 'He has nothing to do with this.'

'Sentiment is a weakness. Isn't it, Zdan?' He nodded to two of the guards. They grabbed Mou and marched him towards the cage. Harry tried to stop them, and more guards rushed in, grabbed his arms, pulled him away.

Mou screamed and fought them, but he was only a child. As the guards got closer, with their little captive, the male lion threw himself against the bars. Dear God. Its claws were almost as long as his forearm. Harry could smell its breath from twenty paces away.

'You have a choice,' Bou Hamra said. 'You can volunteer to be my captain of artillery or you will watch the little boy be consumed before your eyes. You know, sometimes it is very quick. Other times, I have known for the lions to eat away half a man before he stops moving. So captain, what is it to be?'

'Please Harry,' George said. 'Please.'

Harry looked at Bou Hamra and nodded.

'Good. I knew you were a man of reason.' He nodded to the guards who dragged the boy back from the cage.

'Let him go,' Harry said.

'I think not. The boy will stay with me, as my hostage. He is your guarantee of good service until my campaign against Amastan is over. Do we understand each other?'

'I'm going to kill you,' Harry said.

Bou Hamra laughed. 'No, you won't. You will want to, and you will talk about it, but you won't. It is not your destiny. Take them away.'

The guards grabbed them by the arms and manhandled them away. They were taken inside the tower, hauled up the stairs and thrown inside a narrow room stinking of fear and sweat and the all the bodies that had been here before, alive or dead.

And the door slammed shut behind them.

CHAPTER 48

They looked around, at the dank earthen floor and sweating stone walls. There was nothing in the room except two rusted buckets and, Harry suspected, the odd scorpion. Just a meagre pile of straw for sleeping, and one small window, overlooking a walled courtyard. It was breathlessly hot.

'Not quite the palace in Marrakech,' George said.

'But better than Lambeth.'

'Why did you have to antagonise that man? Does it matter who we work for, as long as someone finally rewards us for our efforts?'

Harry threw himself on the floor, his back against the wall. 'I'm sorry, George. I hate to say this, and if you laugh, I will understand. But I think, in the end, it came down to a matter of principle.'

'You could have found a better time to discover principles, Harry.' George examined the contents of the buckets. One was empty, the other was half full of greasy grey water. 'I believe one is for washing in. The other is for our more basic comforts.'

'We'd best remember which is which.'

George slumped down on his haunches next to Harry. 'Do you think he really would have given Mou to the lions?'

'I do not doubt it for a moment. He's mad. You can see it in his eyes.'

'The Sultan's vizier said he was an impostor. Yet he seems convinced he is the real Sultan. Do you think it's true?'

'I think a man can convince himself of anything, whether it's true or not.'

'How in God's name are we going to get out of here?'

'We wait. We'll get our chance.'

George leaned his head back against the wall. 'You must hate me. For dragging you into this.'

'Two thousand pounds dragged me into this, not you. If I hate anyone, it's the Sultan, who passed us around as if we were slave girls. And Zdan. He was the one who sold us out.'

'I don't understand. I thought family was everything to these people.' He turned and looked at Harry. 'Where do you think Bou Hamra got that cannon?'

'There's a French officer, somewhere in Algiers, who is preparing to resign his commission and live happily off the proceeds for the rest of his life, if he avoids prison. Or there's another possibility.'

'What's that?'

'That the French government decided to turn a blind eye to this piece of illegal trade. No doubt they'd like to destabilise Morocco so they can have it for themselves.'

'You're such a cynic, Harry. As if the President of France would consider such a thing. What about the ammunition?'

'Case shot to use on the battlefield isn't hard to get. But if he's going to attack the kasbah at Aït Karim, he'll need eighty-millimetre shells. That will take deep pockets. Though if he has money to buy the latest cannon, I'm sure he can find money for the ammunition.'

'So, in the end we are to go against Amastan and the Sultan. Should we care? Neither of them played right with us.'

'Perhaps. It does not serve to think about it.'

'Once again, we are pawns in the game.'

'We were never pawns, we always had a choice. The first choice was in the Crown, take the money, or not take the money. After that, the rest was just fate and circumstance.'

'I suppose you have a point.'

'What are you going to do with your share.'

'I am going to build a hospital.'

'What?'

'I promised my father I would do it.'

'A hospital?'

'It was his idea. He wanted to set up a children's hospital in the East End of London. He had already found some rich benefactors to underwrite the cost, just before he died. I'd already promised him that I would help him.'

'You were to be the doctor?'

'That was the plan.'

'And what happened?'

'After he died, the benefactors decided I was too young and inexperienced and withdrew their support. They did not have quite the same confidence in my abilities to run things.'

'I see.'

'Well, that's not quite all of it. He owed quite a lot of money when he died. He may have dreamed of building a hospital for the poor but in the end, he could not even stop his own creditors from taking his house. It left my mother penniless. She had to go to live with my sister and I have spent the last two years paying off his debts.'

'But your father was a respected man.'

'He gambled, Harry. Just like you. Not as publicly, perhaps and he didn't lose as spectacularly. But his debts were significant.'

'Ah.'

'For all his faults, I did not want his dream to die with him. This was why I wanted the money, it is why we are here. You were simply a means to an end. I am sorry. Kill me if you wish.'

Harry laughed. 'You shame me, George. You are a far better man than I'll ever be. I want money for booze women and cards, and you want it to save little children. I have no idea how we came to be friends. How much does it cost to build a hospital anyway?'

'Two thousand pounds would have been enough for thirty beds.'

'What about nurses, equipment, supplies?'

'My father had worked out how we could balance the books. We could have had half paying patients, another half of the beds would be for people who could not afford proper medical care, those without means, and the children of the poor.'

'You really thought you could do this?'

'I just had to convince a few rich philanthropist types to donate money for a place on the board, persuade some local companies to donate. If I had enough seed money, it would convince them to give me the rest.'

'And for this you went looking for a burned-out drunk playing baccarat in an illegal gambling den.'

'Not burned out, Harry. You were just resting.'

'Astonishing.'

'What now, do you think?'

'I suppose we just go along with things until we see a chance to escape. Between now and Marrakesh there will be an opportunity and we will take it. Until then we have a single, simple task. We must endure.'

CHAPTER 49

Dawn came slowly, a purple stain behind the mountains, the dark reforming to cedar trees and low scrub. Somewhere down in the valley, Amastan heard a dog barking, the first plaintive song of the *imam* from the balcony of the minaret.

They had run out of the Englishman's elixirs and last night the *djinn* had returned, with vengeance, repaying her doubly for keeping him at bay for so long. Last night had been bad; three times Wafa had fallen, her mouth foaming, eyes rolled back in her head. The spirit had shaken her frail body like a dog shaking a bird in its jaws. Amastan could hardly bear to watch.

When Wafa died, as she surely must, and soon, there would be no one to share her predicament. She would be truly alone.

She would also be free, without her sister to care for, she could do as she wished. What would she do with this freedom?

She went to the window and stared at the moon hurrying behind dark clouds, wondered if the English captain could see sky or stars. Her spies had brought her news of Zdan's betrayal. Had Bou Hamra killed the two Englishmen or was he saving them for some other purpose?

She would know soon enough. Her *chaush* should be here soon.

Perhaps it would be better if the captain were dead. Then perhaps she might stop thinking about him .

Years since she had had such thoughts. It only started again when he had arrived at Aït Karim. Why him, this stranger, this foreigner? Why had he inspired so much turmoil in her? Perhaps it was his strangeness that had set him apart and had caught her in unguarded moments.

She had even dared to daydream about what it might be like to be a woman with him, not for ever, just for a time. After all, when she was done, she could send him away again, back to England, far away, where his knowledge of her could not hurt her. It was a fantasy, no more. But by toying with such an idea, she had allowed it to insinuate itself into her thoughts, and once it was there, she had been unable to rid herself of it.

She heard her father's voice: *You made a choice, you gave me your word, you gave your word to your sisters, you promised would always keep faith with it.*

But something had stirred in her, a *djinn*, like the one that had afflicted Wafa.

You cannot think about this, Amastan, you will risk everything. He could destroy you, and your sisters, your father's entire legacy.

This was a weakness she was supposed to keep hidden. She could not allow herself to linger on it. She had defeated her nature once, and now she must do it again.

She heard a shout from the walls, the clatter of horse's hooves as the guards threw open the gates. Soon after, there were footsteps on the stone stairs that led up from the courtyard. She turned her mind away from uncomfortable thoughts and in moments she was once again Lord of the Atlas.

The rider hurried in, he was filthy and stank of sweat and horse. He executed a hurried *temennah* and went to one knee. 'My Lord.'

'Did you find them?'

'We did, my Lord. The caravan set out from the French fort at Aïn Sefra. We found them two days' ride from Zagora. They had camels and twenty cases of shells.'

'You seized them all?'

'We did.'

'And Bou Hamra's men?'

'Even now, God is welcoming them to Paradise.'

'I doubt they will find much of a welcome there, but that is not our business. You have done well. Go and rest now. There is food waiting for you in the kitchens. You will be rewarded.'

The rider left.

She closed her eyes and let out a long sigh of relief. Two days from Zagora! If the caravan had got through, it might have turned the tide of the rebellion. She could not afford for this to continue much longer. With every passing season, Bou Hamra became more impudent, grew in strength.

It was time to end this.

CHAPTER 50

Zdan licked his lips. His mouth was so dry, he felt like he had been in the desert for a month. Someone had to tell Bou Hamra this news. He wished it wasn't him.

Bou Hamra awaited him under the colonnades, seated on a divan, under a red silk canopy. There were layers of silk rugs under his feet. Two slaves fanned him with palm fronds.

Zdan looked at the two lions. Pray God he does not throw me in there as punishment for bearing this news.

He executed a brief *temennah*, went to his knees, put his forehead to the carpets. I should rather stay like this forever, never have to look up into those mad, terrible eyes.

'Well?'

'The news is not good, lord.'

'Get on with it.'

'Our caravan was intercepted by Amastan's men.'

'And?'

'All lost, except for two men.'

Silence. He finally dared a glance. Bou Hamra was peeling a fig. 'The shells for the cannon?'

'Taken.'

'Then we shall have purchase more.'

Exactly what he was afraid he would say. 'That may not be possiblc.'

Bou Hamra tossed the fig aside. 'I do not think I wish to hear this.'

'The French major, Bartulin. He was recalled to Oran and arrested. He has been sent back to France to face a court martial.'

'They can hang him by his male parts for all that it matters to me. He was vital to our success. How was he betrayed?'

'Someone in Fez heard of our arrangement with him and sent word to the French.'

'The Vizier.'

'He has spies everywhere. The French knew about Bartulin, they may even have encouraged him. Now they are trying to cover it up.'

Bou Hamra strode across the court to the lions' cage, slammed the flat of one massive hand against the bars. The beasts roared and threw themselves at their prison, and he stepped back, laughing at their impotent rage. When they retreated, he did it again, taunting them. Finally, he turned around and kicked Zdan in the ribs, sending him sprawling.

'Could you not have foreseen this?'

'There was nothing I could have done, lord! I spiked the cannons at Aït Karim, I stole the two Englishmen from under Amastan's nose. What more do you want from me?'

Bou Hamra stood over him, scowling. 'I emptied the treasury for that cannon, and without the shells, it is useless to us. What good are the English officers now?' He drew breath. 'No one is to know of this. I have sent messengers all through the *bled es siba,* calling for men to join me in my war on Amastan el-Karim. We will go on as if nothing has happened. Now, get out of my sight.'

Harry and George heard the noise swelling during the afternoon, something was happening outside. They were slumped, bathed in their own sweat, sick from gut rot and lack of water, neither of them had the strength to move. Finally, Harry dragged himself upright. If he stood on his toes, he could just make out the courtyard below their window.

The yard was empty, but it sounded as if there was a vast crowd on the other side of two ancient wooden gates.

Harry slid back down onto his haunches.

'What is it?' George mumbled.

'I don't know.'

Towards evening, they heard digging. Harry again forced himself back to his feet, peered outside.

'It's Mou,' Harry said.

George struggled to his feet. The little boy was down there with Bou Hamra, they had dressed him in fresh white linen robes. Half a dozen slaves were breaking up the dirt with spades.

'What is he doing?' Harry said.

'They're digging a grave,' George said. 'Mou!'

The little boy heard him, looked up and waved. He didn't seem troubled. Bou Hamra had his arm around him, as if he were a favourite son.

The slaves finished digging the hole, it was no more than a foot or so, and Mou happily clambered down into it, and lay there, on his back. Bou Hamra handed him a long piece of bamboo, which he put in his mouth, and another, which he put to his ear. Bou Hamra stood back, and the slaves started to fill sand and dirt back into the hole.

'They're burying him alive,' Harry said.

George slumped back down the wall, put his head in his hands.

'There's something not right here. Why isn't Mou putting up a fight? He's not struggling, it's like he's in on it.'

When they were done, Harry could just see the ends of the two pieces of bamboo protruding from the sand. The slaves used brooms to brush sand and dirt back over the hole, then they were hurried out by the guards.

The sky was getting darker now. Bou Hamra turned and nodded to the men at the gate. They threw them open.

The crowd flooded in.

There were hundreds of them, tribesmen most of them, wild-eyed men carrying ancient flintlocks, curved knives in their belts. They were hard-eyed and weather-bitten, some in rough cloaks trimmed with bright tassels of wool, like Egyptian *fellah*, others looked like cattle thieves from the Rif, braided locks hanging down on one shoulder. Bou Hamra's guards ushered them into a vast semi-circle around their Kaïd, who stood slightly in front of the hole where they had put the boy, his enormous bulk and white kaftan hiding the freshly disturbed dirt and the tips of the two bamboo tubes.

'What the hell is this?' Harry said.

'Zdan said the people down here think Bou Hamra has magical powers. Perhaps it's some sort of show.'

Harry's leg muscles were cramping. He rested them a moment, when he looked again, flaming torches had been lit all around the walls. The flames threw dancing shadows around the court as the sun sunk below the fortress walls. Night fell quickly in the desert. Soon it would be completely dark, it would disguise whatever trickery he was planning.

Bou Hamra started to address the crowd. He had a deep booming voice, and Harry and George could hear him clearly, even from high above in the tower. He began to tell his audience that not only was he the rightful Sultan of Morocco, eldest son of the previous *seigneur*, but that he was descended directly from the Prophet, on his mother's side, and had been gifted with magical powers.

'Join me now in my struggle to regain my rightful position on the throne of Morocco and displace the Sultan's dog Amastan el-Karim as

Lord of the Atlas. Those that do will receive protection from Allah Himself, who will ensure them and their seed riches and prosperity for generations to come. For I have magical powers, granted me by God.'

One of his audience got to his feet, one of the Tuareg Blue Men. He pointed a finger at Bou Hamra and shouted: 'You do not have magical powers! This man is an impostor!'

I'd wager that man had been planted there by Bou Hamra, Harry thought, to rouse the sceptics in the crowd.

Bou Hamra put his hand to his heart, a well-practiced theatrical gesture. 'I do not lie. I can do things that can make you gasp with astonishment, had I the mind to.'

'Talk is cheap! What sort of things?'

'If I wish, I can speak with the dead.'

The man turned to the crowd. 'Speak with the dead? Whoever heard of such a thing?' He turned back to Bou Hamra. 'Only a true descendant of the Prophet could do such a thing.'

'Yet it is true.'

'Prove it!'

'Ah, I would, but it tires me greatly, it requires spiritual energy such as you cannot imagine. Besides, all these men here do not wish to witness such a cheap trick.'

At that, at least a dozen more were on their feet, waving their arms and demanding that Bou Hamra prove to them that he was a divine magician, for they indeed wished to judge for themselves.

'Go on,' they shouted. 'Show us how you raise the dead!'

The whole charade had been well orchestrated. Harry felt his skin crawl.

'It exhausts me to waste my powers on such frivolities. Is this really necessary?'

Half the audience were screaming at him now.

'Very well!' he shouted back at them. 'If that's what you wish!' He spread his hands and raised his face to the darkening sky. Giant shadows danced around the walls. 'Help me, O God, to still these worthless doubters, and show them your will in this!'

He stood quite still, his eyes closed. After a while, the shouting died down and the audience resumed their seats in the circle around him. He waited until there was complete silence, except for the crackling of the torches on the walls.

'I can hear someone,' he said.

'He's making it up!' the Blue Man said, and he turned to the crowd and laughed.

'It is a child, a small boy! He says he is buried somewhere here, near where I stand.'

He waited, long enough for the crowd to again start fidgeting.

'Child,' Bou Hamra called, his voice quavering with emotion. 'Are you here, can you hear me?'

Harry heard Mou answer, his voice muffled through the bamboo tube: 'What do you want of me, Lord?'

'Is your name in life Baragsen al-Nour?'

'That was my name in life.'

'What are you doing here? What do you want?'

'I was murdered long ago and buried here by my wicked stepfather, so that my rightful inheritance could go to his son. I cannot rest until justice is restored, here and everywhere in all Morocco.'

'One day soon, with the help of Almighty God, all such wrongs will be made right again. Sleep in peace, my child.' Bou Hamra stepped back, so that his huge bulk was directly over Mou's grave, his foot covering the bamboo tube.

'No!' Harry said. 'No, you bastard! You godless bastard!'

'What's happening?' George said.

'He's going to suffocate him!'

Harry and George clawed at the bars, screaming at the top of their voices at Bou Hamra, hardly words, trying to get the attention of the rabble watching him. The door crashed open and three of the guards rushed in and dragged them away. They had stout sticks and used them expertly. They smashed the rods into Harry's ribs, around his head, over his back, until he went down and curled into a ball on the floor of the cell. George tried to intervene, so they beat him as well.

When they were done, they went out again.

'Stay away from the window,' one of them said and they heard the key in the heavy iron lock.

After a while, George dragged himself upright again. 'Are you alright?' he said.

Harry sat up. There was blood streaming from a cut over his eye, which had already swollen closed. The rods had torn strips from his shirt, and there were red welts over his ribs and shoulders.

'Mou,' Harry said.

George helped him stand. By the time they got back to the window, Bou Hamra was finishing a long diatribe against his father, the previous Sultan, for his injustices against his family and against the people of Morocco, as well as the wickedness of the man they called Amastan el-Karim, and his offence against the people of the Atlas and against God himself.

When he had finished, there was a long silence, and then one of the men in the audience got to his feet. 'That is all very well,' he said. 'But what of this Baragsen al-Nour?'

'Who?'

'The dead child. You said he was buried here.'

Bou Hamra looked mystified, as if he had quite forgotten all about the boy. He summoned slaves, making it seem an afterthought, had them start digging around the place he had been standing, deliberately sending them to one wrong spot, then another. Finally, just as the crowd were growing restive, they pulled Mou's lifeless body from its shallow grave. One of the slaves carried it to Bou Hamra and put it in his arms.

'Is this what you wanted to see?' he said. 'Now are you convinced?' He turned to the crowd as if they were insufferable for their lack of faith, as if they had somehow killed the boy themselves. In a way, Harry thought, they had.

A sigh passed through the vast crowd, like a ripple on a lake.

The man who had called him an impostor got to his feet once more. He pointed to Bou Hamra. 'Hail the rightful Sultan of Morocco,' he said and fell to his knees, touching his forehead to the earth.'

One by one the rest of the audience followed him, until every man in the crowd had prostrated themselves in front of him. Bou Hamra, with Mou's lifeless body in his arms, smiled and nodded his head.

CHAPTER 51

It was just after dawn when the guards came for him. His hands were tied behind his back with hemp, and he was dragged out.

Bou Hamra was waiting for him in his apartments. He had abandoned the pure white kaftan for something a little more elaborate. His brocaded cloak was embroidered with pearls and sapphires, there were thick silver rings on all his fingers.

He seemed, if anything, jolly.

The room where they had brought him was both remarkable and unexpected. It was filled with clocks, hundreds of them; ornate Boulle mantel clocks, mahogany longcases, several oak Renaissance grandfather clocks, dozens of cuckoo clocks. He saw one that was made from bronze, a Berber warrior on a camel, the shield on the saddle forming the face of the timepiece. They were all set to different times, and the sound of the mechanisms ticking over was deafening. Every few seconds one of the clocks chimed the hour or quarter hour.

Bou Hamra turned from the window and regarded him down the length of his nose. 'Captain Delhaze. I apologise. It seems you have been ill used by my guards. I hope your bruises are not troubling you too greatly this morning?'

'I'll live.'

A hearty laugh. 'I love an optimist. They tell me you were trying to disrupt my performance last night. I am sorry. That could not be allowed.'

'Did you enjoy killing the boy?'

'Did I enjoy it?' A shrug. 'I felt nothing either way about it. He served a purpose. He was dust in the wind, after all. And it was a quick death, many go to Paradise in much harder ways. You seem upset? Is it the beating?'

Harry didn't answer him.

'You're a man of few words. I thought Englishmen liked to talk.'

'I'm not going to waste my breath on you.'

'No, breath should not be wasted. Ask little Mohammed, yes?'

'He thought it was a game, didn't he? He didn't know you were going to suffocate him at the end.'

'Of course he didn't know. Otherwise, he would not have complied.'

'What did you offer him?'

'I said that if he helped me play our little game as I had showed him, then I would let you and your friend go free. He believed me. He was very eager to please. A fine little slave you had there.'

'He wasn't a slave.'

'Whatever he was, he doesn't matter now.' He extended an arm, a curator showing off his treasures. 'Do you like my collection?' The mantel clocks were displayed on low tables, others were nestled in niches on the walls or on the sills of the windows. 'Look at this, Sèvres porcelain from the nineteenth century. It was made in France. Beautiful, isn't it?'

'It's just a clock.'

'No, not just a clock. Not at all. Do you know why I have such a fascination for timepieces, captain?'

'No, but you're going to tell me.'

'It reminds me of the only thing that is important to us all in life. Time. Yet we all waste our greatest treasure. We live as if we have forever, yet with every movement of the mechanism in one of these tiny machines, another moment is lost.'

'You said that if we agreed to help you maintain and fire the cannon, you would not harm the boy.'

'Ah. Circumstances have changed. I no longer need your compliance. But you need mine, if you wish to keep the days and years God has granted you.'

'Do I?'

'Oh, yes. So if I have no further need of you, what should I do with you? Do you have any suggestions?'

'You could let us go. If we serve no further purpose, why bother with us?'

'Let you go?' He pretended to consider this. 'So you can ride back to Amastan el-Karim and help him aim his cannon at the walls of my fortress?'

'You could at least let my friend go. He knows nothing about artillery. He is a magician like yourself.'

'No, not quite like me, I don't think.' He ran a finger down the polished grain of a mahogany grandfather clock. 'Do you know the game of chess?'

'I have played it. My father enjoyed the game.'

'Did you excel at it?'

'Not really. Even my brother used to beat me.'

'You prefer games of chance, with playing cards, don't you? It is how you spent a great deal of your time when you left the army.'

'It seems you know a lot about me.'

'I do not know how you deal with adversity. What about this, we will combine our favourite occupations. Chess is mine, yours is to wager. Toy with the geometry of chance. Yes? I will play a game of chess with you. If you win, I will let your friend go. If you lose, he will die. There. What do you think of that?'

'What I think is that the odds are in your favour.'

'Of course. Why should it be otherwise? You are my prisoner, after all, so I would be a fool to make the game fair. Killing an infidel will raise my prestige among the people here. I shall forego that enhancement to my reputation if you will entertain me for an hour. I may still win but the outcome is by no means certain. Perhaps you will defy the odds.'

'Do I have a choice?'

'Does it seem to you like there is a choice?'

Harry looked around the room. 'Where is the chess board?'

'Well, it's not in here. You don't think I would be as conventional as that. Do you?'

Harry was dragged through the palace, led out to a courtyard of chequered black and white marble, surrounded by shaded arcades. One of the guards cut the hemp rope that tied his hands, and he was pushed forward, in his bare feet.

'Do you like my invention?'

He looked up. Bou Hamra appeared at the gallery above, took his ease on some pillows under a red canopy, which shaded him from the worst of the sun.

The marble had been laid in a pattern of sixty-four squares, eight on each side, after a chessboard. Four lines of black slaves waited in the sun, each having taken their place on one of the marble squares, at opposing ends of the court. They had been dressed to represent the pieces on a chessboard, in black robes or white. There were *askaris*, in nothing more than loincloths; kings and counsellors in silk turbans; elephants and horses and kasbahs in elaborate headdresses, to denote their rank in the game.

Armed guards ringed the walls in the arcades around them.

The sun had only just risen over the walls, a fiery gold, but the shadows were receding quickly and already he could feel the heat building, and the stones warming beneath his feet.

Above them, Bou Hamra sipped on a sherbet. 'The imams forbid using the likeness of a man on chess pieces. I have found my own creative way to overcome their objections. This wretch here is your Kaïd. I admit he looks ridiculous in his jewelled turban and white robes, but we must all make do. The men in the painted headdresses with ivory tusks are your war elephants. The men holding saddles are your cavalry. Knights, you call them in England. Are we ready to begin?'

Harry had to shield his eyes against the sun to look at Bou Hamra. 'As you wish.'

Bou Hamra shouted an instruction, and one of the white *askaris* took two steps forward.

'Now it is your move,' Bou Hamra called down to him. 'I am looking forward to the game!'

'You have the advantage, you can see the board from above,' Harry said.

'Yes, you are right. Life is never fair. If it were, I should be Sultan of Morocco and you would be home in England with two thousand pounds! Get on with it.'

Harry went to one of the *askaris*, took him by the shoulders and moved him a step forward. He was sullen and hard to shift.

'You surprise me,' Bou Hamra said. 'I thought you should be more aggressive, more combative. I shall have to think about this.' He thought about it while he breakfasted, his slaves bringing him pancakes, honey, fruit and more sherbets. The sun continued its steady climb up the sky, heating the marble, he felt it start to burn his skin.

'Is there no time limit?' Harry called up to him.

'Not for me.'

Bou Hamra waited until he had finished his third sherbet, then looked down into the courtyard and snapped an order to one of the *askaris*. The man was wearing a headdress in the likeness of a horse. He squeezed between the two *askaris* in front of him and took a position on one of the black squares.

Harry took another of the *askaris* and pushed him forward one square. The man was also reluctant to move.

He heard Bou Hamra laugh. 'It looks as if you are preparing for a long siege. Is this how you won all your battles, by being so meek?' He rapped out another command and another of his *askaris* took two steps forward. 'I am coming for you, Englishman. I hope you remember what it is at stake if you lose.'

'Let it be me if I lose!'

'For me, it is far more interesting this way. Your move.'

Harry tried desperately to remember everything his father had taught him about the game. He wished now that he had paid more attention, finally there might have been something his father had said that might have been worthwhile.

He turned to his shuffling ranks of men, chose the one wearing the ludicrous tusks and trunk of a war elephant and moved him forward to fill the space left by one of the *askaris*.

Harry had a plan now, a string of moves he remembered from the interminable rainy afternoons in his father's study in Lyon.

He waited. Bou Hamra rapped out another command and one of his cavalrymen in white shuffled forward. Harry immediately took another of his *askaris* by the shoulder and shuffled him forward.

When he looked up, he saw one of Bou Hamra's counsellors whispering in his ear. The big man listened for a moment then got to his feet.

'I am sorry, captain. You must excuse me. I have business to attend to. We shall finish the game when I return.' And he got to his feet and disappeared back into the kasbah.

And so they waited.

The sun continued to climb the sky. Every time he tried to move into the shade, the guards blocked his way. He had nothing to protect his head, he could feel the sun burning his scalp and face.

He looked around at the chessmen, they had hardly moved, they seemed resigned to this, the sweat gleaming on the bare backs of the *askaris*. A couple swayed on the spot, he thought they would fall. The guards prodded them with their swords, there was no mistaking the threat. They would fall at their own peril.

How long did they stand there, in the baking heat like that? Harry had no idea. He could feel the marble scorching the soles of his feet. His eyes hurt from the glare. He didn't know how much longer he could stay upright.

He didn't see Bou Hamra return, suddenly heard his voice, shouting a command to one of his chessmen.

A white elephant shuffled forwards, almost up to the lines of his *askaris*. The man winced as he put his foot on the hot marble. His hands clenched to fists at his sides, and his face contorted in pain.

Bou Hamra clapped his hands. 'Your move!'

His plan, what was his plan, the series of moves his father had taught him? He couldn't remember. His thirst, the sun, they were all he could think about. He moved his counsellor, 'bishop' his father had called it, Bou Hamra moved his.

Harry took his other counsellor by the shoulders, moved him four squares, to displace one of the white *askari* pawns. The man stared at him, his eyes went wide, his face melted into dismay. He shook his head from side to side.

'No,' he said.

'What?' Harry said to him.

One of the guards stepped out of the shade and took off the man's head with a practised sweep of his sword. The head rolled across the marble, and blood gouted out of the severed neck veins. The man's headless body had barely stopped its twitching when other slaves ran on to remove it, and slave women with rags fell on their knees to mop up the blood.

'Did I not explain that to you?' Bou Hamra said. 'I am remiss. In some ways this is a real battle, you see. Your lieutenant is risking his life, why should a few worthless slaves not risk theirs?'

One of the guards picked up the *askari's* head, took it to the rampart and tossed it over the side.

How many innocent men will he make me kill to save George, Harry thought?

Do I have the right to do that, do I even have the nerve?

He staggered in the sun.

'I can see it will soon be too hot to play,' Bou Hamra said. 'We should hurry with our game.' He called down to his chessmen, and one of the slaves, holding a grilled piece of iron to signify the Kasbah, moved a step to the side. He stared right into the face of Harry's counsellor. He saw the man's Adam's apple bob in his throat. He wonders if he will be next, Harry thought.

The counsellor pleaded with him with his eyes. When my father talked of sacrificing a chess piece in order to win the game, he never imagined this, Harry thought. He took him by the shoulders and led him to the side of the marble chessboard, out of harm's way. The man almost collapsed with relief.

Above him, Bou Hamra rapped out an order, and one of the white elephants advanced across the courtyard, to halfway. They are crowding in on me, Harry thought. What does the board even look like? One thing to touch pieces on a board, another to stand here with your throat parched and your flesh burning in the sun and try to understand what is happening.

He went back to the ranks of his chessmen, tried to remember his father's strategies. He went to one man, then another, then another. He needed water. He needed to get out of the sun. He hopped from foot to foot.

I can't think.

He grabbed a tall, stooped man in an elephant headdress and propelled him forward.

Bou Hamra was on his feet now. He leaned on the parapet and a slave hurried forward with a silk parasol to shade him from the sun. Two of his pieces, his Kaïd and his kasbah exchanged their places. What had his father called it, 'castling the king.'

He reached for the nearest man, an *askari*, pulled him two squares across the marble, even though the man was shaking his head, pleading with him, *no, please, please.*

'You are a brave man,' he heard Bou Hamra say above him. 'A bold move but a dangerous one.'

He nodded, and one of the white *askaris* shoved the man Harry had moved off his square. The guards moved in almost languidly to dispatch him. The slave tried to run, and they cornered him against the courtyard wall and slaughtered him.

'I don't think you are thinking clearly. I fear the sun has got to you.'

What must I do now? Harry thought. If I don't try and win this, George is going to die. If I do try, more men will die.

Do I play God, decide who that will be?

'Your move, captain. The longer you take, the longer you stand there in the sun and these men will die anyway, of thirst, or exhaustion. It doesn't take long, not here, not in summer. If you lose, your friend will die anyway. The future is still in your hands. Tick tock. What will it be?'

Harry pulled one of his black *askaris* on to the square diagonal to him. The white *askari*, whose place he was to take, refused to move. His shoulders shook, and he started to wail.

The guards seemed oblivious to it. One slash to take off his head and it was done. Harry's *askari* grimaced as his face was sprayed with the man's hot blood. The game was delayed once more for the removal of the body and the mopping up of the gore.

Around him he heard several of the other slaves start whispering prayers to whatever god or gods they believed in. A pool formed around a kasbah's legs as he lost control of his bladder.

Harry's *askari* had only just wiped the blood from his face when he saw one of Bou Hamra's horses coming for him, nudging him from his spot. There was a collective groan from the men around him as the guards dispatched him with the same casual efficiency as they had the others.

'Come captain, you kill more men than this with one shell from your artillery. Why so pale? Is it worse killing a man when you can see him than when you can't? The result is the same.'

Harry put his hands on his knees, vomited bile onto the marble. He felt light-headed. The thirst, the sun, or his role in the barbarous slaughter going on around him?

Harry straightened, pointed to his 'Kaïd' and the kasbah on the back row of his side of his chessboard, and the two men shuffled their places.

'Ah, finally you have decided to castle. A wise move. You believe you are saving the life of this poor slave in front of your Kaïd. But a bold commander is prepared to sacrifice for victory.'

He barked an order to the man with the horsehead. The man shook his head and started to back away, two guards stepped in, they each grabbed an arm and dragged him forward two squares and then a step to the side to nudge an *askari* from his place. The poor man fell to his knees, held his hands outstretched to Bou Hamra, begging for mercy.

One of the guards slashed his throat with a knife and dragged him to the edge of the court by his hair even before he had finished bleeding out. Harry heard the men behind him start a high-pitched keening, wailing to their gods.

And so it went on. A scream, another gout of blood, one of the white *askaris* retched on the marble, more work for the slave girls. The guards washed their swords in the fountains.

Harry stared at the bubbling water: gore, thirst, all mixed together in his head. He couldn't think anymore. This had to end.

He barely knew what he was doing anymore. Two more men died, horribly. Bou Hamra's counsellor advanced. Harry's own counsellor stood at the far end of the court, shaking with terror, alone, and facing three of Bou Hamra's white men, two *askaris* and one of his kasbahs. Harry hobbled across the marble and dragged him back to stand next to his own Kaïd.

'Are you being tactical or sentimental?' Bou Hamra said, above him. 'I think perhaps you have lost your initiative, captain. Do you wish to concede and save more lives?'

Harry shook himself to try and clear his head. So bright in the courtyard he could barely see, yet his brain felt so thick it was like trying to peer through the fog.

Another of the white *askaris* advanced towards him.

'How many more men will die for your friend? The choice is up to you.'

By instinct Harry moved the man in front of him, the one in black holding the iron grille, moved him to the side to cut off the opposing *askari's* advance.

'You are not thinking clearly, captain. Or perhaps I am being unfair, I really left you no other choice, did I? Elephant, take his kasbah from him.'

The poor man in front of him dropped the grille on his toes and fled to the side of the courtyard. The guards went after him, but he was too fast, he circled and circled, searching desperately for a way out. Finally one of the soldiers caught hold of him and stabbed him with his sword, he went down, purplish and yellow viscera tumbling out of him, sizzling on the hot marble.

He writhed in agony, kicking and screaming, until one of the guards mercifully silenced him.

Harry took hold of the counsellor standing beside his Kaïd, a Sudanese with a milk eye, and shoved him towards the man in the white elephant headdress.

The elephant seemed already resigned to his fate. He went down on his knees, closed his eyes and was halfway through his prayer when the guards slaughtered him.

'I'm not finished yet,' Harry shouted up to the balcony. 'Your attack is blunted. Those men died for nothing.'

Then he saw what Bou Hamra had already seen, from his position at the parapet. A nod and the white counsellor moved to his end of the marble chessboard.

'I think, captain, that the game is over. You may continue, of course, and in six more moves, three more men will die. Or you can concede to me now, and let these poor souls continue their miserable lives. The result will be the same. What do you say?'

Harry slumped onto his knees.

'I have decided I am going to throw your friend into the cage with my lions, captain. It will be entertaining to me. And you will watch. That is your forfeit for losing the game.'

Harry didn't hear all of what he said. He had already slumped onto his side, in a stupor. The guards each took an arm and dragged him away.

CHAPTER 52

Harry gasped, fighting for air. He was drowning. He sat up, brought swiftly back to consciousness. He heard laughter. The guards were crowded around, they had thrown a bucket of water over him to rouse him. One of them knelt down, took a handful of hair to force his head back, and poured more water down his throat.

Harry spluttered and rolled on his side, choking.

He tried to move his hands, but they were tied behind his back. They had thrown him in the shade under one of the colonnades. He remembered where he was now, the courtyard where he and George had first been dragged before Bou Hamra.

He shook his head, dear God, the chess game, I lost.

George, where is George?

He managed to shuffle across the marble, work his way into a sitting position against the wall. The guards had lost interest in him by now and left him to it.

His ran his tongue over his lips, they were cracked and blistered. His hands and feet were the colour of boiled lobster. He felt light-headed. He vomited up the water they had given him.

He squinted against the glare, tried to focus. He heard one of Bou Hamra's lions growling, saw it pacing in its cage on the other side of the courtyard. It had a large head with a tattered mane and there were bald patches on its hide, mange perhaps. Such animals weren't meant to be kept in such small cages.

One of the guards started tormenting it, slapping the flat of his sword against the bars. It drew back its lip and snarled. He did it again and it raised a paw and leaped at him, with terrifying speed. The guard took a step back, shocked, one of the razor-like claws missing his face by inches. His friends laughed.

Harry heard someone yelling, another poor wretch being dragged up from the dungeons. He had been beaten by his guards and could no longer stand, so they were dragging him by the arms.

It was George.

'No,' Harry said, and now he remembered Bou Hamra's threat.

Bou Hamra appeared, he seemed pleased. He stopped in front of Harry, hands on his hips. 'Do you remember that night, you aimed your rifle at my head?'

'I should have finished you.'

'And so you would have done if fate had not intervened on my behalf. I have God on my side, captain. Do you not think so?'

'I think you're just lucky.'

'A compliment indeed, coming from you. Zdan has told me how you have lived your whole life riding your luck, so you should know a lot about it. Including how bitter it is when that luck finally runs out.'

'Let me take his place.'

He pretended to consider. 'I could do that. But I won't. I'm sure you understand why.'

He nodded to the two guards who had George and they dragged him towards the cage.

One of the other soldiers unlocked the door to the cage and waited for the signal. When the two men holding George nodded that they were ready, he threw open the door and they hurled him inside. He quickly shut and locked the gate behind him.

George lay quite still at first, only half conscious, then slowly raised himself on to his hands and knees, didn't seem to know where he was. He crawled to the side of the cage, and lay there, curled up, dazed.

Perhaps the lions won't bother with him, Harry thought.

But then the big male raised his head, his nostrils twitched. He gave a flick of his tail and peered at George, almost as if he were too short-sighted to make out what he was. He became perfectly still.

It was the female that got up, her muscles rippling beneath her yellow coat and padded across the cell. She growled once and stopped, a few feet from where George lay.

'What a shame,' Bou Hamra said. 'I fear they are too well fed. I am overstocked with prisoners and errant slaves. Unlike humans, a wild beast is not predisposed to gluttony. Your friend may escape the consequences of your wager, after all.'

He nodded to one of his black slaves who brought him a gold and crystal timer and placed it at his feet. Bou Hamra set it in motion.

'Let us give your friend's fate over to God. Or chance, whatever you wish to call it. When the sand runs through the hourglass, we will take him from the cage, dead or alive. It will be instructive on the nature of time. As I told you, captain, I am a student of such things. A philosopher if you will. Behold: outside of this cage, the passage of time through the hourglass is nothing, we men waste it freely. Inside the cage, this same handful of time is an eternity. For you too, I believe.'

The female stretched out a massive paw and swiped at George' shoulder, curious.

'Stay still,' Harry said. 'Stay still, George, stay still and you have a chance.'

He could hear George sobbing, knew his nerve was going to break.

'No,' Harry said.

George scrambled to his feet, tried to get away. Pure instinct, for there was nowhere to run. The female swiped at him, almost leisurely, and he saw three red stripes open on George' back. He screamed and fell against the bars.

He got up to run again and the lion pounced on him, bringing him down, her jaws clamped around his arm. He heard George' bones snap between her teeth. She shook him from side to side and then tossed him away as if he were too tiresome to bother with. George lay there, crying with pain, his blood pulsing onto the sand.

The lion fell onto her belly and started to play with something she held propped between her front paws. It was George' hand.

Bou Hamra was right. Hearing George cry out, watching him bleed, it seemed like a lifetime, an eternity.

'Time has run out,' Bou Hamra said, looking down at the hourglass. 'Allah has decided he will live, at least for now.' He turned to the guards. 'Let him out of the cage. Take them down to their new accommodations.' He turned to Harry and executed a swift and ironic *temennah*. 'Thank you for the game, captain. You should practice more if you wish to become a master at it. I bid you farewell. I have business to attend to. My men will escort you to your quarters.'

And he walked away, his white kaftan swishing in the sand.

Their accommodations were not the room in the tower where they had spent the last few days; Harry was dragged to his feet, taken down some steep stone stairs below the kasbah and thrown into an *oubliette*. A few moments later, George was thrown in after him. The guards put leg irons on them, shackling them together by the ankles through an iron ring on the wall. The guards walked out, the heavy iron door slamming shut behind them.

It took some time for his eyes to get accustomed to the gloom. A faint light leaked into the cell, through an iron grille in the door. It came from a torch fixed to the wall outside.

There was an unbearable stench, Harry made out a shape lying on the other side of the room. It was a man's body, lying on his back on the bare earth floor, arms outstretched. He was naked, and his head had been cut off, along with his hands and feet. There were black pools of blood thickening on the floor. It looked as if the body had been there at least a day, rotting in the heat. Flies buzzed in thick clouds over the corpse.

There were bloody handprints on the walls, where the guards had wiped the blood off their hands.

'George?' He touched George' shoulder.

'No! Don't touch me. It hurts. Everything hurts. Dear God.'

'George...'

George started to pant, it reminded Harry of a pet dog he had as a child, it got sick one day and it did this, curled itself up into a ball in the corner, panting, and wouldn't let anyone close.

He tried to make out the extent of George' injuries. Half his arm was gone, between his elbow and his wrist, he could see the dull gleam of jagged bone among the blackened mess. There was a deep laceration on his cheek, he could see his teeth where part of the flesh was missing, there were three deep wounds on his back. It was a miracle he was still alive.

It was a miracle he could do without.

'I'm sorry,' Harry said.

'What for?'

'This is my fault.'

Harry told him about the chess game, about the wager, a gamble that had cost the lives of eleven men. It was his *mea culpa*, but when he finally drew breath, he realised that George could not hear him anyway, he had fallen blessedly unconscious, his breath snoring in his throat.

I hope he never wakes, Harry thought. At least he has escaped from the pain.

Harry gave up, lay on his back, exhausted.

We're going to die here, after all we have been through. I always thought we'd find a way out of this. In the mountains, when we were freezing and exhausted, through all those months captive at Aït Karim I believed there would be a way.

Now it's over. We're finished.

He listened to George moaning and twitching on the floor beside him. Harry slipped into a black and exhausted sleep, when he woke, he didn't know if it was night or day. Once he called for the guards, screaming for someone to come and help George. As if they would. They had left them there to rot. That was how they did things here, when killing became too much trouble.

This time, he really was going to die. After all his playful flirting, the devil had finally taken up his invitation. Dying was something that other people did. It still didn't seem real.

He supposed most people thought this way, were as astounded as he was now, when the end came so soon and in such a vulgar manner. Bou Hamra was right with all his clocks and hourglasses. Time never seemed as precious as when you had none left.

His mind wandered, threw up odd memories, things he had not thought of for years. He pictured his grandfather's funeral, hearing his father read the eulogy. He was young then, barely into his teens, he hadn't thought, oh one day that will be me, someone else will have to look sad and try and make sense of what my life meant, even for a brief and fidgeting hour.

There won't even be that, not for me. Just a rumour, passed along. His family, his friends, his former comrades, would shake their heads in the officer's mess at Aldershot or Cairo or Calcutta, or in the church outside Bristol, and say, well I'm not surprised. It would fall to them to pronounce judgment on his life if they even cared to.

What would he think of their opinions if he were there to hear them?

He saw a rat, heard it first, scuffling and squeaking in the dark, attracted by the smell of blood and the heat of their bodies. He kicked at it with his foot, all he had now to defend them with. It scampered away but he knew it would be back as soon as he fell asleep.

At some point, it might have been a few hours later, or a few days; the guards came in to their cell, sewed the headless body in a winding sheet and carried it out. Harry watched them, didn't even speak to them, he knew it was pointless. They wouldn't help them. Bou Hamra meant for them to die.

'How long before we die of thirst?'

He started, had thought George was still unconscious, his breathing had become so shallow he imagined he might already be dead. He even wondered if he was imagining this.

'Not long.'

Harry opened his mouth wide, tried to gulp in the air, so hot, so thin, he felt as if he was suffocating.

'She's married,' George said.

'What? What did you say?'

'Lucy. She's married.'

'How long?'

'Three years.'

Why did he care? He was dying in a dungeon, for God's sake. Surely, none of that mattered any more. 'Does she have children?'

'Two.'

'Ah.'

'Sorry.'

'What for? You were only ever a friend to me, George.'

'Brought you here.'

'My choices brought me here.'

'Promise me.'

'What?'

'Harry… promise me.'

'Promise what?'

'The hospital.'

'You want me to build the hospital? I can't. I know nothing about hospitals, or medicine.'

'Get the money.'

It's the fever, and the pain, Harry thought. He's gone mad. We're both going to die in here. Build a hospital in London? There's no hope of either of us getting out of this.

'Promise.'

Just promise him, Harry, he thought. Give him some peace before he dies. If that's what it takes. What harm will it do? 'I promise George.'

'Say it.'

'I promise you I'll go back to Lyon and help build a hospital with your share of the money. I'll find your father's sponsors and persuade them to help me do it.'

George made a noise, something between a cry and a grunt, and started jerking around the floor, the leg chains rattling in the hoop as he thrashed about.

When the spasm passed, Harry shuffled towards him, he could see his face, shadowed by the glimmer of the torch through the grille, twisted into a ghastly rictus, his teeth bared, his neck twisted back at an unnatural angle.

Harry had seen men die this way in Tonkin. It started with convulsions, then lockjaw and muscle cramps so violent and vicious that you could hear the bones break. He had seen one man's back arched so far that his spine had cracked. It could go on for days, it wasn't until the breathing muscles failed that the poor bastards suffocated to death while the doctors watched on, helpless.

'Tetany,' George whispered.

His friend's mouth was twisted to one side, and he started gurgling and coughing. Please let this be over quickly, Harry thought. He could feel the heat coming off him. He dared a glance at his arm, the stump stank like rotting meat, it was crusted with blood and something vile was oozing out of it.

'Oh Christ,' Harry said.

CHAPTER 53

As the sun moved down the sky over Zagora, a group of travellers set up their camp in the burial ground under the city walls. Their string of camels lay on the ground, dozing in the sand, their packs piled beside them. Nearby, two donkeys foraged, chewing on God alone knew what. Mange-ridden dogs squabbled over the offal lying among the stripped date branches, until they were shooed away by shadowy wraiths in ragged kaftans, beggar children scavenged for scraps among the clouds of fat blue flies.

An Arab cemetery is never a solitary place at evening. Mourners made their way to a fresh grave in the far corner, the women wailing as the men carried their dead wrapped in a white funeral sheet on their shoulders. Three men sat among the jumble of headstones, smoking kif from a long bone pipe.

More caravans trailed in from the desert, camels and donkeys tramping over the long dead, trailed by peddlers hawking amulets and cold, greasy pancakes.

Mabrouk pulled the hood of his *djellaba* over his face, soon it would be dark, he had to hurry. He made his way towards a *katoob*, an ancient tomb of some long-forgotten saint, its dome half-crumbled away. A solitary date palm grew beside it.

The man he was looking for sat beside the embers of a cook fire, stirring the contents of an iron kettle with a stick. He looked unlike any other camel trader he had ever seen. His black *cheiche* hid his face except for his eyes, which were black and watchful. The other men in the caravan sat a little apart, huddled together, watching them.

Mabrouk sat down at the fire. Without a word, the man in the *cheiche* reached into his robe and tossed a leather pouch to him.

He opened the drawstrings and peered inside. Silver enough for five years' salary and a wife. If he lived to spend it. He thought about the lions in Bou Hamra's cage.

'As much again when you have done as we agreed,' the man in the *cheiche* said.

'This is very dangerous.'

'Do you think you could ever earn this much money doing something that was easy?'

'I cannot stay here after it is done.'

'There will be a horse waiting for you. You can ride with us as far as the Atlas, then you must go your own way.'

Mabrouk licked his lips.

The other man shook his head. They said that the devil could read minds. 'Don't even think about betraying me,' he said.

'I am an honest man.'

'I have heard of honest men, though I have never met one. Let me tell you what will happen if you reveal our plan. Bou Hamra will thank you profusely then feed you to his lions, just for thinking about doing what I have suggested. You know this. But if you do as we have agreed, I will rid the world of Bou Hamra before the summer is out and you will spend the rest of your life as a rich man in Fez or Marrakech or wherever you wish to go. Am I clear?'

Mabrouk's mouth was so dry he couldn't swallow. He nodded.

'Good.'

He clambered to his feet and hurried back through the cemetery. Something dropped to the ground in front of him as he made his way through the gates. It was a blackened head.

Tomorrow evening, that might be me, he thought.

He had made his choice. The gold pouch in his cloak felt reassuringly heavy. Now, may God have mercy, all he had to do was pray everything went according to the plan.

CHAPTER 54

Harry heard footsteps outside, muffled voices. He jerked awake.

'They're coming,' he said.

It had taken hour upon hour, rubbing the hemp rope around his wrists against the rough brick to fray enough of it that he could work it loose. By the time he was free his wrists were raw and bleeding. He was inured to the pain by now.

He only had one thing on his mind now. He wasn't going to let George die like this. He was going to find a way to get them out of here.

'Play dead,' he whispered.

He heard the rattle of keys in the lock. This might be their only chance.

'I just need one of them close enough. If I can get my hands around his neck, I'll choke him and take the keys. Trust me. You'll be cutting the ribbon at your new hospital in no time.'

The door creaked open, two shadows stood in the doorway, silhouetted against the torch on the wall behind them. As the gaoler walked in, Harry swung out his free leg to bring him down, threw himself on him, clamped his left hand around his throat, clawed for his knife with the other.

But then they were on him, there must have been four, five of them, pinning his arms, another with his arm around his neck, there were too many of them, he couldn't do it. He howled in rage and frustration.

He swore and bit and kicked with his free leg, though he knew it was pointless, it was their last chance, and it was gone.

One of the men held up the lantern. 'Gag him, tie him, quickly!'

They dragged Harry off Mabrouk. The old gaoler rolled away, choking, and lay on his back, clutching at his throat.

'He nearly killed me.'

'What do you expect? Get up.'

The leader swung the lantern around. Harry was wide-eyed mad, still struggling with his men, couldn't seem to understand that they were there to get him out. His skin was peeled off in places, he had been terribly burned by the sun, and he stank like a wild animal.

The stench wasn't just him. When they had Harry gagged and trussed, the others reeled back, put the sleeves of their robes over their faces, growling in disgust.

The English doctor was dead, had been dead for a day at least by the look of him. His arm was a putrid mess of maggots, and his body was twisted at an unnatural angle, eyes wide, his lips drawn back from his teeth in a silent scream. Who had the captain been talking to? They had heard his voice clearly through the door.

Must have been hallucinating.

Mabrouk fumbled with his keys, unlocked the irons around Harry's ankle. The men half-carried, half-dragged him to the door.

'Quickly,' Mabrouk said.

He locked the door behind them and led the way back down the passage, lantern swinging, shadows dancing crazily on the walls. The stink of death followed them the whole way.

They reached another iron barred door. Mabrouk swung it open, the six men gulped at the warm night air. They were out of the dungeons, at least.

They hurried through the narrow lanes and alleys of the sleeping city, the men at the front and rear nervously fingered their rifles. They reached another door, Mabrouk put a shoulder to it to open it, the creaking of the rusted hinges was surely loud enough to wake the whole Kasbah.

Running, crouching, below a vault of stars. They were outside the city, back in the cemetery, beyond the walls. There were two silhouettes under the date palms, two men waiting with their horses. The men carrying the English captain grunted under the weight, struggled over the rocky ground to get him there. They threw him over the saddle of one of the old horses like an old carpet, and one of them clambered up after him.

They rode hard, to put as much distance as they could between them and Zagora before dawn. A crescent moon floated over the minaret, the east star below it.

CHAPTER 55

They reached a sparse oasis of date palms by a trickle of river. A rider was waiting for them in the shade of the trees.

Amastan came out to meet them. 'Where's the other one?'

The leading rider shook his head.

Amastan went to the man they had tied and thrown over the poll of one of the horses, felt a rush of relief when she saw it was the captain. She snapped an order and her men hauled him down from the horse, pulled the rags out of his mouth and untied him. He could barely stand. They half-carried him down to the water and plunged him into it, stripped off his clothes and scrubbed the dungeon filth off him. He yelled, his skin was red raw in places where it had been burned by the sun. They gave him a fresh shirt, loose trousers, a rough hooded cloak to keep off the sun, and dragged him back into the shade.

Amastan stood over him. What a mess. There were pink blotches on his face, hands, and feet where the skin had blistered away, his lips were cracked and weeping, bracelets of raw flesh around both his wrists where he had pulled at his bonds. They would get infected if they did not find some help for him.

He lay on his back, hardly breathing, staring through the palm fronds at the sky.

She had a goatskin full of water, poured some of it into a metal cup, sat him up and held it to his lips. He still reeked of decay. The worst of it, though, was his eyes. They were quite empty.

'Your friend,' she said. 'He is dead.'

He gave a slight nod of his head to show that he understood.

'I am sorry.'

'You came back for me.'

'Yes.'

'Why?'

'I need someone to take command of my artillery.'

'No, you don't.'

'I don't have to give you my reasons, Englishman. Just be glad that you are free. We have some hard riding in front of us to return to Aït el-Karim. Are you up to it?'

'He has a cannon. A breech loader. Did you know this?'

'Yes, I know. But the ammunition that was meant for it will no longer be arriving, as he expected. And it has been arranged that he has no way of getting any more.'

'You knew?'

'Our sultan has spies among your countrymen in Algiers. Bou Hamra's source has been arrested and sent back to France. Without ammunition, the gun is just a curiosity, like his clocks.'

'Good.' The light came back to his eyes. 'I should like to return to the Kasbah and fetch our last cannon. We must return with it and blow a hole in the walls and then blow a hole in Bou Hamra.'

'One day you will get your wish. But that day is not today. One of the men will bring you something to eat. You'll need your strength. When worst of the heat is over, we ride again.'

CHAPTER 56

The heat was exhausting. He pulled his *cheiche* tighter over his mouth and nose to keep out the stinging sand and grit, kept the hood of his cloak over his face to shield it from the worst of the sun. His horizon was no broader than the pommel of the saddle, and the black coarse tufts of his horse's mane.

The murmur of the baking wind muffled every other noise. His mind wandered, unrestrained; he thought about riding in the local gymkhana, his parents were behind the rope, watching. By some trick of the mind, he could smell leather and wet grass. He had earned just a polite smattering of applause from the spectators after his round, there was always one jump he missed, and he knew he would have to endure his father's frown of disappointment as he led his horse to the stables.

He passed his brother on his way back, his mare's chestnut coat shining like the mahogany table in their dining room. Tom cantered out, sitting so straight in the saddle, a few minutes later he had scored another faultless round. His father always applauded the loudest, so much so that some of the other fathers gave him a derisory glance.

He remembered what George had said to him: *You can't make up a better past, no matter how many times you go over it in your head.*

He was right. It was time to stop feeling sorry for himself, time to build something, not tear it down. You can't rewrite the past, no matter how hard you try.

They made camp late in the morning to avoid the heat of the day. A stranger would never have found it. The river had cut so deeply in to the plain that the banks either side were the height of two men. It was invisible until you were almost on top of it. This time of year, the river was just a scrap, only ankle deep.

Amastan told him they were barely two days' ride from Aït Isfoul and safety.

He watched her as she helped them make camp for the night, fetching slabs of salted meat from the packs, replenishing the goatskin gourds in the river. An enigma, in so many ways. What went on behind those black eyes? Surely, it would have been better for her to leave him in Bou Hamra's dungeon to die? She had lied when she said she needed him for the guns. And he knew her secret. He was better for her dead than alive.

Was it sentimentality? He found it hard to credit but he could explain what she had done no other way. She would probably call it a weakness.

It was blessedly cooler in the shade of the palms and the men had left their rifles propped against the boles of the trees. They were all the latest Martini-Henry breech-loaders, he supposed they had been supplied to her by the Sultan, to help her in the war against Bou Hamra. If any more Frenchmen decided to line their own pockets by smuggling armaments to the rebels, she would need them.

One of Amastan's men brought him a palm leaf with some of the meat and couscous. He shook his head, and the man shrugged and left it on the sand next to him, anyway.

He couldn't stop thinking about George.

He didn't remember much after the hideous travesty of the chess game. How many men had died for Bou Hamra's perverse enjoyment, and for his own futile attempt to save his friend? Had it been worth it?

In the end, the result would have been the same. More ghosts to haunt his dreams.

He vaguely remembered George being thrown in the cage with the two lions, though only fragments of it, like the disturbed images of a fever-dream. There were snatches of conversations afterwards, in the dungeon, but how much was real, what was imagined? Amastan's men said he was frothing when they dragged him out of the cell, they thought he had gone mad.

'If it had been me,' one of the men had said to him later, 'I would have shot you like you would a mad dog.'

He watched the men eat, then curl up in the shade to sleep through the breathless heat of the afternoon. Amastan sent two of the men to where the horses were tied, for the first watch. Harry was lulled by the sonorous buzzing of flies. He lay down and closed his eyes.

'I'm sorry, George,' he murmured to the hard blue sky. 'I let you down.'

He woke to the sound of someone screaming.

'George?'

He sat up, his heart racing, looked around. There was no one.

He remembered where he was, saw Amastan and the others still asleep, among the saddles and blankets. He looked up at the guards on the first watch, up there on the river bank. God in heaven, they were both asleep, their heads on their chests, rifles cradled between their knees.

In the Army, you could get court-martialled and shot for that. Should he go and kick them awake himself or have Amastan do it? They were her men, after all.

There was that sound again. He hadn't imagined it. He looked around, held his breath, listened.

The drumming of hooves on sand, the sound of a horse. Down here by the river it was impossible to see to the horizon. He was about to shout a warning, but it was already too late.

They appeared suddenly, galloping down the steep river bank. One of the guards woke and jumped to his feet, scrambled for his rifle, but it was already too late. A rider cut him down with his sword before he could shout the alarm. The other guard tried to run, but another of the horsemen reined in, aimed his rifle, and shot him in the back.

Harry counted four others, their stallions snorting and champing at the reins. He crawled behind one of the palm trees, out of sight.

Caught sleeping, it was too late for Amastan or any of her men to go for their rifles now. Their attackers charged in, holding their long guns vertically in their hands, the stocks resting on their thighs. They formed a semi-circle around them, their horses stamping, white-eyed, excited by the noise and the smell of gunpowder.

They had an odd mixture of weapons, mostly muskets, only the leader and one other had modern rifles. They kept the muzzles trained on Amastan and her men.

The leader whipped off his *cheiche*.

It was Zdan.

'Well, it seems your luck has finally turned against you,' he said to Amastan.

Harry realised they still hadn't seen him. He reached for the nearest rifle, and slowly lifted it off the ground and brought it towards him.

The rider who had shot the guard was still fumbling with his gunpowder horn, trying to reload his ancient Jebel on the back of his horse. Six of them, one of them reloading. Five against one, then.

There was a canvas bag full of shells just within his reach. He grabbed one and eased it into the breech. Once he cocked it, they would know he was there. He would have to wait for the right moment.

Another glance around the tree. Mabrouk would be no help to them. Amastan had five men left. If even two of them could reach the rifles, they might have a chance.

Zdan was enjoying his success, leaning on the pommel of his saddle, and staring down Mabrouk, who was visibly shaking with terror.

Zdan laughed. 'Mabrouk, what shall we do with you? Should we let Bou Hamra decide? He tells me he needs some fresh meat for his lions.'

Mabrouk turned and ran.

Where does the fool think he is going to run to? Harry thought.

While Zdan was occupied with the old gaoler, Harry reached for the canvas bag and took out three more shells, put them between the fingers of his left hand, and waited for his chance.

Zdan let Mabrouk get halfway up the nearest sand dune before he raised his rifle, almost languidly, and shot him in the back.

Mabrouk stumbled and fell to his knees. He reached behind him with one hand, as if he thought he could pull the bullet out. He tried to crawl the rest of the way to the top.

Zdan let him do it. He was almost at the crest when he reloaded, aimed, and fired again. Mabrouk slumped onto his face and lay there, not moving.

It was enough of a distraction.

Two of Amastan's men thought so too, they turned and ran to get their rifles. But Zdan's men were ready and opened fire. At that moment, Harry came out from behind the tree, aimed his own rifle and shot Zdan through the chest.

The mistake Zdan's men had made, overconfidence or inexperience, was that they had all fired at the same time at the two men who had made a break for the guns. As they only had muskets, it was impossible for them to reload in time.

Harry's training at Sandhurst came back to him, even though he hadn't fired a breech-loader in anger in years: release the lever, load the second cartridge, stock up to the chin, step out, fire again. A rider was hacking at one of Amastan's men with his sword, Harry walked up and shot him in the chest, the muzzle almost touching the man's robe. He fired and reloaded again, saw one of the riders aiming his rifle at him, heard the bullet slap into the bole of the tree above his head.

The man tried to quickly reload, fumbled the cartridge into the sand in his panic.

Aim.

Fire.

The man jerked in the saddle and fell.

Harry ducked back behind the palm tree to grab more shells from the canvas bag. Where was Amastan?

A quick glance over his shoulder, he saw her run around one of the horses, grab its rider and wrestle him from the saddle.

The last two riders couldn't get a clear shot at her, their aim was obscured by their own horses. They wheeled around in circles, unsure what to do. One of them was struggling to reload his musket, not an easy thing to do on the back of a bucking and panicked horse. The other one had taken out his sword.

Harry reloaded and stepped out. The man with the musket aimed the Jebel at his head, he saw the flash in the pan, but nothing happened. A misfire.

Harry took two steps forward, took careful aim, and shot him between the eyes. The other rider still couldn't steady his horse. Harry took a step towards him, snapped open the breech and loaded another shell. He saw the terror and indecision plain on the other man's face.

The man turned his horse and galloped away.

Amastan had the last of Zdan's men out of the saddle, he saw her knife flash as her hand went around the man's throat. He turned away, didn't want to watch another man die.

He stared at the carnage in front of him. There was no one else left standing.

He heard Amastan's voice, behind him.

'How are you still alive?'

He didn't have an answer for her.

CHAPTER 57

They rode in silence, just the drumming of the night wind and the crunch of the grit and stones under their horses' hooves. They shivered in their cloaks in the deep bone-cold of the desert. When it got too bad, they wrapped themselves in blankets taken from the horses of the dead riders. They had taken four of Zdan's horses, swapping them every few hours to keep them fresh.

Finally, they mounted a plateau of jagged black rock, stopped for a moment to rest. In the moonlight they could see the vast desert behind them, deep shadows tracing the black gullies of rivers and tracks. They were back in Amastan's lands now, in the foothills of the Atlas.

An hour or so later they came to a small outcrop of rocks, honeycombed with caves.

'We are safe now,' she said. 'Bou Hamra's patrols won't dare come this far. We should rest here. Soon we will reach Aït Isfoul and sleep under a proper roof again.'

They carried the water skins and the rest of the dried meat from the horses inside one of the caves, then started gathering wood for the fire. Amastan hung one of their blankets over the entrance to keep out the light so they could sleep through the heat of the day, using rocks to hold it down.

She scattered the rest of the blankets on the floor of the cave, then hobbled the horses and left them to forage.

She made some tea over a small fire as the sun rose over the desert to the east. Afterwards, she took out a bone pipe and passed it to him.

'*Kif*,' she said. 'It will help you relax.'

He took it.

'Tell me something,' he said.

'Is it about Bou Hamra?'

'No, about Zdan.'

'What do you wish to know?'

'Why did he hate you so much? What made him betray you to a man like Bou Hamra?'

'I thought you would understand it better than anyone. I took away his birthright. If I had been born a girl, he would have become the next Kaïd.'

'But you were born a girl.'

'My father said I wasn't. And no one ever disobeyed my father.'

'I thought he was my friend. He betrayed us. What happened to George, it was down to him.'

'I warned you when you first came to Aït Karim. Trust no one.'

'And yet you came back for me.'

'I need someone to fire my cannon.'

'Is that the only reason?'

She took off the *cheiche*. Her hair had been cut short, it only accentuated the smoothness of her cheeks. Then she did something he had not expected. She reached out and took his hand. It was a simple gesture, and it took him off guard.

When he did not respond, she seemed to regret the gesture, busied herself instead with the pipe and relit it. She exhaled the smoke through her nose and handed it to him.

'Why did your father do this to you? Why did he make you into a man? You said your grandmother was a chieftain.'

'Yes, among the Berbers, it would not have been quite so important, but my father's ambitions for me, for the family, for our dynasty, extended far beyond the Atlas Mountains. A woman is nothing in Arab culture compared to a man. They cannot inherit a house, never mind a fortress, a city. They could never become Lord of the Atlas or Pasha of Marrakech. Without me, everything he had, everything he hoped for, would vanish.'

'And your mother couldn't give him a son?'

'There were six girls before me. They say he was a desperate man by the time my mother carried me in her womb. He had tried everything. He consulted fortune tellers, sorcerers, every kind of *fakir*. He even took my mother to the *katoob* of one of the saints, made her stay there for seven days and seven nights with just bread and water. He sprinkled her with urine from a donkey, as a magician told her to do, he bought potions from the sorcerers in the medina. No matter what he did, each time God gave him daughters. All he wanted was a boy who could inherit his ambition.'

'Why didn't he get another wife?'

'His horse stumbled as he was riding down the mountainside near Aït Karim. They carried him back to the Kasbah, they say you could hear his screams in Marrakesh. For months he lay in his bed, he could not move, he lay in terrible pain, everyone thought he would die.'

'But he didn't die.'

'No. But after the bones mended, one leg was shorter than the other so that when he walked, he swayed from side to side like a camel. He also found he could no longer do as a man does when he is with a woman. He thought it was a temporary affliction and that it would pass. But if it didn't, he knew his line would end with me. So, when the time came for my birth, he had already decided. Whatever happened, I was going to be a boy.'

'He decided to play God.'

'In the Atlas, he was God. My mother, my father and the midwife were the only ones present at my birth. Afterwards, my father wrapped

363

me up and told the midwife to tell no one what she had seen and allow nobody near me. And then he went out and announced to everyone that I was boy. Just like that.'

'Your mother went along with this?'

'She did as she was told.'

'No one suspected?'

'Perhaps. But who would dare confront him? From that time on, my father assumed complete responsibility for me. He took more interest in my upbringing and education than any Muslim man would do, I suppose people thought it was because he was so grateful and so blessed to finally have a son.'

'And the midwife?'

'I am told she disappeared soon afterwards. My mother said that my father gave her money and that she went to live in Marrakesh. I am more inclined to suspect that he dealt with the problem in another way.'

'And when you grew up, you accepted what he had done?'

'No, I didn't accept it. I wanted it. I saw how my mother and my sisters were treated by my father, how men treated the women in their families. I embraced my opportunity. It meant I would be free. So, I learned to behave like a man. I mistreated my sisters, had them wait on me at lunch and at dinner, I made them all serve me and fear me.'

'And when your father died, no one challenged you?'

'By then, I had learned enough to make men fear me. My father and I had won many battles together, we had taken land and fortresses. I am a good leader, in peace and in war. Even Zdan, who burned with envy, never dared go against me until now.'

'Have you never regretted your father's decision?'

A brief smile. 'He asked me this same question, just before he died.'

'And what did you say?'

'I said, Father, I am glad for what you did. It has given me opportunity and privilege I would never have had if you had let God decide my fate. To be a woman here in Morocco, it is not enough, not for a life, for a complete life.'

'But the village girls I have seen…'

'They are freer than women in Fez and Marrakesh but do not be fooled. Their life is drawing water and grinding corn in the hand mills.'

He wondered how he might contend with her. Being a man or being a woman: he had never considered this a choice. He had always found women intriguing and beautiful and imagined that they loved compliments, security, children, and family and all the things his mother had enjoyed. Could a woman or a man wish to be other than what they were born to? 'What about your great grandmother? She was a chieftain and a woman.'

'That was a long time ago,' Amastan said. 'I will tell you what my life would have been if my father had not snubbed his nose at God. I would have lived with my mother until I was of an age to marry. I would not have had any education other than learning embroidery and making sweetmeats. And then I would have produced a brood of children and been expected to look after them. And one day I would find myself an old woman, and my life would have counted for nothing. I would have left no mark.'

'But aren't you lonely?'

'Many people are lonely.'

'We cannot deny our true natures forever.'

'Well, you're a man. Of course, you believe that.' Amastan finished the pipe and laid it aside, stared into the dying embers of their fire. 'I am what my father made me. It can never be different. Now, we should sleep. Tomorrow we ride back to Aït Karim.'

Harry couldn't sleep. It was hot inside the cave, airless, his body hurt from the beating he had taken from the guards. Whenever he closed his eyes, he saw George writhing on the floor of the cell, or the face of one of the *askari* the moment before a guard slaughtered him on Bou Hamra's marble chessboard.

He was drained, tormented by ghosts. He just wanted to sleep.

Instead, he lay for hours, tossing, restless. Finally, exhaustion overtook him, and he drifted off; he dreamed of George, in his lieutenant's uniform, playing chess with tiny headless men. Every time he moved one of the pieces, he had to soak up the blood on the board with a rag. George turned around to say something to him, but it wasn't his face, it was Mou's, and his mouth was full of sand and his eyes were bulging, he couldn't breathe.

He sat up, soaked in sweat, his head splitting apart. He reached for the goatskin and tipped it up, his mouth so dry he couldn't swallow, he drank until the water spilled down his chin and soaked his shirt.

Amastan reached out and took the gourd from him, gently, wiped the sweat off his face, stroked his cheek.

'Shh,' she murmured. 'It's alright.'

'Dreams,' he said.

'You have been talking all night.'

'What have I been saying?'

'Sometimes you said your friend's name. Sometimes you said mine.'

Her face was close to his and it seemed the most natural thing in the world to kiss her. He supposed he expected her to pull away, to turn her head, perhaps threaten him with her knife. But she didn't. Instead, she kissed him back, kissed him so hard it bruised his mouth.

When she did finally pull away, it was to sit up and pull her kaftan over her head. He ran his fingers over her skin, licked at the salt of her sweat on her bare shoulder. She had a linen binding around her breasts, and he tried to tear it away, but it was too tight.

'Unwind it,' she said.

It took too long. His hands were shaking. She had to help him.

Her breasts were strikingly pale, and when he touched her, she made a sound like an animal, deep in her throat. She put her hand in his hair and pulled his mouth to her throat. She tore at him with her nails, surprised him with her strength. There was a desperation to it. He winced, there no gentleness in her, and he supposed he had not expected any.

He rolled her onto her back, and she brought up her thighs, squeezed him so that he could scarcely breathe.

'This is all there can ever be,' she said.

'I know,' he said, but he didn't really believe her

'You mustn't leave your seed.'

'I promise,' he said, but he wasn't listening, wasn't thinking. It all seemed so unreal. There was just the desert, the stars, the night, and the desire for something he could never have. He faced his cards, and it was a straight nine, and the croupier gathered the chips in a huge pile and pushed them across the baize towards him.

CHAPTER 58

She did not want to look at him. Even in the long black kaftan, the *cheiche* covering her hair and her face, she felt naked. What had possessed her to give in to such weakness?

She had not found the release she had longed for, only more frustration. She had tried to come closer to how God had made her, but she was as far away as ever.

She could hear her father's voice in her head.

You have disgraced me. You have disgraced yourself.

Everything I did for twenty years, everything you have done since, you have put it all at risk now.

And for what? Will you make this man your master and give up your dominion over the Atlas?

Black clouds towered over the mountains and there was a flash across the sky, like the distant shock of cannon fire. Thunder rolled across the hills after it, she felt the ground shake under her feet.

'There is a storm coming,' Harry said.

They mounted their horses in silence. She removed the hobble, tightened the strappings on her horse. She pulled her *cheiche* over her face, her disguise perfect once more.

Neither of them had said a word. She was once again the Lord of the Atlas.

She turned and spared a look to the desert behind them. Tracks led away in so many directions, you chose your way by the pole star or by the sun. Fate didn't lead you. You decided which way you would go, your fate was just what was at the end of the road.

CHAPTER 59

A slave brought Harry back to his old rooms. He winced at the memory, stood for a long time staring at the place where Mou had slept, and George. Their sleeping mats had been rolled into the corner, next to the trunks of rugs and spare grain.

His rooms now.

They mostly left him alone, slaves brought him trays of fruit and food and jugs of water whenever he required it. There were no guards on the doors. He was neither prisoner nor guest. He was just there.

He left the kasbah once, went down to the *fondak* to stare at the cannon, in its bed of straw, surrounded by offerings of flowers and fruits, disturbed two women praying there. He saw his gun crew, Ramrod and the rest, they raised their hands and cheered when they saw him, he hadn't expected that. They all looked pleased to see him, save for Redbeard, who merely looked sullen.

He had been a curiosity once, the children had tagged him and George wherever they went, the men watching from hooded eyes, muttering among themselves whenever they passed. Now they ignored him. Some even smiled.

It was cool in the alleys, the sunlight could not penetrate there. He wandered aimlessly, found a small boy sitting on a step outside a door with cracked blue paint and iron bossing. A cat had curled itself around his legs.

The boy stared up at him, wide-eyed, this crazy stranger with his sun-blotched face, skin peeling like a leper. For a moment he was too scared to move, his bottom lip curled.

'I have no one to talk with any more,' Harry said. 'My friend is dead. Do you have a friend?'

The boy shook his head.

'Everyone needs a friend.'

The cat got up and coiled itself around Harry's legs, purring. The boy tried to pretend Harry wasn't there, went back to peeling the scrap of orange in his grubby fist.

'It should have been me,' Harry said, in English. 'I watched him get torn to pieces in front of my eyes. I begged Bou Hamra, I said to him, let it be me, put me in the cage. But do you know something? There was another part that was glad. I didn't want to die, and I didn't want to die that way. What does that make me, huh?'

The boy got up and ran back inside.

After that he only went down to the medina after dark, the guards did not trouble him, it was silent and dark, just moon shadow and silhouette, the occasional tap-tap of the watchman with his Mellah lamp. There was no one about, he stumbled down one narrow lane after another, heedless to the fact of being lost.

Because I am lost, he thought. I don't really know how I got here, and I don't know where I shall be a year from now, or a month. There is nowhere I belong. George was my bridge back home, to my family. Now, what am I?

He had come to hate it here, and to love it, this land of sand and ice, dungeons with dead men and black slaves in chains. You recoiled from the salted heads rotting on some gate but then you ducked through a crumbling arch and there in front of you was a desert caravan silhouetted against a sunset mountain, a perfect disc of bright moon hovering above it in a pale evening sky. He could imagine this place unchanged from the days of the testaments, its breathless beauty waved into the choking stench from the tannery, the wail of the blind and limbless beggars at the doors of every mosque.

He could not sleep for more than a few hours. Sometime in the night he would start awake, thinking he heard George moving about the room. Other nights he would think he heard his voice. Once he smelled him, that terrible taint of flesh rotting away.

His father had once told him he was godless, and he supposed in a way it was true. What he had come to believe in, instead of religion, was the sacred geometry of chance. It was the Gambler's Fallacy, wasn't it? Like Amastan's father, railing against God for giving him six daughters, thinking that when the seventh was a girl as well, that it was God punishing him. A good gambler knew that the likelihood of having a son after six daughters was the same as it was for having a son in the first place.

God had nothing to do with anything. It was one chance in two, every single time. In the end, bad things happened to good men as often as they did to bad ones. It should have been him that died, not George. George had so much more to give the world. But then, mathematics was not fair, the turn of a card was not fair.

Unlike a game of cards, he could change his suit, if he wanted. The joker in the pack could as easily become the jack of hearts. He couldn't change luck, but he could change what he did with it.

The knowledge made him only more anxious. He couldn't sit still: he was constantly walking, aimlessly, patrolling the terrace roof, the hood of his *djellaba* pulled down to keep the sun off his face. The skin on his face had healed, though in places it was bright pink, in others there were crusted sores that were slower to heal.

He watched the Berber women going to and from the wells and the fields, hanging clothes on the branches of the oleander and olive trees to dry, splashes of indigo, and black and ruby red.

What was he to make of her? *This is all there can ever be.*

He wanted to build a hospital. He wanted to kill Bou Hamra with his bare hands. He wanted Amastan for himself.

He didn't know what to do to find peace.

Amastan held the letter to the light, read it through carefully, then again. Her hand trembled.

'This is the last letter I shall write to you.
You must stop now. I will not read any more of your missives.
You have known me my whole life, so these words come hard to me.
But I can no longer bear your presence.
You must leave my life now.
I have made my decision. There can be no more idle fancies.
The world is a hard place and there is no room for them.
Go now. Disappear. You are no longer welcome, even as a dream.'

Amastan read what she had written a third time, and carefully signed her name.

CHAPTER 60

The wind brought with it the scent of cumin, sweat and dust. It was baking in the valley, the air so hot and thin it was hard to breathe. A dust devil spun across the *maidan*, a tornado of grit and sand. No sane man would be out here in the middle of the day.

'What are you looking at?' Wafa said.

'The English captain,' Amastan said. 'He's out there, in the *maidan*.'

'Is he down there again? What is he doing?'

'I don't know. The guards think he has gone a little mad. They have all bought themselves amulets to ward off the evil eye.'

'Will you let him go now?'

'He has only to ask.'

'But you won't make him go. Why?'

'There is no reason,' Amastan said, though they both knew that was a lie.

Amastan turned away from the window. Wafa lay on a divan on the far side of the room, away from the window and the light. She had grown thin, cadaverous. She rarely got up from her bed these days, and the *djinn* entered her more often now, shaking her body in his malevolent fist longer and longer each time.

It hurt Amastan to look at her.

'What happened in the desert?'

'Nothing happened.'

'Yes. Something happened with him.'

'No.'

'It's in your face. I can see it.'

'You imagine things.'

'I can't believe you have let him back into your kasbah. He knows too much.'

'He won't say anything.'

'How can you be so sure? And what about the other one, the boy. The one they called Mou.'

'Bou Hamra killed him.'

'He didn't talk?'

'If he had, all of Morocco would know about it by now.'

'So, what do you wish to do?'

'You say it like there is a choice.'

'There is always a choice.'

'I am Lord of the Atlas. I shall stay the course, rid Morocco of Bou Hamra and this time next year I will be pasha of Marrakesh. All our father's dreams for me will be realised. I could not dishonour him now.'

'Yet the English captain has stirred something in you. It is in your cheeks and the way you move.'

'You know more of what it is to be a woman than me, so perhaps you see something that I do not. But my mind is made up. Nothing will change it.'

'This *djinn* will not let me go, Amastan. One day I will fall, and I will not get up. Without the English lieutenant's elixirs, I will get sicker.'

'I know what this medicine is, I have sent to Algiers, a *chaush* will return with more.'

'In the end it will be the same. I will be gone soon, and you will not have to worry. The rest of our sisters have husbands. You will be free to do as you please.'

'I will never be free,' Amastan murmured.

'Yet you wish for a different destiny. Don't you?

'What I wish or do not wish has nothing to do with this. Nothing has changed, Wafa. Nothing.'

For the first time in his life, he carried something in him worse than the dull resentment he had always nursed for his father. What he felt now was different; it was hate, visceral, physical, venomous. What Bou Hamra had done to the boy, what he had done to George, Harry could never take back their suffering, or the years of life that had been stolen from them.

He could not let it be. He could not do nothing.

It would be his revenge, not theirs. He needed to face this man again, destroy him, so he might one day be able to live with what happened, so that when George's ghost moved in the shadows, when Mou moaned and choked in the dark, when they whispered to him in the midnight hours, he would have an answer for them.

Bou Hamra would die at Harry's hand or Harry would die at his. It was the only way he could go forward in this life. It would change nothing for Mou and George, but it would change everything for him.

He spent the next few mornings, before it got too hot, out on the *maidan*, with his gun crew, practising firing drills, until they could load and reload almost as quickly as his battery in the Royal Horse. He endured the scornful stares of Redbeard for as long as he could, and finally he took him aside, intending to have rid of the ingrate for good and all.

'What is wrong with you, you son of a dog?'

'My father,' Redbeard said, 'was a chieftain, in the Rif mountains.'

'What has that to do with firing a cannon?'

'This is beneath me. All you have me do is put my finger over a hole. I might as well stick it up a donkey's ass.'

'The thought had occurred to me. If you wish, I will even buy you your own mule.'

'You insult me. I am better than this. You won't give me the chance.'

He was about to walk away, tell Amastan to give him another man, but something made him hesitate. 'What is your name?'

'Mohammed.'

Mohammed, the first born son. Of course. He wondered what his story was; had his father rebelled and died in disgrace, or had he also been overlooked?

'What is it you think you can do?' Harry said.

'I should be the commander.'

'The commander?'

Redbeard pointed a finger at him. 'I should be you.'

'Do you know how long I trained to become a captain of artillery?'

The man looked at him down the length of his nose. 'Show me. I can do it.'

If George had been alive, he would have scoffed and walked away, got himself a new man. Against his better judgment, Harry relented.

He didn't know why he did it, perhaps as much to keep himself distracted, it was something to occupy his mind, keep from thinking about George, the noise his bones made when they cracked from one of the spasms brought on by the tetany. Stop thinking about Mou, how he laughed when he jumped down into the grave that Bou Hamra's slaves had dug for him.

'Alright' Harry said. 'I will teach you as much as you are able to learn.'

In the next few days, he showed him topography, how to think not like a man, but like a bird, imagine the battlefield from above. He pointed to the storks in their huge nest at the top of the kasbah tower. 'You must be like them,' he told Redbeard, every morning before he began his lessons. 'You must see the world like they do.'

They stood out on the *maidan* below the fortress and Harry showed him the main features of the landscape and drew a map in the sand with a stick. If you had a cannon at this point here, could you bring fire to bear on the kasbah here and be out of range of the rifles on the wall here?

If you had your cannon at the spur of the mountain there, would you be in range of a gun in the shepherd's hut in the valley there?

Could you place a forward scout in the forest over there, unseen by a battery at the redoubt on the ridge in the lee of that mountain?

He showed him how to measure distances by counting out the paces, how to use a prismatic compass, and sketch the contours of the landscape with his Watkins clinometer. He let him use his pocket sextant and theodolite, taught him what he must do to make an accurate representation of the terrain from the saddle under fire.

Redbeard was a more than willing student. Not that he showed the slightest inclination towards friendliness or gratitude for his tuition. He remained as sullen as ever. Harry told himself he did not do it for favour; in the end, it was for the benefit of Amastan.

She would need men like Redbeard after he was gone.

CHAPTER 61

Amastan received him, finally, in the eyrie at the top of the kasbah. She indicated the cushions on the floor beside her, and he sat down. She clapped her hands and a slave appeared, with porcelain bowls of water and towels so they could wash their hands.

Another slave brought tiny cups, poured the coffee. She put one in front of him and one in front of Amastan, who showed no inclination to drink it. He supposed it was a formality, nothing else.

'I have prepared your payment,' Amastan said without preamble. 'The equivalent of two thousand British pounds in silver. I will provide you with an escort to Tangier. You may leave when you wish.'

Harry sipped the coffee. It was scalding hot and spiced with cinnamon. 'But I have not fulfilled my contract.'

'I am releasing you from your obligations to me. You have given me good service, and suffered greatly on my behalf, for which you deserve reward.'

'No.'

'No?'

'Bou Hamra is still alive.'

'Bou Hamra is no longer your concern.'

'Your gun crew cannot maintain and operate the remaining cannon. You still need me, Amastan.'

'Bou Hamra is finished.'

'What do you mean?'

'I mean he has overreached himself. A few days ago, a *chaush* brought me news. There are lead and copper mines that belong to one of the tribes that supports him. He sold their rights to a consortium of French and Spanish businessmen, right from under their noses. They are rightfully aggrieved and have threatened to drive him out of Zagora.'

'Why would he do such a thing? He did not strike me as a stupid man.'

'He needed the money to buy the cannon. If he had been able to use it against me, perhaps his avarice might have been overlooked. He would have had the means to compensate his supporters. Now he doesn't.'

'Where is he now?'

'He is still at Zagora. My spies tell me he is planning to make his way south of the Atlas towards the Tuareg. He still has *chereefs* sympathetic to his cause down there.'

'You want him out in the open.'

'As soon as he leaves Zagora, I will destroy him.'

'No, let it be me.'

'You?'

'You want Bou Hamra dead? Very well. Let it be at my hand.'

'I thought you were tired of killing men?'

'Just one more.'

Amastan considered. 'Very well,' she said, finally.

'And then?'

'And then, when he is dead, I will be second only to the Sultan in all Morocco. My son may rise even higher.'

'But he's not your son.'

'He is if I say he is.'

She seemed so calm, so unaffected. He wished there were a way to make her rage at him again, make her say his name, even one more time. He lowered his voice. 'Come back to England with me.'

'Be careful, captain. Do not mistake passion for sentimentality. I will kill you if you put me in danger.'

'Did you mean it? Is one night really all there will ever be, all that you ever want?'

'Didn't I already tell you that? Thank you, captain. You can go. Be ready. When Bou Hamra makes his move, we will leave to intercept him. Until then, we will wait.'

Harry couldn't sit still, there was a pain in his gut, twisting, twisting. He stood by the orange tree in the courtyard, but he could still smell the dungeon, and George, writhing, his muscles taut as steel wire.

He heard a voice behind him. '*God save the Queen.*'

He was going mad. Had he imagined it?

'God save the Queen!'

He spun around, as if he expected to see George standing there in the courtyard, hands on his hips, laughing.

It was the parrot, Algernon. It rolled its head and blinked at him, flapped its wings.

'George, you owe me five guineas,' he said aloud and slumped onto his haunches. He didn't know whether to laugh or cry. A slave, sweeping the steps, saw the crazy English officer, sitting with his head in his hands, shoulders heaving. He made the sign against the evil eye and fled back up the stairs.

'*Bou Hamra!*' Algernon said and laughed, laughed just like George. '*Fuck off!*'

CHAPTER 62

A gate at the rear of the harem led to a traceried cloister overlooking an orange grove. They had brought Wafa there to recover from the latest depredations of the *djinn* that tormented her. They had propped her on a divan, with silk cushions, in the shade. There were two slaves with her.

'You have had another fall,' Amastan said.

She looked utterly drained and there were deep hollows under her eyes. 'I do not think I will be a burden to you for much longer.'

'Don't say that. You were never a burden.'

'Let's not spoil this beautiful morning talking about this. You have news of Bou Hamra?'

'Bou Hamra has been forced to flee Zagora. The cockroach is out in the open and we have only to stamp on him.'

'And the English captain?'

'He wishes to come with me and finish the usurper, even though I have offered him his commission and free passage to Tangier. He is no longer a mercenary, but a true Berber. He believes in vengeance.'

'He will do well here if he stays.'

Amastan sat down beside her. She dismissed the slaves with a motion of her hand. 'There is a complication,' she murmured, after they had gone.

'What complication?'

Amastan did not know how to say the words.

'I have been betrayed.'

'Betrayed? Who by?'

'By myself. I allowed myself to be a woman, for one night.'

'I knew it. Oh, Amastan.'

Amastan expected her scorn, her disgust. She was shaken by the tender look on her sister's face. It wasn't even pity.

'Just once?'

'Yes.'

'And?'

'And it was one time too many.'

Wafa caught her breath, put a hand to her mouth.

Amastan nodded.

'What will you do?'

'There is a witch in the medina who can fix these things. You know of her?'

'I have heard of her. Amastan, it is dangerous.'

'More dangerous than doing nothing?'

They were silent with their thoughts. Amastan had expected more questions, more recriminations, from her sister. Instead, all she said was: 'You must not blame yourself.'

'Who else is there to blame?'

'Father.'

'No. I went along with it.'

'Well, whoever is at fault, I envy you. I am trapped in a body I don't want also. At least you found a way out.'

'It is hardly a way out, Wafa.'

'It could be.'

'No.'

'Father is dead, and you won't have to protect me much longer. You don't have to live your own dreams.'

'There is more at stake than that. Rest now, Wafa. I need to think.'

'Don't.'

'Don't?'

'Don't go to the witch until you've talked to me again.'

Amastan shrugged her shoulders. 'There is nothing more to say about it.'

'There is everything to say! Our father was wrong. He should not have laid such a burden on you.'

'It is no burden, Wafa. I would have had it no other way.'

Amastan left her there, in the garden, knowing there was only one way out of this for her now.

It was a part of the medina where she rarely came, and never dressed like this, like an ordinary Berber woman, barefoot, her eyes streaked with kohl, her hands and face tattooed with henna. She wore a blue headscarf and a stained black smock, the silver trinkets on the sash at her waist jingled as she walked.

Ragged children played in the dirt, old women, bent double by the loads on their back, jostled her as they went past. Smithies hammered at horseshoes and scythes and axes in black and baking foundries. The laneways smelled of smoke and piss.

She went down a series of narrow alleys, shaded from the sun by makeshift roofs of ancient planks and woven date palms, past doors with peeling blue and green paint, until she reached a deserted courtyard with a single withered fig tree. She went through a hole in the wall, ducking her head under the ancient lintel.

She waited for her eyes to grow accustomed to the gloom. An old woman sat on a thin carpet, surrounded by some evil smelling herbs, tied together in bunches. She was ancient, her skin brown and wrinkled as old leather, and she had barely any teeth, just a few rotten stumps like old tombstones.

Amastan crouched down, whispered what she wanted. The old woman didn't say anything, sorted among the herbs and jars around her until she found what she needed. She put some leaves in the stone bowl with powder and a splash of water from a rusted kettle and ground it into a paste with a stone pestle. She used her fingers to scoop the mixture into a small stone jar and handed it to Amastan.

'I have to swallow this?'

The old woman nodded.

'It's safe?'

A shrug.

'Will it work?'

'Of course.'

They were the only words the old woman spoke. Amastan paid her and left.

She hurried back through the medina, no one took any notice, just another poor Berber peasant girl, the shame was all in her mind.

Only her father paying any attention. He followed her all the way back to the kasbah, through the secret door and up to her eyrie high above the town. He moaned and wrung his hands, his ghost whispering: *What have you done, my shameful daughter, my errant son?*

CHAPTER 63

The twilight was nipped with the smell of thyme, a dog barked somewhere down the valley. A donkey munched at some grass a few yards away, its owner would be searching frantically for it. A yellow finch darted between the bushes.

She stared at the tall squat tower of the kasbah, its walls steeped in pink by the setting sun, the cedar forests behind it turned black in the shadows of the mountain. All that she could see, the mud wattle walls, the ramparts, the great tower of the fortress, the flat-roofed town nestled below it down the mountain, had been built by her father or her father's father. And all of it, in the end, soluble in water.

It had been their dream, all of this, and she had given herself readily to it. It was what she wanted.

She turned and looked down the valley, the rich red brown earth, the onion fields and olive groves, the swathes of cloth of black and ruby red, drying on the bushes. Down that narrow track between the moss-covered boulders lay Marrakesh, and the road to Mogador and the ocean. Finally, if you rode long and hard enough, you would come to Tangier and another life, another future.

She stared at the ceramic pot she held in her hand. It was her future. Swallow the evil-smelling stew inside it, and these mountains as far as she could see would always be hers. Hurl it into the ravine over there and another future waited for her, in the gathering dusk down that road.

Her father had been just another tribal chieftain, once, she could scarcely imagine his will, his determination, the sacrifices he had made, to forge a destiny such as this.

Over decades, he had won wars, made alliances with every other Kaïd in the Atlas so that he could one day become overlord. She had followed his example, becoming more like the Arab sultans in Fez, taking a harem, helping the Sultan with his wars, every day proving herself stronger, tougher, wilier, than any of the other Kaïds.

This was the life she had cherished as a precious gift from her father. He had saved her from an ordinary life and now she held in her hands not only his dreams but their family's history. Their name, if not their blood, might endure for centuries still.

A future always happens softly, without blast of trumpets or beating of drums. She could walk back to the kasbah or ride to the sea, and she had only a moon to decide. Delay too long and life would decide for her.

She stared at the potion in her hand. The sun dipped below the mountain and shadows raced towards her. She felt her father watching her, urging her to end this madness once and for all.

CHAPTER 64

Harry sat up and gasped, heart racing.

He thought the dreams would pass. It had been weeks now, he was exhausted, never enough sleep and terrified to ever close his eyes.

He heard a noise outside in the passage. Perhaps one of the guards. It came closer and he heard the door creak as it edged open. He reached underneath his pillow for his knife.

'Harry?'

'Amastan? What are you doing here?'

She went to the shutters, took off the latch, opened it to the moonlight. She took off her *cheiche* then her kaftan. She was naked underneath, there were bangles on her wrist and silver anklets, like a Berber girl.

'Do you want me to go?'

'Of course not,' he said.

'Good,' she said, 'then I'll stay.' And she lay down beside him

Sometime during the night, he woke and found her lying on her side, her leg lying over his thigh, watching him. Her eyes were luminous in the moon shadow.

'What will you do when we have vanquished Bou Hamra?'

'I will go back to England.'

'Go back to your old life?'

He shook his head.

'What then?'

'I told George I would use the four thousand pounds to build a hospital in the poor part of London. I gave him my word. I will keep it.'

'No, you won't. You'll step off the train, take one look around you, then get back on again. You'll find some other place with a bar and a card game and that will be that.'

'Not this time.'

He heard a dog barking through the open window and sat up. 'I saw something yesterday. A procession, it seemed like the whole city out on the *maidan*, in single file.'

'Yes. It was a funeral.'

'Who died?'

'Wafa. The *djinn* took her in the end.'

'When did this happen?'

'Yesterday morning. Our custom is to bury the dead quickly.'

'I'm sorry.'

A shrug. 'It is written. She has been dying for a long time. I have already wept all my tears.' She rolled away from him, put her head on the cushion, closed her eyes.

'Will you come back to England with me?' he said. When she did not answer, he said: 'Perhaps this is the way God wants it. Marry me. Be a wife. Be a mother to our children. You don't have to spend your life alone.'

'Suddenly you are pious.' She sat up. 'Which do you think fits my nature best? The wife of an English administrator who runs a small hospital in London or the pasha of Marrakesh, the most powerful *Kaïd* in all Morocco?'

'At least you will live the life you were meant for.'

'The life I was meant for is the life I choose. As pasha or wife, I am the one that must make the sacrifice. Whatever I decide, you will still go on being a man.'

'You were born a woman.'

'You have seen what it means to be a woman here in Morocco. Would you wish it for yourself?'

'At least, in England, you would be free.'

'Would I? I have spoken with one of the sultan's counsellors who has been to your country. They tell me that being a woman in your country is very much the same as it is here, whether it is as one wife or as one of a hundred. If I go back with you, you will always be my lord. Here, no man has power over me except for the sultan.'

'But you would have a husband and a family!'

'You say it as if it is all I have ever dreamed of.'

'I know that there is a part of you longs for it, anyway. And I would never let you down, Amastan'

'When I am pasha of Marrakesh, no one would dare let me down. Not even a good husband.' She stroked his cheek. 'I am an exotic bird to you. Once you have me in a cage, I fear you will tire of me.'

'That won't happen.'

She got up from the bed and slipped on her kaftan. 'Bou Hamra has left Zagora. Has been chased out, in fact. The *chereef* at Taroudant has offered him refuge but I will not let him get that far. You still want your revenge for what he did to your friend?'

'Yes. Oh, yes.'

'Good. Be ready to ride.'

The moon came out from behind a cloud. He saw her staring hard at him, as if she were committing his face to her memory. Then it shifted behind a cloud, her shadow moved, and he heard the door open and swiftly close again and she was gone.

CHAPTER 65

They came upon Bou Hamra in the Sous valley, ten leagues east of Taroudant. The *chereef*, sensing the shift in the wind, had instead sent a messenger to the Lord of the Atlas, pledging his eternal loyalty. He had offered some of his men to confront the Muslim Antichrist before he reached his safe haven in the Tuareg.

Bou Hamra now had only a few hundred men from his original army. He still had the eighty-millimetre cannon, which had impressed the peasants in the villages he had travelled through, though there was no ammunition for it, not even case shot. He had his harem, and his jewels, and not much else.

Harry sat on a horse next to Amastan, on a ridge overlooking the sandy plain, saw the dust from the column making its way towards the village oasis below them. Behind the village the great dunes of the Sahara rose like a golden, rippled sea.

'This time, we will destroy him,' Amastan said.

They had spoken little on the journey. For now, Harry had only one thing on his mind, getting justice for George and for Mou. When it was done, he would go back to London, build the hospital. Alone or with a wife? He didn't know.

'What do you think?' she asked him.

'They'll form a skirmish line at the edge of the village. They can't escape to the south because of the dunes. They have to fight it out if they have the appetite for it.'

'Good. Set up the cannon. We'll find out how hungry they are for battle.'

It was already mid-morning by the time they reached the outskirts of the village. Bou Hamra had made camp there, he couldn't march through the heat of the day, even the camels would have protested. The heat was stupefying.

Amastan had sent out her riders to form a ring around the town. They had found a goatherd who had been too slow to return to his village. They sent him into the village with a message for Bou Hamra and his men: come out with your heads bowed, or you will come out with no heads at all.

The horse and caisson galloped into position, *al-raed* coming up directly behind. The gun crew had been drilled for weeks now at Aït Karim, they had the gun set up in minutes, well out of range of Bou Hamra's rifles. They fetched the ramrods and rail levers from the caisson, stood at attention in their positions beside it, as Harry had taught them to do.

He climbed down from his horse and strode over. He took out his eyeglass and studied the layout of the village, the plain in front of it was quite flat, there was no natural advantage, he could make out Bou Hamra's men taking up position inside the huddle of mud brick houses, their rifles propped at the windows, as if that would do them any good. There was a saint's tomb, a *katoob*, just outside the village, but it seemed to be deserted.

He picked up his field glasses to take a closer look. It was one of the most beautiful *katoobs* that he had seen, shaded by a forest of date and fan palms and shrouded in vine creepers. Pieces of coloured rags had been tied to the leaves of the lowest branches, as was the custom. He could make out a bone white dome through the rampant greenery, a horseshoe arch and the visceral glitter of green ceramic.

Amastan rode down the column towards him, her black cloak billowing behind her. 'Captain,' she said.

'What do you want me to do?'

'My forward scouts say he is inside the building to the right of the mosque.'

'Who else is in there?'

'It doesn't matter. Once Bou Hamra is dead, this is over.'

He went back to the cannon. Redbeard was watching him, eager to be at it. Harry nodded and the gunners went to work, loading *al-raed* with powder and shot. Redbeard stepped forward, thinking he would sight her. Harry shoved him aside.

'I know how to do it,' Redbeard said. 'You showed me.'

'Not today. This is too important.'

Harry adjusted the elevation with the screw under the breech and had Redbeard adjust the trails to the right with an iron lever.

He would test the range first, it would serve as a warning shot to the defenders. He didn't want more men to die than was necessary.

He gave the order to fire

Al-raed spat flame from the muzzle and jumped back on her rails. Harry watched through the eyeglass as the ground erupted about twenty yards in front of the mosque, snapping a palm tree off at the base.

He heard screams, and a pall of smoke drifted through the village. People ran from the buildings in panic. Most of them were villagers.

Come on, Bou Hamra, show yourself.

The gunners were busy cleaning the breech, getting ready to fire another round. Amastan walked her horse forward and leaned from the saddle.

'Your aim is off,' she said.

'Just getting my range.'

'No, you did it deliberately.'

'Why would I do that?'

'Because you are sentimental.'

'Is it sentimental not to wish to slaughter innocent women and children?'

He heard Redbeard say, behind him: 'Let me aim the cannon. The captain has shown me how to do it!'

'You dog,' Harry murmured, under his breath. He turned back to Amastan. 'This fellow here has spent most of his life herding goats. He couldn't hit a camel with a watermelon if he were standing next to one.'

Amastan laughed and said to Redbeard. 'Get back to your position or the captain here will have you flogged.'

Harry raised his eyeglass. Men were running out of the village with their hands in the air, a rabble of rough-looking tribesmen and Tuaregs, the remnants of Bou Hamra's army, by the looks of them.

'You see,' Harry said. 'They have no appetite at all. Why should they? They know it's all over.'

'Look,' Amastan said.

A man had run out of one of the buildings, ushering a gaggle of heavily veiled women and small children scuttling in front of him towards the *katoob*. Even at this distance there was no mistake who it might be, by the sheer bulk of him.

'Bou Hamra,' he said.

Bare ground, the dome of the tomb bone-white, the shadow of the aged fig tree and its twisted limbs almost blue-black in the rippling heat. A single branch explored the hole where the roof had collapsed, twisting among the tracery of vaulting and broken arches.

'What is he doing in there?' Harry said.

'It is the tomb of a saint. By tradition, he can claim sanctuary there.'

Amastan's riders had ridden out and herded the remnants of Bou Hamra's army away from the village. They had them tied with ropes, ready to be led away. Most of them looked in a bad way, as if they hadn't eaten for weeks.

Through the eyeglass Harry saw some of the villagers scuttling across the plain towards the *katoob*. Some of them had weapons. What were they doing?

Amastan raised her hand. A cohort of her best riders charged past towards the tomb. She joined them. They got to within fifty paces, and Harry saw puff after puff of black smoke, heard the concussion of the musket shots a moment later. Two of the riders fell from their saddles and lay face down in the dirt. Amastan raised her hand again and the riders turned and followed her back towards their lines.

'What happened?' Harry shouted, as she reined in her horse, next to the cannon. 'I thought Bou Hamra's men had surrendered.'

'They're not Bou Hamra's men. They're the villagers. All I can think, they don't want us to desecrate the tomb. I'll not sacrifice my men's lives for something that can be settled with one cannonball.'

'He has women and children in there with him,' Harry said.

'Then what do you suggest? I can go back with more men, and dozens more will die. Do you have an answer, captain?'

He snatched up the field glasses. The white dome was a tempting target. If Bou Hamra was in there on his own, it would have posed no problem. But his women, their children, they were innocents and he had murdered enough of those in his life. He had promised himself there would be no more ghosts to haunt his sleep.

He made up his mind. He went to his horse, took his rifle from the holster on the saddle and set off across the plain towards the tomb.

'What are you doing, captain?'

'I'm going to get the bastard out of there.'

'I'll help you,' Redbeard said, and he drew the sword at his belt and set off after him.

Ripples of heat rose off the desert. Harry held the rifle loosely at his side, wondered with every step if the villagers would open fire on him. They weren't hardened soldiers, so he was banking on them being prepared to see what he had to say before they let loose with their muskets.

Redbeard kept pace beside him.

'What are you up to now?' Harry said.

Redbeard said nothing, appeared to be mumbling something to himself under his breath.

Harry stepped over one of the fallen riders. The man had a bullet hole clean through him.

A man with a grey beard and a scrappy turban stepped out from behind the fig tree, his ancient musket aimed at Harry's head. Harry supposed he was the *sheikh*, the village chief. The gun he was holding would not have looked out of place in a museum, but as the dead man lying a few feet away could attest, it was still a deadly threat.

Other villagers rose to their feet from behind the fallen tree. A handful of them had muskets, others were armed with rusted swords and hatchets and chains. Only two of them had breech loading rifles. He supposed that Bou Hamra's men had left them behind.

As the old man took a step forward, Redbeard turned and took off at the run, headed back to their lines. Harry watched him go. Strange. He never took him for a coward.

The *sheikh* took in Harry's blue and red field uniform and then looked down at the Martini-Henri, held loosely at his side.

'What is it you want?' he said, in Arabic.

'I want Bou Hamra.'

'What is he to you?'

'He killed my friend.'

A shrug. 'He has taken sanctuary in the tomb. You cannot go in.'

'Very well, I'll settle with him outside.'

The *sheikh* and some of the other older men held a quick debate between themselves in a language he didn't understand. They seemed to come to a decision.

'Leave your rifle here,' the *sheikh* said.

'Why?'

'We will protect our saint with our lives. If you try to sully the tomb, we will shoot you. You have your sword. If Bou Hamra wants to come out and face you, he can.' He nodded at Harry's rifle. 'Leave the rifle there,' he repeated.

Harry supposed he didn't have much choice. If they had wanted to shoot him, they would have done it by now. He laid his rifle in the sand.

Without another word, he strode across the sand towards the tomb. The doorway was black and empty and there was no sign of life from inside. He swayed a little in the heat. If he didn't get back into the shade soon, he would faint.

'Bou Hamra! You remember me?'

There was no answer.

If he doesn't come out, Harry thought, what will I do? The villagers won't let me take even a step inside the *katoob*. I must get him out here.

'Bou Hamra! Do you want the whole world to see what a coward you are?'

He thought he heard something, a child's voice, or perhaps a woman.

'You beat me once at chess. I want to see if you are as apt with a sword.'

He heard the familiar sound of a shell being loaded into a breech and Bou Hamra appeared at the doorway of the tomb, a rifle at his shoulder, the muzzle aimed at Harry's chest.

He looked none the worse for his travails, in his white kaftan and turban. He had lost a little weight and there were no jewels on his fingers. But hardly bowed and beaten. He even managed a smile.

'You. Englishman. What are you doing here?' He edged out into the sunlight.

Harry drew his sword. 'Put the rifle down, let's settle this like men.'

'Is that what you think I will do? You are mad.'

'You can die like a man or crawl like a dog. You can't get away from here. If Amastan's soldiers get their hands on you, you know what they'll do to you.'

Bou Hamra looked up at the sky. 'Look. The sun is past its zenith. I don't have to hold out here for long. These people won't let anyone inside their *katoob,* and when the night falls, let's see if Amastan and his soldiers can find me then. I am the master of illusion, and the darkness is my friend. I only have to reach my friends in the Tuareg, and I will rise again, like your Jesus. It's not over for me. But it is over for you.'

He saw Bou Hamra's finger tense around the trigger, and he closed his eyes waiting for the crack of the rifle. He wondered if there would be much pain. When it came, the explosion was deafening, louder than any rifle and pure instinct made him throw himself face first in the dirt.

He felt a blast of heat roll over his body. The ground shook underneath him and afterwards the silence was shocking, and complete.

When he finally sat up, the *sheikh* and his men were already scrambling back to their village, over the splintered wreckage of the fig tree. The dome of the old tomb was gone, and smoke rose from the wreckage of ancient stones.

He looked down and was shocked not to see blood. His arms and legs were still there. He stumbled to his feet, but he couldn't seem to get his balance, and sat down again. He couldn't hear a damned thing.

He looked around for Bou Hamra, saw an arm, holding a rifle, buried under the rubble where the door of the tomb had been. He managed to get up the second time and staggered towards it. It was Bou Hamra's right arm, the arm he owed George.

He stepped over the hot stones, looking for the rest of him. The tomb was gone, anyone inside it would have been blown to bits. The shell must have landed on the roof.

He remembered Redbeard volunteering to step out with him, how he was muttering under his breath the whole way. Now he realised what he had been doing. He was counting out the paces, like the good artillery cadet that he was, getting the range.

A piece of rubble shifted; someone was buried underneath it. He saw the dirt spill, a massive slab of rock moved, just a little. A bloodied hand twitched. The big man was buried under there somewhere.

Harry put his fingers under the slab of rock, straining, dragged it clear. Bou Hamra, or what was left of him, lay underneath it. Both his legs and an arm were gone. Apart from the sheer bulk of him, Harry wouldn't have recognised him, would not even have known the mass of heaving flesh, covered in blood and dust, was even human.

He saw his lips moving. 'Help me.'

'No one can help you now.'

The fingers of his one remaining hand twitched. He pointed to the rifle. 'Please.'

The kind thing, the merciful thing, would be to put a bullet in him, end it now. He would not survive long like this and if Amastan's soldiers found him, before he died, it would not go easy on him. They would try and keep him alive a little longer, for their sport.

Then he thought about Mou, and he thought about George and there was no kindness left in him, not today.

Bou Hamra's mouth opened again, his white teeth broken and bloody. He kept saying, over and over: '*Please.*'

Harry saw the Berbers riding towards him. Amastan got down from her horse and came over. She saw what he was looking at.

'At last,' she said. 'It's finished.'

He saw her lips moving, but he couldn't hear her. He put a hand to his right ear, and his fingers came away stained with blood. His ear drums had burst. He had seen it happen before, in Tonkin, when someone got too close to an exploding shell. He knew it would be weeks before he could hear properly again.

She looked over her shoulder to make sure no one could see her, then she pulled aside her *cheiche* from her face, the first time he had ever seen her do it outside of her harem.

'Why did you do that?' she said, thinking he might be able to read her lips. 'Why did you face him with just a sword?'

'I don't know,' he said.

He walked back to the lines, saw Redbeard and his gunners standing around *al-raed*, they looked furtive when they saw him. Harry stopped in front of Redbeard.

He stared back at him, as insolent as he had been that very first day. What could you expect of first sons?

'Who gave the order to fire the gun?' he said. 'Was it Redbeard. Or was it the Kaïd?'

They would not answer him, and he couldn't have heard them, even if they had.

He threw Redbeard the leather satchel with the compass and eyeglass and the rest of his equipment. 'Welcome to it,' Harry said, and walked away.

CHAPTER 66

Marrakesh

It was over a year since Harry first stood on the roof watching the Sultan's fireworks sparkle and crack over the Koutoubya mosque. He thought about the man he had been then. He had seen a full turn of the seasons in this beautiful and barbarous country but now there was a change coming, the heat of the afternoon was almost bearable, a few more months and the snows would return to the mountains. He would be long gone.

A caravan had arrived from the south, a long train of mules with panniers of almonds, the staple trade of the Atlas Mountains, from here they would go to Mogador and then by ship to Europe. And life went on.

He stared at the distant ramparts of the Atlas, ghostly in the heat haze that clung to the plain. He had left a part of himself up there, along with George. One of them he would mourn for ever; the other he was glad to leave behind.

He heard music from the warren of sandy lanes close to the palace walls, saw a man in an elaborate kaftan, riding a black stallion, caparisoned in silks and silver. In front of the man, on the peaked saddle, sat a small boy in an embroidered orange Kaftan. The man held a Koran open in front of him as he rode.

The boy looked frightened and a little bewildered.

They were followed by what looked to be a dozen or so *mullahs*, all in white, riding mules, musicians with flutes and drums marching behind. He knew enough of the country by now to recognise it as a circumcision procession, on its way to the mosque.

It was the order of things that Amastan's father had dreamed of overcoming.

It was getting on for sunset, and the people of Marrakesh came out onto their roofs, veiled women gossiped to each other from the rooftops, children laughed and screamed.

He watched the Sultan's ragged *askari*, in their red and blue, kneeling in unison down in the courtyard for the evening prayer. Once again, the Sultan was in residence, but there would be no fireworks, and no *harka* into the Atlas Mountains and the deserts beyond. He had come with just his bodyguard and a handful of counsellors to meet with Amastan. She had brought the wild lands under control, had had Bou Hamra's head salted and prepared, and the *grand seigneur* was there to bestow his thanks, and his rewards.

Harry hadn't seen her since the battle at the saint's tomb. The next day she had headed for Marrakesh with a dozen of her fastest riders, to that she could send a *chaush* to Fez with the news that she had finally rid the Sultan of the *roguis*, Bou Hamra. Harry had followed behind later, with the rest of her Berber army.

It was not an experience he would remember fondly. Without Amastan to enforce restraint, her men had taken their reward for the victory in the time-honoured way, helping themselves to Bou Hamra's harem of boys and young women.

By the time he reached Marrakesh, Harry could hear again. He had spent the last two nights in the palace, an honoured guest, but still no word from Amastan. Finally, this afternoon, a slave had come to his quarters and told him that the new pasha of Marrakesh would receive him in audience after the evening prayer.

He watched the setting sun turn the pink bricks of the mosque to flame.

CHAPTER 67

It had all seemed so majestic, so exotic, when they first came here. He saw beyond the opulence now. He noticed the broken floor tiles and once splendid cedar doors hanging crookedly from their hinges. There was a family of mice living in the torn upholstery of one of the divans in his room. The swallows and wild pigeons that nested in the rafters in the gallery outside his room, left droppings on the marble that looked as if they had been there for weeks.

He followed the slave into the audience chamber where he was to meet Amastan. Looking at the moth-eaten rugs and the broken chandelier it was clear to him that the new pasha would have to have deep pockets to maintain it all. The Sultan's gift was a poisoned chalice.

He was not sure what kind of welcome to expect. Amastan was waiting for him on a low divan, her black *cheiche* in place, as always, so he could not read anything on her face.

'The Sultan has kept his word,' she said. 'He has offered me everything my father dreamed of. The Lord of the Atlas is now also Pasha of Marrakesh.' She went to the window. 'Everything you see, the city, the mosque, the mountains, they all belong to me now.'

'Is it enough?'

'I have a choice of two birthrights, one given me by my father, and one given me by God. Whatever I choose, I leave a great part of myself behind.'

He came to stand behind her. He hesitated to touch her. He thought of the mirage in the desert. If he came too close, he knew it would disappear into the dust haze.

'You will leave here tomorrow, at dawn. I will send my men to fetch you from your apartments. They will escort you to the coast.'

'I don't know if I want to leave.'

'There is another way. You could stay.'

'And be what? Your husband?'

It seemed to him she was struggling for the right words, something she had never done before. 'You cannot be a husband to a Pasha, Harry. No, no one can ever know the truth. But we would be together. When circumstances allowed.'

'I would slip into the harem by a little known door, like Zdan.'

'We would have to be more... careful, in our relations. We would steal a few moments from under God's very nose.'

He took a step towards her, then drew back. 'I made a promise,' he said. 'I have to keep it.'

'We both have promises to keep,' she said.

He stopped at the door. 'One day, I'll come back,' he said.

CHAPTER 68

Harry didn't sleep again that night. He tossed and turned for hours, eventually went up to the roof, stared at the moon hanging fat and silver over the minaret.

The Timbuctians, Zdan had told him once, said of their history: 'Gold comes from the south, salt comes from the north, and Divine Knowledge comes from within.'

He had travelled many miles since he had first set foot here, and he had seen gold and salt.

He thought about Bou Hamra's room of clocks and his grandiose pronouncements about time. His world turned on tomorrow. For everyone else sleeping tonight in this dun and dark city, it was just another day. The beggars outside the mosque dreamed of the coins that would rattle in their cups, the snoring rug merchants slept on and imagined customers flocking to their wooden kennels in the medina.

Such a long night, and not a moment's sleep, but the dawn came far too soon.

It was yet dark. He was dressed and ready to leave.

He heard a gentle tapping at the door and leaped to his feet. A tall Berber stood there, in a red *cheiche*. Wordlessly, Harry followed him down the stairs and into the courtyard below.

There were other Berbers waiting, their horses stamping on the hard sand, eager to be on their way. He mounted the black stallion they had brought for him, and they rode through the gates into the waking city.

Amastan stood at the window, saw the guards shut the gates behind the riders as they made their way to the medina. So, he was leaving, after all. Even to this moment she thought he might change his mind. It seemed Harry was finally listening to his head, in the moment that she had found her heart.

This was the right choice, the only choice. Why then could she see her future stretching away to the distant horizon as arid as a gravel plain. She was suddenly overcome with a desolation so profound that for a moment, she could not breathe.

'Please don't go,' she murmured.

She made for the door, thinking to go after him, then stopped herself. It could not be any other way.

She put a hand to her belly. It was a girl, she knew it, she could feel it. She took the potion the witch had given her and unscrewed the cork. *Insh'allah*. It is written. It is what God wants.

She dropped the bottle on the flagstones and crushed the splinters of glass and paste under the heel of her boot.

In a few months she would ride back into the mountains, and have her daughter in secret, bring her back to her harem. And one day, when she was grown, she would let her choose her own path.

The African sky was pale and powder blue, cloudless, the last stars quickly fading. The Jemma el-Fnaa was deserted, littered with the detritus from yesterday's market, melon rinds, horse dung, beggars sleeping where they could. A few merchants slept under the canvas sheets of their makeshift stalls.

When they reached the square, Harry reined in his horse, and the Berbers clustered around him, their horses stamping their feet, eager to be on their way. He checked the saddlebags on his horse. They were inordinately heavy, weighted with silver. How much silver? Four thousand pounds of sterling, he supposed, and probably a lot more. Enough to build George's hospital.

He twisted around in the saddle, his eyes searching the pink walls of the palace. He thought he saw her, up there on the roof. Then she was gone.

He would be his own man from now on. And perhaps one day, when all promises were kept, he would come back.

The riders waited patiently for him. Then the one with the red *cheiche* said: 'We must go, captain.'

Harry nodded, and they set off, galloping past the Koutoubya, headed for the northern gates.

He had told her that one day he would come back, but he knew he wouldn't. You can never step in the same river twice. People, places, they are weathered by time, and should you ever look back, they are no longer what they were.

One day he would wake up in London, and Morocco would seem like an exotic dream. But a dream that had finally woken him to his life.

EPIC ADVENTURE SERIES

Colin Falconer's EPIC ADVENTURE SERIES of historical thrillers draws inspiration from many periods of history. Visit the fabled city of Xanadu, the Aztec temples of Mexico, or the mountain strongholds of the legendary Cathars. Glimpse Julius Caesar in the sweat and press of the Roman forum, ride a war elephant in the army of Alexander the Great, or follow Suleiman the Magnificent into the forbidden palace of his harem.

2000+ five-star reviews.
Translated into 25 languages.
3000+ pages.

'A fantastic read' - Wilbur Smith

The series is available in Kindle eBook or 6x9 inch paperback.at Amazon.com, Amazon.co.uk and Amazon.ca.

A WORD FROM COLIN

Thank you for reading this book. I hope you enjoyed it. It's part of a series of fast paced thrillers that take you all around the world and through many periods of history.

SILK ROAD sees Templar knight, Josseran Sarrazini faced with a formidable task - to ride the treacherous Silk Road to the edge of the known world to forge a crucial allegiance with a people who do not honor his cause, or his God.

LORD OF THE ATLAS finds ex-soldier Harry Delhaze battling the wild bandit armies of ruthless prophet-warlord, Bou Hamra, through the snows of the Atlas Mountains and the baking deserts of the Sahara.

And FEVER COAST is a quest, from the African savannah and the slave markets of Mozambique to the Moghul palaces and British redcoat forts of Carnatic India, that forces Lachlan McKenzie to decide between the life that he always dreamed of and a sworn promise of vengeance.

The books are all stand-alone stories and can be read in any order.

View the whole series here: Epic Adventure Series.

SPECIAL PRICES AND NEW RELEASES

I send monthly newsletters with details on new releases, special offers and other bits of news relating to my books.

Just sign up to my COLIN FALCONER BOOKS <u>mailing list</u> to stay in the loop.

ENJOY THIS BOOK?

You can make a big difference.

Honest reviews of my books help bring them to the attention of other readers.

If you've enjoyed this book I would be very grateful if you could spend a few minutes leaving a review (it can be as short as you like) on the book's Amazon page. You can jump right to the page by clicking below.

Write a book review.

If you've read a few books in the series please would you consider writing a brief series review on the Amazon SERIES PAGE?

Write a series review (scroll to the very bottom of the series page to write your review).

MANY THANKS!

ABOUT THE AUTHOR

Born in London, Colin Falconer started out in advertising, then became a freelance journalist. He worked in radio and television before writing his first novel. He has published over forty books, and is best known for historical adventure thrillers – stories on an epic scale, inspired by his passion for history and travel. His books have been translated into 24 languages.

Colin stays in touch with readers and answers questions on Facebook and via his website www.colinfalconer.org.

Printed in Great Britain
by Amazon

33758215R00229